'Mainly,' I said. 'In time it will be nothing but a memory of sadness and disturbance. It is good that Vashu should have such memories.'

'Yes.' She nodded. 'It is good. Come – let us ride to the Calling Hills as we used to when we first met.'

Together we urged our daharas forward through the quiet morning, riding through the lovely streets and out towards the Calling Hills.

With my beautiful wife riding beside me, and with the exhilaration of the fast ride, I knew that I had won something of immense value – something that I might well have lost if I had not come to Mars as I did.

The cool scents of the Martian autumn in my nostrils, I gave myself up to the joy that comes from true and simple happiness.

Epilogue

I HAD LISTENED with keen interest to Michael Kane's story and it had moved me to a deeper emotion than any I had experienced before.

Now I realised why he seemed so much more relaxed than he had ever been before. He had found something – something rare on Earth.

At that point I was tempted to ask him to let me return to Mars with him, but he smiled.

'Would you really like that?' he asked.

'I – I think so.'

He shook his head.

'Find Mars in yourself,' he said. Then he grinned. 'It is far less strenuous, for one thing.'

I thought this over and then shrugged.

'Perhaps you're right,' I said. 'But at least I'll have the pleasure of committing your story to paper. So others will have the pleasure of sharing a little of what you found on Mars.'

'I hope so,' he said. He paused. 'I suppose you think me rather sentimental.'

'What do you mean?'

'Well, trying to describe all my emotions to you – the bit I told you about our ride to the Calling Hills.'

'There is a great difference between sentimentality and honest sentiment,' I told him. 'The trouble is that people tend to confuse one for the other and so reject both. All we seek is honesty.'

'And an absence of fear.' He smiled.

'That comes with honesty,' I suggested.

'Partly,' he agreed.

'What a mistrusting lot we are on Earth,' I said. 'We are so blind that we even distrust beauty when we see it, feeling that it cannot be what it appears to be.'

'A healthy enough feeling,' Kane pointed out. 'But it can, as you say, go too far. Perhaps the old medieval ideal is not such a bad one – moderation in all things. So often that phrase is taken to apply to just the physical side of mankind, but it is just as important to his spiritual development, I think.'

I nodded.

'Well,' he said. 'For fear of boring you further, I will return to the basement and the matter transmitter. I find that Earth is a better place every time I return – but I find Mars the same, also. I am a lucky man.'

'You are an exceptionally lucky man,' I said. 'When will you come back? There must be more adventures yet to come.'

'Wasn't that one enough?' He grinned.

'For the moment,' I told him. 'But I will soon want to hear more.'

'Remember,' he joked, pretending to wag a warning finger. 'Moderation in all things.'

'It will comfort me as I wait for your next visit,' I said, smiling.

'I will be back,' he assured me.

And then he had left the room – left me sitting beside a dying fire, still full of memories of Mars.

There would be even more memories for me soon. Of that I was sure.

MICHAEL MOORCOCK (1939–) is one of the most important figures in British SF and Fantasy literature. The author of many literary novels and stories in practically every genre, he has won and been shortlisted for numerous awards including the Hugo, Nebula, World Fantasy, Whitbread and Guardian Fiction Prize. He is also a musician who performed in the seventies with his own band, the Deep Fix; and, as a member of the space-rock band, Hawkwind, won a platinum disc. His tenure as editor of NEW WORLDS magazine in the sixties and seventies is seen as the high watermark of SF editorship in the UK, and was crucial in the development of the SF New Wave. Michael Moorcock's literary creations include Hawkmoon, Corum, Von Bek, Jerry Cornelius and, of course, his most famous character, Elric. He has been compared to, among others, Balzac, Dumas, Dickens, James Joyce, Ian Fleming, J.R.R. Tolkien and Robert E. Howard. Although born in London, he now splits his time between homes in Texas and Paris.

For a more detailed biography, please see Michael Moorcock's entry in *The Encyclopedia of Science Fiction* at: http://www.sf-encyclopedia.com/

For further information about Michael Moorcock and his work, please visit www.multiverse.org, or send S.A.E. to The Nomads Of The Time Streams, Mo Dhachaidh, Loch Awe, Dalmally, Argyll, PA33 1AQ, Scotland, or P.O. Box 385716, Waikoloa, HI 96738, USA.

Kane of Old Mars

The Michael Moorcock Collection

The Michael Moorcock Collection is the definitive library of acclaimed author Michael Moorcock's SF & fantasy, including the entirety of his Eternal Champion work. It is prepared and edited by John Davey, the author's long-time bibliographer and editor, and will be published, over the course of two years, in the following print omnibus editions by Gollancz, and as individual eBooks by the SF Gateway (see http://www.sfgateway.com/authors/m/moorcock-michael/ for a complete list of available eBooks).

ELRIC

Elric of Melniboné and Other Stories

Elric: The Fortress of the Pearl

Elric: The Sailor on the Seas of Fate

Elric: The Sleeping Sorceress

Elric: The Revenge of the Rose

Elric: Stormbringer!

Elric: The Moonbeam Roads
comprising –
Daughter of Dreams
Destiny's Brother
Son of the Wolf

CORUM

Corum: The Prince in the Scarlet Robe
comprising –
The Knight of the Swords
The Queen of the Swords
The King of the Swords

Corum: The Prince with the Silver Hand
comprising –
The Bull and the Spear
The Oak and the Ram
The Sword and the Stallion

HAWKMOON

Hawkmoon: The History of the Runestaff
comprising –
The Jewel in the Skull
The Mad God's Amulet
The Sword of the Dawn
The Runestaff

Hawkmoon: Count Brass
comprising –
Count Brass
The Champion of Garathorm
The Quest for Tanelorn

JERRY CORNELIUS

The Cornelius Quartet
comprising –
The Final Programme
A Cure for Cancer
The English Assassin
The Condition of Muzak

Jerry Cornelius: His Lives and His Times (short-fiction collection)

A Cornelius Calendar
comprising –
The Adventures of Una Persson and Catherine Cornelius in the Twentieth Century
The Entropy Tango
The Great Rock 'n' Roll Swindle
The Alchemist's Question
Firing the Cathedral/Modem Times 2.0

Von Bek
comprising –
The War Hound and the World's Pain
The City in the Autumn Stars

The Eternal Champion
comprising –
The Eternal Champion
Phoenix in Obsidian
The Dragon in the Sword

The Dancers at the End of Time
comprising –
An Alien Heat
The Hollow Lands
The End of all Songs

Kane of Old Mars
comprising –
Warriors of Mars
Blades of Mars
Barbarians of Mars

Moorcock's Multiverse
comprising –
The Sundered Worlds
The Winds of Limbo
The Shores of Death

The Nomad of Time
comprising –
The Warlord of the Air
The Land Leviathan
The Steel Tsar

Travelling to Utopia
comprising –
The Wrecks of Time
The Ice Schooner
The Black Corridor

The War Amongst the Angels
comprising –
Blood: A Southern Fantasy
Fabulous Harbours
The War Amongst the Angels

Tales from the End of Time
comprising –
Legends from the End of Time
Constant Fire
Elric at the End of Time

Behold the Man

Gloriana; or, The Unfulfill'd Queen

SHORT FICTION
My Experiences in the Third World War and Other Stories: The Best Short Fiction of Michael Moorcock Volume 1

The Brothel in Rosenstrasse and Other Stories: The Best Short Fiction of Michael Moorcock Volume 2

Breakfast in the Ruins and Other Stories: The Best Short Fiction of Michael Moorcock Volume 3

Kane of Old Mars

Warriors of Mars
Blades of Mars
Barbarians of Mars

MICHAEL MOORCOCK

writing as Edward P. Bradbury

Edited by John Davey

This edition published in Great Britain in 2015 by
Gollancz
An imprint of the Orion Publishing Group
Orion House, 5 Upper St Martin's Lane,
London WC2H 9EA

An Hachette UK Company

The authorised representative in the EEA is Hachette Ireland,
8 Castlecourt Centre, Dublin 15, D15 XTP3, Ireland (email: info@hbgi.ie)

10

A CIP catalogue record for this book is
available from the British Library

ISBN 978 0 575 09252 5

Typeset by Jouve (UK), Milton Keynes

Printed and bound in Great Britain by Clays Ltd, Elcograf S.p.A.

www.multiverse.org
www.sfgateway.com
www.gollancz.co.uk
www.orionbooks.co.uk

Introduction to *The Michael Moorcock Collection*

John Clute

HE IS NOW over 70, enough time for most careers to start and end in, enough time to fit in an occasional half-decade or so of silence to mark off the big years. Silence happens. I don't think I know an author who doesn't fear silence like the plague; most of us, if we live long enough, can remember a bad blank year or so, or more. Not Michael Moorcock. Except for some worrying surgery on his toes in recent years, he seems not to have taken time off to breathe the air of peace and panic. There has been no time to spare. The nearly 60 years of his active career seems to have been too short to fit everything in: the teenage comics; the editing jobs; the pulp fiction; the reinvented heroic fantasies; the Eternal Champion; the deep Jerry Cornelius riffs; NEW WORLDS; the 1970s/1980s flow of stories and novels, dozens upon dozens of them in every category of modern fantastika; the tales of the dying Earth and the possessing of Jesus; the exercises in postmodernism that turned the world inside out before most of us had begun to guess we were living on the wrong side of things; the invention (more or less) of steampunk; the alternate histories; the *Mitteleuropean* tales of sexual terror; the deep-city London riffs: the turns and changes and returns and reconfigurations to which he has subjected his oeuvre over the years (he expects this new Collected Edition will fix these transformations in place for good); the late tales where he has been remodelling the intersecting worlds he created in the 1960s in terms of twenty-first-century physics: for starters. If you can't take the heat, I guess, stay out of the multiverse.

His life has been full and complicated, a life he has exposed and hidden (like many other prolific authors) throughout his work. In *Mother London* (1988), though, a non-fantastic novel published at what is now something like the midpoint of his career, it may be possible to find the key to all the other selves who made the 100 books. There are three protagonists in the tale, which is set from about 1940 to about 1988 in the suburbs and inner runnels of the vast metropolis of Charles Dickens and Robert Louis Stevenson. The oldest of these protagonists is Joseph Kiss, a flamboyant self-advertising fin-de-siècle figure of substantial girth and a fantasticating relationship to the world: he is Michael Moorcock, seen with genial bite as a kind of G.K. Chesterton without the wearying punch-line paradoxes. The youngest of the three is David Mummery, a haunted introspective half-insane denizen of a secret London of trials and runes and codes and magic: he too is Michael Moorcock, seen through a glass, darkly. And there is Mary Gasalee, a kind of holy-innocent and survivor, blessed with a luminous clarity of insight, so that in all her apparent ignorance of the onrushing secular world she is more deeply wise than other folk: she is also Michael Moorcock, Moorcock when young as viewed from the wry middle years of 1988. When we read the book, we are reading a book of instructions for the assembly of a London writer. The Moorcock we put together from this choice of portraits is amused and bemused at the vision of himself; he is a phenomenon of flamboyance and introspection, a poseur and a solitary, a dreamer and a doer, a multitude and a singleton. But only the three Moorcocks in this book, working together, could have written all the other books.

It all began – as it does for David Mummery in *Mother London* – in South London, in a subtopian stretch of villas called Mitcham, in 1939. In early childhood, he experienced the Blitz, and never forgot the extraordinariness of being a participant – however minute – in the great drama; all around him, as though the world were being dismantled nightly, darkness and blackout would descend, bombs fall, buildings and streets disappear; and in the morning, as though a new universe had taken over from the old one and the world had become portals, the sun would rise on glinting rubble, abandoned tricycles, men and women going about their daily tasks as though nothing had happened, strange shards of ruin poking into altered air. From a very early age, Michael Moorcock's security reposed in a sense that everything might change, in the blinking of an eye, and be *rejourneyed* the next day (or the next book). Though as a writer he has certainly elucidated the fears and alarums of life in Aftermath Britain, it does seem that his very early years were marked by the epiphanies of war, rather than the inflictions of despair and beclouding amnesia most adults necessarily experienced. After the war ended, his parents separated, and the young Moorcock began to attend a pretty wide variety of schools, several of which he seems to have been expelled from, and as soon as he could legally do so he began to work full time, up north in London's heart, which he only left when he moved to Texas (with intervals in Paris) in the early 1990s, from where (to jump briefly up the decades) he continues to cast a Martian eye: as with most exiles, Moorcock's intensest anatomies of his homeland date from after his cunning departure.

But back again to the beginning (just as though we were rimming a multiverse). Starting in the 1950s there was the comics and pulp work for Fleetway Publications; there was the first book (*Caribbean Crisis*, 1962) as by Desmond Reid, co-written with his early friend the artist James Cawthorn (1929–2008); there was marriage, with the writer Hilary Bailey (they divorced in 1978), three children, a heated existence in the Ladbroke Grove/Notting Hill Gate region of London he was later to populate with Jerry Cornelius and his vast family; there was the editing of NEW WORLDS, which began in 1964 and became the heartbeat of the British New Wave two years later as writers like Brian W. Aldiss and J.G. Ballard, reaching their early prime, made it into a tympanum, as young American writers like Thomas M. Disch, John T. Sladek, Norman Spinrad and Pamela Zoline found a home in London for material they could not publish in America, and new British writers like M. John Harrison and Charles Platt began their careers in its pages; but before that there was Elric. With *The Stealer of Souls* (1963) and

Stormbringer (1965), the multiverse began to flicker into view, and the Eternal Champion (whom Elric parodied and embodied) began properly to ransack the worlds in his fight against a greater Chaos than the great dance could sustain. There was also the first SF novel, *The Sundered Worlds* (1965), but in the 1960s SF was a difficult nut to demolish for Moorcock: he would bide his time.

We come to the heart of the matter. Jerry Cornelius, who first appears in *The Final Programme* (1968) – which assembles and co-ordinates material first published a few years earlier in NEW WORLDS – is a deliberate solarisation of the albino Elric, who was himself a mocking solarisation of Robert E. Howard's Conan, or rather of the mighty-thew-headed Conan created for profit by Howard epigones: Moorcock rarely mocks the true quill. Cornelius, who reaches his first and most telling apotheosis in the four novels comprising *The Cornelius Quartet*, remains his most distinctive and perhaps most original single creation: a wide boy, an agent, a *flaneur*, a bad musician, a shopper, a shapechanger, a trans, a spy in the house of London: a toxic palimpsest on whom and through whom the *zeitgeist* inscribes surreal conjugations of 'message'. Jerry Cornelius gives head to Elric.

The life continued apace. By 1970, with NEW WORLDS on its last legs, multiverse fantasies and experimental novels poured forth; Moorcock and Hilary Bailey began to live separately, though he moved, in fact, only around the corner, where he set up house with Jill Riches, who would become his second wife; there was a second home in Yorkshire, but London remained his central base. *The Condition of Muzak* (1977), which is the fourth Cornelius novel, and *Gloriana; or, The Unfulfill'd Queen* (1978), which transfigures the first Elizabeth into a kinked Astraea, marked perhaps the high point of his career as a writer of fiction whose font lay in genre or its mutations – marked perhaps the furthest bournes he could transgress while remaining within the perimeters of fantasy (though *within* those bournes vast stretches of territory remained and would, continually, be explored). During these years he sometimes wore a leather jacket constructed out of numerous patches of varicoloured material, and it sometimes seemed perfectly fitting that he bore the semblance, as his jacket flickered and fuzzed from across a room or road, of an illustrated man, a map, a thing of shreds and patches, a student fleshed from dreams. Like the stories he told, he seemed to be more than one thing. To use a term frequently applied (by me at least) to twenty-first-century fiction, he seemed equipoisal: which is to say that, through all his genre-hopping and genre-mixing and genre-transcending and genre-loyal returnings to old pitches, *he was never still*, because 'equipoise' is all about *making stories move*. As with his stories, he cannot be pinned down, because he is not in one place. In person and in his work, it has always been sink or swim: like a shark, or a dancer, or an equilibrist...

The marriage with Jill Riches came to an end. He married Linda Steele in 1983; they remain married. The Colonel Pyat books, *Byzantium Endures* (1981), *The Laughter of Carthage* (1984), *Jerusalem Commands* (1992) and *The Vengeance of Rome* (2006), dominated these years, along with *Mother London*. As these books, which are non-fantastic, are not included in the current *Michael Moorcock Collection*, it might be worth noting here that, in their insistence on the irreducible difficulty of gaining anything like true sight, they represent Moorcock's mature modernist take on what one might call the rag-and-bone shop of the world itself; and that the huge ornate postmodern edifice of his multiverse *loosens* us from that world, gives us room to breathe, to juggle our strategies for living – allows us ultimately to escape from prison (to use a phrase from a writer he does not respect, J.R.R. Tolkien, for whom the twentieth century was a prison train bound for hell). What Moorcock may best be remembered for in the end is the (perhaps unique) interplay between modernism and postmodernism in his work. (But a plethora of discordant understandings makes these terms hard to use; so enough of them.) In the end, one might just say that Moorcock's work as a whole represents an extraordinarily multifarious execution of the fantasist's main task: which is to *get us out of here*.

Recent decades saw a continuation of the multifarious, but with a more intensely applied methodology. The late volumes of the long Elric saga, and the Second Ether sequence of meta-fantasies – *Blood: A Southern Fantasy* (1995), *Fabulous Harbours* (1995) and *The War Amongst the Angels: An Autobiographical Story* (1996) – brood on the real world and the multiverse through the lens of Chaos Theory: the closer you get to the world, the less you describe it. *The Metatemporal Detective* (2007) – a narrative in the Steampunk mode Moorcock had previewed as long ago as *The Warlord of the Air* (1971) and *The Land Leviathan* (1974) – continues the process, sometimes dizzyingly: as though the reader inhabited the eye of a camera increasing its focus on a closely observed reality while its bogey simultaneously wheels it backwards from the desired rapport: an old Kurasawa trick here amplified into a tool of conspectus, fantasy eyed and (once again) rejourneyed, this time through the lens of SF.

We reach the second decade of the twenty-first century, time still to make things new, but also time to sort. There are dozens of titles in *The Michael Moorcock Collection* that have not been listed in this short space, much less trawled for tidbits. The various avatars of the Eternal Champion – Elric, Kane of Old Mars, Hawkmoon, Count Brass, Corum, Von Bek – differ vastly from one another. Hawkmoon is a bit of a berk; Corum is a steely solitary at the End of Time: the joys and doleurs of the interplays amongst them can only be experienced through immersion. And the Dancers at the End of Time books, and the Nomad of the Time Stream books, and the Karl Glogauer books, and all the others. They are here now, a 100 books that make up one book. They have been fixed for reading. It is time to enter the multiverse and see the world.

September 2012

Introduction to *The Michael Moorcock Collection*

Michael Moorcock

By 1964, after I had been editing NEW WORLDS for some months and had published several science fiction and fantasy novels, including *Stormbringer*, I realised that my run as a writer was over. About the only new ideas I'd come up with were miniature computers, the multiverse and black holes, all very crudely realised, in *The Sundered Worlds*. No doubt I would have to return to journalism, writing features and editing. 'My career,' I told my friend J.G. Ballard, 'is finished.' He sympathised and told me he only had a few SF stories left in him, then he, too, wasn't sure what he'd do.

In January 1965, living in Colville Terrace, Notting Hill, then an infamous slum, best known for its race riots, I sat down at the typewriter in our kitchen-cum-bathroom and began a locally based book, designed to be accompanied by music and graphics. *The Final Programme* featured a character based on a young man I'd seen around the area and whom I named after a local greengrocer, Jerry Cornelius, 'Messiah to the Age of Science'. Jerry was as much a technique as a character. Not the 'spy' some critics described him as but an urban adventurer as interested in his psychic environment as the contemporary physical world. My influences were English and French absurdists, American noir novels. My inspiration was William Burroughs with whom I'd recently begun a correspondence. I also borrowed a few SF ideas, though I was adamant that I was not writing in any established genre. I felt I had at last found my own authentic voice.

I had already written a short novel, *The Golden Barge*, set in a nowhere, no-time world very much influenced by Peake and the surrealists, which I had not attempted to publish. An earlier autobiographical novel, *The Hungry Dreamers*, set in Soho, was eaten by rats in a Ladbroke Grove basement. I remained unsatisfied with my style and my technique. *The Final Programme* took nine days to complete (by 20 January, 1965) with my baby daughters sometimes cradled with their bottles while I typed on. This, I should say, is my memory of events; my then wife scoffed at this story when I recounted it. Whatever the truth, the fact is I only believed I might be a serious writer after I had finished that novel, with all its flaws. But Jerry Cornelius, probably my most successful sustained attempt at unconventional fiction, was born then and ever since has remained a useful means of telling complex stories. Associated with the 60s and 70s, he has been equally at home in all the following decades. Through novels and novellas I developed a means of carrying several narratives and viewpoints on what appeared to be a very light (but tight) structure which dispensed with some of the earlier methods of fiction. In the sense that it took for granted the understanding that the novel is among other things an internal dialogue and I did not feel the need to repeat by now commonly understood modernist conventions, this fiction was post-modern.

Not all my fiction looked for new forms for the new century. Like many 'revolutionaries' I looked back as well as forward. As George Meredith looked to the eighteenth century for inspiration for his experiments with narrative, I looked to Meredith, popular Edwardian realists like Pett Ridge and Zangwill and the writers of the *fin de siècle* for methods and inspiration. An almost obsessive interest in the Fabians, several of whom believed in the possibility of benign imperialism, ultimately led to my Bastable books which examined our enduring British notion that an empire could be essentially a force for good. The first was *The Warlord of the Air*.

I also wrote my *Dancers at the End of Time* stories and novels under the influence of Edwardian humourists and absurdists like Jerome or Firbank. Together with more conventional generic books like *The Ice Schooner* or *The Black Corridor*, most of that work was done in the 1960s and 70s when I wrote the Eternal Champion supernatural adventure novels which helped support my own and others' experiments via NEW WORLDS, allowing me also to keep a family while writing books in which action and fantastic invention were paramount. Though I did them quickly, I didn't write them cynically. I have always believed, somewhat puritanically, in giving the audience good value for money. I enjoyed writing them, tried to avoid repetition, and through each new one was able to develop a few more ideas. They also continued to teach me how to express myself through image and metaphor. My Everyman became the Eternal Champion, his dreams and ambitions represented by the multiverse. He could be an ordinary person struggling with familiar problems in a contemporary setting or he could be a swordsman fighting monsters on a far-away world.

Long before I wrote *Gloriana* (in four parts reflecting the seasons) I had learned to think in images and symbols through reading John Bunyan's *Pilgrim's Progress*, Milton and others, understanding early on that the visual could be the most important part of a book and was often in itself a story as, for instance, a famous personality could also, through everything associated with their name, function as narrative. I wanted to find ways of carrying as many stories as possible in one. From the cinema I also learned how to use images as connecting themes. Images, colours, music, and even popular magazine headlines can all add coherence to an apparently random story, underpinning it and giving the reader a sense of internal logic and a satisfactory resolution, dispensing with certain familiar literary conventions.

When the story required it, I also began writing neo-realist fiction exploring the interface of character and environment, especially the city, especially London. In some books I condensed, manipulated and randomised time to achieve what I wanted, but in others the sense of 'real time' as we all generally perceive it was more suitable and could best be achieved by traditional nineteenth-century means. For the Pyat books I first looked back to the great German classic, Grimmelshausen's *Simplicissimus* and other early picaresques. I then examined the roots of a certain kind of moral fiction from Defoe through Thackeray and Meredith then to modern times where the picaresque (or rogue tale) can take the form of a road movie, for instance. While it's probably fair to say that Pyat and *Byzantium Endures* precipitated the end of my second marriage (echoed to a degree in *The Brothel in Rosenstrasse*), the late 70s and the 80s were exhilarating times for me, with *Mother London* being perhaps my own favourite novel of that period. I wanted to write something celebratory.

By the 90s I was again attempting to unite several kinds of fiction in one novel with my Second Ether trilogy. With Mandelbrot, Chaos Theory and String Theory I felt, as I said at the time, as if I were being offered a chart of my own brain. That chart made it easier for me to develop the notion of the multiverse as representing both the internal and the external, as a metaphor and as a means of structuring and rationalising an outrageously inventive and quasi-realistic narrative. The worlds of the multiverse move up and down scales or 'planes' explained in terms of mass, allowing entire universes to exist in the 'same' space. The result of developing this idea was the *War Amongst the Angels* sequence which added absurdist elements also functioning as a kind of mythology and folklore for a world beginning to understand itself in terms of new metaphysics and theoretical physics. As the cosmos becomes denser and almost infinite before our eyes, with black holes and dark matter affecting our own reality, we can explore them and observe them as our ancestors explored our planet and observed the heavens.

At the end of the 90s I'd returned to realism, sometimes with a dash of fantasy, with *King of the City* and the stories collected in *London Bone*. I also wrote a new Elric/Eternal Champion sequence, beginning with *Daughter of Dreams*, which brought the fantasy worlds of Hawkmoon, Bastable and Co. in line with my realistic and autobiographical stories, another attempt to unify all my fiction, and also offer a way in which disparate genres could be reunited, through notions developed from the multiverse and the Eternal Champion, as one giant novel. At the time I was finishing the Pyat sequence which attempted to look at the roots of the Nazi Holocaust in our European, Middle Eastern and American cultures and to ground my strange survival guilt while at the same time examining my own cultural roots in the light of an enduring anti-Semitism.

By the 2000s I was exploring various conventional ways of story-telling in the last parts of *The Metatemporal Detective* and through other homages, comics, parodies and games. I also looked back at my earliest influences. I had reached retirement age and felt like a rest. I wrote a 'prequel' to the Elric series as a graphic novel with Walter Simonson, *The Making of a Sorcerer*, and did a little online editing with FANTASTIC METROPOLIS.

By 2010 I had written a novel featuring Doctor Who, *The Coming of the Terraphiles*, with a nod to P.G. Wodehouse (a boyhood favourite), continued to write short stories and novellas and to work on the beginning of a new sequence combining pure fantasy and straight autobiography called *The Whispering Swarm* while still writing more Cornelius stories trying to unite all the various genres and sub-genres into which contemporary fiction has fallen.

Throughout my career critics have announced that I'm 'abandoning' fantasy and concentrating on literary fiction. The truth is, however, that all my life, since I became a professional writer and editor at the age of 16, I've written in whatever mode suits a story best and where necessary created a new form if an old one didn't work for me. Certain ideas are best carried on a Jerry Cornelius story, others work better as realism and others as fantasy or science fiction. Some work best as a combination. I'm sure I'll write whatever I like and will continue to experiment with all the ways there are of telling stories and carrying as many themes as possible. Whether I write about a widow coping with loneliness in her cottage or a massive, universe-size sentient spaceship searching for her children, I'll no doubt die trying to tell them all. I hope you'll find at least some of them to your taste.

One thing a reader can be sure of about these new editions is that they would not have been possible without the tremendous and indispensable help of my old friend and bibliographer John Davey. John has ensured that these Gollancz editions are definitive. I am indebted to John for many things, including his work at

Moorcock's Miscellany, my website, but his work on this edition has been outstanding. As well as being an accomplished novelist in his own right John is an astonishingly good editor who has worked with Gollancz and myself to point out every error and flaw in all previous editions, some of them not corrected since their first publication, and has enabled me to correct or revise them. I couldn't have completed this project without him. Together, I think, Gollancz, John Davey and myself have produced what will be the best editions possible and I am very grateful to him, to Malcolm Edwards, Darren Nash and Marcus Gipps for all the considerable hard work they have done to make this edition what it is.

Michael Moorcock

Contents

Warriors of Mars

Dedicated to the memories of Edgar Rice Burroughs and H.G. Wells, with thanks and admiration

Prologue

I WAS ENDING the season at Nice – being fortunate enough to possess a small private income. It was the lovely summer of 1968 and the crowds were greater than normal – so much so that I found it necessary to take long walks along the coast and inland if I desired a little comparative solitude.

I am thankful now to those crowds – had they not forced me away from the main centres I should never have met Michael Kane, that strange, enigmatic character in whose life I was soon to become closely involved.

Lemontagne is situated about twelve miles along the coast from Nice. A small but picturesque village on the cliff-top, I had discovered it several years before and found it a pleasant, restful place. There was a white-walled café where the coffee was excellent and from its terrace you could look out over the blue Mediterranean. Unspoiled by tourists, untouched by the passing of time, Lemontagne with its café-terrace was a peaceful haven for me.

The date, I remember, was 15 July – one of the best days of the year, warm and bright and soporific. I was sitting at my usual table sipping a cool Pernod and looking out over the blue, blue sea when I first noticed the big man. He came and sat down at a table close to mine, ordering a light beer in a quiet, American accent.

A tall, slim-hipped giant, bronzed and handsome and with the appearance of a man of action, he looked like a young god in those surroundings. Yet there was a haunted look about the eyes that seemed to speak of some strange tragedy – perhaps mystery – in his past.

I am something of a literary dabbler, having already written one or two small volumes of travel and reminiscence, and my literary instincts were instantly alerted. My curiosity overcame normal good manners and I decided to try to engage him in conversation.

'A pleasant day, sir,' I said.

'Very pleasant.' His tone was friendly but distant, his smile somewhat half-hearted.

'You are an American, I would guess. Are you staying in the village?'

He nodded abstractedly, then looked away and stared out to sea. Perhaps it was boorish of me to continue – perhaps I intruded. But if I had not I should have deprived myself of an incredible experience and missed the strangest story that has ever been told to me.

When the waiter came for my next order I told him to bring the American another beer. When it came I took my own drink over to his table and asked if I might join him.

'Forgive me,' he said, looking up suddenly and giving me one of those friendly, half-sad, mysterious smiles which were soon to become familiar. 'I was dreaming. By all means sit down. I would like someone to talk to.'

'Have you been here long?' I asked.

'Where – on Earth?'

It was a strangely startling answer. I laughed. 'No, no – of course not. In the village.'

'No,' he said, 'not long. Though –' he sighed deeply – 'far too long, I regret to say. You are English, aren't you?'

'Actually born in New England,' I said, 'but English by adoption. Where are you from in America?'

'America? Oh, Ohio originally.'

I was baffled by his oddly oblique replies and his detached way of speaking. Why had he wondered if I meant the planet itself when I asked him if he had been in the village very long? The question piqued my curiosity further.

'Do you work in America?' I pressed on.

'I did once, yes.' Suddenly he looked directly at me, his diamond-blue eyes seeming to bore into my brain. I felt as if an electric current had surged through me. Then he continued: 'That was the whole start of it, I suppose. I could tell you a tale that would send you running to the nearest lunatic asylum and have me put away!'

'You intrigue me. By the look of you it is some tragedy. Have you been crossed in love – is that it?' I was beginning to wonder just how impertinent my rising curiosity was making me. But he did not seem offended.

'In a sense, you could say that. My name is Michael Kane. Does that mean anything to you?'

'It rings a faint bell,' I admitted.

'Professor Michael Kane of the Chicago Special Research Institute.' He sighed again, his manner retrospective. 'We were doing top-secret research on matter transmitters.'

'Matter transmitters?'

'I shouldn't really be telling you this, but it doesn't seem important now. We were trying to build a machine that, by a combination of electronics and nucleonics, could break down the atoms of an object and translate them into a series of waves that could be transmitted across great distances like radio waves. There was a receiver which could, theoretically, re-translate the waves back into the object.'

'You mean an apple could be broken down into particles, transmitted like, say, a radio-picture, and become the same apple again at the receiving end? I have read something about it, now you mention it. I had thought such a machine was still only theoretical.'

'It was until comparatively recently – in your recent past, that is.'

'My past? Isn't it essentially the same as yours?' I was again surprised.

'I am coming to that,' he said. 'If perfected, a machine of the type we've discussed could take even a *human being*, break him down into atoms, transmit him across any selected distance, and have the "receiver" at the other end put him together again!'

'Astounding! How did you make this discovery?'

'It became possible to build such a machine following completion of some research on lasers and masers. I will not bore you with a series of obscure equations, but our work on light waves and radio waves was of great help. I was the physicist in charge of the work. I was obsessed with the idea…' His voice trailed off and he looked thoughtfully down at the table, clenching his long-fingered hands together tightly.

'What happened?' I asked eagerly.

'We got the machine working. We sent a few rats and mice through it – successfully. Then we had to test it on a human subject. It was dangerous – we couldn't ask for volunteers.'

'So you decided to test it yourself?'

He smiled. 'That's right. I was eager to prove it would really work, you see, though I was convinced it would.' He paused, then added: 'But it *didn't* work.'

'You survived, however,' I pointed out. 'Unless I'm talking to a ghost!'

'You're closer to the truth than you think, my friend. Where would you say I went after I entered the matter transmitter?'

'Well, it seems natural that you went to the receiver and were – um – put together again.'

'You think me sane?' Again this strange man was off at a slight tangent.

'Eminently sane,' I said.

'You would not say I had the appearance or manner of a liar?'

'Far from it. Where is this leading? Where did you go?'

'Believe me,' he said seriously. *'I left this planet altogether!'*

I gasped. For a moment I thought my confidence in his sanity and his word had been misplaced. But then I saw that it had not been. His whole manner was that of a man speaking sane truth. 'You went into *space*?' I said.

'I went *through* space – and time as well, I think. *I went to Mars, my friend.'*

'Mars!' I was now even more incredulous. 'But how could you have survived? Mars is lifeless – a waste of dust and lichen!'

'Not this Mars, my friend.'

'There is *another* Mars?' I raised my eyebrows.

'In a sense, yes. The planet I visited was not, I am convinced, the Mars we can see through our telescopes. It was an older Mars, aeons in the past, yet still ancient. It is my theory that our own ancestors originated on the planet and came here when Mars was dying millions of years ago!'

'You mean you met people on the Red Planet?'

'People very similar to us. More – I encountered a strange romantic civilisation totally unlike any we have ever had on Earth. Perhaps our most ancient legends hint at it – legends that we brought with us from Mars when our race fled from there to Earth and degenerated into savagery before beginning the upward climb towards civilisation again. Ah, it was beautiful, fantastic, breathtaking – a place where a man could *be* a man and survive and be recognised for his true qualities of character and prowess. And then there was Shizala...'

I recognised the look in his eyes this time. 'So there was a woman,' I said softly.

'Yes, there was a woman. A girl – young, ravishingly attractive, a tall Martian girl, an aristocrat from a line that would have made the dynasties of Egypt appear trifling by comparison. She was Princess of Varnal, City of the Green Mists, with its spires and colonnades, its ziggurats and domes, its strong, slender people – and the finest fighting men in that martial world...'

'Go on,' I breathed, entranced.

'It seems like a splendid dream now.' He smiled sadly. 'A dream that I may yet recapture.' Then his lips set firmly and his diamond-blue eyes gleamed with determination. 'I *must*!'

'And I must hear the whole story,' I said excitedly. Although my reason rejected his fantastic tale, my emotions accepted it. He was right, I was almost sure. 'Will you come with me to my hotel? I have a tape recorder there. I should like to hear everything you can tell me – and record it.'

'You are certain I'm not mad or lying?'

'Fairly certain,' I said with a self-deprecating smile. 'I am not quite sure. You must let me judge when I have heard all.'

'Very well.' He got up abruptly.

I am by no measure a short man, but he was a full head and shoulders taller.

'I should like you to believe me,' he said. 'And...' He broke off, controlling himself from saying something he evidently dearly wanted to say.

'What is it?' I urged as we settled the bill and began to walk to the nearby taxi rank, where stood one decrepit cab.

'I cannot return to my laboratory, you understand,' he said. 'And yet to build another transmitter would be expensive. I – I need help.'

'I am a man of comfortable means,' I told him, leaning forward in the cab to give the driver instructions. 'I may be able to help in some way.'

'You will probably not believe me,' he said with that half-smile of his, 'but it will be a relief to find an ear which is at least sympathetic.'

We were driven back to my hotel in Nice – the Hotel de la Mer. In my suite I ordered a meal to be brought to us. As ever, the food was excellent and had a mellowing effect on us both. When we had finished, I switched on my machine and he began to talk.

As I have said, I could not at first unreservedly believe his strange narrative. Yet, as he spoke on, the tape recording all he said, I became convinced that he was neither a madman nor a liar. He had experienced everything he told me. When he finished speaking, after many hours long into the night, I felt that I, too, had experienced the wild and remarkable adventures of Michael Kane, American physicist and – *Warrior of Mars!*

What you are about to read is essentially what he told me. The few omissions and clarifications I have made are in the cause of readability and to conform to the laws of Britain and the United States – laws for the most part involving scientific secrets. You must judge Kane as I judged him. However you feel, I must add, do not condemn him at once as a liar, for if you had seen him as I saw him in that hotel room in Nice, speaking in flowing, controlled sentences, his eyes staring up at the ceiling as if at Mars herself, and his whole attitude one of reminiscence, changing with the moods he felt as he recalled this scene or that, you would have believed him as implicitly as I did.

E.P.B.,
Chester Square,
London, S.W.1.
April 1969.

Chapter One
My Debt to M. Clarchet

THE MATTER TRANSMITTER is both villain and hero of this story (began Kane) for it took me to a world where I felt more at home than I shall ever feel here. It brought me to a wonderful girl whom I loved and who loved me – and then took it all away again.

But I had better begin at the beginning.

I was born, as I told you, in Ohio – in Wynnsville – a small, pleasant town that never changed much. Its only unusual feature was in the person of Monsieur Clarchet, a Frenchman who had settled there shortly after the First World War. He lived in a large place on the outskirts of town. M. Clarchet was a cosmopolitan, a Frenchman of the old school – short, very straight-backed, with a typically French, waxed moustache and a rather military way of walking.

To be honest, M. Clarchet was something of a caricature to us and seemed to illustrate everything we had learned about the French in our dime novels and comic books. Yet I owe my life to M. Clarchet, though I wasn't to realise it until many years after the old gentleman had passed on, and when I found myself suddenly transported to Mars... But again I am getting ahead of myself.

Clarchet was an enigma even to me though, as boy and youth, I probably knew him better than anyone else. He had been, he said, a fencing master at the Court of the Tsar of Russia before the Revolution and had had to leave in a hurry when the Bolsheviks took over.

He had settled in Wynnsville directly because of this experience. It had seemed to him at the time that the whole world was in chaos and was being turned upside down. He had found a small town that was never likely to change much – and he liked it. The way of life he led now was radically different from the one he had been used to, and it seemed to suit him.

We first met when I had accepted a dare by my young pals to climb the fence of his house and see if I could observe what M. Clarchet was up to. At the time we were all convinced he was a spy of some description! He had caught me, but instead of shooting me, as I half-expected, he had laughed good-naturedly and sent me on my way. I liked him at once.

Soon after that we kids had a phase which was a sequel to seeing Ronald Colman in *The Prisoner of Zenda*. We all became Ruperts and Rudolfs for a time. With long canes for swords, we fenced one another to exhaustion – not very skilfully but with a lot of enthusiasm!

On a sunny afternoon in early summer, it so happened that I and another boy, Johnny Bulmer, were duelling for the throne of Ruritania just outside M. Clarchet's house. Suddenly there came a great shout from the house and we wheeled in astonishment.

'*Non! Non! Non*!' The Frenchman was plainly exasperated. 'That ees wrong, wrong, wrong! That ees not how a gentleman fences!'

He rushed from his garden and seized my cane, adopting a graceful fencing stance and facing a startled Johnny, who just stood there with his mouth open.

'Now,' he said to Johnny, 'you do ze same, *oui*?'

Johnny inelegantly copied his posture.

'Now, you thrust – so!' The cane darted out in a flicker of movement and stopped just short of Johnny's chest.

Johnny copied him – and was parried with equal swiftness. We were amazed and delighted by this time. Here was a man who would have been a good match for Rupert of Hentzau.

After a while M. Clarchet stopped and shook his head. 'It ees no good with thees sticks – we must have real foils, *non*? Come!'

We followed him into the house. It was well furnished though not lavishly. In a special room at the top we found more to make us gasp.

Here was an array of blades such as we'd never even imagined! Now I know them to be foils and épées and sabres, plus a collection of fine, antique weapons – claymores, scimitars, Samurai swords, broadswords, Roman short swords – the *gladius* – and many, many more.

M. Clarchet waved a hand at the fascinating display of weapons. 'Zere! My collection. Zey are sweet, ze little swords, *non*?' He took down a small rapier and handed it to me, handing a similar sword to Johnny. It felt really good, holding that well-balanced sword in my hand. I flexed my wrist, not quite able to get the balance. M. Clarchet took my hand and showed me the correct way of grasping it.

'How would you like to learn properly?' said M. Clarchet with a wink. 'I could teach you much.'

Was it possible? We were going to be allowed to wield these swords – taught how to sword-fight like the best. I was amazed and delighted – until a thought struck me, and I frowned.

'Oh – we don't have any money, sir. We couldn't pay you and our moms and pops aren't likely to – they're mean enough as it is.'

'I do not wish for payment. The skill you acquire from me will be reward enough! Here – I will show you zee simple parry first...'

And so he taught us. Not only did we learn how to fence with the modern conventional weapons – foils, épées and sabres – but also with the antique and foreign weapons of all shapes, weights, sizes and balances. He taught us the whole of his marvellous art.

Whenever we could, Johnny and I attended M. Clarchet's special Sword Room. He seemed grateful to us, in his way, for the opportunity to pass on his skill, just as we were to him for giving us the chance to learn. By the time we were around fifteen we were both pretty good, and I think I probably had the edge on Johnny, though I say it myself.

Johnny's parents moved to Chicago about that time so I became M. Clarchet's only pupil. When I wasn't studying physics at high school and later at university, I was to be found at M. Clarchet's, learning all I could. And at last the day came when he cried with joy. I had *beaten* him in a long and complicated duel!

'You are zee best, Mike! Better zan any I have known!'

It was the highest praise I have ever received. At university I went in for fencing, of course, and was picked for the American team in the Olympics. But it was a crucial time in my studies and I had to drop out at the last moment.

That was how I learned to fence, anyway. I thought of it in my more depressed moments as rather a purposeless sport – archaic and only indirectly useful, in that it gave me excellently sharp reactions, strengthened my muscles and so on. It was useful in the Army, too, for the physical discipline essential in Army training was already built into me.

I was lucky. I did well in my studies and survived my military service, part of which was spent fighting the Communist guerrillas in the jungles of Vietnam. By the time I was thirty, I was known as a bright boy in the world of physics. Because of my ideas on matter transmission I was appointed Director of the department responsible for developing the machine.

I remember we were working late on it, enlarging its capacity so that it could take a man.

The neon lights in the lab ceiling illuminated the shining steel and plastic cabinet, the great 'translator cone' directed down at it, and all the other equipment and instruments that filled the place almost to capacity. There were five of us working – three technicians and Doctor Logan, my chief assistant.

I checked all the instruments while Logan and the men worked on the equipment. Soon all the gauges were reading what they should read, and we were ready.

I turned to Doctor Logan and looked at him. He said nothing as he looked back at me. Then we shook hands. That was all.

I climbed into the machine. They had tried to talk me out of it earlier but had given up by this time. Logan reached for the phone and contacted the team handling the 'receiver'. This was situated in a lab on the other side of the building.

Logan told the team we were ready and checked with them. They were ready, too.

Logan walked to the main switch. Through the little glass panel in the cabinet I saw him switch on gravely.

My body began to tingle pleasantly. That was all at first. It is difficult to describe the weird sensation I experienced as soon as the transmitter began to work. It was literally true that every atom of my body was being torn apart – and it felt like it. I began to get light-headed; then came the sensation of frightful pressure building up inside me, followed by the feeling that I was exploding outwards. Everything went green and I felt as though I was spreading gently in all directions. Then came the riot of colour blossoming around me – reds, yellows, purples, blues.

There was an increasing sense of weightlessness – *mass*lessness even. I felt I was streaming through blackness and my mind began to blank out altogether. I felt I was hurtling over vast distances, beyond time and space – covering an incredible area of the universe in every direction in a few seconds.

Then I knew nothing more!

I came to my senses – if senses they were – under a lemon-coloured sun blaring down on me from out of a deep blue, near-purple, sky. It was a colour more intense than any I had ever seen before. Had my experience enabled me to see colour with greater sharpness?

But when I looked around I realised that it was more than intensity which had changed. I was lying in a field of gently swaying, sweet-smelling ferns. But they were ferns unlike any I had ever seen!

These ferns were an impossible shade of crimson!

I rubbed my eyes. Had the transmitter – or rather the receiver – gone wrong and put me together slightly mixed up, with my colour sense in a muddle?

I got up and looked across the sea of crimson ferns.

I gasped.

My whole sight must somehow have been altered!

Cropping at the ferns, with a line of yellowish hills in the background, was a beast as large as an elephant and of roughly the same proportions as a horse. Yet here the similarity to any beast I knew ended. This creature was a mottled shade of mauve and light green. It had three long, white horns curling from its flat, almost catlike head. It had twin, somewhat reptilian, tails spreading to the ground behind it, and it had one huge eye covering at least half the area of its face. This was a faceted eye that shone and glinted in the sunlight. The beast looked rather curiously at me and lifted its head, then began to move towards me.

With, I suspect, a wild yell, I ran. I felt convinced I was experiencing some sort of nightmare or paranoiac delusion as a result of a fault in the transmitter or receiver.

I heard the beast thundering on behind me, giving out a strange mooing sound, and increased my pace as best I could. I found I could run very easily indeed and seemed to be lighter than normal.

Then to one side of me I heard musical laughter, at once merry and sympathetic. A lilting voice called something in what was to me a strange, unearthly language, trilling and melodic. In fact, the sound of the language was so beautiful that it did not seem to need words.

'Kahsaaa manherra vosu!'

I slowed my pace and looked towards the source of the voice.

It was a girl – the most wonderful girl I have ever seen in my life.

Her hair was long, free and golden. Her face was oval, her white skin clear and fresh. She was naked, apart from a wispy cloak which curled round her shoulders and a broad, leather belt around her waist. The belt held a short sword and a holster from which jutted the butt of a pistol of some kind. She was tall and her figure was exquisite. Somehow her nakedness was not obvious and I accepted it at once. She, too, was totally unselfconscious about it. I stopped still, not caring about the beast behind me so long as I could have a few seconds' glimpse of her.

Again she threw back her head and laughed that merry laugh.

Suddenly I felt something wet tickling my neck. Thinking it must be an insect of some sort, I put up my hand. But it was too large for an insect. I turned.

That strange mauve-and-green beast, that monster with the flylike, cyclops eye, two tails and three horns, was gently licking me!

Was it tasting me? I wondered vaguely, still concentrating on the girl. Judging by the way she was laughing, I thought not.

Wherever I was – in dream or lost world – I knew that I had fled in panic from a tame, friendly, domestic animal. I blushed and then joined in the girl's laughter.

After a moment I said: 'If it's not a rude question, I wonder, ma'am, if you could tell me where I am.'

She wrinkled her perfect brow when she heard me and shook her head slowly. '*Uhoi merrrash? Civinnee norshasa?*'

I tried again in French but without any luck. Then in German – again no success. Spanish was equally ineffective at producing communication between us. My Latin and Greek were limited, but I tried those, too. I am something of a linguist, picking up foreign tongues quickly. I tried to remember the little Sioux and Apache I had learned during a brief study of the Red Indians at college. But nothing worked.

She spoke a few more words in her language which seemed to me, when I listened very carefully, to have certain faint similarities to classical Sanskrit.

'We are both, it seems, at a loss,' I remarked, standing there with the beast still licking me lovingly.

She stretched out a hand for me to take. My heart pounded and I could hardly make myself move. '*Phoresha*,' she said. She seemed to want me to go somewhere with her, and pointed towards the distant hills.

I shrugged, took her hand and went along with her.

So that was how, hand in hand with its loveliest resident, I came to Várnal, City of the Green Mists – most splendid of the splendid Martian cities.

Oh, how many thousands upon thousands of years ago!

Chapter Two

The Astounding Truth

VARNAL IS MORE real to me, even in my memories, than ever Chicago or New York can be. It lies in a gentle valley in the hills, which the Martians term the Calling Hills. Green and golden, they are covered with slender trees and, when the wind passes through them, they sound like sweet, distant, calling voices as one walks past.

The valley itself is wide and shallow and contains a fairly large, hot lake. The city is built around the lake, from which rises a greenish steam, a delicate green that sends tendrils curling around the spires of Varnal. Most of Varnal's graceful buildings are tall and white, though some are built of the unique blue marble which is mined close by. Others have traceries of gold in them, making them glitter in the sunlight. The city is walled by the same blue marble, which also has golden traceries in it. From its towers fly pennants, gay and multicoloured, and its terraces are crowded with its handsome inhabitants, the plainest of whom would be a sought-after beau or belle in Wynnsville, Ohio – or, indeed, Chicago or any other great city of our world.

When I first came upon the city of Varnal, led by that wonderful girl, I gasped in awed admiration. She seemed to accept my gasp as the compliment it was and she smiled proudly, saying something in her then incomprehensible language.

I decided that I could not be dreaming, for my own imagination was simply not capable of creating such a vision of splendour and loveliness.

But where was I? I did not know then. How had I got there? That I still cannot answer fully.

I puzzled over the second question. Evidently the matter transmitter had had a fault. Instead of sending me to the receiver on the other side of the lab building it had sent me hurtling through space – perhaps through time, too – to another world. It could not be Earth – not, at least, the Earth of my own age. Somehow I could not believe it was any Earth, of the past or the future. Yet it could not be the only other obvious planet in our solar system – Mars – for Mars was a dead, arid planet of red dust and lichen. Yet the size of the sun and the fact that gravity was less here than on Earth seemed to indicate Mars.

It was in a daze of speculation that I allowed the girl to lead me through the golden gates of the city, through its tree-lined streets, towards a place of shining white stone. People, men and women dressed – if dressed is the word – similarly to the girl, glanced in polite curiosity at my white lab coat and grey pants which I was still wearing.

We mounted the steps of the palace and entered a great hall, hung with banners of many colours, on which were embroidered strange emblems, mythical beasts and words traced out in a peculiar script which also reminded me of Sanskrit.

Five galleries rose around the hall and in the centre a fountain played. The few simply dressed people who stood conversing in the hall waved cheerfully to the girl and gave me that same look of polite curiosity I had received in the streets.

We walked through the hall, through another doorway and up a spiral staircase of white marble. Here she paused on the landing and opened a door that at first looked like metal but on closer observation proved to be wood of incredible hardness and polish.

The room in which I found myself was quite small. It was barely furnished, with a few rugs of brightly dyed animal skins scattered about and a series of cupboards around the walls.

The girl went to one of these cupboards, opened it and took out two metal circlets in which were set radiant gems of a kind completely unknown to me. She placed one of these on her head and indicated that I should imitate her with the second. I took the circlet and fitted it over my own head.

Suddenly a voice spoke inside my skull. I was astonished for a second, until I realised that here was some kind of telepathic communicator which we physicists had only speculated about.

'Greetings, stranger,' said the voice, and I could see the girl's lips move, framing those lovely, alien syllables.

'From where do you come?'

'I come from Chicago, Illinois,' I said, more to test the device than to convey information which I guessed would be meaningless to her.

She frowned. 'Soft sounds and very pleasant, but I do not know that place. Where in Vashu is that?'

'Vashu? Is this city in a land called Vashu?'

'No – Vashu is the whole planet. This city is called Varnal, capital of the nation of the Karnala, my people.'

'Do you have astronomy?' I asked. 'Do you study the stars?'

'We do. Why do you ask?'

'Which planet is this in relation to the sun?'

'It is the fourth from the sun.'

'Mars! It *is* Mars!' I cried.

'I do not follow you.'

'I am sorry. Somehow I have arrived here from the third planet, which we call Earth. That is where Chicago is!'

'But there are no men on Negalu, the third planet. Only steamy jungles and monstrous beasts!'

'How do you know so much about the planet?'

'Our ethercraft have visited it and brought back pictures.'

'You have spaceships – but…' I was at a loss. This was too incredible for me to accept all at once. I questioned her more closely and soon learned that the Earth her people knew was not the Earth I had left. It seemed to be an Earth that had existed millions of years ago, during the Age of Reptiles. Somehow both space and time had been crossed. That matter transmitter had more to it than we'd guessed!

Another thing puzzled me. The people did not appear to have a great deal of technology visible in the city yet they had spaceships.

'How could this be?' I asked her.

'We did not build the ethercraft. They were a gift from the Sheev – as were these mind-crowns. We have a science of our own but it cannot compare to the great wisdom and knowledge of the Sheev.'

'Who are the Sheev?'

'They are very great and few of them still live. They are remote and of an older race than any on Vashu. Our philosophers speculate on their origin, but we know little about them.'

I let that go for the time being and decided it was about the moment to introduce myself.

'I am called Michael Kane,' I said.

'I am Shizala, Bradhinaka of the Karnala, and ruler in the absence of the Bradhi.'

I learned that the Bradhi was about the equivalent of our 'king', although the title did not suggest that the man who held it possessed absolute power. Perhaps Guide would be a better one – or Protector? Bradhinaka meant, roughly, Princess – daughter of the King.

'And where is the Bradhi?' I asked.

I saw her face become sad and she glanced at the ground.

'My father disappeared two years ago – on a punitive expedition against the Argzoon. He must have been killed or, if he was captured, killed himself. It is better to die than become a prisoner of the Blue Giants.'

I expressed my sympathy and did not feel the time right to ask what the Argzoon or Blue Giants were. She was evidently deeply moved by the memory of the loss of her father, but showed great self-control in refusing to burden someone else with her grief.

I felt immediately like trying to offer her some comfort. But, considering I knew nothing of the moral code and customs of her people, that might perhaps have been disastrous.

She touched her circlet. 'We only need to wear these for the time being. The Sheev have given us another machine which should be able to teach you our spoken language.'

We conversed a little longer and I learned much of Mars – or Vashu, as I was already beginning to think of it.

There were many nations on Mars, some friendly towards the Karnala, some not. They all spoke recognisable versions of the same root language. This is supposedly true of Earth – that our language was originally a common one; but in our case the changes have been extreme. This was not the case, I learned, on Vashu.

The seas of Mars still existed, Shizala told me, though apparently they were not so vast as Earth's. Varnal, capital of the Karnala nation, was one of a number of countries, with rather hazily defined borders, which existed on a large land mass bigger, but in roughly the same geographical position, than the whole of the American continent.

Travel was effected in two main ways. Most ordinary travel relied on the *dahara*, a riding and carriage beast of great strength and endurance. But many nations had a few aircraft. As far as I could make out, these relied on atomics – which none of the Vashu peoples understood. These had not been gifts of the Sheev, I learned, but must once have belonged to the Sheev. They were incredibly ancient by all accounts and could not be replaced when destroyed. Thus they were only used in emergencies. There were also ships incorporating some sort of atomic engine, and sailing ships of various kinds. These plied the few rivers of Vashu – rivers which were shrinking with almost every year that passed.

For arms, the Vashu warriors relied primarily on the sword. They had guns – Shizala showed me hers. It was a long-barrelled, finely made weapon with a comfortable grip. I could not quite see what it fired or on what principle it worked, but as Shizala tried to explain haltingly I concluded that it was some sort of laser-gun. What an incredible amount of power, I thought, was packed into its chambers, for we scientists had always argued that a laser-handgun was out of the question, since the power required to produce the laser ray – tightly focused light which could cut through steel – relied on a very big generator. Wonderingly, I handed the gun back to her. These guns, not gifts of the Sheev but probably looted from their now lost or completely ruined cities by Shizala's remote ancestors, were also used infrequently, since once the charge was finally expended it could not be replaced.

Their *akashasard* – or ethercraft – apparently numbered five in all. Three of these belonged to the Karnala and one each to friendly, neighbouring nations – the Iridala and the Walavala. Although there were pilots who could operate them, none of the folk of Vashu had any idea how they worked.

Other benefits which a few chosen nations had received from the mysterious Sheev included a longevity serum which, once taken, did not need to be taken again. Everyone was allowed to use it and it gave up to two thousand years of life! Because of this very few children were born, so the population of Vashu remained comparatively small. No bad thing, I reflected. I could have listened to Shizala for hours, but at length she stopped my questions with a smile.

'First we must eat. The evening meal will be served soon. Come.'

I followed Shizala as she led me from the little room and down into the main hall, which was now furnished with several large tables at which sat men and women of Karnala, all handsome and beautiful and chatting gaily.

They all rose politely, though not servilely, as Shizala took her place at the head of one of the tables. She indicated the chair on her left and I sat down. The food looked strange but smelled good. Opposite me, on Shizala's right, sat a dark-haired man, superbly muscled. He wore a simple gold bangle on his right wrist and he put his arm on the table in such a way as to show it off.

Evidently he was proud of it for he wanted me to see it. I guessed it to be a decoration of some kind and thought no more of it.

Shizala introduced the man as Bradhinak – or Prince – Telem Fas Ogdai. The name did not sound like a Karnala name, and it soon transpired that Bradhinak Telem Fas Ogdai was from the city of Mishim Tep, a friendly nation some two thousand miles to the south. He was, so it seemed, a witty talker though, of course, I could not understand what he said. Only a person wearing a circlet could communicate with me.

On my left was a pleasant-faced young man with long, almost

white, fair hair. He seemed to be making a special effort to make me feel at home, offering food and drink, asking polite questions through Shizala, who translated for us. This was Darnad, Shizala's younger brother. Apparently the succession to the throne of Varnal was determined by age and not by sex.

Darnad was apparently chief Pukan-Nara of Varnal. A Pukan, I learned, was a warrior, and a Pukan-Nara a warrior leader. The chief Pukan-Nara was elected by popular vote – by civilians and warriors alike. I assumed from this that Darnad's position was therefore no honorary one, and that he had earned it through prowess and intelligence. Though he was personable and charming, the people of Varnal did not judge a man merely on his appearance but on his merit and record.

I was already beginning to pick up a few words of the Vashu tongue by the time the meal was over, and we adjourned into an anteroom to drink a beverage called basu, a sweetish drink I found quite palatable but which, frankly, did not at that time seem as good to me as good, old-fashioned coffee. Later I was to discover that basu grew on one and then I preferred it to coffee. Like coffee, it is a mild stimulant.

In spite of the basu, I began to feel quite sleepy and, as always alert to her guests' needs, Shizala sensed this.

'I have had a room prepared for you,' she telepathed. 'Perhaps you would like to retire now.'

I admitted that the day's surprising experiences had taken a lot out of me. A servant was called and Shizala went with us up the stairs to the second floor of the palace. A dim bulb burned in the room, giving adequate light.

Shizala showed me a bell rope very like old-fashioned bell ropes on Earth. It was close to the bed and was used to summon a servant. She left her circlet behind when she left. Before she did so she told me that anyone could use the circlet and the servant would know how.

The bed consisted of a wide, hard bench, on which was a thin mattress. A large fur rug was laid over this, and it seemed rather too heavy, since the day had been very warm. To some, perhaps, the bed would have been too austere but, as it happened, it was of the kind I preferred.

I fell asleep immediately, having shed my clothes, and I awoke only once in the middle of the Martian night – which is, of course, longer than ours – feeling very cold. I had not realised how much the temperature could change. I pulled the rug about me and was soon asleep again.

Chapter Three

The Invaders

A FEMALE SERVANT entered in the morning, after knocking lightly on the door. I was standing at the window looking out over the beautiful streets and houses of Varnal. At first I felt embarrassed by my nakedness. But then I realised that there was no need since it was abnormal here to wear many clothes, and then, it seemed, only for decoration.

What did continue to embarrass me, however, was the look of open admiration she gave me as she handed me my breakfast tray of fruit and basu.

After she had gone I sat down to eat the fruit – a large one very similar to grapefruit but with a slightly less bitter taste – and drink the basu.

I was just finishing when there was another knock on the door. I called 'Come in!' in English, thinking that this would do the trick. It did. In walked Shizala, smiling.

Seeing her again, it seemed that I had dreamed of her all night for she was as beautiful – if not more so – as I remembered her. Her blonde hair was swept back from her shoulders and back. She had on a black, gauzy cloak and at her waist was the wide belt containing holstered gun and short sword. These, I gathered, were ceremonial weapons of office, for I could not imagine such a graceful girl having much familiarity with the artefacts of war. On her feet she wore sandals, laced up the calf almost to the knee. That was all she was wearing – but it was enough.

She picked up the circlet she had worn the day before and put it on.

'I thought you might wish to ride around the city and see everything,' I heard her voice say in my head. 'Would you like that?'

'Very much,' I replied. 'If you can spare the time.'

'It would please me to do so.' She gave me a warm smile.

I could not make up my mind whether she felt as attracted to me as I was to her, or whether she was just being normally polite. It was a puzzle which was already beginning to fill a great deal of my thoughts.

'First,' she continued, 'it would be better if you spent a couple of hours with the Sheev teaching machine. After that you will be able to converse in our language without recourse to these rather clumsy things.'

As she led me down corridors and staircases, I asked her why, if the tongue of Vashu were common, there should be such a thing as a language-teaching machine. She replied that it had been designed for use on other planets but, since the other planets in the solar system only appeared to be inhabited by animals, it had never been used.

She led me below ground. The cellars of the place seemed to go down many levels, but at last we reached a place lighted by the same sort of dim bulb as the one in my room. These bulbs were also of Sheev manufacture, Shizala told me, and had once burned much brighter than they did now. The room was small and contained a single piece of equipment. It was large and made of metal I did not recognise – probably an alloy. It glowed a little, adding to the light in the room. It seemed to consist of a cabinet with an alcove moulded to accommodate the form of a seated human being. I could see no other machinery and I would dearly have loved to strip the cabinet down to see what was inside – but curbed my impatience.

'Please sit there,' said Shizala, indicating the cabinet. 'According to what I have been told, the cabinet will be activated immediately you do so. You may feel yourself black out, but do not be disturbed.'

I did as she asked and, sure enough, as soon as I was seated the cabinet began to hum softly. A cap came down from above and fitted itself over my head, then I began to feel dizzy and soon became unconscious.

I did not know how much time had passed until I came to,

finding myself still seated in the now no longer activated cabinet. I looked at Shizala a little dazedly. My head was aching slightly.

'How do you feel?' she asked.

'Fine,' I said, getting up.

But I had not said 'fine' at all, I realised. I had said *vrazha* – the Martian word that was its nearest equivalent.

I had spoken Martian!

'It works!' I cried. 'What sort of machine is it that can achieve that so swiftly?'

'I do not know. We are content simply to use the things of the Sheev. We were warned in the far past never to tamper with their gifts since it might result in disaster for us! Their mighty civilisation once suffered a disaster, but we have only a few legends which speak of it and they are bound up in talk of supernatural entities in whom we no longer believe.'

Respecting what was evidently a deeply rooted custom never to question the Sheev inventions, I remained silent, though every instinct made me want to get at the language-teaching machine, probably a highly sophisticated computer containing an hypnotic device of some kind.

My headache had gone by the time we reached the upper levels of the palace and walked through the great hall out into the city. At the bottom of the wide, white steps two strange beasts were waiting.

They were about the same size as shire-horses – the famous English Great Horse which had once borne knights into battle. But horses they were not. Their origin seemed to stem from the same basic root as Man! They were apelike creatures with wide kangaroo tails, their hind legs larger than the forelegs. They were on all fours now and saddles were on their backs. Their great heads, placid and intelligent, turned to look at us as we came down the steps.

I had a few qualms about mounting mine, since it *did* bear certain affinities to my own race, but once aboard it seemed natural that I should ride it. Its back was wider than that of a horse and involved stretching one's legs out in front, and cupping the feet in the stirrups attached to another part of the harness up ahead. The saddle had a solid support allowing the rider to stretch backwards at ease. It was rather like being seated in a sports car, and was very comfortable.

In a kind of holster on my right were several lances, though I had no idea of their purpose. I found that by gentle tugs on the reins, the dahara would respond quickly to any command I made.

With Shizala leading the way, we trotted off through the plaza and down the main street of Varnal.

The city was as exquisite as ever under the deep yellow sun. The sky was cloudless and I began to relax, feeling that I could spend the rest of my life in Varnal and its surrounds. Here a dome caught the light and flashed brightly; there a little white house nestled between an impressive ziggurat on one side and a slender tower on the other. People moved about in a leisurely yet purposeful way. A fruit market was busy, but there was none of the noise and bustle of a similar Earthly market place. As we rode around the city, Shizala told me much about it.

The Karnala as a race had always been primarily traders. Their origins were the same as many races – they had started off as barbarian raiders and finally settled on one part of the country they had liked. But instead of turning to farming they had continued to travel as traders instead of raiders. Because of daring expeditions to far parts of Vashu, they had become very rich, trading Southern artefacts for Northern precious metals, and so on.

The Karnala were also great artists, musicians and – what was highly worthwhile in terms of trade as well as everything else – the finest book producers in their world. The printing presses of Karnala, I learned, were of a flatbed type, not so fast as the rotary machines on Earth, but producing what appeared to my eye much sharper printing. The Sanskrit-like lettering I still could not read but as Shizala took me round a small press, showing me some of the beautifully made books it produced, I soon learned to recognise many words as she pointed them out to me.

These books were in great demand across the whole continent and were a great asset to the Karnala, as were their artists and writers who produced the raw material.

Other industries thrived in Varnal. Their swordsmiths were also renowned throughout the world, I learned. The smiths still worked by the old methods, using furnace and anvil much as smiths on Earth worked – an Earth that was yet to come, I realised.

Some farming was done now, but on a big scale and not by private landowners. Square miles of cereals were sown, I was told, and harvested all at once by volunteers from all over the Karnala nation. What was not used was stored in case of hard times, for the Karnala were well aware that a nation based on trade and industry cannot buy food in famine and will only survive if it can produce its own.

The absence of any places of worship was noticeable and I asked Shizala about this. She replied that there was no official religion of any kind, but for those who wanted to believe in a higher being it was better to look for Him or Her in their own minds and hearts, not to seek Him or Her in the words of others.

On the other hand, there were public schools, libraries, clinics, social centres, hotels and the like, and no-one seemed underprivileged or unhappy in Varnal.

The Karnala political philosophy seemed to be one of armed neutrality. They were a strong nation and prepared for any attack. Besides this, an old-fashioned martial code still seemed to exist, because an aggressor never attacked without good warning.

After telling me this, Shizala added: 'Apart from the more savage tribes, and they are no threat. Those – and the Blue Giants.'

'Who are the Blue Giants?' I asked.

'The Argzoon. They are fierce and without code or conscience. They dwell in the far North and only venture out on raids. They have only once come this far south, and then my father's army drove them away…' She bowed her head and tightened her grip of the reins.

'And never returned?' I said sympathetically, feeling I had to say something.

'Just so.'

She jostled the reins and the dahara began to trot faster. I imitated her and we were soon galloping along the wide streets through which the delicate green mist wound, and up towards the golden hills – the Calling Hills.

We were soon out of the city and rushing through the strange trees which seemed to be calling for us as we moved among them.

After a while Shizala slowed her steed and I did likewise. She turned to me with a smile.

'I acted wilfully – I hope you will forgive me.'

'I could forgive you anything,' I said, almost without thinking.

She gave me a quizzical, intelligent look which again I could not interpret.

'Perhaps,' she said, 'I should mention...'

Again I spoke on impulse. 'Let us not talk – we are interrupting the voices of the trees. Let us just ride and listen.'

She smiled. 'Very well.'

As we rode I suddenly began to wonder how I was going to live on Mars. I had accepted that I would like to stay in the idyllic city of Varnal – I would never willingly leave a place which sheltered such a graceful beauty as the girl riding beside me at that moment – but how was I going to earn my living?

As a scientist I could probably contribute something to the industries. It struck me that Shizala might be interested if I suggested that she elect me as some sort of Court Scientific Advisor! This would allow me to serve a useful function in the community and at the same time enable me to be close to her and see a great deal of her.

At that time, of course, I was acting almost intuitively. I had not as yet wondered if the customs of the Karnala would even permit me to propose marriage to Shizala – and, anyway, there was a very good chance that Shizala would want nothing to do with me. Why should she? Although she had not questioned what I had told her about where I had come from and how I had arrived on her planet, for all she knew I might be a lunatic.

My mind was confused as I rode along. At length we decided we had best return to the city and the palace, and I directed my strange steed back with some reluctance.

The visiting Prince of Mishim Tep, Telem Fas Ogdai, was

waiting on the steps of the palace when we arrived. He had one foot on a higher step and his hand rested on the hilt of his long, broad-bladed sword. He wore soft boots and a heavy cloak of dark material. He looked both angry and impatient, and twice as I dismounted and walked up the steps towards him, he removed his hand from his sword hilt to finger the plain gold bangle on his wrist.

He ignored me but flashed a glance at Shizala and then turned his back on both of us, rumbling up the steps into the palace.

Shizala looked at me apologetically. 'I am sorry, Michael Kane – but I had better speak to the Bradhinak. Will you excuse me? You will find food in the hall.'

I bowed. 'Of course. I hope to see you again later.'

She gave me a quick, half-nervous smile and then she was tripping up the steps after the Bradhinak.

Some diplomatic problem, I guessed, since the prince was evidently an emissary of some kind and was here on diplomatic business as well as a friendly visit.

Perhaps Karnala's strength had been sapped in the battle and the following expedition which had lost them their king. Perhaps they were forced to rely on stronger allies while they built up their strength again – and perhaps Mishim Tep was one of these allies. All this speculation seemed likely – and much of it was subsequently proved correct.

I entered the great hall. A kind of buffet meal had been laid out on the table by servants. Cold meat, fruit, the inevitable basu, sweetmeats and so forth. I sampled a little of everything and found almost all of it to my liking. I exchanged small-talk with some of the men and women around the table. They were evidently very curious about me but too polite to ask too many direct questions – which I did not feel in any mood to answer at that moment.

As I munched at a particularly tasty piece of meat wrapped in a green, lettucelike leaf, I suddenly heard an odd sound. I was not sure what it was, but I listened carefully so that I should hear it again if it came.

The courtiers had fallen silent and were listening. Then the sound came again.

A muffled cry.

The courtiers looked at one another in apparent consternation but made no move towards the source of the cry.

It came a third time and now I was sure I recognised the voice. It was Shizala's!

Although there were guards at intervals around the hall, none of them moved and no orders were given to go to Shizala's assistance.

Desperately, I looked round at the courtiers. 'That is your Bradhinaka's voice – why don't you help her? Where is she?'

One of the courtiers looked very disturbed and pointed to a door leading off the hall. 'She is there – we cannot help her unless she summons us. It is a very delicate matter involving the Bradhinak Telem Fas Ogdai...'

'You mean he is causing her pain! I will not allow it! I thought you were people of character – but you just stand here...'

'I told you – the situation is delicate. We feel very deeply... But etiquette...'

'To hell with etiquette,' I said in English. 'This is no time for niceties – Shizala may be in danger.'

And with that I strode towards the door he had pointed to. It was not locked and I flung it open.

Telem Fas Ogdai was holding Shizala's wrists in a cruel grip and she was struggling. He was speaking to her in a low, urgent tone. When she saw me she gasped:

'No, Michael Kane – go from here. It will mean more trouble.'

'I will not leave while I know this boor is troubling you,' I said, flicking him a look of scorn.

He frowned, then he grinned evilly and his teeth flashed.

He still held her wrists.

'Let her go!' I warned, stepping forward.

'No, Michael Kane,' she said. 'Telem Fas Ogdai means me no harm. We are having an argument, that is all. It will end...'

But I had put my hand on the prince's shoulder now and I let it lie there heavily.

'Release her,' I ordered.

He released her all right – and at the same time swung both his fists round to catch me on the head, sending me reeling. That was it! My temper got the better of me and I surged back in. A punch on the chest winded him and a following punch on the jaw knocked him back. He tried to retaliate so I punched him on the jaw again. He went down with a clatter and stayed down.

'Oh!' cried Shizala. 'Michael Kane, what have you done?'

'I have dealt with a brute who was hurting a very beautiful and sweet young lady,' I said, rubbing my fists. 'I am sorry that it had to happen, but he deserved it.'

'He has a bad temper sometimes, but he is not evil. I am sure you did what you thought was best, Michael Kane, but now you have made things even worse for me.'

'If he is here on diplomatic business he should behave like a diplomat and with dignity,' I reminded her.

'Diplomat? He is no emissary from Mishim Tep. He is my betrothed – did you not see the armlet on his wrist?'

'Armlet – so that's what it is! Your betrothed! But – but he can't be! Why would you consent to marry such a man?' I was horrified and bewildered. There was no chance of making her mine! 'You could not love him!'

Now she frowned and it sent a shudder through me to see that I had angered her. She drew herself up and pulled a bell-cord. 'You do not behave as befits a stranger and a guest,' she said coldly. 'You presume too much!'

'I am sorry – deeply sorry. I was impulsive. But…'

In the same emotionless voice, she said: 'It was my father's wish that when he died and I succeeded him I should marry the son of his old ally, thus making sure of the Karnala's security. I intend to respect my father's wish. You are presumptuous to make any comment concerning my relationship with the Bradhinak of Mishim Tep.'

This was a side of Shizala I had not seen before – the regal side. I must have offended her deeply for her to adopt this manner and tone, for I knew it was not natural.

'I – I am very sorry.'

'I accept your apology. You will not interfere again. Now, please leave.'

In confusion, I turned and left the room.

Bewildered, I walked straight from the great hall, down the steps of the palace to where a servant was just leading away the dahara I had been riding earlier.

With a muttered word to the servant I mounted the beast and shook its reins, making it gallop away down the main street towards one of the gates of the city.

I had to go right away from Varnal for the time being, had to go somewhere where I could be alone to collect my thoughts and pull myself together.

Shizala betrothed! A girl whom, I knew now, I had loved from the moment I saw her. It was too much to bear!

My heart beating much more rapidly than normal and my thoughts racing, my whole being seething with anguish, I rode blindly from the city, past the Green Lake and out into the Calling Hills.

Oh, Shizala, Shizala, I thought, I could have made you so happy.

I believe that I was close to crying then. I, Michael Kane, who had always prided himself on his self-control.

It was some time before I slowed my pace and began to make myself think levelly.

I did not know how far I had ridden. Many, many miles, I suspected. My surroundings were unfamiliar. There were no landmarks I could recognise.

It was then that I saw a movement to the north. At first I thought I was looking at a distant herd of beasts galloping towards me but, shading my eyes from the sun, I soon realised that these were riders mounted on some sort of beast similar to my dahara. Many riders.

A horde!

Knowing so little of Martian geography or, for that matter, politics, I did not know whether these riders threatened danger or not.

I sat my beast, watching them advance at a tremendous pace.

Even so far away from them I could feel the ground faintly trembling, reverberating to the sound of the thundering animals.

Something seemed a little strange as they approached closer. I guess they still could not see me – one solitary figure – but I could see them.

The scale was wrong. That was it.

Judging the average height of man and mount against the average height of trees and shrubs, I knew that these riders and their steeds were gigantic! Not one of their daharas was less than twice the height of mine; not one rider under eight feet tall.

My memory worked swiftly and came up with only one answer.

These were invaders!

More – I thought I knew them.

They could only be those fierce, Northern raiders Shizala had mentioned. *The Blue Giants – the Argzoon!*

Why had the city had no warning of the horde's approach?

How had they managed to come this far undetected?

These questions rose in my mind as I watched, but I dismissed them as useless. The fact was that a mounted force of warriors – thousands of them, it seemed – was riding towards Varnal!

Quickly, I turned my beast, all thoughts of my grief now forgotten. I was obsessed by the emergency. I must warn the city. At least they would have a little time!

I checked my position from the sun and guided the swiftly moving dahara back the way I had come.

But I had not reckoned with the Argzoon outriders. Though I had observed the main horde, the scouts sent ahead had evidently observed *me*!

As I ducked to avoid the low branches of the slim trees and emerged into a wide glade, I heard a huge snort and a strange, wild, gusty laugh.

Then I was staring at a mounted giant towering above me on his great beast. In one hand he held an enormous sword and in the other an oval-headed mace of some kind.

I was unarmed – save for the slender lances that still reposed in the holster at my side.

Chapter Four
The Attack

MY MIND RACED. For a moment I felt completely overwhelmed, staring up into the face of a being that was to me as impossible as the unicorn or the hippogriff.

His skin was a dark, mottled hue. Like the folk of Varnal, he did not wear what we should think of as clothing. His body was a mass of padded leather armour and on his seemingly hairless head was a tough cap, also of padded leather, but reinforced with metal.

His face was broad yet tapering, with slitted eyes and a great gash of a mouth that was open now in laughing anticipation of my rapid demise. A mouth full of black teeth, uneven and jagged. The ears were pointed and large, sweeping back from the skull. The arms were bare, save for wrist guards, and strongly muscled on a fantastic scale. The fingers were covered – encrusted would be a better description – with crudely cut precious stones.

His dahara was not the quiet beast that I rode. It seemed as fierce as its rider, pawing at the delicate moss of the glade, its head sporting a metal spike and its body partially protected by the same dark brown, padded leather armour.

The Argzoon warrior uttered a few guttural words which I could not understand, though they were clearly in the same language that I now spoke so fluently.

Fatalistically feeling that if I must die I would die fighting, I reached for one of the lances in the holster.

The warrior laughed again jeeringly and waved his sword, clapping his massive legs to his mount's side and goading it forward.

Now my reactions came to my rescue.

Swiftly, I plucked one of the lances from the holster and almost in the same motion got its balance, then swung it at the giant's face.

He roared as it hurtled towards him but with incredible speed for one so huge he struck it aside with his sword.

But by that time I had another lance in my hand and turned my jittery mount away as the warrior advanced, his sword swooping down towards me.

I ducked and felt it pass within an inch of my scalp.

Then he had thundered past, carried on by the weight of his own momentum. I wheeled my beast and flung another lance at him as he tried to turn his mount, which was evidently less trained than mine.

The lance caught him in the arm.

He yelled in pain and rage and this time his speed was even faster as he bore down on me again.

I had only two lances left.

I flung the third as he came in with his sword held out in front of him, like a cavalryman on Earth might once have held his sword in a charge.

The third lance missed. But at least my second had wounded his mace-arm and I only had the sword to contend with. I could not duck this one. But what could I do? There were split seconds in which to decide!

Grabbing the remaining lance, I flung myself off the beast and fell to the ground just as the sword met air where I would have been.

Bruised, I picked myself up. I still gripped the last lance.

I would have to use it with certainty if I were to win this duel.

I crouched, waiting as he turned, poised on the balls of my feet, watching the gigantic, snorting brute as he fought his dahara, turning it round again.

Then he paused, laughing that gusty, animal laughter, his blue head flung back and his vast chest heaving beneath its armour.

It was his mistake.

Thanking providence for this opportunity, I hurled the lance with all my force and skill – straight at the momentarily exposed neck.

It went in some inches and for a brief instant the laughter still came from his mortally wounded throat. The noise changed to a shocked gurgle, a high sigh, and then my opponent pitched backward off his dahara and lay dead on the ground.

As soon as it was relieved of its rider, the dahara galloped away into the forest.

I was left, panting and dazed but grateful for the fortuitous opportunity I had been given. I should have been dead. Instead, I was alive – and still whole.

I had expected to die. I had not counted on the incredible stupidity of an adversary who had been so sure of victory he had exposed a vital spot which could only have been reached by the very weapon I happened to possess.

I stood over the great hulk. It lay spread out on the moss, the sword and mace still attached by wrist thongs to its arms. There was a stink about it not of death but of general uncleanliness. The slitted eyes stared, the mouth still a grinning gash, though now it grinned in death.

I looked at his sword.

It was, of course, a great weapon, such as only a nine-foot giant would use. Yet, proportionately, it was almost a short sword – just over five feet long. Fastidiously I bent down and unhooked the thong from the creature's wrist. I picked the sword up. It was very heavy, but finely balanced. I could not use it in one hand as the Argzoon scout had done, but I could use it as a broadsword with two hands. The grips were just right. I hefted it, feeling better, thanking heaven for M. Clarchet, my old fencing master, who had taught me how to get the most out of any blade, no matter how strange or crude it at first seemed.

Holding it by its thong, I remounted my beast and lay the sword across my legs as I rode in that still-peculiar riding position back towards the city.

There was a long way to go and I had to hurry – even more so now – to warn the city of the imminent attack.

But as I rode up hill and down dale for what seemed like hours, I was to be threatened once again by an Argzoon giant who came riding at me from my right flank as I rode down one of the last hillsides before Varnal.

He did not laugh. Indeed, he uttered no sound at all as he came at me. Evidently so near the city he did not wish to alert anyone who might be close by.

He had no mace – just a sword.

I met his first swing with my own recently acquired weapon. He looked at it in surprise, clearly recognising it as one forged by his own folk.

His surprise served me well. These Argzoon were swift movers for their size, but poor thinkers – that had already been made quite plain.

While he was staring at my sword and at the same time bringing his own round for another blow, I did not swing up to protect myself but drove the sword towards where I hoped his heart would be. I also prayed it would pierce the armour. It did, though not as swiftly as I had hoped and, as the blade struck through leather and then flesh, bone and sinew, his sword came down in a convulsive movement and grazed my right arm. It was not a bad wound but, within a moment, it was painful.

His sword dropped from inert fingers, dangling by its thong as he sat in his saddle, rocking dazedly and looking at me groggily.

I could see that he was badly wounded, though not mortally, I guessed.

As he began to topple from his saddle I reached out and tried to take his weight to stop him from falling. With my own wounded arm it was difficult, but I managed to hold him there while I inspected the injury I had inflicted.

Turned slightly by the padded armour, the sword had gone in just below the heart.

I managed somehow to dismount, still holding him, and lifted him down and laid him out on the moss.

He spoke to me then. He seemed very puzzled.

'What –?' he said in his thick, brutish accent.

'I am in a hurry. There, I have stopped the bleeding, it doesn't look fatal. Your own folk must look after you.'

'You – you do not kill me?'

'It is not my way to kill if I do not have to!'

'But I have failed – the warriors of the Argzoon will torture me to death for that. Slay me, my vanquisher!'

'It is not my way,' I insisted.

'Then...' He struggled up, reaching towards a knife in his belt. I forced the huge hand away and he sank back, exhausted.

'I will help you to that undergrowth,' I pointed to some thick shrubbery nearby. 'You can hide there and they will not find you.'

I realised I was showing him more mercy than he expected, even from the folk of Varnal. And in helping him I was slowing myself up. Yet a man is a man, I thought – he cannot do what is contrary to his own feelings and principles. If he has a code of honour he must adhere to it. The moment he forgets that code, then all is lost, for even though he forgets on one occasion, it is the beginning of the end. Bit by bit the code will be qualified, any break with it justified, until the man is no longer a man, in truth, at all.

That is why I helped the odd being I had vanquished. I could do nothing less. As I had told him – it was my way. Such emotions may sound old-fashioned, even prudish, in this modern age where values are changing – many think for the worse – or things are losing their values altogether. But though I realise I may sound stiff and peculiar to many of my contemporaries, I am afraid that then, in that gentle valley on ancient Mars, just as now, on Earth, I had a set of principles – call it what you will – that I knew I must abide by.

As soon as I had hauled the creature to cover, I sent his dahara galloping away and mounted my own.

Within a few minutes I had reached the gates of the city and was riding desperately through them, shouting my warning.

'Attack! Attack! It is the hordes of Argzoon!'

The men looked startled but evidently they, too, recognised the type of sword I was carrying. The gates began to close behind me.

Straight to the palace steps I rode and flung myself from the exhausted dahara, running up the steps, half staggering with pain, exhaustion and the weight of the sword – proof of what I had to tell!

Shizala came running into the main hall. She looked dishevelled and her face still bore traces of her earlier anger.

'What is it? Michael Kane! What means this disturbance?'

'The Argzoon!' I blurted out. 'The Blue Giants – your enemies – a great horde of them attacks the city!'

'Impossible! Why have we not heard? We have our mirror posts that signal messages from hill to hill. We should have heard. Yet...'

She frowned thoughtfully.

'What is it?' I asked.

'The mirrors have had no messages for some time. Perhaps the stations were destroyed by the wily Argzoon.'

'If they have reached this far before, they will have known roughly what to expect.'

'But from where comes their strength? We had thought them beaten and quiescent for at least another ten years. They were all but wiped out by my father's army and its allies! My father headed the army which hunted down the survivors!'

'Well the horde he defeated must have been only a fraction of the Argzoon strength. Perhaps this raid is part of a consistent strategy of surprise, meant to weaken you.'

'If that is their plan,' she sighed, squaring her beautiful creamy shoulders, 'then it was a good one, for in truth we are unprepared!'

'No time for self-recrimination now,' I pointed out, 'Where is your brother Darnad? As chief Pukan-Nara of Varnal it is up to him to direct preparations for defence. What of the other warriors of Karnala?'

'They patrol borders, keep the peace against roaming bandit bands. Our army is scattered, but even if it were all assembled in Varnal it might not suffice to meet an Argzoon horde!'

'It seems impossible that you received no warning at all – not even a runner from another city. How have the Argzoon been able to get this far south without you knowing?'

'I cannot think. As you say, it could be that they have been planning this for years, that they have had spies not of their own race working for them, travelled in small groups under cover at night and in disguise, assembling in some nearby remote quarter of our land – and now ride on the city with none of our allies knowing our fate.'

'The walls will resist heavy siege,' I pointed out. 'You say you have some aircraft. You can bombard them from the air, using your Sheev-guns. That is one advantage.'

'Our three aircraft will not achieve much against so large a force.'

'Then you must send one of them to your nearest ally. Send your – your...' I paused as memory flooded back. 'Send the Bradhinak of Mishim Tep to summon his father's aid – and seek help from your other, weaker, allies on the way.'

She frowned thoughtfully and then looked up at me with a strange, half-puzzled look. She pursed her lips.

'I will do as you suggest,' she said at length. 'But even at their fastest our aircraft will take several days to reach Mishim Tep – an army will take even longer getting here. We will have difficulty resisting so long a siege!'

'But outlast it and resist it we must – for Varnal and for the security of your neighbouring states,' I told her. 'If the Argzoon conquer the Karnala, then they will sweep on across other nations. They must be stopped at Varnal – or your entire civilisation could go under!'

'You have a clearer idea of what is at stake than I.' She smiled, slightly. 'And you have only been with us a short time.'

'Warfare,' I said quietly, thinking of my own experiences, 'does not seem to change much anywhere. The basic issues remain much the same – the strategy, the aims. I have already encountered two of your Blue Giants and hate to think of this lovely city being ruled by them!'

I did not add that it was not only the city I feared for but Shizala, too. Try as I might, I could not make myself forget the emotion I felt for her. I knew now she was betrothed to another and that whatever she or I felt it was impossible that anything could come of it. Evidently her code was quite as strong as mine and would not let her weaken, just as I did not intend to weaken.

For a long moment we looked into each other's eyes and all this was there – the pain, the knowledge, the resolution.

Or did I simply imagine that she was to some degree attracted to me? I must not think such thoughts, in any case. It was over – and Varnal must be protected.

'Have you more suitable arms for me than this?' I said, indicating the Argzoon sword.

'Of course. I will call a guard. He will take you to the arms room where you can select whatever weapons you wish.'

At her command, one of the guards stepped forward and she ordered him to take me to the arms room.

He led me down several flights of steps until we were deeper below the palace than I had been before.

At last he stopped at two huge, metal-studded doors and cried:

'Guard of the Tenth Watch – it is Ino-Pukan Hara with the guest of the Bradhinaka! Please open.' An Ino-Pukan, I now knew, was a warrior with a rank about equivalent to sergeant.

The doors moved slowly open and I stood in a long hall of great size, dimly lit by the waning blue bulbs in the roof.

The guard who admitted us was an old man with a long beard. At his belt were twin pistols. He carried no other weapons.

He looked at me quizzically.

The Ino-Pukan said: 'The Bradhinaka wishes her guest to arm himself as he pleases. The Argzoon attack!'

'Again? But I thought them finished!'

'Not so,' said the Ino-Pukan sadly. 'According to our guest here, they are almost upon us.'

'So the Bradhi died in vain – we are still to be vanquished.' The old man's voice sounded hopeless as he let me wander up the hall admiring the great assortment of weapons.

'We are not defeated yet,' I reminded him, staring at rack upon rack of fine swords. I took several down, testing them for length, weight and balance. At last I selected a long, fairly slim sword, rather like a straight sabre, with a blade as long as the sword I had taken from my Argzoon opponent.

It had a beautiful balance. It had a basket hilt and, as with swords on Earth of the same kind, one curled two fingers, the index and the one next to it around the crosspiece, gripping it with the thumb along the top of the hilt with the remaining two fingers curled under. That may seem an awkward grip to some, but it is actually quite comfortable and also has the advantage of making sure that the sword is not easily knocked from the grasp.

I found a belt for the sword with a loop of leather about six inches broad. It seemed traditional in Varnal that swords were carried naked and not scabbarded – some old custom from less peaceful times internally, I gathered.

There were also guns that seemed operated by a combination of spring and air. I took one of these from its place and turned to the old keeper of the arms room.

'Do many use these?' I asked.

'Some, our guest.' He took the gun from my hand and showed me how it loaded. A magazine of steel darts was exposed. These, in the manner of air-gun darts, could be slid automatically into the breech. The air was automatically repressured after a shot – this was done by means of the spring attachment. A very fine piece of craftsmanship but, as the old man demonstrated, the accuracy was all but nil! The gun bucked so much as it shot its missile that the target had to be very close indeed if one was to have much success in hitting him!

Still, my arms belt had a place for a gun – another leather loop – so I slipped the air-gun in. Now with the gun and sword I felt better and was eager to rejoin Shizala to see how the preparations were progressing.

I thanked the old man and, accompanied by the Ino-Pukan, strode back up to the ground level of the palace. Shizala was not in the hall, but another guard led me up many flights of stairs that grew increasingly narrower until we were standing outside a room that obviously was in one of the circular towers rising from the main building of the palace.

The guard knocked.

Shizala's voice called for us to enter.

We did so and Shizala stood there with Telem Fas Ogdai and

her brother, the Bradhinak Darnad. Darnad darted me a quick smile of acknowledgement. Shizala's welcome was a gracious movement of the head, but Telem Fas Ogdai's smile was stiff and frosty. He evidently had not forgotten our earlier encounter that day. I couldn't blame him now, though I still disliked him greatly. I put my feelings about him down to the situation and made an effort to dismiss them as best I could.

Darnad had spread out a map. It was a little strange to me, this method of map-making. The symbols for cities, forests and so on were not pictorial as ours tend to be, but at last I had some idea of where we were in relation to the rest of that mighty continent – and to Mishim Tep and our other allies. I could also point out where I had seen the Argzoon and at what speed they had been travelling and so on.

'Little time,' Darnad murmured thoughtfully, running his fingers through his long, near-white hair. His other hand gripped his sword hilt. He seemed very young just then – probably little more than seventeen. A boy playing at soldiers, one would have thought at first glance. Then I noted the look of responsibility he wore, the confident way he carried himself, the unselfconscious, unstudied mannerisms.

He began to speak rapidly to us, suggesting where the weakest points would be in the city walls and how they would best be defended. Having had some training in warfare, I was able to make some suggestions which he found useful. He looked at me with something like admiration and I accepted the look as a compliment, for I might have been doing much the same. His essential manliness and clear-headed, objective attitude to the task ahead made me feel that he was ideal as a military leader, and I felt that to fight beside him would be reassuring, to say the least. It would also be, in its way, a pleasure.

Shizala turned to Telem Fas Ogdai.

'And now, Telem, you have seen what we shall try to do and will have some idea of what our chances are of holding off the Argzoon. An aircraft awaits you at the hangars. Luckily, its motor has been prepared, since we planned to show it to our guest. Go swiftly and make sure that reinforcements are sent at once from all cities allied to Varnal. And tell them if Varnal falls, their chances of withstanding the Argzoon are lessened.'

Telem bowed slightly, formally, looked deep into her eyes, darted me another of his looks and left the chamber.

We returned to the study of the map.

From the balcony of the tower it was possible to see the whole lovely city laid out beneath us – and we could see the surrounding countryside.

After a while we took the map out onto the balcony. It was as if we felt something was imminent – as, indeed, something was!

A short time later Darnad pointed.

'Telem leaves,' he said to his sister.

Although there had been talk of aircraft I had not expected the sight which greeted me.

The aircraft was of metal, but it rose and navigated like an old-fashioned airship – gracefully, slowly. It was oval in shape and had portholes dotted along its length. It gleamed like richly burnished gold and was heavily ornamented with pictures of strange beasts and symbols.

It swung in the air as if defying the very laws of gravity and then began to move towards the south, travelling rapidly by my standards, but with a stately dignity which could not be matched by any aircraft ever known to Earth.

It was not out of sight before Darnad pointed again – this time to our north-east.

'Look!'

'The Argzoon!' gasped Shizala.

The horde was coming. We could see the first wave clearly, looking like an army of marching ants from where we stood, yet the menace implicit in its steady progress could not be ignored. We all felt it.

'You did not exaggerate, Michael Kane,' Darnad said softly. I could see his knuckles whiten on his sword hilt.

The air was still and very faintly we could hear their shouts. Thin shouts now – but, having already had some experience of the sounds that the Argzoon warriors could make, I imagined what the noise must be like at source!

Darnad stepped back into the room and came out onto the balcony again, clutching what was obviously a megaphone.

He leaned over the balcony, peering down into a courtyard where a group of guards stood ready.

He put the megaphone to his mouth and shouted to them.

'Commanders of the wall – to your posts. The Argzoon come.' He then relayed specific orders based on what we had discussed a short time before.

As the commanders marched away to take charge of their men and position them, we watched in awful fascination as the horde approached.

Rapidly – too rapidly for us – they began to near the walls. We saw movement from within the city, saw warriors taking up their posts. They stood still, awaiting the first attack.

There were too few of them, I thought – far too few!

Chapter Five
A Desperate Plan

At least we held the wall against the first wave.

The whole city seemed to shake at their onslaught. The air was ripped by their great, roaring shouts, polluted by the stink of their incendiary bombs launched from catapults, and by the odour of their very bodies. Flame licked here, crackled there – and the women and children of Varnal struggled valiantly to extinguish it. The sounds of clashing steel, of dying or victorious war-cries, the swish of missiles – blazing balls of some pitchlike substance – as they hurtled overhead and dropped in streets and on roofs. Shizala and I still watched from the balcony but I felt impatient, anxious to join the brave warriors defending the city. Darnad had already gone to rally his men.

I turned to Shizala, feeling moved, in spite of myself, at her closeness. 'What of your remaining aircraft? Where are they?'

'We are keeping them in reserve,' she told me. 'They will be of better use as a surprise later.'

'I understand,' I told her. 'But what can I do? How can I help?'

'Help? It is not for you – a guest – to concern yourself with our problems. I was thoughtless – I should have sent you away with Telem Fas Ogdai.'

'I am not a coward,' I reminded her. 'I am a skilled swordsman and have been shown great kindness and hospitality by you and your folk. I would regard it as an honour to fight for you!'

She smiled then. 'You are a noble stranger, Michael Kane. I know not how you came to Vashu but I feel it was good that you should be here now. Go then – find Darnad and he will tell you how you can help.'

I bowed briefly and left, running down the stairs of the tower until I had reached the main hall, now in confusion, with men and women rushing this way and that.

I made my way through them, asking a warrior if he knew where I might find the Bradhinak Darnad.

'I heard that the east wall is weakest. You will probably find him there.'

I thanked the warrior and left the palace, heading for the east wall. The main buildings of the city, sturdily built of stone as they were, were not damaged by the fire-bombs hurled by the Argzoon catapults, but here and there bundles of fabric and dry sticks had caught, and single pumps were being operated by women in an effort to put them out.

Thick smoke burned my lungs and made my eyes water. My ears were assailed by cries and shouts from all sides.

And outside – outside the mighty hordes of Blue Giants battered against the city walls. An invincible force?

I did not let my thoughts dwell on *that* idea!

At last I saw Darnad through the smoke near the wall. He was in consultation with two of his officers who were pointing up at the walls, evidently showing him the weakest points. He was frowning thoughtfully, his mouth set in a grim line.

'How can I assist you?' I asked, clapping him on the shoulder.

He looked up wearily.

'I do not know, Michael Kane. Could you magically bring half a million men to our aid?'

'No,' I said, 'but I can use a sword.'

He deliberated. Plainly he was unsure of me and I could not blame him for wondering about one who was, after all, untried.

Just then there came an exultant shout from the wall – a shout that did not issue from a Karnala throat.

It was one of those roaring, triumphant shouts I had heard earlier.

All eyes turned upward.

'Zar! The devils have breached a section of our defence!'

We could see them. Only a few of the blue warriors had gained the top of the wall but, unless they were halted, I knew that soon hundreds would be stepping over.

Scarcely stopping to think, I drew my blade from my belt and leapt for the nearest ramp leading to the wall-top. I ran up it faster than I had ever thought possible.

A blue Argzoon warrior, towering above me, turned as I shouted a challenge from behind.

Again he voiced that deep, maniacal laugh. I lunged with my blade and he parried the thrust with a swift movement of his own thick sword. I danced and saw a slight chance as his arm came round. I darted my sword at the exposed upper arm and was fortunate enough to draw blood. He yelled an oath and swung at me with his other weapon, a short-hafted battle-axe. Again my faster speed saved me and I ducked in under his clumsy guard to take him high in the belly. The sword flashed into his flesh and came out again. His eyes seemed to widen and then, with a dying growl, he toppled from the wall.

Another came at me, more cautiously than his comrade. Again I took the attack to the towering monster.

Twice I lunged, twice he parried, then he lunged at me. I blocked his thrust and saw that my blade was only an inch from his face. I pressed the blade forward and took him in the eye.

I had now got the feel of my sword – a marvellous weapon, better even than the best I had used on Earth.

Now reinforcements had come to my aid. I glanced down on the other side of the wall at what seemed to be a great tide of turbulent blue flesh, leathern armour and flashing steel. A scaling ladder had been raised. More of the Argzoon were scaling it.

That ladder had to be destroyed. I made it my objective. Although the scene was so confused and I could hardly tell what the general situation was, I felt a peculiar calmness sweep over me.

I knew the feeling. I had experienced it before in the jungles of Vietnam – had even experienced something like it in a particularly difficult engagement while fencing for sport.

Now that I had a few comrades at least, I felt even better. I stumbled on something and looked down. One of my assailants had lost his battle-axe. I picked it up in my left hand, testing its weight, and found it was not too badly balanced for me if I held it fairly close to the blade.

Both weapons ready, I moved forward in a half-crouched position towards the next blue invader.

He was leading his fellows along the wall towards the ramp. The wall was wide enough to take three of us, and two warriors ranged themselves on either side of me.

I felt rather like Horatius holding the bridge at that moment, but the Blue Giants were unlike Lars Porsena's men in that none of them was crying 'back'. They all seemed to have the same obsession – to press forward at all costs.

Their huge bodies came towards us, lumbering, powerful. Their slitted eyes stared black hatred at us and I shuddered as, for an instant, I stared directly into one face. There was something less than human, something primeval about that gaze – something so primitive that I felt I had a vision of Hell!

Then they were upon us!

I remember only a fury of fighting. The rapid cut and thrust of the duel; the desperate sense of *having* to hang on, *having* to win, *having* to bring out every ounce of energy and skill if we were to drive them back to the ladder – and destroy it.

Yet it seemed at first as if the most we could do was hold the wall against these huge beast-men looming above us with their great, corded muscles rolling under blue skins, their hate-filled, slitted eyes, their teeth-filled gashes of mouths, and their heavy weapons, the weight of which alone could sweep us from the wall to our doom!

I remember that my wrists, my arms, my back, my legs – my whole body – were aching. Then the aching seemed to stop and I felt only a strange numbness as we fought on.

I remember the killing, also.

We fought against their superior strength and numbers – and we killed. More than half a dozen Blue Giants fell beneath our blades.

We had more to fight for than just a city. We had an ideal, and this gave us a moral strength which the Argzoon lacked.

We began to advance, driving the giants back towards their ladder. This advantage gave us extra strength and we redoubled our attack, fighting shoulder to shoulder like old comrades though I was a stranger from another planet, another time even.

And as the sun began to sink, staining the sky a deep purple shot with veins of scarlet and yellow, we had reached their ladder.

Holding the ladder we were able to stop the giants as they attempted to climb up.

While the others concentrated on stopping any more of the Argzoon gaining the wall, I chopped at the ladder as far down as I could, shortening it so that it no longer topped the wall. Spears clattered around me, but I worked on desperately.

At length my task was as finished as I could make it. I stood up, ignoring the missiles that flew about my body, took careful aim with the axe, aiming at the middle section of the ladder. Then I flung it.

It hit a main strut about halfway down and it went in deep. Several Argzoon warriors were above the place where I had hit the ladder. Their weight completed my work for me – the ladder cracked, splintered and then broke.

With horrible screams the Argzoon fell upon the heads of their comrades crowding the ground below.

Luckily it was the only ladder they had managed to raise, and only because the halberd-type weapons the defenders used to push the ladders back had not been available on this section.

This was rectified as two halberdiers took up their positions.

I was feeling somewhat shaky after my efforts and turned to grin at my comrades. One of them was a boy, even younger than Darnad – a red-headed youngster with freckles and a snub nose. I gripped his hand and shook it, though he was not familiar with the custom. Nonetheless, he responded in the right spirit, guessing the meaning of the gesture.

I reached out my hand to grasp that of the other man. He gave me a glazed look, tried to stretch out his own arm and then pitched forward towards me.

I knelt beside him and examined his wound. A blade had gone right through him. By rights he should have been dead an hour before. Head bowed, I paid my silent respects to such a brave fighter.

Then I was up again, looking around for Darnad, wondering how the battle went.

Night soon fell and flares were lighted.

It seemed we were to have some relief, for the Argzoon horde retreated some distance from the walls and began to pitch tents.

I staggered along the wall and down a ramp. I learned from a wall commander that Darnad had been called to the south wall but would be returning to the palace soon.

Rather than seek him along the wall, I went wearily back to the palace.

In the anteroom off the main hall, I found Shizala. The guard who had brought me here left and I was again comfortably alone with her. Even in my exhausted condition I could not help admiring her tall beauty. At her silent indication I sank upon cushions that had been heaped on the floor.

She brought me a flask of basu. Thankfully I drank it down, almost in a single draught. Then I handed the flask back to her, feeling a little better.

'I have heard what you did,' she said softly, not looking directly at me. 'It was an heroic deed. Your action may have saved the city – or at least a large number of our warriors.'

'It was necessary, that is all,' I replied.

'You are a modest hero.' She still did not look my way but raised her eyebrows a little ironically.

'Merely truthful,' I replied in the same manner. 'How goes the defence?'

She sighed. 'Satisfactorily, considering our shortage of men and the size of the Argzoon horde. Those Argzoon, they are fighting well and cunningly – with more cunning than I had suspected they possessed. They must have a clever leader.'

'I did not think cleverness was an Argzoon quality,' I said, 'from what I have experienced myself.'

'Neither did I. If only we could reach their leader – to destroy him would probably defeat the entire plan of attack and the Argzoon, leaderless, might disperse.'

'You think so?' I said.

'I think it likely. The Argzoon can rarely be persuaded to fight with overall strategy of the sort they are applying now. They pride themselves on their individuality – refuse to fight as an army or under any commander. They enjoy fighting, but not the discipline demanded for ambitious fighting involving armies and planned strategy. They must have a superior kind of leader if he has persuaded them to fight as they are doing now.'

'How could we reach the leader?' I enquired. 'We cannot disguise ourselves as Argzoon – we could dye ourselves blue but could not add eight or ten *kilodas* to our height –' a kiloda is about a third of a foot – 'so an attempt to reach his tent would be impossible.'

'Yes.' She spoke tiredly.

'Unless –' a thought had suddenly struck me – 'unless we could attack him from the *air*!'

'The air – yes...' Her eyes gleamed. 'But even then we do not know who their leader is. They seem to be one great tide of warriors – I saw no obvious commanders. Did you?'

I shook my head. 'And yet he must be out there somewhere. It was too confused today. Let us wait until dawn, when we will be able to see their camp before they resume the attack.'

'Very well. You had better go to your room and sleep now – you have exhausted yourself and will need all your strength for tomorrow. I will have a guard wake you just before dawn.'

I got up, bowed and left her. I went up to my room and stood for a moment at the window. The sweet smell of the Martian night – cool, somehow nostalgic – was tinged now by the stink of war.

How I hated those Blue Giants!

Someone had left some meat and fruit on the table next to my bed. I did not feel hungry but common sense told me to eat. I did. I washed the dried blood, dirt and sweat of the day's warfare from me, climbed beneath that heavy fur and was asleep immediately I lay down.

Next morning the same girl servant awakened me. I received glances from her which were even more overtly admiring than before. It seemed I was something of a talking point in Varnal. I felt flattered but a little bewildered. After all, I had only done what anyone else would have done. I knew I had done my chosen task well, but that was all. I felt myself grow a trifle red with embarrassment as I accepted the food she brought me.

It was not yet dawn, but would be in a very short time – less than two *shatis*, I guessed. A shati is roughly an eighth of an Earth hour.

Just as I was buckling on my sword belt, a light knock sounded on the door. I opened it and faced a guard.

'The Bradhinaka awaits you in the tower,' he told me.

I thanked him and made my way up to the tower chamber where we had met the previous day.

Shizala and Darnad were both there, already on the balcony, tense and waiting for the sun to rise.

It began to rise as I joined them. They said nothing as we exchanged nods.

Soon the sun was flooding golden light over the scene. It struck the lovely walls of Varnal, gleamed on water and illuminated the dark camp of the Argzoon surrounding our city. I say 'our' city because that is how I was already thinking of it – more so now.

The Argzoon tents were affairs of skin stretched on wooden frames – oval in shape mainly, though a few were circular or even square. Most of the warriors seemed to be sleeping on the ground and were beginning to stir as light pervaded the scene.

But from one tent – no larger than the others – a banner flew. All the others were undecorated and tended to surround that solitary oval tent sitting in their centre. There was no doubt in my mind that the cunning Argzoon leader slept there.

'So now we know where their leader is,' I said, staring hard at the waving Argzoon banner. It seemed to depict some sort of writhing, snakelike creature with eyes not unlike those of the Argzoon themselves.

'The N'aal Beast,' Shizala explained with a shudder when I asked her what it symbolised. 'Yes, it is the N'aal Beast.'

'What –?' I broke off as Darnad pointed.

'Look,' he cried, 'they are already preparing to attack!'

He rushed back into the room and came out bearing a long, curling trumpet. He blew on this with all his might and a high, melancholy note echoed through the city. Other trumpet calls sounded in reply.

The warriors of Varnal – many of whom had slept at their posts – began to make ready for another day's fighting. It could well be their last.

Shizala said: 'Although it will take Telem Fas Ogdai another day before he reaches Mishim Tep, he will have stopped off at nearer cities on the way and relief might come by tonight or tomorrow morning. If we can hold out until then...'

'We may not need to if I can borrow one of your aircraft,' I said. 'It only needs one man to drop from the air onto the Argzoon commander – and dispatch him.'

She smiled. 'You are very brave. But the aircraft motors take the best part of a day to warm up. Even if we switched them on now they would not be ready before evening.'

'Then I suggest that you order them to be switched on at once,' I said disappointedly, 'for the opportunity might still arise and be welcomed by you when it does.'

'I will do as you say. But you would perish in a venture such as you contemplate.'

'It would be worth it,' I said simply.

She turned away from me then, and I wondered why. Perhaps she thought me stupid – an unintelligent boor who only knew how to die. After all, I had offended her earlier by behaving tactlessly and unsubtly. Again I controlled my thoughts. It did not matter what she thought, I told myself.

I sighed. Knowing nothing of the science that had developed

the aircraft, I could not suggest any way of getting their motors ready faster. Obviously, I thought, it was some sort of slow reaction system – probably very safe and foolproof, but at a time like that I would have preferred something faster even if more dangerous.

I felt as if Shizala were deliberately hampering me for some reason, as if she did not want me to put my plan into operation. I wondered why.

Darnad now put down the trumpet and clapped me on the shoulder. 'Do you want to come with me?'

'Willingly,' I said. 'You must tell me how I can be most useful.'

'I was unsure of you yesterday,' he said with a smile. 'But that is not true today.'

'I'm glad. Farewell, Shizala.'

'Farewell, sister,' said Darnad.

She replied to neither of us as we left. I wondered if I had offended her in some way. After all, I was unfamiliar with the customs of Vashu and might have done so unknowingly.

But there was no time for such speculation.

Soon the walls of the city were shaking again to another Argzoon attack. I helped with the siege weapons, tipping cylinders of flaring fat down on the attackers, hurling stones on them, flinging their own javelins back into their ranks.

They seemed to care little for their own lives and even less for the lives of their comrades. As Shizala had pointed out, they were individualistic warriors and, though they were taking part in an organised mass attack, you could still see that they were having to control their own instincts. Once or twice I saw a couple of them fighting between themselves while their fellows milled around them and our missiles rained down.

By midday little had been gained or lost, save that whilst the defenders were weary almost to the point of dropping the attackers could bring in fresh reserves. I learned that the system of reserves was alien to the Argzoon normally, and this was another puzzling factor of their attack.

Though fierce and feared, the Argzoon had never been a really important threat since they could not be organised into one mass for long enough. Also this monstrous attack so far from their homeland – an attack without warning – spoke of fantastic planning and ingenuity. It might also speak of treachery, I thought privately – an ally letting the horde through his land by pretending to ignore it. But I still did not know enough of Vashu politics to make any fair guesses.

In the afternoon I helped the members of an engineering squad force up special barriers in places where the wall had been badly weakened by Argzoon rams and catapults.

Turning and wiping sweat from my brow after a particularly difficult piece of manipulating, I discovered Shizala at my side.

'You seem able to turn your hand to anything.' She smiled.

'The test of a good scientist – the test of a good soldier,' I replied, returning her smile.

'I suppose it is.'

'How is the aircraft coming along?'

'It will be ready just before dusk.'

'Good.'

'You will need a specially trained pilot.'

'Then I hope you'll supply one.'

She dropped her gaze. 'That will be arranged.'

'Meanwhile,' I said, 'have you stopped to think that the Argzoon may have been able to arrive undetected here through the connivance of one of your "allies"?'

'Impossible. None of our allies would stoop to such treachery.'

'Forgive me,' I said, 'But though I am impressed by the code of honour possessed by Karnala, I am not sure that all the races of Vashu possess it – particularly since I have seen another Vashuvian race almost as unlike the Karnala as it could possibly be.'

She pursed her lips. 'You must be wrong.'

'Perhaps. But my explanation seems the likeliest. What if Mishim Tep were...?'

Her eyes blazed. 'So that is the foundation of your suspicion – jealousy of Telem Fas Ogdai! Well, let me point out that the Bradhi of Mishim Tep is my father's oldest friend and ally. They have fought many a battle together. The bonds of mutual help that exist between the two nations are centuries old. What you suggest is not only impertinent – it is base!'

'I was only going to say...'

'Say no more, Michael Kane!' She turned on her heel and left.

I may tell you, I had little stomach for further fighting just then.

Yet, scarcely three shatis later, I was part of a small body of warriors defending a breach that the Argzoon had made in the wall.

Steel clashed, blood spilled, the stench of death was everywhere. We stood on the broken masonry and fought off ten times our number of Blue Giants. Brave and ferocious as they were, the Blue Giants lacked our intelligence and speed – as well as our burning ideal to hold the city at all costs. These three advantages just seemed to balance the savage attacks which we somehow managed to withstand.

At one time I was engaging an Argzoon even larger than most of his kind. Around his huge throat he wore a necklace of human bones and his helmet seemed constructed of several large wild-beast skulls. He was evidently some sort of local commander.

He carried two large swords, one in each hand, and he whirled them before him so that facing him was rather like facing a propeller-driven plane!

I stumbled before the force of his attack and my foot slipped on a blood-wet stone. I fell backwards and lay there while, grinning jubilantly, he prepared to finish me.

He raised both swords to hack at my prone figure, and then somehow I swivelled my body and cut at his calves, deliberately slashing at the muscles just behind the knees.

One leg bent and he opened his mouth wide in a great roar of pain. Then the other leg bent and suddenly he was falling towards me.

Hastily I scrambled up and flung myself out of his path. With a tremendous crash he fell to the broken stones and I turned to finish him with a single sword-thrust.

Luck, providence – perhaps justice – were on our side that day.

I cannot explain how else we managed to hold the city against the invaders.

But we did. Then just four shatis before sunset, I left the wall and headed for the aircraft hangars that had been pointed out to me the day before.

The hangars were domed buildings near the central square of the city. There were three of them, side by side. The domes were not of stone, but of some metallic substance, another alloy with which I was unfamiliar.

The entrances were small, barely wide enough or high enough for a man of my size to squeeze through. I thought this strange, and wondered how the aircraft could get out.

Shizala was in the first hangar I tried, supervising some male servants who were swinging one of the heavy aircraft around on davits. It was cradled in the davits, which swung slightly as they moved it.

The strange oval ship was even more beautiful at close view. It was evidently incredibly ancient. There was this aura of millennia of existence about it. I looked at it in fascination.

Shizala, tight-lipped, did not welcome me as I entered.

I gave her a slight bow, feeling uncomfortable. A low thrum of power came from the ship. It looked more like a piece of sculpture in bronzelike substance than a vehicle. The complicated, raised designs spoke of a creative intelligence superior to any in my experience.

A simple rope ladder led to the entrance. I walked up to this in silence and tested it.

I darted a look of enquiry at Shizala.

At first she refused to meet my glance, but at length she did and said with a gesture at the ship: 'Go aboard. Your pilot will join you in a moment.'

'There is not much time,' I reminded her. 'This should be accomplished before nightfall.'

'I am aware of that,' she replied coldly.

I began to climb the swaying ladder, reached the top and entered the ship.

It was richly furnished, with padded couches of some deep green and gold material. At the far end were controls, as beautifully made and as finely decorated as the rest of the ship, with levers of brass – perhaps even gold – instruments encased in crystal. There was a small screen in a cabinet – some kind of television equipment which gave a wider view of what lay outside the ship than could be obtained through one of the rather small portholes.

After inspecting the interior of the ship I sat on one of the couches to work out my plan of assassination – for that, in essence, was what it was – and wait impatiently for my pilot to join me.

In a while I heard him climbing the rope ladder. My back was to the entrance so I did not see him as he entered.

'Hurry,' I said. 'We have very little time!'

'I am aware of that,' came Shizala's voice as she walked towards the controls and seated herself at them!

'Shizala! This is dangerous! It is no job for a woman!'

'No? Then who else do you suggest? Only a few pilots exist for the ships – and I am the only one available.'

I was not sure that she spoke the truth, but there was no time to waste.

'Then be very careful,' I said. 'Your people need you more than I do – do not forget your responsibility to them.'

'That I could never do,' she said. For some reason I thought she spoke bitterly, though I could not determine why at that time.

Now she operated the controls and the ship began to rise, light as a feather, towards the roof. As the roof slid open, I realised how the ships left the hangars. The dark blue sky of late evening was above us. The ship's motors began to murmur with greater intensity.

Soon we were winging over the city towards the camp of the Argzoon. We noticed that they were beginning to retreat again, as was their night-time custom.

Our plan was simple. The ship would swoop down over the tent of the Argzoon commander. I would drop swiftly down the rope ladder. The oval tent had holes at the top, covered with thin gauze – presumably for better ventilation. The hole would just take a man. I had to drop through it and thus surprise the commander, engage him quickly and dispatch him with expediency.

A simple plan – but one that would require swift reactions, excellent timing and absolute accuracy.

As we began to move over the enemy camp, their great catapults sent huge stones hurtling into the air towards us. We had expected this. But we had also expected what happened next – the falling stones, of course, landed back in the Argzoon camp and the warriors naturally objected to being crushed by the artillery of their own forces. Soon the barrage ceased.

Within a short time our objective was reached.

At a signal from Shizala, I went to the entrance – began to pay out more of the rope ladder from the drum near the door.

I darted a glance at her but she did not turn to look at me. I gazed down. I could see the Banner of the N'aal Beast stirring in the faint breeze that was beginning to blow.

The faces of hundreds of Argzoon were watching me, of course, for they had expected some sort of attack from us. I hoped they didn't realise what form it would take.

Looking down at them, I felt like a fly dropping into a nest of giant spiders. I gathered my courage, made sure of my sword, drawing it in a single gesture, shouted once to Shizala and swung down the rope ladder until I was directly over the gauze-covered opening of the leader's tent.

Argzoon were shouting and milling about. Several spears flashed past me. More than ten feet over the opening I decided it was now or never.

I let myself go and dropped towards the tent.

Chapter Six

Salvation – And Disaster!

THERE WAS A momentary roaring in my ears and then I was plummeting through the opening, dragging the gauze cover with me.

I landed on my feet but staggered as the air was forced from my lungs. Then I whirled to confront the occupants of the tent.

There were two of them – a large, battered Argzoon warrior, resplendent in rudely beaten bangles and rough-hewn gems – and a woman! She was black-haired, dark-complexioned and had a haughty bearing. She was wrapped in a thick, black cloak of some velvetlike material. She stared at me in surprise. She was as far as I could tell an ordinary human woman! What was she doing here?

Outside came yells from the Argzoon warriors.

Ignoring the woman, I gestured to the battered Argzoon to draw his sword. He did so with a sharp grin and came at me suddenly.

He was an excellent swordsman and, still recovering from my drop into his tent, I was forced to fight a defensive duel for a few moments.

I had little time to do what I had come to accomplish. I met his thrusts with the fastest parries I have ever made, returned them with thrusts and lunges of my own. Our swords crossed perhaps a score of times before I saw a break in his guard and moved in swiftly, catching him in the heart and running him through.

At that moment several more Argzoon rushed into the tent. I turned to meet them but before we could engage the woman cried imperiously:

'Enough! Do not kill him yet, I wish to question him.'

I remained on guard, suspecting a ruse of some sort, but the warriors seemed to be in the habit of obeying the woman's orders. They stood their ground.

Cautiously I turned to look at her. She was exotically beautiful in her wild, dark way, and her eyes smouldered mockingly.

'You are not of the Karnala,' she said.

'How do you know that?'

'Your skin is the wrong texture, your hair is short – there is something about the set of your shoulders. I have never seen a man like you. Where are you from?'

'You would not believe me if I told you.'

'Tell me!' She spoke fiercely.

I shrugged. 'I come from Negalu,' I said, using the Martian name for Earth.

'That is impossible. There are no men on Negalu.'

'Not now. There will be.'

She frowned. 'You seem to speak truthfully, but in some sort of riddle. You are perhaps a – a...' She seemed to regret what she was about to say, and stopped.

'A what?'

'What do you know of Raharumara?'

'Nothing.'

This seemed to satisfy her. She put her knuckles to her mouth and seemed to gnaw them. Suddenly she looked up at me again.

'If you are not of the Karnala, why do you fight with them? Why did you jump into this tent and kill Ranak Mard?' She indicated the fallen Argzoon.

'Why, do you think?'

She shook her head. 'Why risk your life just to kill one Argzoon captain?'

'Is that all I did?'

She smiled suddenly. 'Aha! I think I know. Yes, that is all you did.'

My spirits sank. So I had been wrong. The tent did not hold some great Argzoon battle-leader. Perhaps it was a deliberate blind and the leader was elsewhere.

'What of you?' I said. 'Are you a prisoner of these folk – a prisoner with some power?'

'Call me a prisoner if you like. I am Horguhl of the Vladnyar nation.'

'Where lies Vladnyar?'

'You do not know? It lies to the north of Karnala, beyond Narvaash. The Vladnyar are ancient enemies of the Karnala.'

'So Vladnyar has struck up an alliance with Argzoon?'

'Think what you like.' She smiled secretively. 'And now, I think, you will d –' She broke off as there came a great sound of fighting outside the tent. 'What is that?'

I could not think. It was impossible that the small force of Karnala warriors in the city had attacked the Argzoon – that would have been folly. But what else?

As Horguhl and the Blue Giants turned towards the sound, I seized my opportunity, stepped forward and ran one of the Argzoon through the throat. I fought my way through the others and found myself outside the tent, staring into the darkness as the remaining warriors came after me.

I ran in the general direction of the noise of battle. I darted a quick glance back above the tent, looking to see if Shizala had made good her escape.

The ship was still there – hovering above the tent!

Why hadn't she left? I stopped, uncertain what to do, and in a second found myself engaging several of the gigantic warriors. It was all I could do to protect my own life, but as I fought I got the impression that something was happening close by and suddenly, out of the corner of my eye, I saw a group of splendidly armoured warriors of about my own height break through a mass of blue swordsmen.

The warriors were not from the city, that was plain. They wore helmets, for one thing – helmets from which nodded brightly coloured plumes. Phobos and Deimos, coursing across the heavens, gave illumination to the scene around me. The new warriors also had lances and some carried what looked like metal crossbows.

Soon their foreguard had pressed forward until I found myself with several allies helping me to engage the Argzoon who were attacking me.

'Greetings, friend,' said one of them in an accent only slightly different from the one I was familiar with.

'Greetings. Your presence here has saved my life,' I replied in relieved gratitude. 'Who are you?'

'We are from Srinai.'

'Did Telem Fas Ogdai send you here?'

'No.' The man's voice sounded a trifle surprised. 'We were originally on our way to deal with a large force of bandits who fled into Karnala. That is why there are so many of us. A detachment of your border patrol were about to help us when a messenger came with news that the Argzoon were attacking Varnal – so we left the bandits and rode to Varnal as fast as we could.'

'I am glad you did. What do you think our chances are of defeating them?'

'I doubt that we can – not completely. But we might be able to drive them away from Varnal and give your reinforcements time to come to your aid.'

This conversation was carried on while fighting Argzoon warriors. But the Argzoon were becoming increasingly few and it seemed we were winning in that particular area, anyway.

At last we had them on the run and the combined force of Srinai and Karnala chased the retreating Argzoon towards the Calling Hills whence they had come.

The Argzoon stood their ground on the crest of the first range of hills, and then we withdrew to count our strength and plan fresh strategy.

It was soon obvious that the Argzoon still outnumbered us and that the Srinai and Karnala who had attacked them from behind had the advantage of being fresh and able to take the Argzoon by surprise.

But I felt much better. Now, I decided, we could withstand the next attack and hold the Argzoon off until help came.

Then I remembered the ship and Shizala. I returned to the now ruined Argzoon camp. The tent with the banner was still standing, unlike most of the others and, rather strangely, the ship still hovered above it. It seemed to me, peering through the moonlit darkness, that the ship was now lower above the roof, the rope ladder brushing the top of the tent.

I called her name, but silence greeted me. With a feeling of foreboding I climbed up the yielding sides of the tent. It was a hard climb, but I made it rapidly, almost in panic. Sure enough, the rope ladder was closer, the ship lower. I grabbed the ladder and began to clamber up it.

Soon I was inside the ship.

A brief glance showed me that it was empty.

Shizala had gone!

How? Where?

What had happened to her? What had she done? Why had she left the ship? What reason was there for doing such a thing?

All these thoughts raced through my brain and then I was dropping down the rope ladder again, hand over hand, until I was above the now uncovered roof-opening. I dropped through it as I had done earlier.

Save for the corpse of Ranak Mard the tent was empty. Yet there were signs of a struggle and I noticed that Ranak Mard's sword had been removed from his dead grasp and now lay on the other side of the tent.

Something else lay beside it.

A gun.

A gun of the Sheev.

It could only be Shizala's gun.

The mysterious, dark-haired woman Horguhl and the Argzoon warriors must have taken part in a struggle soon after I had left.

For some reason best known to herself, Shizala had decided to follow me into the tent. She had found me gone, of course, and confronted Horguhl and the Argzoon. There had probably been a fight and Shizala had been overpowered and captured. She had not been killed – that was a mercy – or I should have found her corpse.

Abducted, then?

My misguided plan to kill the absent mastermind behind the

Argzoon had been worthless. All my plan had succeeded in doing was putting a hostage in the hands of the Argzoon.

The best hostage they could ever hope for.

The ruler of Varnal.

I began to curse myself as I would never curse another, even my greatest enemy.

Chapter Seven
The Pursuit

THEN I WAS running from the tent, blind with remorse and anger. I rushed through the corpse-strewn field towards the Calling Hills, bent on Shizala's rescue!

I ran past startled warriors of the Srinai and the Karnala, who called after me enquiringly.

I began to run up the hill towards the spot the Argzoon had taken their stand.

I heard more shouts behind me, the sound of fast-moving feet. I refused to pay them any attention.

Ahead and above, the Argzoon stirred, evidently thinking that we were launching another surprise attack on them.

Instead of holding their ground as I expected, they began to turn and run in twos and threes.

I yelled at them to stop and fight. I called them cowards.

They did not stop.

Soon it seemed that the whole Argzoon force was in full flight – pursued by one man with a sword!

Suddenly I felt something grapple my legs. I turned to meet this new adversary, wondering where he had come from. I raised my sword, striving to keep my balance.

More men jumped on me. I growled in fury, trying to fight them off. Then my head cleared for a moment and I realised that the one who had grappled me was none other than Darnad – Shizala's brother!

I could not understand why *he* should be attacking me. I cried out:

'Darnad – it is Michael Kane. Shizala – Shizala – they have...' Then came a blow on my head and I knew no more.

*

I awoke with a throbbing headache. I was in my room in the palace at Varnal. That much I could understand. But why?

Why had Darnad attacked me?

I fought to think clearly. I sat up rubbing my head. The door suddenly opened and my attacker entered looking worried.

'Darnad! Why did you –?'

'How do you feel?'

'Worse than I would if your comrade had not knocked me out. Don't you realise that…'

'You are still excited, I see. We had to stop you, even though your madness resulted in the Argzoon fleeing in complete disorganisation. As far as we can tell, they are now scattered. Your plan to slay their leader must have worked. They seem to have broken up completely. They no longer represent a threat to Varnal.'

'But I slew the wrong man. I –' I paused. 'What do you mean, my *madness*?'

'It sometimes happens that a warrior who has fought long and hard, as you did, is gripped by a kind of battle-rage in which – no matter how tired he might be – he cannot stop fighting. We thought this was what happened to you. There is another thing that concerns me. Shizala –'

'Don't you realise what you have done?' I spoke in a low, angry voice. 'You speak of Shizala. Is she here? Is she safe?'

'No – we cannot find her. She piloted the ship that took you to the Argzoon camp, but the ship was empty when we recovered it. We think that…'

'I *know* what has happened to her!'

'You know? Then why did you not tell us? Why –?'

'I was seized by no battle-rage, Darnad. I discovered that Shizala had been abducted. I was on my way to try to rescue her when you set upon me. How long ago was this?'

'Last night – about thirty-six shatis ago.'

'Thirty-six!' I got up, giving an involuntary groan. Not only my head ached. The exertions of the previous two days had taken their toll of my body. It seemed a mass of bruises and minor wounds. My worst wound – the one on my arm – was throbbing painfully. Thirty-six shatis – more than four hours ago!

As quickly as I could, I told Darnad all the details of what I had learned. He was as surprised as I had been to learn of Horguhl the Vladnyar woman.

'I wonder what part she plays in this?' he said with a frown.

'I have no idea. Her answers were ambiguous, to say the least.'

'I am sorry that I made that mistake, Michael Kane,' he said. 'I was a fool. I heard you shouting something. I should have listened. With luck we should have rescued Shizala and all would be over. The Argzoon are scattered. We and our allies will soon have cleansed Karnala of them. We will be able to question prisoners and discover how they managed to reach Varnal undetected.'

'But while we are doing this Shizala could be taken anywhere! North – south – east – west. How are you to know where they will carry her?'

Darnad dropped his eyes and stared at the floor.

'You are right. But if you think Shizala is with this Vladnyar girl, then we must hope that some of our prisoners will have seen which way they went. There is also the chance that in our general routing and capturing of the Argzoon we will manage to rescue Shizala.'

'There is no time for recriminations of any kind,' I said. 'So let us forget the errors of judgement we have both made. The heat of the battle must be held to account. What do you intend to do now?'

'I shall be leading a force with the specific intention of capturing Argzoon and questioning them on the whereabouts of Shizala.'

'Then I shall accompany you,' I told him.

'That is what I hoped you would say,' he said, patting my shoulder. 'Rest while the last preparations are being made. I will call for you when we are ready to leave – there is nothing else you can do until then, and you had better regain as much strength as possible – you are going to need it. I will have food sent.'

'Thank you,' I said gratefully. He was right. I must make myself relax – for Shizala's sake.

As I lay back on the couch, I again wondered just why she had risked such danger by going into the Argzoon tent. There had been no need for it – and as ruler of her folk she should have returned at once to Varnal.

I decided that the sooner we found her the sooner we should have answers to these and other questions.

I slept until a servant entered with food. Then I ate the food and, on receiving a message that Darnad and his warriors were ready, washed hastily and went down to join them.

The day should have been grim and stark and full of storm clouds. It was not. It was a lovely, clear day with the pale sun brightening the streets of the city and obscuring most traces of the strife that had so recently ended.

At the foot of the palace steps was a company of warriors mounted on dahara. Darnad was at their head, holding the reins of a dahara that was evidently meant for me.

I mounted the beast, stretching my legs out along it. Then the whole company turned into the street leading towards the main gate.

We were soon riding across the Calling Hills, tracking our fleeing enemy.

It was still a mystery why the Argzoon had fled so precipitately – particularly in the face of such a small force.

But we did not ask ourselves these questions as we rode grimly after our quarry, even though it seemed that Ranak Mard had, indeed, been the mastermind behind the Argzoon attack – for it was plain that he was dead and the Argzoon were now in confusion.

Yet why had Horguhl told me otherwise?

No questions. Not yet.

Find the Argzoon – they will answer our questions.

On we rode.

It was not until late in the afternoon that we managed to surprise a group of some ten weary Argzoon who had camped in a shallow valley far, far from the Calling Hills.

They rose up at our approach and stood ready to fight. For

once *we* outnumbered *them*. Normally, this would not please me but I felt that in this case it made a pleasant change to have the advantage over the Argzoon.

They put up a token fight as we attacked them. About half were killed and then the others lay down their arms.

The Argzoon have no code of loyalty such as we understand it, and little sense of comradeship with one another. This made it easier to question them in one way – but harder in another.

They did not stay silent because they did not wish to betray their fellows. They stayed silent out of stubbornness.

It was not until Darnad significantly fingered his long dagger and hinted that, since they were no use to us, it would be as well to dispose of the Argzoon, that one of them broke.

We were lucky. He knew a great deal more than we had expected one simple warrior to know.

They had not crossed from Argzoon to Karnala by land at all but had spent over a year travelling by sea and river. They had gone round the coast, thousands of miles out of their way – for Varnal lay many thousands of miles inland – and then sailed down the Haal River, the largest of the rivers on the continent. They had assembled in a place called the Crimson Plain and then gone in small groups from there, moving at night all the time, until they reached Karnala undetected. We learned that one or two parties of Karnala warriors had discovered detachments of Argzoon, but the Karnala had been wiped out.

'Simple,' Darnad mused after hearing this. 'And yet we never credited the Argzoon with such ingenuity or patience. It just isn't in their nature to spend so much time and thought on a raid. It is good that you slew Ranak Mard, Michael Kane. He must have been a strange sort of Argzoon.'

'Now,' I said, 'let us try to discover where Shizala has been taken.'

But the Argzoon could not help beyond telling us that as far as he knew all the Argzoon were fleeing north. It seemed instinctive for them to go north, back to their mountains, in defeat.

'I think he is right,' said Darnad. 'Our best chance would be to try the North.'

'North,' I said – 'that takes in a lot of territory.'

Darnad sighed.

'True – but...' He looked at me directly and there was a misery in his eyes that was only half hidden.

I reached out and grasped his shoulder. 'But all we can do is search on,' I said. 'We will take more prisoners soon and with luck we shall be able to get a better indication of where they have taken Shizala.'

Our prisoners were tied securely and one of our number undertook to escort them back to Varnal.

Now we rode across a vast plateau of short, waving crimson fern. It was the Crimson Plain. It was like a great sea of bright blood, stretching in all directions, and I began to feel hopeless of ever finding Shizala.

Night fell and we camped, building no fires for fear of ambush from Argzoon or from the marauding bandits who apparently roamed these plains, nomadic bands made up from the riff-raff of all the nearby nations. The Crimson Plain was a kind of no man's land hardly touched by law of any sort – save the savage dog-eat-dog, weakest-to-the-wall law of the lawless.

I slept little. I was beginning to feel frustrated, wanting to find more Argzoon to question.

We moved off early, almost before dawn. It was no longer fine and the sky was full of grey clouds, a light drizzle falling.

We saw nothing of bandits or Argzoon until the next afternoon when suddenly in front of us some fifty Blue Giants rose up in our path. They looked ready for a fight – ready for vengeance on us for their defeat!

We scarcely paused as we drew lances and swords and goaded our mounts towards them, yelling as fiercely as they did.

Then we clashed and the fight was on.

I found myself engaged with a blue warrior who wore around his waist a girdle of grisly spoils from the earlier encounter – severed human hands.

I decided to claim some recompense for those hands.

Being mounted, I was more at an advantage than I had been,

for the Argzoon were not. Apart from the advance guard I had originally seen, there seemed to be few mounts among them and I concluded that their need for secrecy had made them wary of using too many.

The warrior struck at me left-handed, catching me by surprise. The weapon was a battle-axe, and it took all my skills to block the blow and at the same time avoid the lunge of his sword.

He pressed down on my sword with both weapons and we remained in that position for several moments, testing each other's strength and reflexes. Then he tried to raise the sword to aim a blow at my head, but I whipped my own blade out from under his axe and he was unbalanced for a second. I used that second to pierce him in the throat.

Meanwhile there was general confusion around me. Though it seemed we were beating the Argzoon, we had many casualties. It seemed we had only about half our original strength left.

I saw Darnad having trouble with a couple of blue warriors and rode in to help him.

Together we quickly dispatched our opponents.

From the fifty Argzoon we had fought, only two had surrendered.

We used the same technique on them as we had used with the previous prisoners. At last they began to answer our questions surlily.

'Did you see any of your comrades take a Karnala woman with them?'

'Perhaps.'

Darnad fingered his knife.

'Yes,' said the Argzoon.

'In which direction were they riding?' I said.

'North.'

'But where did you think they were going?'

'Maybe towards Narlet.'

'Where is that?' I asked Darnad.

'About three days' ride – a brigand town near the borders of the Crimson Plain.'

'A brigand town – dangerous for us, eh?'

'It could be,' Darnad admitted. 'But I doubt it if *we* don't make trouble. They prefer not to antagonise us if we make it plain we are not seeking any of their number. In fact,' Darnad laughed, 'I have a friend or two in Narlet. Rogues, but pleasant company if you forget that they are thieves and murderers many times over.'

Again we put the prisoners in charge of one man and our somewhat depleted force moved on towards Narlet.

At least we had some definite information and our spirits rose as we rode full speed towards the City of Thieves.

Twice more en route we were forced to stop and engage Argzoon and the prisoners we took confirmed that in all likelihood Shizala had been taken to Narlet.

Less than three days later we saw a range of hills in the far distance, marking the end of the Crimson Plain.

Then we saw a small walled city – its wall seeming to be built of logs covered with dried mud.

The buildings were square and seemed solid enough, but they had little beauty.

We had reached Narlet, City of Thieves.

But would we find Shizala?

Chapter Eight

The City of Thieves

It would not be true to say that we received a joyous welcome in Narlet but, as Darnad had said, they did not immediately set upon us, though they gave us looks of intense suspicion and tended to avoid us as we entered the city's only gate and made our way through the narrow streets.

'We'll get no information from most of them,' Darnad told me. 'But I think I know where I can find someone who will help us – if old Belet Vor still lives.'

'Belet Vor?' I said questioningly.

'One of those friends I mentioned.'

Our little party emerged into a market square of some sort and Darnad pointed to a small house sandwiched between two ramshackle buildings. 'When I used to patrol these parts he saved my life once. I had the good fortune to return the favour – and somehow we struck up a strong friendship. One of those things.'

We dismounted outside the house and from it an old man emerged. He was toothless and wrinkled and incredibly ugly, yet there was a jaunty appearance about him which made one forget his unwholesome visage.

'Ah, the Bradhinak Darnad – an honour, an honour.' His eyes twinkled, belying his servile words. He spoke ironically. I could see why Darnad had liked him.

'Greetings, you old scoundrel. How many children have you robbed today?'

'Only a dozen or so, Bradhinak. Would this friend of yours like to see my spoils – some of the sweetmeats are only half-eaten. Heh – heh!'

'Spare us the temptation.' I smiled as he ushered us into his hovel.

It was surprisingly clean and orderly and we sat on benches while he brought us basu.

Drinking the sweet beverage, Darnad said seriously: 'We are in haste, Belet Vor. Have any warriors of the Argzoon been seen in Narlet recently – coming here perhaps a day or so before us?'

The old rogue cocked his head to one side. 'Why, yes – two Argzoon warriors. Looked as if they'd taken a beating and were scampering back to their mountain lairs.'

'Just two warriors?'

Belet Vor chuckled. 'And two prisoners, by the look of them. I'm thinking they wouldn't have chosen such company of their own free will.'

'*Two* prisoners?'

'Women, both of them. One fair, one dark.'

'Shizala and Horguhl!' I cried.

'Are they still here?' Darnad asked urgently.

'I'm not sure. They could have left early this morning, but I think not.'

'Where are they staying?'

'Ah – there you have it, if you seek the prisoners. The Argzoon warriors seem to be of high rank. They are guests of our city's noble Bradhi.'

'Your Bradhi – not Chinod Sai?'

'Yes. He has now chosen to call himself the Bradhi Chinod Sai. Narlet is becoming respectable, eh? He is one of your peers now, Bradhinak Darnad – not so?'

'The scoundrel. He gives himself airs.'

'Perhaps,' said old Belet Vor musingly, 'but I seem to remember that many of the established nations in these parts had origins similar to ours.'

Darnad laughed shortly. 'You have me there, Belet Vor – but that's for posterity. I know Chinod Sai for a bloodthirsty slayer of women and children.'

'You do him an injustice.' Belet Vor grinned. 'He has killed at least one youth in a fair fight.'

Darnad turned to me, speaking seriously. 'If these Argzoon

have Chinod Sai's protection, then we will have greater difficulty getting Shizala – and this other woman – out of their power. We are in a bad position.'

'I have a suggestion, if you will hear it,' Belet Vor insinuated.

'I'll listen to anything reasonable,' said Darnad.

'Well – I would say that the Argzoon and their ladies are guesting in the special chambers set aside for sudden visitors of some standing.'

'What of it?' I said, a trifle tersely.

'Those chambers are conveniently placed on the ground floor. They have large windows. Perhaps you could help your friends without – er – actually disturbing our royal Bradhi?'

I frowned. 'But aren't they guarded?'

'Oh, there are guards surrounding the great Bradhi's palace at intervals. He fears, possibly, that there may be robbers in these parts – such little faith does he have in his subjects.'

'How would we enter the guest rooms without the guards seeing us?' I rubbed my chin.

'You would have to dispose of them – they are very alert. After all, some of the best thieves of the Crimson Plain have tried to help themselves to Chinod Sai's booty from time to time. A few have even succeeded. Most have helped decorate the city walls – or at least their heads have.'

'But how could we silence the guards easily?'

'That,' said Belet Vor with a wink, 'is where I can help you. Excuse me.' He got up and hobbled from the room.

'I think he's a likeable old bandit, don't you?' Darnad said when Belet Vor had left.

I nodded. 'But he puts himself in danger, surely, by helping us. If we are successful this Chinod Sai's men are bound to suspect that he had a hand in it.'

'True. But I doubt whether Chinod Sai would do anything about it. Belet Vor knows many secrets and some of them concern Chinod Sai. Also, Belet Vor is very popular and Chinod Sai sits his self-made throne rather uncertainly. There are many who would usurp him if they could gain a popular following. If anything happened to Belet Vor it would be just the excuse needed by some would-be Bradhi of Thieves. Chinod Sai knows that well enough.'

'Good,' I replied. 'But nonetheless, I think he risks more than he needs for our sake.'

'I told you, Michael Kane – there is a bond between us.'

That simple statement meant a great deal to Darnad, evidently, and I think I knew how he felt. Such virtues as loyalty, self-discipline, temperance, moderation, truthfulness, fortitude and honourable conduct to women are apparently outmoded in the societies of New York, London and Paris – but on Mars, my Vashu, they were still strong. Is it any wonder I should prefer the Red Planet to my own?

Soon Belet Vor returned carrying a long tube and a small, handsomely worked box.

'These will silence your guards,' he said, flourishing the box. 'And more – they will not actually kill them.'

He opened the box carefully and displayed the contents. About a score of tiny, feathered slivers lay there. At once I guessed that the tube was a blowpipe and these were its ammunition. The slivers must be tipped with some poison that would knock the guards out.

In silence we accepted the weapon.

'There are some eight shatis until nightfall,' Belet Vor said. 'Time to exchange reminiscences, eh? How many men came with you?'

'There are six left,' I said.

'Then there is room enough in here for them. Invite them in for a cup of basu.'

Darnad went outside to extend Belet Vor's invitation to his men.

They came in and accepted the cups gratefully. Belet Vor also brought food.

The eight shatis passed with incredible slowness and I spent them, for the most part, in thoughtful silence. Soon, if providence were on our side, I would see Shizala again! My heart pounded in spite of myself. I knew she could never be mine – but just to be near her would be enough to know that she was safe, to know that I would always be nearby to protect her. When it was dark Belet Vor glanced at me.

'Eight is a good number,' he said. 'Not too small a force if you run into trouble, not so large as to be easily detected.'

We rose, our war-harness creaking, our accoutrements jingling. We rose in silence save for those small sounds.

'Farewell, Darnad,' Belet Vor grasped the young Bradhinak's shoulder and Darnad grasped the old man's. There seemed to be something final about that parting, as if Belet Vor knew they would never meet again.

'Farewell, Belet Vor,' he said softly. Their eyes met for an instant and then Darnad was striding for the door.

'Thank you, Belet Vor,' I said.

'Good luck,' he murmured as we left and followed Darnad towards Chinod Sai's 'palace'.

The building we finally came upon was situated in the centre of the city. It was only two storeys high and while it had some stone in its construction it was mainly of wood.

It stood in an open square from which several narrow streets radiated. We hugged the shadows of the streets and watched the guards as they patrolled the grounds of the palace.

Belet Vor had told Darnad exactly where the guest rooms were and when the Argzoon were likely to retire. We assumed that Shizala and Horguhl would not be dining with Chinod Sai. At this time it was likely that the Argzoon were eating in the main hall of the building. This meant we must be able to rescue the two women without arousing the suspicion of those inside and thus avoid a noisy fight.

After we had ascertained the exact movements of the patrolling guards, Darnad placed the first dart carefully in the blowpipe and took aim.

His aim was accurate. The dart winged its way towards the guard. I saw him clutch his neck and then fall almost soundlessly to the ground.

The next guard – there were four we needed to attend to in all – saw his comrade fall and rushed towards him. We heard him lean over him and speak casually. 'Get up, Akar, or the Bradhi will have your head. I told you not to drink so much before we went on guard!'

I held my breath as Darnad aimed another dart, expelled it softly – and the second guard fell.

The third guard turned a corner and paused in astonishment on seeing the bodies of his fallen comrades.

'Hey! What's this –?'

He would never fully know, for Darnad's third dart took him in his naked shoulder. The drug was quick. The guard fell – Darnad grinned at me – we seemed near to success.

The fourth guard was disposed of even before he saw his fellows.

Then the eight of us moved in, cat-footing it towards the guest rooms.

Soon, soon, I thought, all this would be over and we could return to Varnal to live in peace. I could study the sciences of the mysterious Sheev, increase the inventions that the Karnala would be able to use. With my help, the Karnala need never fear attack again. They had the basic technology necessary for building internal-combustion engines, electric power generators, radios – I could accomplish all that for them.

Those were the thoughts – inapt, perhaps, for the moment – that coursed through my brain as we crept towards the guest-room windows.

The windows were not glazed, only shuttered, and one of these was drawn back. Luck seemed to be on our side that night.

Cautiously I peered into the room. It was richly furnished, though somewhat vulgarly, floors heaped with furs, carved chests and benches. In a bracket a torch flared, illuminating the room. It was empty.

I swung my leg over the low sill and entered the room as quietly as I could.

Darnad and the others followed me.

Then we all stood there, staring at one another, listening intently for some sound that might indicate where the women were imprisoned.

It came at last – a low tone that could have been anything. All we could be sure of was that it issued from a human throat.

It came from a room on our left.

Darnad and I went towards the room with the warriors following. We paused at the door which, surprisingly, was unbarred.

Now from within came a sound that seemed like a soft laugh – a woman's laugh. But it could not be a laugh. I must have misheard. The next sound was a voice, pitched low and impossible to make sense of.

Darnad looked at me. Our eyes met, and then with a concerted movement we flung open the door.

Torchlight showed us the two within.

One was Horguhl, standing close to the window.

The other was Shizala – my Shizala!

Shizala was bound hand and foot.

But Horguhl was unfettered. She stood with hands on hips smiling down at Shizala, who glared back at her.

Horguhl's smile froze when she saw us. Shizala gave a glad cry: 'Michael Kane! Darnad! Oh, thank Zar you have come!'

Horguhl stood there expressionlessly, saying nothing.

I stepped forward to untie Shizala. As I worked at the bonds I kept a suspicious eye on the Vladnyar girl, uncertain of her part in this. Was she or was she not a prisoner?

It did not seem likely now. Yet...

Horguhl suddenly laughed in my face.

I finished untying Shizala's bonds. 'Why do you laugh?' I asked.

'I thought you were dead,' she replied, not answering my question. And then she lifted her head and let out a piercing shriek.

'Silence!' Darned said in a fierce whisper. 'You will alert the whole palace. We intend you no harm.'

'I am sure you do not,' she said as Darnad stepped towards her. 'But I mean *you* harm, my friends!' Again she shrieked.

There was a disturbance outside in the corridor.

Shizala's eyes glistened with tears – but with gladness also – as she stared up into my face. 'Oh, Michael Kane – somehow I knew you would save me. I thought they had killed you – and yet...'

'No time for conversation,' I said brusquely, trying to hide the emotion that her closeness brought to my breast: 'We must escape.'

Darnad had his hand over Horguhl's mouth. He looked unhappy, not used to treating a woman so.

'Horguhl is no prisoner,' Shizala said. 'She –'

'I can see that now,' I said. 'Come – we must hurry.' We turned and left the room. Darnad released his hold on Horguhl and followed us.

But before we could reach the window a score of men, led by the two Argzoon giants and another who wore a bright circlet on his matted, greasy hair, burst into the room.

Darnad, myself and our six warriors turned to face them, forming a barrier between them and Shizala.

'Leave quickly, Shizala,' I said softly. 'Go to the house of Belet Vor.' I gave her brief instructions how to find the old man.

'I cannot leave you. I cannot.'

'You must – it will serve us better if we know you, at least, are safe. Please do as I say.' I was staring at the Argzoon and the others, waiting for them to attack. They were moving in cautiously.

She seemed to understand my reasoning and it was with relief that I saw her from the corner of my eye clamber over the sill and disappear into the night.

Horguhl emerged from the other room, pointing an imperious finger at us. Her face was flushed with anger.

'These men sought to abduct me and the other woman,' she said to the greasy-haired man who stood there with drawn sword.

'So – did you not know,' he said, addressing us with a leer, 'that Chinod Sai values the safety of his guests and resents the intrusion of riff-raff such as you?'

'Riff-raff, murderer of children,' said Darnad. 'I know you, upstart – you who calls himself Bradhi of a collection of cutthroats and pilferers!'

Chinod Sai sneered. 'You speak bravely – but your words are hollow. You are all about to die.'

Then he and his unholy allies were on us, his guards supporting them.

The duel began.

I found myself fighting not only Chinod Sai but one of the Argzoon, and it was all I could do to defend myself, even though I knew I outmatched them both in swordsmanship.

However, they tended to crowd each other and this, a least, was to my advantage.

I held them off as best I could until I saw my chance. Rapidly I flung my sword from my right hand to my left. This foxed them for a second. Then I lunged at the Argzoon, who was slower than Chinod Sai, and caught him in the breast. He fell back groaning. That left the self-styled Bradhi of Narlet.

But seeing the great blue warrior fall, Chinod Sai evidently lost his stomach for battle and backed away, letting his hired guards take his place.

It was my turn to sneer.

One by one our own warriors went down until only Darnad and myself were left standing.

I hardly cared if I died. So long as Shizala were safe – and I knew that the wily old Belet Vor would see to that – I was prepared to die.

But I did not die. There were so many warriors pressing in towards us that we could hardly move our sword-arms.

Soon we were not so much sword-fighting as wrestling.

Their weight of numbers was too great. After a short time we were engulfed and, for the second time in the space of a week, I received a blow on the head – and this second blow was not meant in kindness as the first had been!

My senses fled, blackness engulfed me, and I knew no more.

Chapter Nine
Buried Alive!

I OPENED MY eyes but saw nothing. I smelt much. My nostrils were assailed by a foul, damp, chilly smell that seemed to indicate I was somewhere below ground. I flexed my arms and legs. They were unbound, at least.

I tried to get up but bumped my head. I could only crouch on the damp, messy ground.

I was horrified. Had I been incarcerated in some tomb? Was I to die slowly of hunger, or have my senses leave me? With an effort I controlled myself. Then I heard a slight sound to my left.

Cautiously I felt about me and my hand touched something warm.

Someone groaned. I had touched a limb. It stirred.

Then a voice murmured: 'Who is there? Where am I?'

'Darnad?'

'Yes.'

'It is Michael Kane. We seem to be in some sort of dungeon – with a very low ceiling indeed.'

'What?' I heard Darnad move and sit up, perhaps reaching with his hands above him. 'No!'

'Do you know the place?'

'I believe I have heard of it.'

'What is it?'

'The old heating system.'

'That sounds very innocuous. What's that?'

'Narlet is built on the ancient ruins of one of the Sheev cities. Hardly anything of it exists, save the foundations of one particular building. Those foundations now make up Chinod Sai's foundations for his palace. Apparently the slabs forming the floor of the palace lie over an ancient, sunken pool which could be filled with hot water and made to heat the ground floor of the palace – perhaps the whole of it – by means of pipes. From what I hear, the Sheev abandoned this particular city well before their decline, for they later discovered better methods of heating.'

'And so we are buried under the floor of Chinod Sai's palace?'

'I've heard it gives him pleasure to imprison his enemies here – having them permanently at his feet, as it were.'

I did not laugh, though I admired the fortitude of my friend in jesting at a time like this.

I put my hands up and felt the smooth, damp slabs over my head, pressing on them. They did not budge.

'If he can raise the slabs, why can't we?'

'There are only a few loose ones, I've heard – Belet Vor told me all this – and very heavy furniture is placed over those when prisoners have been incarcerated.'

'So we *have* been buried alive,' I said, suppressing a shudder of terror. I admit that I was horrified. I think any man – no matter how brave – would have been at the thought of such a fate.

'Yes.' Darnad's voice was a thin mutter. It seemed that he, too, had no liking for what had happened to us.

'At least we have saved Shizala.' I reminded him, 'Belet Vor will see that she returns safely to Varnal.'

'Yes.' The voice sounded slightly less strained.

Silence for a while.

Later I made up my mind.

'If you will stay where you are, Darnad,' I said, 'so that I may keep some sort of bearing, I will explore our prison.'

'Very well,' he agreed.

I had to crawl, of course – there was no other way.

I counted the number of 'paces' as I moved across that horribly wet and foul-smelling floor.

By the time I had counted to sixty-one I had reached a wall. I then began to crawl round this, still counting.

Something obstructed me. I could not tell at first what it was. Thin objects like sticks. I felt them carefully and then withdrew my hand suddenly as I realised what they were. Bones. One of Chinod Sai's earlier victims.

I encountered several more skeletons on my circuit of the walls.

From where I had started, the first wall measured ninety-seven 'paces'; the second only fifty-four. The third was, in all, a hundred and twenty-six. I began to wonder why I was doing this, save to keep my mind occupied.

The fourth wall. One 'pace', two, three...

On the seventeenth 'pace' along the fourth wall my hand touched – nothing!

Surely this could not be a means of escape? By touch I discovered that some sort of circular hole led off from the fourth wall – perhaps a pipe that had once brought water into the chamber. It was just wide enough to take a man.

I put my head inside and reached my arms along it. It was wet and slimy but nothing stopped me.

Before I raised Darnad's hopes, I decided to see whether the pipe really offered a chance of escape.

I squeezed my whole body into it and began to lever myself forward, wriggling like a snake.

I begin to feel elated when nothing obstructed me. Soon my whole body was in the pipe. I wriggled on. I hate being so confined normally, but if the pipe meant escape it was worth suffering my claustrophobia.

But then came disappointment.

My questing hands found something – and I knew at once what they touched.

It was another human skeleton.

Evidently some other poor soul – perhaps many – had sought this means of escape and been disappointed – and not had the energy or inclination to return.

I sighed deeply and begin to wriggle back down.

But as I did so I suddenly heard something from behind me. I paused. It was the sound of grating stone. A little light filtered up the pipe and I heard someone chuckle.

I did not move. I waited.

Then came Chinod Sai's jeering voice. 'Greetings, Bradhinak – how are you enjoying your stay?'

Darnad did not reply.

'Come up, come up – I wish to show my men what a real Bradhinak of the Karnala looks like. A little befouled, perhaps – I am sorry my accommodation is not quite what you are accustomed to.'

'I'd rather stay here than be subjected to your insults, you scum,' Darnad replied levelly.

'And what of your friend – the strange one? Perhaps he would like a little respite. Where is he?'

'I do not know.'

'You do not know! But he was put down there with you. Do not lie, boy – where is your companion?'

'I do not know.'

The light increased, probably because Chinod Sai was peering into this horrible crypt, using a torch for illumination.

His voice rose querulously. 'He *must* be down there!'

Darnad's tone seemed lighter now. 'You can see he is not unless one of these skeletons is his.'

'Impossible! Guards!'

I heard the faint sound of feet above me.

Chinod Sai continued: 'Take up some more of these stones – see if the other prisoner is hiding in a corner. He is down here somewhere. Meanwhile, bring up the Karnala.'

More sounds, and I gathered that Darnad had been escorted away.

Then I heard the guards beginning to tear up other slabs and I grinned to myself, hoping that they would not think of looking in the pipe. Then something occurred to me. It was not a pleasant thought but it might save me and give me, in turn, a chance to save Darnad.

I wriggled up the pipe again and reached up to take hold of some of the bones of the unfortunate who had been there before me. He had not been lucky but, even though dead some years, he might be able to help me now – and help me avenge him if and when the opportunity came.

Squeezing myself up against one section of the pipe as tightly as I could, I began to pass bones down in front of me until quite a heap lay below my feet. I did this as soundlessly as possible, and any noise I did make was probably drowned by the racket the desperate guards were making pulling up flagstones and crawling around in the semi-darkness trying to find me.

'He isn't here,' I heard one of them say.

'You are a fool,' answered another. 'He must be here!'

'Well, I tell you he isn't. Come and look for yourself.'

Another guard joined the first and I heard him stumbling around, too.

'I don't understand – there is no way out of here. We've put enough of them down here one time or another. Hey – what's this?'

The guard had found the pipe. The light increased.

'Could he have gone up here? If he did it won't do him any good. It's blocked at the other end!'

Then the guard found the bones. 'Ugh! He didn't go up but someone else tried to. These bones are old.'

'What are we going to tell the Bradhi?' The first guard spoke nervously. 'This smacks of magic!'

'There's no such thing!'

'So we're told these days, but my grandfather says there are stories...'

'Shut your mouth! Magic – ghosts. Nonsense... Still, I must admit that he had a strange look about him. He seemed to belong to no nation I've ever seen. And I have heard that beyond the ocean lies another land where men have powers greater than normal. And then there are the Sheev...'

'The Sheev! That's it!'

'Hold your tongue. Chinod Sai will tear it out if he hears such language spoken in his place!'

'What do we tell him?'

'Only the facts. The man *was* here – but he is no longer here.'

'But will he believe us?'

'We must hope that he does.'

I heard the guards clamber up and march away. The instant they had gone I slipped down the pipe as fast as I could and was soon standing up in what had been my prison, my head just above the level of the floor. Flagstones had been ripped out and the whole floor was in a mess. I was glad of that, at least.

No-one was in the room, which seemed to be some sort of throne room judging by the huge, ornately carved, precious-metal-gilded chair at one end.

I heaved myself up and stood in the room. As slowly and as silently as I could, I ran towards the door and stood by it, listening.

It was half open. Angry voices came from the other side.

There were more sounds coming from outside the palace itself – shouts, cries. They sounded angry.

Somewhere in the distance several pairs of fists began to beat on a door.

Then I stepped back as, suddenly, someone came into the room.

It was Chinod Sai.

He stared at me in horror for a moment.

That moment was all I needed. In a flash I darted forward and snatched his own sword from his belt!

I pressed the point gently against his throat and said with a grim smile on my lips: 'Call for your guards, Chinod Sai – and you call for death!'

He paled and gurgled something. I gestured for him to come into the room and shut the door. I had been lucky. Everyone had been too busy with whatever else they were concerned with to notice what had happened to their 'Bradhi'. 'Speak in a low voice,' I ordered. 'Tell me what is happening and where my comrade is.'

'How – how did you escape?'

'I am asking the questions, my friend. Now – answer!'

He grunted. 'What do you mean?'

'Answer!'

'The scum are attacking my palace,' he said. 'Some petty dahara-thief seeks to replace me.'

'I hope he makes a better chief than you. And where is my comrade?'

He waved a hand behind him.

'In there.'

Suddenly someone entered. I had expected the guards to knock and had intended that Chinod Sai should tell them not to enter.

But this was not a guard.

It was the surviving Argzoon. He looked astonished to see me. He turned, giving a roar of warning to the men in the room.

They came in and I backed away, looking around for a means of escape, but all the windows in this room were barred.

'Kill him!' screamed Chinod Sai, pointing a shaking finger at me. 'Kill him!'

Led by the blue Argzoon, the guards came at me. I knew that I faced death – they would not take me prisoner a second time.

Chapter Ten

Into the Caves of Darkness

SOMEHOW I MANAGED to keep them at bay, though I will never know how. Then I saw Darnad appear behind them, waving a sword he had got from somewhere.

Together, one on each side, we took on Chinod Sai and his men, but we knew we must be beaten eventually.

Then there came a sudden, elated roar, and bursting into the throne room came a wild mob waving swords, spears, and halberds.

They were led by a good-looking young man, and by the gleam in his eyes – at once calculating and triumphant – I guessed him to be the next contender for the paltry throne of the City of Thieves.

Now, while the others helped Darnad deal with the Argzoon and the guards, I concentrated on Chinod Sai. This time, I promised myself, he would not retreat.

Chinod Sai realised my intention and this seemed to improve his skill.

Back and forth across the broken floor of the throne room, over the bones of the wretches he had incarcerated for his own perverted pleasure, we fought.

Lunging, parrying, thrusting, the steel of our blades rang through the hall while to one side the mob fought, a thick mass of struggling men.

Then came disaster for me – or so I thought. I tripped over one of the flagstones and fell backwards into the pit!

I saw Chinod Sai raise his arm for the thrust that would finish me as, sprawled out on the slime, I stared up at him.

Then, as the sword came towards my heart I rolled away, under part of the floor that was still intact. I heard him curse and saw him drop down after me. He saw me and lunged. Raising myself on my left arm, I returned his lunge and caught him exactly in the heart. I pushed home my thrust and he fell back with a groan.

I climbed from the pit. 'A fitting burial place, Chinod Sai,' I said. 'Lie with the bones of those you have slain so horribly. You had a swifter death than you deserved!'

I was just in time to see Darnad dispose of the last Argzoon.

The fight was over and the young leader of the mob raised his right hand high, shouting:

'Chinod Sai is defeated – the tyrant dies!'

The mob replied exultantly: 'Salute Morda Kohn, Bradhi of Narlet!'

Morda Kohn swung round and grinned at me. 'Enemies of Chinod Sai are friends of mine. Indirectly you helped me gain the throne. But where is Chinod Sai?'

I pointed at the floor. 'I slew him,' I said simply.

Morda Kohn laughed. 'Good, good! You are even more of a friend for that little service.'

'It was no service to you,' I said, 'but something I had promised myself the pleasure of accomplishing.'

'Quite so. I was truly sorry about the death of your friend.'

'My friend?' I said as Darnad joined us. He had a flesh wound on his right shoulder but otherwise seemed all right.

'Belet Vor – did you not know?'

'What has happened to Belet Vor?' Darnad asked urgently.

I must admit I was not only thinking of Belet Vor – but of the girl I had sent to him, Shizala.

'Why, that is what enabled me to arouse the people against Chinod Sai,' Morda Kohn said. 'Chinod Sai and his blue friend learned that you had been seen in the house of Belet Vor. They went there and they ordered him to be beheaded on the spot!'

'Belet Vor, dead? Beheaded – oh, no!' Darnad's face turned pale with horror.

'I am afraid so.'

'But the girl we rescued – the one we sent to him?' I spoke in some trepidation, almost afraid to hear the answer.

'Girl? I do not know – I heard nothing of a girl. Perhaps she is still at his house, hiding somewhere.'

I relaxed. That was probably true.

'There is still another missing,' Darnad said. 'The Vladnyar woman – Horguhl. Where is she?'

Together we searched the palace but there was no sign of her.

Night was falling as we borrowed mounts from the new 'Bradhi' and rushed to Belet Vor's house.

Inside, it had been torn apart. We called Shizala's name but she did not answer.

Shizala had gone – but where? And how?

We stumbled out of the house. Had we fought and risked so much only to fail now?

Back to the palace to see if Morda Kohn could help us.

The new Bradhi was supervising the replacement of the flagstones.

'They will be securely cemented down,' he said. 'They will never be put to the same dreadful use again.'

'Morda Kohn,' I said desperately, 'the girl was not at Belet Vor's house. And we know she would not have gone anywhere of her own accord. Did any of Chinod Sai's guards survive? If they did, one of them may be able to tell us what happened.'

'I think there are several prisoners in the anteroom.' Morda Kohn nodded. 'Question them if you like.'

We went to the anteroom. There were three sulking, badly wounded prisoners.

'Do any of you know where Shizala is?' I asked.

'Shizala?' One of them looked up with a frown.

'The blonde girl – the prisoner who was here.'

'Oh, her – I think they both went off together.'

'Both?'

'Her and the dark-haired woman.'

'Where did they go?'

'What's it worth to tell you what I know?' The guard looked cunningly at me.

'I will speak to Morda Kohn. He owes us a favour. I will ask him to show mercy to you.'

'You'll keep your word?'

'Of course.'

'I think they went to the Mountains of Argzoon.'

'Ah – but why?' Darnad broke in. 'Why should a Vladnyar willingly go to Argzoon? The Blue Giants are no-one's friends.'

'There is something mysterious about Horguhl's association with the Argzoon. Perhaps when we find her we will learn the answer,' I said. 'Could you lead us to the Mountains of Argzoon, Darnad?'

'I think so.' He nodded.

'Come, then – let's make haste after them. With luck we may even catch them before they reach the mountains.'

'Best that we did,' he said.

'Why?'

'Because the Argzoon literally dwell in the mountains – in the Caves of Darkness that run *under* the range. Some say it is really the Bleak World of the Dead, and from what I've heard it's possible!'

We spoke briefly to Morda Kohn, telling him to show the guard mercy. Then we strode outside, mounted our daharas and rode into the night – heading for the dreadful Caves of Darkness.

We were not lucky. First Darnad's beast cut its foot on a sharp rock and went lame. We had to travel at walking pace for a full day until we came to a camp where we could exchange Darnad's prime mount for a rather stringy beast that looked as if it had little stamina.

Then we lost our bearings on a barren plain known as the Wilderness of Sorrow – and we could understand why anyone would feel sorrowful on encountering it.

On the other hand, the mount that Darnad had exchanged was in fact very strong – and my own beast wearied before his did!

We finally crossed the Wilderness of Sorrow and emerged on the shores of an incredibly wide river – wider even than the Mississippi.

Another pause while we borrowed a boat from a friendly fisherman and managed to cross. Luckily Darnad had a precious ring on his finger and was able to convert this into pearls, which were the general currency of these parts.

We bought supplies in the riverside town and learned – to our relief, for there had always been the chance that the guard was lying maliciously – that two women answering to the description of Horguhl and Shizala had passed that way. We enquired if Shizala had seemed to be under restraint, but our informant told us that she did not appear to be bound.

This was puzzling and we could not understand why Shizala should seem to be travelling to the terrible domain of the Argzoon of her own free will.

But, as we told ourselves, all this would be learned the quicker if we caught up with them. They were still some three days ahead of us.

So we crossed the Carzax River in the fisherman's boat, ferrying our mounts and provisions with us. It was a difficult task and the current drew us many miles downriver before we reached the other side. The fisherman would collect the boat later. We pulled it ashore, strapped our provisions to our animals and mounted.

It was forest land now, but the trees were the strangest I had ever seen.

Their trunks were not solid like the tree trunks on Earth, but consisted of many hundreds of slender stems curling around one another to form trunks some thirty or forty feet in diameter. On the other hand, the trees did not reach very high, but fanned out so that sometimes when passing through a particular grove of low-growing trees our heads actually stood out above the trees. It made me feel gigantic!

Also, the foliage had a tinge similar to the ferns of the Crimson Plain – though red was only the main colour. There were also tints of blue, green and yellow, brown and orange. It seemed, in fact, that the forest was in a perpetual state of autumn and I was pleased by the sight of it. Strange as the stumpy trees were they reminded me, in some obscure way, of my boyhood.

Had it not been for the object of our quest, I would have liked to relax more and spend longer in that strange forest.

But there was something else in the forest that I was to meet shortly – and that decided me, if nothing else could have done, on the necessity of moving on.

We had been travelling in the forest for two days when Darnad suddenly pulled his mount up short and pointed silently through the foliage.

I could see nothing and shook my head in puzzlement.

Darnad's beast now seemed to move a little restlessly, and so did mine.

Darnad began to turn his dahara, pointing back the way we had come. The peculiar, apelike beast obeyed the guiding reins and my own followed suit, rather quickly, as if glad to be turned back.

Then Darnad stopped again and his hand fell to his sword.

'Too late,' he said. 'And I should have warned you.'

'I see nothing – I hear nothing. What should you have warned me of?'

'The *heela*.'

'Heela – what is a heela?'

'That –' Darnad pointed.

Skulking towards us, its hide exactly the same mottled shades as the foliage of the trees, came a beast out of a nightmare.

It had eight legs and each leg terminated in six curved talons. It had two heads and each head had a broad, gaping mouth full of long, razorlike teeth, glaring yellow eyes, flaring nostrils. A single neck rose from the trunk and then divided near the top to accommodate the heads.

It had two tails, scaly and powerful-looking, and a barrel-shaped body rippling with muscle.

It was unlike anything I could describe. It could not exist – but it did!

The heela stopped a few yards away and its twin tails lashed as it regarded us with its two pairs of eyes.

The only thing to its disadvantage, as far as I could see, was that it measured only about half the size of an ordinary dahara.

Yet it still looked dangerous and could easily dispose of me, I knew.

Then it sprang. Not at me and not at Darnad – but at the head of Darnad's dahara.

The poor animal shrieked in pain and fear as the heela sank its eight sets of talons into its great flat head and simply clung there, biting with its two sets of teeth at the dahara's spinal cord.

Darnad began to hack at the heela with his sword. I tried to move in to help him but my animal refused to budge.

I dismounted – it was the only thing I could do – and paused behind the clinging heela's back. I did not know much about Martian biology, but I selected a spot on the heela's neck corresponding to the place where he was biting the dahara. I knew that many animals will go for a spot on other species which corresponds with their *own* vital spots.

I plunged my sword in.

For a few moments the heela still clung to the dahara's head; then it released its grip and with a blood-curdling scream of anguish and fury fell to the mossy ground. I stood back, ready to meet any attack it might make. But it got up, stood shakily on its legs, took a couple of paces away from me – then fell dead.

Meanwhile, Darnad had dismounted from the dahara, which was moaning in pain and stamping on the moss.

The poor beast's flesh had been ripped away from a considerable area of its head and neck. It was beyond any help we could give it – save to put it out of its pain.

Regretfully, I saw Darnad place his sword against the creature's head and drive it home, wincing as he did so.

Soon dahara and heela lay side by side. A useless waste of life, I reflected.

What was more, we should now have to ride double and though my dahara was strong enough to carry both of us, we should have to travel at about half our previous speed.

Bad luck was dogging us, it seemed.

Riding double, we left the heela-infested forest behind. Darnad informed me that we had been lucky to meet only one of the beasts since there had been others of its pack about. Apparently it was quite common amongst heelas for the leader to attack the victim first and, if successful, lead the rest in for the kill, having tested the victim's strength. If, on the other hand, the heela-leader were killed, then the pack would skulk off, judging the enemy too strong to risk attacking. Besides which they would feed off their dead leader's corpse. In this case, the corpse of the dahara, too.

It seemed that, like hyaena, the heelas were strong but cowardly. I thanked providence for this trait, at any rate!

Now the air grew colder – we had been travelling for well over a month – and the skies darker. We began to cross a vast plain of black mud and obsidian rock, stunted, sinister shrubs and ancient ruins. The feet of our single dahara splashed in deep puddles or waded through oozing mud, slipped on the glassy rock or stumbled over great areas of broken masonry.

I asked Darnad if these were the ruins of the Sheev but he muttered that he did not think so.

'I suspect that these ruins were once inhabited by the Yaksha,' he said.

I shivered as cold rain fell on us.

'Who were the Yaksha?'

'It is said they are ancient enemies of the Sheev but originally of the same race.'

'That is all you know?'

'Those are the only facts. The rest is superstition and speculation.' He seemed to shudder inwardly, not from the cold but from some idea that had occurred to him.

On we went, making slower and slower progress over that dark wasteland, taking shelter at night – scarcely distinguishable though it was from day! – under half-fallen walls or outcrops of rock. Strange, livid beasts prowled that plain; peculiar cries like the voices of lost souls; queer disturbances that we *felt* rather than heard or saw.

It was like that for another two weeks until the looming crags of Argzoon became visible through the dim, misty light of the Wastes of Doom.

The Mountains of Argzoon were tall and jagged, black and forbidding.

'Seeing their environment,' I said to Darnad, 'I can understand why the Argzoon are what they are, for such landscapes are not conducive to instilling a sense of sweetness and light into one.'

'I agree,' he replied. Then a little later: 'We should reach the Gates of Gor Delpus before nightfall.'

'What are they?'

'The entrance to the Caves of Darkness. They are, I've been told, never guarded, for few have ever dared venture into the Argzoon's own underground land – they let our normal fear of dark, enclosed spaces do their work for them.'

'Are the Caves very dangerous?'

'I do not know,' he said. 'No-one has ever returned to tell…'

By nightfall we made out the Gates by means of Deimos's very dim moonlight. They were mainly natural cave mouths widened and made taller by crude workmanship. They were dark and gloomy and I could understand what Darnad had told me.

Only my mission – to rescue the woman I loved but would never be able to make mine – would induce me to enter.

We left our faithful dahara outside to fend for himself until we returned – if ever we should.

And then we entered the Caves of Darkness.

Chapter Eleven
Queen of the Argzoon

THEY WERE COLD, those caves. A chill pervaded them greater than anything we had experienced on the Wastes of Doom.

Down and down we went, along a smooth, broad, winding track that had torches lighting it at wide intervals. We caught glimpses of vast grottoes and caverns, as it were within the great caverns; of stalactites and stalagmites; of jumbled, black rock and rivulets of ice-cold water; of a bitter-smelling slime that clung to the rocks; of small pallid animals that scuttled away at our approach.

And deeper down, the sides of the path had been decorated with trophies of war – here a skeleton of an Argzoon in full armour, with sword, shield, spear and axe, grinning down at us from its great height; there several human skulls piled into a rough pyramid. Dark trophies brought alive sometimes by the flickering torchlight, but fitting decoration for this strange place.

Then at length we felt the path turn sharply to the left. Following it round, we suddenly came upon a monstrous cave, its walls so far away they were invisible. We stood above it, looking down. The path led to it, we could see, twisting down for perhaps two miles. Huge fires flared at intervals on the floor of the cave and there were complete villages dotted across it. Fairly close to our side of the cave there was a stone city – a city that seemed piled on blocks of stone heaped almost haphazardly one upon the other. A heavy city, a cold, strong, bleak city. A city to suit the Argzoon.

Moving about in the city and the surrounding villages, we saw Argzoon men, women and children going about their business. There were also pens of dahara and some sort of small creature that seemed to be a domestic version of the heela.

'How can we get in there?' I whispered to Darnad. 'They will realise who we are immediately!'

Just then I heard a noise behind us and pulled him into the shadows of the rock.

A few moments later a group of some thirty Argzoon warriors stumbled past. They looked as if they had been through an ordeal. Many bore untreated wounds, others had had their armour almost completely cut to shreds, and all were weary.

I realised that these were probably survivors of the 'mopping up' operation instituted from Varnal the day we had left.

That was another reason why we should not expose ourselves! The Argzoon would enjoy taking vengeance on members of the race that had defeated them.

But these warriors were too tired even to notice us. They just staggered on down the twisting path towards the cavern world, where the great bonfires crackled and attempted to heat and light the place with little success.

We could not wait for nightfall here, for it was perpetual night! How *could* we reach the city and discover where Shizala was imprisoned?

There was nothing for it but to begin creeping down the path, keeping to the shadows as best we could, hoping that the Argzoon would be too busy with their own affairs, treating their wounded, assessing their strength and so on, to notice us.

Not once did either of us think of returning to find help. It seemed too late for that. We must rescue Shizala ourselves.

But then it occurred to me!

Who else knew where Shizala was held? Who else had all the information concerning the Argzoon that we had?

The answer was plain – none.

When we had gone a little distance I turned to Darnad and said bluntly:

'You must go back.'

'Go back? Are you mad?'

'No – I'm perfectly sane for once. Don't you realise that if we are both killed in this attempt, then there can be no further attempts to save Shizala – for what we know will die with us!'

'I had not thought of that,' he mused. 'But why should I go back? You go. I will try to…'

'No. You know the geography of Vashu better than I. I might easily get lost. Now you have led me to the Mountains of Argzoon you must return to the nearest friendly settlement, send messengers to tell where I am, where Shizala is – get the news out as fast as you can. Then a big force of warriors can come here while the Argzoon are still depleted and recovering and wipe out the threat of the Blue Giants once and for all!'

'But it will take me weeks to get back to civilisation of any sort. If you get into trouble here you will be dead long before I can bring help.'

'If personal safety were our first consideration,' I reminded him, 'neither of us would be here now. You must see the logic of what I say. Go!'

He thought deeply for a moment, then clapped me on the shoulder, turned and began to make his way rapidly back in the direction we had come.

Once made up, Darnad's mind made him act swiftly.

Now I crept on, feeling somehow even smaller and weaker in the face of monstrous nature now that Darnad gone.

Somehow I managed to get to the base of the path without being seen.

Somehow I managed to dash from cliff-wall to the shadow of the city and hug myself close to the rough-hewn stone.

And then, all of a sudden, it became darker!

I could not at first understand the cause of my good luck. Then I saw that they were damping down the big fires!

Why?

Then I realised what must be happening. Fuel itself must be scarce so, for a period corresponding to night-time on the surface, the fires were damped while the Argzoon slept. In the almost pitch-black darkness I decided that this was my chance to explore the city and try to find out where Shizala was imprisoned.

Perhaps, if luck continued to stay on my side, I would even

have a chance to rescue her, and together we could leave the gloomy cavern-world of the Argzoon and ride back to Varnal.

I hardly dared consider this as I began slowly to climb the rough sides of the city wall.

It was a stiff climb, but not too difficult. Both my hands and my feet had been hardened over the long weeks of our quest and so I found I could grip the rock like a Gibraltar monkey.

The darkness brought its own dangers, of course, and I was forced to climb largely by touch, but soon I was on top of the wall.

Crouching, sword in hand just in case I should be surprised, I sidled along the wall, peering down into the city, trying to make out the likeliest place where Shizala might be held.

Then I saw it!

One building was fairly well illuminated by torches from within and brands on the ramparts. But this is not what I noticed so much as the great, brooding banner that flew from a mast on the central keep of the building.

It was the N'aal Banner that adorned Horguhl's tent on the battlefield outside – a larger version, but the same design.

It was little to go on – but it was something. I would make for the building with the banner.

I resheathed my sword and clambered over the other side of the wall, beginning to climb slowly down towards the ground.

I was nearly at the bottom with perhaps only a dozen feet to go when a detachment of Argzoon warriors suddenly rounded a building near the wall and marched towards me. I wondered if I had been seen – whether they had been sent to deal with me. But then they began to pass beneath me. I was only a couple of feet above the head of the tallest as he passed. I clung like a fly to the wall, praying that I would not slip and betray myself.

As soon as they were out of sight, I climbed the remaining distance to the ground and dashed across to the cover of a building, fashioned from the same roughly heaped stone as the wall.

Knowing that the Argzoon warriors had not had many mounts, I guessed that only a few had returned as yet, which explained why the city seemed virtually deserted.

This was another thing that I welcomed and which was to my advantage.

Soon I had reached the building I was headed for.

The sides of this were somewhat smoother, but I thought I could tackle it. The only problem here was that the walls were fairly well illuminated and I might be seen. There was nothing for it but to risk it, for no other time would be better. I would try to reach a window and swing myself in. Once inside the building I might be able to hide myself better and at least discover something, by watching and listening, of where Shizala was being kept.

I got a hold on a piece of projecting stone and hauled myself up, inch by inch. It was slow going and increasingly difficult. All the windows – little more than holes in the rock – were some distance above the ground, none less than twenty feet, and the one I had decided to try was probably higher. I deduced that fear of attack was the reason why the windows were positioned so high.

But at last I managed to make the window and peered over the sill to see if the room was occupied. It did not appear to be.

I entered quickly.

It appeared that I was in a storeroom of some kind, for there were wicker baskets of dried fruit and meat, herbs and vegetables. I decided to make use of some of the food stuff, obviously looted in an earlier raiding expedition. I selected the most palatable items and ate them. I was thirsty, too, but there was no readily available source of water. I would have to wait for a drink.

Feeling refreshed, I explored the room. It was fairly large and very draughty. Perhaps because of the draughts, it had not been used as living accommodation for a long while – judging by the old and near-rotted pieces of basket that littered the floor.

I found the door and tried it.

To my great disappointment it was locked – barred from the outside, probably as a precaution against thieves!

I was very weary and my eyes kept closing involuntarily as I fought sleep. The pursuit had been long and arduous; we had allowed ourselves little time for rest. I decided that I would be more use to Shizala if I were rested.

I clambered over the baskets and made myself a kind of nest in the centre by removing some baskets and piling them around me. That way I would be warmer, and if anyone entered the room they would not see me. Feeling fairly secure, I lay down to sleep.

An increase in the glow of firelight entering the window told me that it was a new Argzoon 'day'. But, I realised immediately, that was not what had awakened me.

There was someone else in the room.

Very cautiously, I stretched my cramped limbs and began to stand up, peering through a crack in my barricade.

I was astonished.

The man collecting food from the baskets was not an Argzoon. He was a man similar in build to myself, but with a pale complexion – perhaps caused by living in the sunless vaults of the Blue Giants.

His face had a strange, dead appearance. His eyes were dull, his features frozen as he mechanically transferred meat and vegetables from the baskets to a smaller basket he held in his left hand.

He was unarmed. His shoulders were bowed, his hair lank and uncared for.

There was no questioning his situation and function in the cavern-world of the Argzoon.

The man was a slave and seemed to have been one for a long time.

Being a slave he would, of course, have no love for his masters. On the other hand, how much had he been cowed by them? Could I reveal myself in the hope of receiving help from him, or would he be frightened and shout for help?

I had taken many risks to get this far. I must take a further risk now.

As silently as I could I climbed from cover and crept across the tops of the baskets towards him. He was half turned away from me and only seemed to notice me when I was almost on top of him.

When he saw me, his eyes widened and his mouth dropped, but he made no sound.

'I am a friend,' I whispered.

'F-friend...?' He repeated the word dully as if it meant nothing to him.

'An enemy of the Argzoon – a slayer of many of the Blue Giants.'

'Aah!' He backed away in fear, dropping his basket.

I leapt to the ground and dashed towards the door, closing it. He turned to face me, his mouth trembling now, his eyes still wide in ghastly fear. It was evidently not me he feared so much as something that I represented to him.

'Y-you must go to the Queen – y-you must surrender yourself. D-do that and y-you may escape the N'aal Beast!'

'The Queen? The N'aal Beast? I've heard the name – what is it?'

'O-oh, d-do not ask me!'

'Who are you? How long have you been here?' I tried a different line of questioning.

'I – I think my name was Ornak Dia... Y-yes, that was it, that was my name... I d-do not know h-how long since w-we f-followed the Argzoon h-here and w-were led into ambush. Th-they had only sent half their strength against the lands of the South – we did n-not r-realise...' With these memories he seemed to remember something of the man he must have been previously, for his shoulders straightened a little and he held his mouth better.

'You were part of the force led by the Bradhi of the Karnala – is that right?' I asked him. I wondered what kind of hardships could have turned a warrior into this servile thing in such a comparatively short space of time.

'Th-that is right.'

'They lured you down here where the rest of their army was waiting – it had been a calculated tactic – and when you reached the floor of the cavern-world they attacked you and wiped out your army. Isn't that what happened?' I had already guessed most of this, of course.

'Y-yes. They took prisoners. I am among the last of them left alive.'

'How many prisoners?'

'Several hundreds.'

I was horrified. Now it was plain that, as I had surmised, this move of the Argzoon had been carefully planned for years. The first force had been badly defeated, but it had severely weakened the strength of the Southern nations. Secondly, the Southern army's punitive force that had followed the Argzoon here had been led into a carefully laid trap and the weary warriors must have been fairly easy game for a force of fresh Argzoon warriors waiting in ambush. Then the Argzoon had put the second half of their strategy into operation, going secretly south in small numbers with the object of taking the South by surprise, beginning with Varnal. Something had disrupted this strategy – my slaying of their mastermind – and the plan had broken down. But much damage had been done. The South would take years recovering from the blow and while recovering would face constant danger from other, stronger would-be aggressors. The Vladnyar, for instance.

Now I asked the slave the leading question:

'Tell me – have two women been brought here recently? A dark one and a fair one.'

'There h-has been a woman prisoner...'

Only one! I prayed that Shizala had not been killed on the way.

'What does she look like?'

'She is very beautiful – fair-haired – a Karnala woman, I think...'

I sighed my relief. 'But what of Horguhl the Vladnyar – the dark-haired woman?'

'Ah!' His voice was a muted scream. 'Do not mention th-that name. Do not mention it!'

'What is wrong?' I could see that he was in an even worse state now than when I had originally confronted him. Spittle ran down his chin and his eyes flickered crazily. He was trembling in every part of his body. He hugged himself, hunched and twitching. He began to moan softly.

I seized his shoulder, trying to shake some self-control into him, but he fell to the floor and continued to moan and tremble.

I knelt beside him. 'Tell me – who is Horguhl – what is her part in this?'

'Ah! P-please – leave me. I will not tell them you are here... Y-you must go. L-leave!'

I continued to shake him. 'Tell me!'

Suddenly a new voice spoke from behind me. A cool, mocking voice full of controlled, malicious humour...

'Leave the poor wretch alone, Michael Kane. I can answer your question better than he. My guards mentioned a disturbance in the storeroom so I came to investigate myself. I have been half-expecting you.'

I whirled, still in a crouching position, and looked up to stare into the deep, evil eyes of the dark-haired woman whose rôle had been such a mystery. It was to be a mystery no longer.

'Horguhl! Who are you?'

'I am Queen of the Argzoon, Michael Kane. It was I who commanded the army you defeated, not poor Ranak Mard. My army dispersed before I could recall it because that bitch-dahara Shizala attacked me soon after you had left. In the struggle she knocked me unconscious but she was then captured by some of my men. When I awoke, my army was in confusion, so I decided to take vengeance on her instead of her city...'

'You! All this was your doing! But how are you Queen of those giant savages – what power can one woman wield over them?'

'It is my power over something else that they fear,' she smiled.

'What is that?'

'You will learn soon enough.' Blue Giants were beginning to swarm into the room behind her. 'Seize him!'

I tried to stand up but stumbled against the prone and shaking body of the slave. Before I could recover my position half a dozen Argzoon were piling on top of me.

I fought back with fists and feet, but soon they had bound my arms behind me and Horguhl was laughing in my face, her white, sharp teeth flashing in the gloom.

'And now,' she said, 'you will learn the punishment meted out to the man responsible for disrupting the plans of the Queen of the Argzoon!'

Chapter Twelve
The Pit of the N'aal Beast

'BRING HIM TO my chambers,' Horguhl ordered the guards. 'I will question him first.'

I was forced to walk behind her, following her through a maze of bleak and draughty corridors lit by guttering torches, until we came to a large door apparently made of heavy wood covered with silver hammered into some crude semblance of a design.

This door was opened and the big room we entered was warmed by a huge fire roaring in a grate at one side. The room itself was rich with rugs of fur and heavy cloth. Covering the walls were tapestries, obviously booty from raided cities, for the workmanship was exquisite. Even the windows were covered, and this explained the warmth of the room.

A heavy chest, about the height of my waist, stood near the fire. On this stood jugs of wine and bowls of fruit and meat. A large, fur-strewn couch was on the other side of the room opposite the fire, and there were a few benches and carved wooden chairs dotted about.

Though not particularly lavish by the standards of the civilised South, the queen's chambers were luxurious compared with what I had witnessed of the living standards of the Argzoon peoples.

Over the fireplace hung a tapestry much less well executed than the others. It depicted the creature I had already seen on the queen's banner – the mysterious N'aal Beast. It looked menacing and I noticed the guards avert their eyes from it as if afraid of it.

I was still tightly bound, of course, and when Horguhl dismissed the guards she was in no danger from me. I stood straight-backed, staring over her head as she paced before me, darting me strange, curious looks. This went on for some time, but I kept my expression blank and my eyes fixedly ahead.

Suddenly she faced me, swept back her right hand and slapped me stingingly across the mouth. I kept my features rigid as before.

'Who are you, Michael Kane?'

I did not answer.

'There is something about you. Something I have never sensed in any other man. Something I could learn to – to like.' Her voice became softer and she took a step closer to me. 'I mean it, Michael Kane,' she said. 'Your fate will not be pleasant if I order it to be carried out. But you could avert it...'

I still remained silent.

'Michael Kane – I am a woman. A – a sensitive woman.' She laughed lightly, somewhat self-mockingly, I thought. 'I am what I am through no circumstances of my own making. Would you like to hear why I am Queen of the Argzoon?'

'I would like to know where Shizala is, that is all,' I said at length. 'Where is she?'

'No harm has come to her yet. Perhaps none will. I have thought out an interesting fate for her. It will not kill her, but it will help me turn her into a willing hand-maiden, I think. I would rather keep the ruler of Varnal as my cringing slave than have her dead...'

My mind raced. So Shizala was not to die – yet, at any rate. I was relieved, for that would give time for Darnad to come and try to rescue her. I relaxed a little – perhaps I even smiled.

'You seem in good humour. Do you not feel anything for the woman then?' Horguhl sounded almost eager.

'Why should I?' I lied.

'That is good,' she said, almost to herself. She strode panther-like to the couch and spread her beautiful body upon it. I continued to stand where I was, but looked directly into those smouldering eyes. After a while she dropped her gaze.

Staring at the floor, she said: 'I was only a child of eleven when the Argzoon attacked the caravan in which I and my parents were travelling through the northern borders of Vladnyar. They killed many – including my mother and father – but took slaves as well, I was one of those slaves...'

I knew she was trying to touch me in some way, and if her story were true I felt sorry for the child she had been. But I could not, considering her later crimes, justify them.

'In those days the Argzoon were divided amongst themselves. Often the cavern was a battlefield between warring factions. They could not unite. The Argzoon were split into scores of family clans, and blood feuds were normal, day-to-day happenings. The only thing that could unite them for a short while was the common fear of the N'aal Beast which haunted the subterranean passages below the floor of the Great Cavern. It fed on the Argzoon who were its natural prey. It would slither up and attack then slither away again. The Argzoon believe that the N'aal Beast is an incarnation of Raharumara, their chief deity. They dared not make any attempt to kill it. Whenever possible they would sacrifice slaves to it.

'When I was sixteen years old, I was chosen as one of those who would feed the N'aal Beast. But already I had felt this power in me – some ability to make others do my will. Oh, not in large ways – I was still a slave – but in ways that made my lot a little easier. Strangely, it was the N'aal Beast which brought this power out of me in strength.

'When news came that the N'aal was slithering up into the Great Cavern, I and a number of others – folk like myself and Argzoon criminals – were bound and placed in its supposed path. Soon it appeared and I watched in horrified dread as it began to seize my companions and swallow them. I started to stare into its eyes. Some instinct made me croon at it. I – I don't know what it was, but it responded to me. Through my mind, I was able to communicate with it, give it orders.'

She paused and looked up at me. I did not react.

'I returned to this city – the Black City – with the N'aal Beast following me like a pet. I ordered a deep hole to be made, in which the beast was imprisoned. The Argzoon regarded me with superstitious awe – they still do. By controlling the N'aal Beast, I control them. Later I decided to make up for my years of misery and hardship and planned conquest of this entire continent. By several methods I got news of the South and her defences. Then I put the first stage of my plan into operation. I was prepared to wait years for victory – but instead…'

'Defeat,' I said. 'A well-deserved defeat. Your years with the Argzoon have warped you, Horguhl – warped you beyond hope of salvation!'

'Fool!' She was off the couch and pressing her voluptuous body against me, stroking my chest. 'Fool! I have other plans – I am not defeated. I know many secrets; I have much power that you do not dream of. Michael Kane, you can share all this. I told you I have never known a man like you – brave, handsome, strong-willed. But you also have something else – some mysterious quality that makes you as different from the ordinary riff-raff of Vashu as I am. Become my King, Michael Kane…'

She was speaking softly, her hypnotic eyes staring into mine, and something seemed to be happening to my brain. I felt warm, euphoric. I began to think her proposal was attractive.

'Michael Kane – I love you!'

Somehow that statement saved me – though I will never know why. It jerked my mind back to sanity. Bound as I was, I shrugged her clinging hands away.

'I do not love you, Horguhl,' I said firmly. 'Neither could I feel anything but loathing for someone who has done what you have done. Now I realise how Shizala was so easily brought here – that hypnotic power of yours! Well, it will not get the better of me!'

She released me and when she spoke again her voice was low, vibrant. 'Somehow I knew that. Perhaps that is what attracts me to you – the fact that you can resist my power. Few others can – not even that primordial beast, the N'aal.'

I took several steps backwards. I was still looking around for some means of escape. She seemed to realise this and looked up suddenly.

Her face was now a mask of hatred!

'Very well, Michael Kane – by refusing me you are accepting the fate I had planned for you. Guards!'

The huge Argzoon warriors entered.

'Take him! Send messengers to all the Argzoon who have returned. There are not many as yet – but tell them all to come. Tell them they are going to witness a sacrifice to Raharumara!'

With that, I was led away.

I spent a short time with my guards when they paused in a chamber near the exit of the castle. Then they led me out through the smoky, evil-smelling streets of the Black City. Behind us, in twos and threes at first, then in increasing numbers, there began to follow a procession of Argzoon. One blue warrior who strode beside my guards, keeping pace with me, darted me a strange glance which I could not interpret. The warrior did not wear armour – I assumed he had lost it during the flight back to the Black City – and he had the signs of a recent wound on his breast. Then we were passing from the city and I forgot about him.

The scene beyond the city was like a medieval painting representing Hell. The great bonfires roared, sending flickering, smoky light across the rocky plain that was the cavern floor. The giant Argzoon looked like demons as they escorted me over the plain. The fires were the fires on which the damned were roasted. And I was soon to meet a creature very like an ancient representation of Satan!

Horguhl was already there, standing on a dais that was reached by a flight of about sixty steps. Her back was turned to us and her arms were outstretched. On either side of her were braziers, flaring brightly to show her to all. The Argzoon began to form a semicircle at the bottom of the steps, and spread out along the sides of what was plainly a pit, now that we were closer. The steps terminated at the dais and the dais looked down on the pit.

My guards halted and waited expectantly just before the first step. We all looked up at Horguhl. She was crooning something. The words – sounds, rather, for I did not recognise them – sent a shudder through me and I noticed that many of the Argzoon were similarly affected.

There came a peculiar, slithering sound from the pit and from it, just to one side of the dais, I saw a great flat serpent head rise up and begin to sway in rhythm to Horguhl's crooning.

The Argzoon muttered in superstitious fear and began to chant and sway in time to the movement of the serpent head. It was of a sickly yellowish colour, with long fangs curving out of its mouth from the upper jaw. There was a stale, unwholesome smell about it, and once it opened its great jaws and gave forth a horrid hissing, revealing a gaping red maw and a huge forked tongue.

Then Horguhl's crooning became softer and softer, the swaying more gentle, the humming of the spectators almost inaudible, and then – it came almost as a shock to me – absolute silence.

Suddenly this silence was broken as from behind me there came a cry.

'No! No!'

I turned my head and saw who it was that had cried out.

'Shizala!' I shouted involuntarily. The fiends had brought her here to witness my death – that was obvious. Even from that distance I could see her cheeks were streaked with tears and she struggled in the grasp of two massive blue warriors. I tried to break away and run towards her, but my bonds and my guards stopped me.

'Stay alive!' I shouted to her. 'Stay alive! Do not fear!' I could not tell her that Darnad was even now riding for civilisation, bent on bringing help to rescue her. But perhaps my cry would mean something to her. 'Stay alive!'

Her voice answered faintly: 'Oh, Michael Kane, I – I –'

'Silence!' Horguhl had turned and was addressing her subjects as much as myself and Shizala. 'Take the prisoner to the pit's edge!'

I was hustled forward and stared down to where the N'aal Beast was coiled. Its oddly intelligent eyes stared up at me – and I shuddered at this – almost with malicious humour!

'The N'aal Beast is in a playful mood today,' Horguhl said from above me. 'He will play with you for some time before devouring you.'

I resolved to show no sign of the horror within me.

'Throw him down!' Horguhl ordered.

Bound and helpless, I was thrown into the Pit of the N'aal Beast!

I managed to land on my feet some yards away from where the huge snake-creature still lay coiled, looking at me with those terrible eyes.

And then, suddenly, from above I heard a cry and looked up. An Argzoon warrior was staring down at me – the one I had seen earlier who had looked at me so strangely. He had a sword in one hand and a battle-axe in the other. What was he doing?

I heard Horguhl shriek to her guards: 'Stop him!'

And then the Argzoon was leaping into the pit to stand beside me. He raised his sword and I suddenly realised the truth of what was happening.

Chapter Thirteen
An Unexpected Ally

At first I had thought that the warrior was going to slay me himself for some obscure reason. But this was not the case. Swiftly he slashed my bonds.

'I know you,' I said in surprise. 'You are the warrior I fought near Varnal.'

'I am the warrior whose life you refused to take – whom you spared from the insults and swords of his comrades. I have thought much on what you did, Michael Kane. I admired what you did. It meant something to me. And now – I can at least help you to fight for your life against this creature.'

'But I thought your folk feared it because of its supposed supernatural character.'

'True. But I begin to doubt that this is true. Quickly – take this sword, I have always been a better axeman than a swordsman.'

With this unexpected – and welcome – ally, I turned to face the N'aal Beast.

The beast seemed put out by this turn of events. Its gaze went from one to the other of us as though uncertain which one to attack first, for we had spaced out now – both crouching, waiting.

The beast's great head suddenly whipped towards me. I stumbled backwards until I stood against the wall, desperately hacking at its snout with the great Argzoon blade.

It was evidently unused to its victims retaliating and it hissed in apparently puzzled anger as my sword gashed a wound in its snout.

It drew back its head and began to uncoil so that soon the head had risen high above me and I was in its shadow. Down came the gaping maw and I thought it would take me in one gulp. I raised the sword point first and as the mouth was almost upon me, the foetid breath almost overpowering, I dug the sword point into the beast's soft palate.

It screamed and threshed backwards. Meanwhile, the Argzoon warrior had come in and hacked at the beast's head with his axe. It turned on him and the sweeping head caught him off balance.

He fell and the N'aal Beast opened its mouth, about to snap off his head.

Then I saw my chance. I leapt *on* the N'aal Beast's back – onto its upper head and, running over that flat head, straddled it just above the eyes.

All this took only a few seconds, as the Argzoon below tried desperately to fend off the ripping jaws.

I raised my sword in both hands over the creature's right eye.

I plunged the blade downwards.

The steel sank in. The head jerked backwards and I was flung – swordless now – from my perch.

The N'aal Beast turned again towards me. The sword still protruded from its eye so that it made an even more grotesque sight as it came at me.

The Argzoon axeman leapt up again and came to stand by me, evidently intending to protect me now that I was unarmed.

The beast let out a chilling, reverberating scream, and the gaping mouth, forked tongue flicking rapidly, flashed down on us.

Only inches before it reached us, the head suddenly turned and flung itself upwards. The beast uncoiled its whole length and began to shoot up so that I felt it would leave the pit altogether. I caught a glimpse of spectators scattering – and then it flopped down, almost striking us and finishing us by being crushed beneath its weight.

My sword had done the trick. I had killed it. It had clung on to life longer than anything should have. I half-credited its supernatural origin then!

I bent towards the great head and removed my sword. It slid out easily.

Then I realised that nothing was really saved. I was still

imprisoned and, though armed, there were some two hundred Argzoon above us, ready to destroy us at a word from Horguhl.

'What do we do?' I asked my new friend.

'I know,' he said, after some thought. 'There is a small opening – look there, at the base of the pit on the other side.' I followed his pointing finger. He was right. There was an opening large enough to take a man but not large enough for the head of the N'aal Beast.

'What is it?' I asked.

'A tunnel that leads to the slave pens. Sometimes slaves are forced down it from the other side to feed the beast.' My new friend chuckled grimly. 'It will feast no more on human flesh! Come, follow me. We have slain the N'aal Beast – that will impress them. They will be even more impressed when they see we have vanished from the pens. With luck, we shall escape in the confusion.'

I followed him into the tunnel.

As we moved along it, he told me his name. Movat Jard of the Clan Movat-Tyk – one of the great Argzoon clans in the old days, before Horguhl had reorganised the Argzoon nation. He told me that though the Argzoon feared Horguhl's power, they were now muttering against her. Her ambitious schemes of large-scale conquest had come to nothing – and Argzoon was decimated.

After some time, the dark tunnel became a little lighter and ahead I saw some sort of slatted grating. It was of wood. Peering through it I saw a cavern lighted by a single torch.

Lying about on the floor, in attitudes of the utmost dejection, closely packed like cattle, naked and dirty, bearded and pale, were the remains of the great army that had been ambushed here earlier. Some hundred and fifty undernourished, spiritless slaves. I felt pity for them.

Movat Jard was hacking at the wooden grille with his axe. It soon fell and some of the slaves looked up in surprise as we entered. The smell of humanity was almost too much to bear, but I knew it was not their fault.

One fellow, who held himself straighter than the rest and was as tall as I, stepped forward. He had a heavy beard which he had endeavoured to keep clean, and his body rippled with muscle as if he had been deliberately keeping himself in training.

When he spoke his voice was deep and manly – even dignified.

'I am Carnak,' he said simply. 'What means this? Who are you and how came you here? How did you evade the N'aal Beast?'

I did not only address him. I addressed them all, since they were all looking at us with something akin to hope in their eyes.

'The N'aal Beast is dead!' I announced. 'We slew it – this is Movat Jard, my friend.'

'An Argzoon your friend? Impossible!'

'Possible – and my life is witness to that!' I smiled at Movat Jard, who made an attempt to smile back, though when he bared his teeth he still looked menacing!

'Who are you?' asked the bearded man, Carnak.

'I am a stranger here – a stranger to your planet, but I am here to help you. Would you be free?

'Of course,' he said. A murmur of excitement ran round the cavern. Men began to get up, a new liveliness in their manner.

'You must be prepared to win such freedom dearly,' I told them. 'From somewhere we must get weapons.'

'We cannot fight the whole Argzoon nation,' Carnak said in a low voice.

'I know,' I said. 'But the whole Argzoon nation is not here. There are perhaps two hundred warriors in all – and they are demoralised.'

'Is this true? Really true?' Carnak was grinning excitedly.

'It is true,' I said, 'but you are outnumbered as well as unarmed. We must think carefully – but first we must escape from here.'

'That should not be difficult in our present mood,' replied Carnak. 'There are usually more guards, but at present there are only two.' He pointed to the other entrance to the cave. It was made of wickerwork, that was all. 'Normally the cave beyond is thick with guards and all who have tried to escape that way have been cut down or forced back and sacrificed to the N'aal Beast. But now…'

With Movat Jard close at my heels, I strode to the door and immediately began hacking at it with my sword.

Movat Jard joined me, using his axe. The prisoners crowded eagerly behind us, Carnak well to the fore.

From the other side of the door we heard a grunt of surprise. Then an Argzoon yelled:

'Cease – or you'll be food for the N'aal!'

'The N'aal is dead,' I replied, 'You address the two who slew it.'

We forced the door down. It fell outwards and crashed to the floor, revealing two baffled-looking guards, their swords in their hands.

Movat Jard and I rushed at them instantly and had soon dispatched them in as swift a series of strokes as I shall ever witness.

Carnak bent down and took one of the swords from the fallen guard. Another man also took a sword and two others helped themselves to a mace and an axe respectively.

'We must go to the Weapon Chambers of Argzoon,' Movat Jard said. 'Once there, we can equip ourselves properly.'

'Where lie these dungeons?' I asked.

'Why, under the Black City. There are several entrances.'

'And where lie the Weapon Chambers?'

'In the castle – Horguhl's castle. If we are quick we can get there before they return to the city. They must be in some confusion.'

'Movat Jard, why do you help us against your own folk?' Carnak asked. He seemed just a little suspicious, for he had already experienced one clever Argzoon trap.

'I have learned much from a little that Michael Kane here said, and what he did, once, for me. I have learned that *ideas* can sometimes rise above blood loyalties. And besides, it is Horguhl whom I fight, not the Argzoon. If we beat her, then I shall have to decide again what my attitude is – but not until she no longer rules the Argzoon!'

Carnak seemed convinced by this. We rushed up the slopes leading away from the dungeons and had soon reached an iron gate kept by a single watchman. When he saw us and noted, perhaps, the desperate looks in our eyes, he did not draw his weapons but flung out his hands before him.

'Take my keys – do not take my life.'

'A fair bargain,' I said, accepting his keys and unlocking the iron gate. 'We will also borrow your weapons.' Two more men were armed with a sword and an axe – making eight in all. We bound the Blue Giant and passed on into the streets.

Beyond the walls of the Black City we heard the confused babble of voices, but the Argzoon had not yet reached the gates. We headed towards the nearby castle, pouring through the streets towards the Weapon Chambers, with Movat Jard, Carnak and myself in the lead.

We swarmed into the castle, cutting down the few guards who attempted to stop us.

Just as we were breaking into the Weapon Chambers, the first of the Argzoon returned and shouted the alarm.

We burst into the Weapon Chambers, less well laid-out but not unlike the Weapon Room of Varnal in appearance, though the weapons were, of course, more barbaric.

While the joyful prisoners went to arm themselves with the best weapons of the Argzoon – not to mention the heaps of captured weapons they found lying therein – we eight, who were already armed, met the initial wave of Argzoon warriors.

We must have made a strange sight, the three of us who led – a blue man of the Argzoon nearly ten feet in height; a wild-eyed, naked man covered in hair; and a tanned swordsman who was not even of that planet. But one thing we all had in common – we could use swords.

We stood shoulder to shoulder, fending off our attackers while our comrades armed themselves. It seemed that I faced a veritable wall of swords raining down upon me from the Blue Giants.

Somehow we held them off – and succeeded in depleting our enemies.

Then, from behind us, came a great roar!

The prisoners were all armed and ready to fight. The slaves had become warriors again – warriors with a lust for vengeance for the years of servitude and fear, revenge for the treacherous ambush which had wiped out a great percentage of the flower of Southern manhood.

We pressed forward now, driving the Argzoon before us!

Along the corridors of the castle we fought. In halls and rooms we fought. In Horguhl's deserted throne room we fought, and in her private rooms, too. At one stage I took the opportunity to tear down the N'aal tapestry hanging there.

Out into the streets until the whole of the Black City seethed with fighting men.

Our numbers were few. Our men had all but forgotten their old training. But our hearts were full of exultant battle-lust, for at long last we were able to strike back at our old enemies.

By the time all our force was in the streets, the Argzoon had cut down more than a third of our men – but we had taken more of them!

And the longer we fought, the more of their old skills the ex-slaves remembered. The fighting in the city became more sporadic as the Argzoon attempted to re-form.

We used the pause to stress our own strength and discuss strategy. We held a large area around the castle, but the Argzoon still held most of the city. Somewhere were Horguhl and Shizala. I prayed that Horguhl would not order Shizala slain in the pique of defeat; that the queen still had confidence in her warriors' ability to win.

The Argzoon attacked first, but we were ready for them, with warriors deployed in every street.

For a time neither side gained any advantage. We held our position and the Argzoon held theirs.

'It is deadlock,' said Movat Jard as he, Carnak and I conferred.

'How can we break it?' I asked.

'We must get a fairly large party of warriors into position behind them,' Carnak said. 'Then we can attack them from two sides and drive a wedge through their ranks.'

'A good plan,' I agreed. 'But how can we move that party of warriors? We cannot fly.'

'True,' Movat Jard said, 'but we can go *under* them. Remember the slave pens? Remember that I said there were several entrances and exits?'

'Yes,' I replied. 'Could we go through one of these and emerge behind the enemy?'

'Unless they are ready for that trick,' he said, 'we could. But if they have blocked the entrances, we stand to lose more – since we will have a force of good warriors stranded down there unable to help defend the area we have gained. Is it worth the risk?'

'Yes,' I said. 'For if we do not gain an advantage soon our men will tire. They are already weak from the sojourn. We cannot afford to waste any more time.'

'Who will lead them?' Carnak stepped forward, evidently thinking of himself.

'I will,' I said. 'You are both needed here to rally the defenders.'

They understood the necessity of this.

Within a shati, I was leading a force of some thirty warriors towards the slave-pen entrance Movat Jard had indicated.

Down the winding ramps we went at a loping run.

And we ran straight into a detachment of Argzoon coming the other way!

Almost before we knew it we were wasting time and men in a battle for the underground passage.

The Argzoon seemed to be fighting with little will, and I had killed two myself and disarmed several more before the rest lay down their arms, holding out their hands in a gesture of surrender.

'Why do you give up so easily?' I asked one of them.

He answered in the coarse, guttural accent of his people.

'We are tired of fighting battles for Horguhl,' he said. 'And she does not lead us even – she disappeared after you killed the N'aal Beast. We only followed her because we thought Raharumara dwelt in the N'aal Beast and she was stronger than Raharumara. But now we know that Raharumara does not dwell in the N'aal Beast, else you could not have killed it. We do not wish to lose our lives for her schemes any longer – too many of our brothers have died over the years to satisfy her ambitions. Now it has all come to this – a few warriors fighting in the streets of the Black City, defending themselves against slaves. We wish a truce!'

'How many others feel as you do?' I asked.

'I do not know,' he admitted. 'We have not talked – too much has happened too swiftly.'

'You know the fair-haired girl Horguhl brought here and who was at the ceremony of the N'aal Beast earlier?' I questioned him.

'I saw her, yes.'

'Do you know where she is?'

'I think she is in the Tower of Vulse.'

'Where is that?'

'Near the main gate – it is the tallest tower in the city.'

We took their arms from them and continued on through the slave pens emerging at last in a part of the city almost immediately behind the rear lines of the battling Argzoon.

We attacked at once.

With cries of surprise the Argzoon turned. Then we were locked in combat, driving through their midst in an effort to link up with our comrades on the other side.

I myself was engaged with one of the largest Argzoon I had encountered. He was almost twelve feet high and fought with a long lance and a sword.

At one stage he flung the lance at me. By chance, I grabbed it in mid-air, turned it and flung it back at him. It caught him in the belly. I finished him with my sword. If it had not been for that lucky catch, I doubt if I should have survived the encounter.

Now I could see that we were almost linked with our fellows on the other side.

Certain that the tactic had succeeded, I left my men in charge of a dark-skinned warrior who had shown skill and intelligence in the fighting, and left the fray, sheathing my sword.

I was running for the Tower of Vulse near the main gate. Here I hoped that I would at least find Shizala and make myself responsible for her safety, if I could do nothing else.

I saw the tower soon and noted that its entrance seemed unguarded.

But I saw something else. Something that sent a shock of surprise thrilling through me.

What I saw I thought impossible – some trick of the light, some illusion.

What I saw was an aircraft tethered near the top of the tower – an aircraft similar to the one in which Shizala and I had flown when we went to the camp of the Argzoon.

How did it come to be there?

I reached the entrance of the tower and ran inside. There I found a set of winding, stone steps leading up and up. There seemed to be no rooms in the lower part of the tower. I began to run up the steps.

Near the top of the tower I found a door. It was unbarred and I flung it open.

I felt shock as I saw the two within the room.

One of them was Shizala.

The other –? The other was Telem Fas Ogdai, Bradhinak of Mishim Tep, Shizala's betrothed.

He had one arm around Shizala and his other hand held a sword as he looked warily towards the door through which I had burst.

Chapter Fourteen

Sweet Joy and Bitter Sorrow

FOR A MOMENT I confess that my emotion was one of dreadful disappointment rather than joy that Shizala was safe in the arms of a protector.

I dropped my guard and smiled at Telem Fas Ogdai.

'Greetings, Bradhinak. I am glad to see that you have managed to keep the Bradhinaka from danger. How did you get here? Did you hear something of where we had gone in Narlet, perhaps? Or was Darnad able to get word to you more swiftly than I had supposed?'

Telem Fas Ogdai smiled and shrugged. 'Does it matter? I am here and Shizala is safe. That is the important thing.'

I felt the answer rather unnecessarily oblique but accepted it.

'Michael Kane,' Shizala said, 'I was sure you had been killed by now.'

'Providence is on my side, it seems,' I said, trying to hide the expression in my eyes, which must have added – 'save in the most important matter of my life.'

'I hear you've performed miracles of daring.' Telem Fas Ogdai spoke somewhat ironically. My dislike for him increased in spite of my effort to take an objective attitude to him. He was not helping me.

'Providence again,' I said.

'Perhaps you will leave us for a moment,' Telem Fas Ogdai said. 'I would like to have some words with Shizala in private.'

I would not be boorish a second time. I bowed slightly and went out of the room.

As the door closed I heard Shizala's voice suddenly scream loudly.

It was too much. In spite of my earlier encounter at the palace of Varnal, I could not control myself. I sprang back into the room.

Shizala was struggling in the grasp of a scowling Telem Fas Ogdai. He was trying to drag her towards the window to where his aircraft waited.

'Stop!' I ordered levelly.

She was sobbing. 'Michael Kane – he –'

'I am sorry, Shizala, but no matter what you think of me for it, I will not stand by and see a brute handle a lady so!'

Telem Fas Ogdai laughed. He had sheathed his sword, but now he released Shizala in order to draw it.

To my surprise she ran immediately to me!

'He is a traitor!' she shouted. 'Telem Fas Ogdai was in league with Horguhl – they planned to rule the continent together!'

I could hardly believe my ears. I drew my own blade.

'He threatened to kill you unless I remained silent just now,' she went on. 'I – I did not want that.'

Telem Fas Ogdai chuckled. 'Remember your bond, Shizala. You must still marry me.'

'When the world learns that you are a traitor,' I said, 'she will not.'

She shook her head. 'No, a bond of the kind we made goes higher than ordinary law. He is right. He will be exiled and I with him!'

'But that is a cruel law!'

'It is tradition,' she said simply. 'It is a custom of our folk. If tradition is ignored society will crumble, we know that. Therefore the individual must sometimes suffer unjustly, for the sake of the Great Law.'

It was hard for me to argue against this. I may be old-fashioned, but I have great respect for tradition and custom as pillars of society.

Suddenly Telem Fas Ogdai laughed again, a somewhat unhinged chuckle, and lunged towards me.

I thrust Shizala behind me and met his lunge with parry.

Back and forth across the room we fought. I had never encountered such a skilled swordsman. We were evenly matched, save that I had earlier exerted myself a great deal. I began to feel that he must win and Shizala would be condemned to spending her life with a traitor she hated!

Soon I was actually retreating before a whirlwind of steel and found myself with my back not against the wall – but worse – my back was to the window. A drop of a hundred feet was behind me!

I saw Telem Fas Ogdai grin as he forced me further back. I became desperate. From somewhere I called on extra reserves of energy. In a final, desperate bid I hurled myself forward, straight into that network of flashing steel!

I took him by surprise. It saved my life and cost him his.

He stumbled backward for a moment.

I thrust rapidly at his throat. The point met flesh and he fell with a great roar of baffled rage.

I knelt beside him as the life bubbled from him. I could not save him. We both knew he was going to die. Shizala came and knelt by him, too.

'Why, Telem,' she said, 'why did you do such a despicable thing?'

He turned his eyes towards her, speaking with difficulty.

'It was an expedition I undertook in secret more than a year ago. I thought I would try to discover what had happened to your father. Instead, I was captured and brought to Horguhl.'

'You were brave to attempt such a thing,' I said softly.

'She – she seduced me somehow,' he said. 'She told me secrets – dark secrets. I became completely in her power. I helped her plan the final stages of the attack on Varnal. I deliberately went to Varnal at the time of the attack, knowing that I would be asked to carry a message for help to Mishim Tep and your other allies.' He began to cough horribly, then rallied himself.

'I – I could not help myself. I expected you to be defeated, but you were not. Your folk learned that I had not taken the message to Mishim Tep – m-my father asked why I had not. I – I could not reply. People talked – soon it was common knowledge that I had betrayed Varnal, though – though none knew *why*. It was that woman – it is like a dream – I – I was a traitor and a fool – she – she –'

He raised himself up then, his eyes staring blankly out at nothing.

'She is evil!' he cried. 'She must be found and killed. Until she is, all that we love and hold valuable on Vashu will be in danger of corruption. Her secrets are terrible – they give her an awful power! *She must die!*'

And then he fell back – dead.

'Where is Horguhl?' Shizala asked me.

'I do not know. I think she has escaped – but to where is a mystery. This cavern-world is not fully known even to the Argzoon!'

'Do you think he exaggerated – that his mind was clouded?'

'I think it possible,' I said.

And then, quite suddenly, she was in my arms, sobbing and sobbing.

I held her close, whispering words of comfort into her ear. She had been through incredible hardships and terrors and had borne them all bravely. I did not blame her for crying then.

'Oh, Michael Kane – oh – my love!' she sobbed.

I could scarcely believe my ears. I felt that the day's trials had turned my brain!

'Wh – what did you say?' I asked softly, bewildered.

She controlled her sobbing and looked up at me, smiling through her tears, 'I said, "my love",' she repeated. 'Michael Kane, I have loved you ever since we first met. Remember, when the mizip chased you?' I laughed and she joined in.

'But that is when I fell in love with you,' I gasped. 'And – I thought you loved Telem Fas Ogdai!'

'I admired him – then,' she said, 'but I could not love him – particularly after I had seen you. But what could I do? Tradition had bound me to him and I could not break with tradition –'

'Nor would I expect you to,' I said. 'But now –'

She put her arms around me and I drew her close. 'Now,' she breathed, 'we are free to marry as soon as the betrothal day can be arranged!'

I bent to kiss her and then realised that I was not yet sure how the battle had gone.

'We must see how our men are dealing with the Argzoon,' I said.

She knew nothing of what had happened – or at least little. Quickly I told her. She smiled again and slipped her hand in mine. 'I will not be parted from you again,' she said. I knew I should have left her in the tower – or better still in the aircraft, where she would be safest – but I could not bear the thought of something else separating us. The aircraft reminded me of the time we had flown together over the Argzoon camp and I asked her why she had left the security of the ship.

'Did you not realise?' she asked as we moved down the steps, hand in hand. 'I wished to help you – or die with you, if that was to be. But when I got there you had already done your work and gone!'

I squeezed her hand affectionately and with gratitude. I knew the rest from Horguhl.

In the street we discovered that the Argzoon were laying down their arms, evidently losing all stomach for fighting now that they had learned their queen had fled.

Towards us, marching in excited triumph, came a detachment of warriors headed by Movat Jard and Carnak, the ex-slave.

We waited to meet them and I felt suddenly weary as I realised that we had won and that I need do no more fighting that day.

Tired as I felt, my heart was bounding with gladness. We had won – and Shizala had promised to be mine. I wished nothing else!

Then, suddenly, Carnak came rushing forward, a smile on his lips and his hands outstretched.

'Shizala!' he cried. 'Shizala – is it really you? What are you doing here?'

She looked puzzled, not recognising the bearded man. I wondered if it was an old friend and hoped it might not be some previous fiancé or someone who would shatter my happiness!

'Carnak – you know Shizala?' I said in surprise.

'Know her!' Carnak laughed heartily. 'I should think I do!'

'Carnak!' It was Shizala's turn to laugh. 'Is that your name? Is it?'

'Of course!'

I watched with some jealousy, I don't mind telling you, as the older man took my Shizala in his arms. And then all was revealed in a single word.

'Father!' she cried. 'Oh, Father, I thought you were dead!'

'So I would have been in a very short time had it not been for this young man with the strange-sounding name – and this fierce savage, his friend.' Carnak cocked a thumb at Movat Jard.

Shizala turned to me.

'You saved my father's life?' She hugged my arm. 'Oh, Michael Kane – the House of Varnal owes its very existence to you!'

I smiled. 'Thank you – if it did *not* exist I would be a very sad man.'

Carnak patted my shoulder. 'What a champion – I've known none like him in all my days – and I've known some good warriors, too.'

'You are a fine warrior yourself, sir,' I said.

'I'm not so bad, young man – but I was never so good as you.' Then he looked regretfully at his daughter and me. 'I can see that you feel – um – some emotion for one another. But you realise, Shizala, that there is nothing you can do about it?'

'What?' I was almost beside myself with horror at this. What new factor had arisen to become a barrier between my love and me?

Carnak shook his head. 'There is the matter of the Bradhinak Telem Fas Ogdai. He –'

'He is dead,' I said. I felt relief. Of course, Carnak knew nothing of what had happened recently. Quickly I told him.

He frowned as he listened. 'I knew the lad was headstrong – and I knew Horguhl could use those eyes and that voice of hers to put anyone in her power – but I never thought that the son of my oldest friend could...' He cleared his throat... 'It was, in a sense, my fault – for he came to see if I still lived, a prisoner, with the intention of saving me.' Carnak – or the Bradhi of Varnal, as he was – shook his head. 'We shall tell his father that he died on our behalf,' he decided. 'As, in an indirect sense, he did.'

He looked at us and smiled. 'Then you can announce your betrothal as soon as we return to Varnal, if that is what you wish.'

'It is what we wish,' we replied in unison, smiling at one another.

It took only a short time to round up the rest of the demoralised Argzoon and it was decided that we three – Carnak, Shizala and myself – should leave the Black City in the charge of Movat Jard, thus making the Argzoon's defeat less bitter. We announced that Movat Jard was temporary ruler of the Argzoon until some vote could be taken after a treaty had been drawn up.

Realising that the Argzoon had been led to this situation by Horguhl's schemings, we were not as hard on them as we might have been.

Soon we were entering the aircraft, bidding farewell for the moment to Movat Jard.

Carnak took the controls of the ship and guided it through the difficult twists and turns of the tunnel leading to the open air.

Soon we were passing over the Wastes of Doom, over the stunted forests, the wide river, the wilderness and the Crimson Plain.

The journey took many days, but we spent it making plans for the future, discussing all that had passed while we had been parted.

Then soon we were hovering over Varnal.

When the city discovered who we were, it went mad with joy and we were received with great ceremony. The betrothal was fixed for the following day and I went to my old room that night in a state of tremendous happiness.

But after all this came the bitterest blow of all. It was as if Fate had decided to make me go through all those trials simply to snatch away my reward at the final moment – for, in the night I felt a strange, familiar sensation come over me.

I felt my body seeming to break apart, felt as if, once again, I was drawn across space and time at fantastic speed. Then it was over and I was lying down again. I smiled, thinking that it had been a dream. I felt a light on my eyes and thought it must be morning – the morning of my betrothal.

I opened my eyes and looked into the smiling face of *Doctor Logan* – my chief assistant at the laboratories!

'Logan!' I gasped. 'Where am I – what has happened?'

'I don't know, professor,' he said. 'Your body is a mass of scars – but you've put on extra muscle from somewhere. How do you feel?'

'What has happened!' I repeated loudly.

'You mean this end? Well, it took us about seven hours, but we finally picked you up again on some funny wavelength – we thought we'd lost you altogether. Something went wrong with the transmitter. Some jamming perhaps – I don't know.'

I got up and seized him by his lab coat.

'You've got to send me back! You've got to send me back!'

'Hey – your experiences haven't done you any good, prof,' one of the technicians said. 'You're lucky to be alive at all. We've been working for seven hours – you were as good as dead!'

'I still am,' I said, my shoulders sagging. I let go of Logan's coat and stood there looking at the equipment. It had taken me to a place of high adventure and a lovely woman – and it had brought me back to this drab world.

I was hustled away to the sick bay and they wouldn't let me out for weeks what with the doctors and psychologists trying to discover what had 'really' happened to me. I was judged unfit for work and they'd never let me get near the transmitter, of course – though I tried several times. Finally they sent me to Europe – on extended leave.

And here I am.

Epilogue

AND THAT, SUBSTANTIALLY, was the testament of Professor Michael Kane, physicist and swordsman – scientist on Earth, warrior on Mars.

Believe it, as I believed it, if you will. Do not believe it if you can.

After hearing Kane's story I asked his permission to do two things.

He wanted to know what they were.

'Let me publish this remarkable story of yours,' I said, 'so that the whole world might judge your sanity and truthfulness.'

He shrugged. 'I suspect few will make the correct judgement.'

'At least those few will prove me right.'

'Very well – and the other request?'

'That you let me finance a *privately* built matter transmitter. Can it be done?'

'Yes. I am, after all, the inventor of the machine. It would require a great deal of money, however.'

I asked how much. He told me. It would make a large hole in my income – really rather more than I could afford, but I did not tell him that. I was ready to back my faith in his story with a great deal of money.

Now the transmitter is almost finished. Kane says he thinks he can tune it to the correct frequency. We have worked like dogs for weeks to complete it, and I hope he is right.

This machine is in some ways more sophisticated than the first one, in that it is really a type of 'transceiver' being permanently tuned on this special wave.

Kane's idea is that if he can return to Mars – however many centuries in the past it lies – he will be able to build another machine there and thus travel back and forth at will. That side of it seems, perhaps, a little too ambitious, but I have developed a great respect for his scientific mind.

Will it work?

I do not yet know. As this manuscript goes to press, we still have a week or so in which to test the machine.

Perhaps, soon, will I have more to write about the Warriors of Mars?

I hope so.

Blades of Mars

For Henry Morrison and Robert Silverberg

Prologue

'WE MUST NOT fail!' I looked up sharply. The speaker was a handsome giant of a man with burning, diamond-blue eyes. He was bending over one of the strangest devices I had ever seen. About the size of a telephone box, it was covered with dials and switches. A large coil suspended above it pulsed with power and on the right, in a dark corner, a dynamo of unusual design fed it with energy.

The tall man sat in a kind of cradle affair that was suspended from the roof of the makeshift laboratory – really the cellars of my Belgravia house. I stood beneath the cradle, reading out to him the information given on the dials.

We had been at work on the machine for many weeks – or rather *he* had been at work. I had merely put up money for the equipment he needed, and followed his instructions in doing the simple tasks he permitted me to do.

We had met fairly recently in France, where he had told me a strange and wonderful story about his adventures in – of all places – the planet Mars! There he had fallen in love with a beautiful princess of a city called Varnal of the Green Mists. He had fought against gigantic blue men called Argzoon, finally succeeding in saving half a continent from their savage domination.

Put as baldly as this, the whole thing sounds like the paranoiac ravings of a madman or the lurid tales of a smooth-tongued tale-teller. Yet I believed it – and still do.

I have already recounted this first meeting and what became of it – of how Michael Kane, the man who now worked in the cradle above my head, had been a physicist in Chicago doing special research on something he called a 'matter transmitter'; of how the early experiment had gone wrong and he had been transmitted not to another part of the lab, but to *Mars*!

It was a Mars, we believed, aeons in the past, a Mars that thrived before Man ever walked this planet, a Mars of strange contrasts, customs, scenery – and beasts. A Mars of warring nations possessing the remnants of a once mighty technical civilisation – a Mars where Kane had come into his own. An expert swordsman, he had been a match for the master swordsmen of the Red Planet; a romantic despising his own dull environment, he had rejoiced at the luck which Fate brought him.

But Fate – in the guise of his fellow scientists – had also brought him back to Earth – back to here-and-now, just as he was about to marry his Martian sweetheart! The other scientists in Chicago had adjusted the fault in the transmitter and managed to recall Kane. One moment he had been sleeping in a Martian bed – the next he was back in the laboratory looking into the smiling faces of his fellow researchers! They thought they had done him a favour!

No-one had believed his story. This brilliant scientist had been discredited when he had tried to convince the others that he had really been to Mars – a Mars that had existed millions of years ago! He was not allowed near his own invention and he was given indefinite 'leave of absence'. Weighed down with despair of ever seeing his beloved Mars again, Kane had taken to wandering the world, aimlessly, thinking always of Vashu – the native name for Mars.

Then we had met by accident in a small café overlooking the French Mediterranean. He had told me the whole story. At the end of it I had agreed to help him build privately a transmitter similar to the one in Chicago so that, with luck, he would be able to return.

And now the device was almost ready!

'*We must not fail!*' He repeated the phrase, speaking half to himself as he worked with frowning concentration.

He would be taking his life in his hands if the experiment went wrong. He could have been flung through time and space at random the first time – he had only the flimsiest evidence to support his theory of spacial-temporal warp being affected by a special tuning of the transmitter, tuning which had existed during the first experiment. I had reminded him of this – that even if the transmitter worked there was scant likelihood of it sending him to Mars again. Even if it *did* send him to Mars, what chance was there of it being the same Mars of the time he had left?

But he held to his theory – a theory based, I felt, more upon what he wished than what actually was – and he placed all his faith on it working – if he picked the right time of year and day, and the right geographical position.

Apparently a spot near the city of Salisbury would be ideal – and tomorrow at eleven-thirty p.m. would be an excellent time. That was why we worked with such frantic haste.

So far as the actual equipment was concerned, I was sure it was all right. I did not pretend to understand his calculations but I trusted his character and his reputation as a physicist.

At last Kane looked away from the cone he'd been tinkering with and fixed me with that melancholy yet burning gaze with which I had become so familiar.

'That's it,' he said. 'There's nothing else we can do except ship it to our location. Is the power-wagon ready?'

'It is,' I replied, referring to the transportable dynamo we would use to power his device. 'Shall I phone the agency?'

He pursed his lips, frowning. He swung himself out of the cradle and dropped to the floor. He looked up at his brainchild and then his face relaxed. He seemed satisfied.

'Yes. Better phone them tonight rather than the morning.' He nodded.

I went upstairs and put through a call to the employment agency, who were hiring us the 'muscle-power' we needed to get our equipment to its ultimate destination on Salisbury Plain. The men would be at my front door in the morning, the agency assured me.

When I returned I found Kane slumped in a chair, half asleep.

'Come along, old man,' I said. 'You'd better rest now or you'll be unable to do your best tomorrow.'

He nodded mutely and I helped him upstairs to bed. Then I retired myself.

Next morning the men arrived with a large van. Under Kane's

somewhat nervous supervision the matter transmitter was taken out and secured inside the van.

Then we set off for Salisbury with me driving behind the larger vehicle in what Kane had chosen to call our power-wagon.

We had selected a spot not far from the famous Circle of Stones, Stonehenge. The great, primitive pillars – thought by many to be one of the earliest astronomical observatories – stood out boldly in the sharp light of early morning. We had brought a large tent to protect our equipment both from the weather and from prying eyes. We erected this with the help of the men, who then drove off with our instructions to return with their van in the morning.

It was a restless day and the wind beat at the canvas of the tent as Kane and I worked to set up the equipment and give it a few tests to make sure it was working efficiently. This took us the best part of the day, and night was falling as I went to the van to switch on the dynamo in order to test the transmitter.

As the hours slipped by, Kane's face set more and more grimly. He was tense and kept reminding me of what I had to do when the time came. I knew it by heart – a simple business of checking certain instruments and pressing certain switches.

Shortly before eleven-thirty I went outside. The moon was high, the night wild and stormy. Great banks of black clouds scudded across the sky. A night of portent!

I stood there smoking for a few minutes, huddled in my overcoat. My mind was half numb from the concentration of the previous weeks. Now that the experiment was about to take place I was almost afraid – afraid for Kane. He stood to lose if not his life, at least his hopes if we failed. And with the loss of hope, I felt, Kane would cease to be the man I admired.

He called me from inside the tent.

When I went back I could see that his normal calmness was still not so apparent, partly due to his near-exhaustion, partly to evident realisation of the same things I had been thinking.

'We're almost ready, Edward.'

I stamped out my cigarette and looked at the weird machine. The matter transmitter was alive now, humming with power. The scanner-cone at the top glowed a ruby red, giving the interior of the tent a bizarre appearance. Reflected in this glow, Kane's handsome face looked like that of some noble but unearthly demigod.

'Wish me luck.' He smiled with an attempt at lightness. We shook hands.

He entered the transmitter and I closed the panel behind him, sealing it shut. I glanced at my watch. One minute to go. I dared not think – dared not consider, now, what I was about to do!

As the seconds ticked by I carefully recalled all his instructions, studied the instruments as needles quivered and dials glowed. I reached out my hand and depressed a button, flicked a switch. Simple actions, but actions which could either kill a man, or consign him to limbo, either physical or mental.

There came a sudden, shrill note from above and the needles flickered frenetically. I knew what it meant.

Kane was on his way!

But where? When? Perhaps I would never know!

But now it was done. I walked slowly from the tent.

I lit another cigarette and smoked it. I thought about Kane, about his tales of high adventure and romance on an ancient planet. I wondered, as I had done before, if I had been right to believe him and help him. I wondered if I had been wrong.

Also I felt a loss – as if something strong and important had been removed from my life. I had lost a friend.

Then, suddenly, I heard a voice from within the tent!

With a shock I recognised Kane's voice – though now it had a different note to it.

So we had failed. Perhaps he had not gone anywhere. Perhaps his calculations had been wrong. Half in relief and half in trepidation, I stumbled back into the tent – to receive another shock!

The man who stood there was almost naked.

It was Kane – but not the Kane with whom I had shaken hands only minutes before.

I stared in astonishment at this apparition. It was clad in a leather harness of some sort, and it was decorated with strange, glowing gems which I could not recognise as any I knew. Across the broad, muscular shoulders was draped a light cloak of a wonderful blue colour. At its left hip the figure wore a long sword with a basket hilt – a sword suspended from a wide loop of thick leather but naked, unscabbarded. On his feet were heavy sandals laced up the calves to just below the knee. His hair, I now noticed, was longer, too. Upon his body were scars, some old and some fresh. He smiled strangely at me, as if greeting an old acquaintance from whom he had been separated for some time.

I recognised the gear from Kane's earlier descriptions. It was the gear of a *pakan* – a Warrior of Mars!

'Kane!' I gasped. 'What has happened? Only a few moments ago you were...' I broke off, unable to speak, able only to stare!

He strode forward and grasped my shoulder in his powerful grip.

'Wait,' he said firmly, 'and I will explain. But first, can we return to your house in London? You might need that tape recorder again!'

By means of the power-wagon we drove back to Belgravia, this strange, naked warrior with his long blade and alien, jewelled war-harness, sitting next to me.

Luckily we were unobserved as we entered my house. He moved lithely, his bronzed muscles rippling – a graceful superman, a hero from the pages of Myth.

My housekeeper does not live in so I prepared him a meal myself and brought him some strong, black coffee which he seemed to relish a great deal.

I switched on the tape recorder and he began to talk. Here is the tale he told me, edited only as to my questions and his asides – and some of the more secret scientific information – so as to present his own continuous narrative.

E.P.B.,
Chester Square,
London, S.W.1.
April 1969

Chapter One
The Barren Plain

After I had entered the matter transmitter I felt a tinge of fear. I realised fully for the first time just what I could lose.

But then it was too late. On your side of the transmitter you had done your work. I began to experience the familiar sensations associated with the machine. There was no difference save that this time I had no certainty of where I was going – you will remember that on my first trip I had thought I was merely being transmitted to a 'receiver' in another part of the laboratory building. Instead, I had been transported to my Mars. Now where was I bound? I prayed that it should be Mars again!

Strange colours spread themselves before my eyes. Again I felt weightless. There came a period during which I felt in communion with – *everything*. Then came the feeling of being bodiless, and yet hurtling through blackness, at incredible velocities. My mind blanked out.

This time I awoke to comparative darkness. I lay face down on a hard, stony surface. I felt a little bruised, but not badly. I rolled over on my back.

I was on Mars!

I knew it the moment I saw the twin moons – Urnoo and Garhoo in Martian, Phobos and Deimos in English – lighting a desolate landscape of chilly rocks and sparse vegetation. Over to the west something glinted – something that might have been a vast stretch of placid water.

I was still in the clothes I was wearing when I entered the transmitter. Its scanner broke down and translated into wave-form everything placed inside the machine. I even had some loose change in my pockets, and my watch.

But something was wrong.

Gingerly I sat up. I was still a little dazed but already the suspicion was dawning on me that something had gone seriously wrong.

On my first two-way trip I had arrived just outside the city of Varnal on Southern Mars. And it was from Varnal that I had been snatched when my 'helpful' brother scientists drew me back to Earth.

But this wasteland was unlike any I had seen on *my* Mars!

Mars it was, of course – the moons proved that. Yet it did not seem to be the Mars of the age I had known – a Mars that had existed when dinosaurs still walked the Earth and Man had yet to come to dominance on my home planet.

I felt desperate, helpless, incredibly lonely. I had cut off all hope of ever seeing my beloved, betrothed Shizala again or of living in peace in the City of the Green Mists.

The Martian night is long and this seemed the longest of all until, when dawn began to appear, I finally rose and looked about me.

Nothing but sea and rock greeted my gaze whichever way I turned!

As I had guessed, I stood on a barren plain of brown-orange rock that stretched inland from a great, cold sea that moved slightly but restlessly, grey under a bleak sky.

Whether this was in the past or future of the Mars I knew I cared not. I only knew that if I was, as I suspected, on the exact geographical spot where once had stood – or once *would* stand – Varnal of the Green Mists and the Calling Hills, then all was lost to me! Now a sea rolled where the hills had rolled, rock occupied the place of the city.

I felt betrayed. It is difficult to describe why I should feel this. It was my own fault that I was here – and not even now embracing my sweetheart in the palace of the rulers of the Karnala.

I sighed, suddenly weary. Uncaring of what befell me, I began gloomily to walk inland. I had no purpose, it seemed, but to walk until I dropped from weariness and hunger. The barrenness of the landscape seemed to reflect the barrenness of ambition in myself.

All hope was dashed, all dreams vanished. Despair alone consumed me!

It was perhaps five hours – or approximately forty Martian *shatis* – later that I saw the beast. It must have been stalking me for some time.

The first thing I noticed about it was its weird, coruscating skin that caught the light and reflected it with all the colours of the rainbow. It was as if the beast were made of some kind of viscous, crystalline substance, but that was not so. Strange as it was, a second glance showed it to be of flesh and blood.

It was about eighteen to twenty *kilodas* – roughly six feet – high and thirty *kilodas* long. It was a powerful beast with a huge, wide mouth full of teeth that gleamed like crystal too. It had a single, many-faceted eye – an attribute of several Martian animals – and four short, heavily muscled legs ending in big, clawed paws. It had no tail, but a kind of crest, perhaps of matted fur, oscillated along its back.

It was bent on having me for its lunch, that was clear.

Now my mood of despair left me as this danger threatened. I had no weapon, so I stooped and grabbed large rocks in each hand.

With a effort of will I faced the beast as it began to stalk slowly towards me, the crest oscillating quicker and quicker as if in anticipation of its meal. Yellowish saliva dripped from the open mouth and the single eye was fixed intently on me.

Suddenly I yelled and flung my first rock, aiming at the eye, following this shot with my second. The creature vented an incredible wailing cry, half of pain, half of anger. It reared on its hind legs and made lashing movements with its forelegs.

I picked up two more rocks and flung them at its soft underbelly. Evidently these did not have the same effect as those I had hurled at the eye. The beast dropped to all fours again and held its ground – as I held mine – regarding me balefully.

It seemed to be stalemate for the moment.

Slowly I stooped and felt around for more ammunition. I found one rock – there were no more.

Now the crest trembled and fluttered, the mouth opened still wider and the drooling increased. Then the creature took several steps backward but I could tell it was not retreating, merely preparing to spring.

I tried a trick which I knew had worked on Earth when men had been in a similar position confronted by wild beasts. I shouted at the top of my voice and ran towards it, the hand holding the rock upraised.

I ran full tilt almost into its horrid maw.

The beast had not moved an inch!

Now I was in worse straits than I was before!

Deciding to sell my life dearly, I flung my last rock at the eye and dashed past to get behind it. The beast screamed, wailed and reared again. Then I saw thick blood beginning to ooze down its muzzle. It scuttled round, still on its hind legs, forelegs waving, claws slashing at air. I had hit the lower part of the eye. I must have inflicted some damage, for the blood was evident, but the beast could still see.

I stooped towards another rock and then, with a speed I had not expected, it was dashing towards me, jaws gaping!

I flung myself out of its path just in time – but already it was whirling round and coming at me again. I knew I hadn't a chance.

I remember lying on the rock trying to turn over and get to my feet, fearfully aware of that great bulk rushing down on me, the shining teeth, the saliva...

And then, only inches from me, the beast fell to the ground, threshed and was still.

What had happened? I thought at first that my rock must have done more damage than I had suspected but when I got up I saw long, heavy lance jutting from the beast's side.

I looked around, saw the figure standing there – and was instantly on my guard again. This was a Blue Giant – an Argzoon. I had previously experienced their savagery – I knew they attacked men such as me on sight.

The Argzoon was well armed, with sword and mace at left and right hips. He was magnificently muscled and almost ten feet tall.

What confirmed my suspicion that I was in a different era was the fact that instead of wearing the normal Argzoon leather breastplate his was of fine metal, as were his wrist guards and greaves.

Perhaps he had saved my life in order to have some sport with me. I began attempting to wrench his lance from the corpse of the beast so that I would have something with which to defend myself when he attacked.

I got the lance free as he came close. He smiled and stood regarding me with some puzzlement in his manner, arms akimbo, head slightly to one side.

'I am ready for you, Argzoon,' I said in Martian.

He laughed then – not the savage, animal laugh of the Argzoon but a good-humoured laugh. Had the Argzoon changed so much?

'I saw you fight with the *rhadari*,' he said. 'You are very brave.'

Warily I lowered my lance, saying nothing. The voice, too, had been unlike the Argzoon guttural which I knew.

He pointed at me, smiling again. 'Why are you swathed in that bulky cloth? Are you ill?'

I shook my head, feeling a little embarrassed already, both by my appearance – which was odd on Mars, to say the least – and my assumption that he was a foe.

'I am called Hool Haji,' he said. 'Your name and your tribe?'

'Michael Kane,' I said, finding my tongue at last. 'I have no native tribe, but am an adopted member of the Karnala nation.'

'A strange name – but I know of the Karnala. By reputation, they are as brave as you have shown yourself to be.'

'You'll pardon me,' I said, 'but you do not seem typical of the Argzoon nation.'

He laughed good-humouredly. 'Thank you. That is because I am of the Mendishar.'

I seemed to have heard vaguely of the Mendishar, but could not remember what I had been told – by Shizala probably, I thought.

'Is this Mendishar?' I asked.

'I wish it were. We are nearly there, however.'

'Where is Mendishar in relation to Argzoon?'

'Oh, we lie well to the north of the Caves of Darkness.'

The discrepancy in time could not be as great as I had at first thought then. If the Karnala and the Argzoon's underground world, the Caves of Darkness, still existed, then the spot – this barren waste – on which I had found myself was not typical of the planet I knew.

Hool Haji reached out his hand. 'Perhaps I could have my lance now?'

I apologised and handed it to him.

'You look exhausted,' he said. 'Come – I have a camp nearby – we'll eat a little of your late adversary.' He bent down and lifted the great beast's carcase easily, flinging it over his shoulder.

I walked beside him and he deliberately shortened his pace so that I might find it easier to keep up with him. He did not seem to tire beneath his burden.

'I was graceless,' I said. 'I did not thank you for saving my life. I am in your debt.'

'May you have an opportunity to repay it,' he replied, using a formal reply which I had only heard in the South until now.

We reached Hool Haji's camp – a low tent pitched beside a small stream that ran through the rocks. A fire was burning and giving off a great deal of ill-smelling smoke, but Hool Haji explained that the only fuel in these parts was in the *oxel*, the brownish, brackenlike plant that sprouted among the rocks.

Hool Haji began to skin the beast and as he did so, preparing it most deftly with a special knife he wore in his upper harness, he explained the similarities between his race and the Argzoon. I was interested to hear it, especially since it also told me a little more about the earlier history of Vashu – or Mars, as they call it on Earth.

It seems that in the dim and distant past of Vashu the Mendishar and the Argzoon were one people, living close to the sea from which, their legends said, they had originated. They were fishermen and boat builders, pirates and coastal raiders, sea traders, *inrak* divers – the inrak being a rare shellfish regarded as a delicacy by all, it appeared, but the blue men themselves.

They lived in a part of the planet which at that time was remote. Their lives were parochial, their trading and raiding confined mostly to nearby places.

Then came the Mightiest War. About the cause of this war and its protagonists Hool Haji was rather vague. It was between the Sheev and the Yaksha, he said. I had heard of the Sheev. This mysterious people had given many benefits to the Karnala – they had once possessed a grand civilisation, understood nuclear energy and the like, were more advanced than Earthmen of my own time. The ruins of their cities were still sometimes to be found here and there. Hool Haji appeared to know little more than I did. The Yaksha and the Sheev were of similar origins, he said, but the Yaksha were considerably less wholesome.

The Mightiest War was waged across the planet for decades. Soon even the remote blue men heard of it. Soon they even suffered from its effects, many dying from a strange disease borne on the wind from the West.

Then the Yaksha came to the settlements of the blue folk. They had many wonderful weapons but they seemed beaten and desperate. The handful of Yaksha offered the blue men great chances of plunder if they would help them attack a Sheev position inland. Many had agreed and had set off for the mountains where the Sheev were. Apparently they had found the Sheev in underground chambers blasted from the rock, and had attacked. The Sheev had held them off until only three of the Sheev survived. Then these escaped in a flying boat of some kind. The Yaksha, also few in number, had followed them, telling the blue folk to hold the position until they returned.

They had not returned. The blue folk settled in the cavern-world. Some had brought women. They adapted to the environment and had even seemed to thrive on it. The caverns were an ideal place from which to conduct raids on the smaller, lighter-skinned races – so they had raided. That had been the origin of the Argzoon millennia before.

The Mendishar were those who had remained. They had taken no part in the Mightiest War, but had prospered, trading amongst far islands and a continent which lay beyond the sea to the north.

'That is,' Hool Haji said as he set the meat on a spit over the fire, 'until the Priosa gained too much power.'

'Who are they?' I asked.

'Originally they were simply a royal guard – a ceremonial force attached to our Bradhi's house.' A Bradhi was a kind of Martian king who tended to rule by heredity but could be deposed and replaced by popular vote. 'They were made up of young warriors who had won honour among our people. They were idolised by the populace who began, by degrees, to attach an almost mystical significance to them. In the minds of the ordinary folk they became more than men, almost deities – they could do what they liked virtually with impunity. Then, about forty years ago, the warrior who was then Pukan-Nara –' this meant, roughly, warrior leader – 'of the Priosa began to say that he was receiving messages from higher beings.

'Realising that the whole system of the Priosa offered danger to the Mendishar nation, the Bradhi and his council decided to disband it. But they had reckoned without the power the Priosa now held over the ordinary folk. When they announced the decision to disband the force the people refused to hear of it. The Bradhi was deposed and the Pukan-Nara – Jewar Baru – was elected Bradhi. The old Bradhi and his council all died mysteriously in different ways, the Bradhi's family was forced to flee and the new Bradhi Jewar Baru began his unhealthy reign.'

'In what way is it unhealthy?' I asked.

'They have brought superstition back into the lives of the Mendishar. They perform "miracles" and claim clairvoyance; they receive "messages" from "higher beings"... it is religion debased to its lowest level.'

I knew the pattern. It was not unlike similar episodes in my own planet's chequered history.

'They are now a caste of warrior-priests milking the nation of its riches,' Hool Haji continued, 'to the point where many are now disillusioned. But Jewar Baru and his "more-than-men" have total power and those who are disillusioned and say so publicly soon find themselves taking part in one of their barbaric ritual sacrifices where a man's – or a woman's – heart is torn out in the central square of Mendisharling, our nation's capital city.'

I was disgusted. 'But what part do you play in this?' I asked him.

'An important one,' he said. 'A rebellion is planned and many rebels wait in the small hill villages beyond Mendisharling. They need only a leader to unite under and march against the Priosa.'

'And that leader is not forthcoming?'

'I am that leader,' he said. 'I hope their faith in me will be justified. I am the last of the line of the old Bradhis – my father was slain on Jewar Baru's orders. My family wandered the wastelands, seeking refuge and finding none, hunted by bands of Priosa. Those who were not killed by the Priosa died of malnutrition and disease, of attacks by wild beasts such as our friend there.' He pointed at the carcase which was now beginning to roast well.

'At length only I, Hool Haji, remained. Though I yearned for Mendishar I could think of no way of returning – until a messenger found me wandering, many days' journey from this spot, and told me of the rebels. Of their longing for a leader, how as last of the old line I would be ideal. I agreed to go to the hill village he told me of – and I am now on my way.'

'Since I have no aims,' I said, 'perhaps you will allow me to accompany you.'

'Your presence will be welcome. I am a lonely man.'

We ate and I told him my story, which he did not find as incredible as I had suspected he would.

'We are used to strange happenings on Vashu,' he said. 'From time to time the shadows of the older races pass across us in the form of rediscovered marvels, strange inventions of which we know little. Your story is unusual – but possible. Everything is possible.'

I realised once again that the Martians are a philosophical folk on the whole – somewhat fatalistic in our terms, I suppose, yet with a strong tradition and moral code that save them from any hint of decadence.

After our meal we slept, and it was night again by the time we set off for the hills of Mendishar.

Dawn rose on those hills which marked the border of the Mendishar nation, and Hool Haji had to restrain himself from lengthening his steps.

It was as we set foot on blue-green sward that two riders, mounted on the huge, apelike *daharas*, riding beasts of almost all Martian nations, topped the nearest hill, paused for a moment when they saw us and then rode full tilt at us.

They were gaudily dressed, with brightly lacquered armour and long, coloured plumes in close-fitting helmets. Their swords flashed in the early-morning sun.

They were clearly bent on taking our lives!

Hool Haji cried one word as he flung me his long lance and drew his sword.

That word was – '*Priosa!*'

The pair thundered down on us and I held my lance ready as my opponent's great sword swung up, preparing to crash down and cleave my skull.

It swept towards me. I deflected it with my lance but the force of his blow knocked my weapon from my hands and I was forced to leap out of the warrior's path, dashing to retrieve the lance as he wheeled his mount and grinned with narrowed eyes, sure of an easy victory.

Chapter Two

Ora Lis

THE GIANT BLUE warrior now aimed his sword at me as if to impale me – I was sure that was his intention.

My lance was only a short distance from me but there was no time to pick it up. When the point of his sword was almost at my throat I flung myself backwards, feeling the metal literally part my hair! Then I grabbed for the lance and leapt to my feet.

He was once again turning his mount when I saw my opportunity and hurled my lance at him.

It took him in the face and killed him instantly. He fell back, the lance quivering in his head. His sword dropped from his hand and hung by its wrist throng. The unruly dahara reared up, sensing that its master no longer controlled it, and the corpse toppled from the saddle.

Glancing about me, I saw that Hool Haji had not had my good luck – for luck it had been. He was defending himself from a rain of blows his attacker was aiming at him. He had dropped to one knee.

Snatching up my late opponent's sword, I ran forward with a yell. I must have looked a peculiar sight, still in jacket, shirt and trousers, armed with a huge blade, running to the aid of one of two battling Blue Giants!

Foolishly, Hool Haji's antagonist half-turned at my yell. My blue ally needed only that momentary diversion. He sprang up, knocked aside his opponent's weapon and plunged his sword into the Priosa's throat.

The giant was scarcely dead before Hool Haji was grasping the dahara's harness and steadying the beast as its late master fell sideways from the saddle. Somewhat contemptuously, the ex-Bradhinak freed the feet of the corpse from the stirrups and let it drop to the ground.

I realised what my friend had in mind and turned towards the other dahara, which had moved a short distance away and was nervously looking about. Without its rider it looked even more curiously manlike than ever. The dahara was descended from the common ape-ancestor of Man. If anyone had said of it, as is sometimes said of dogs and horses on Earth, that it was 'almost human', that person would have stated a plain fact! Their intelligence varied according to species, the intelligence of the smaller Southern variety being greater than that of this much larger Northern variety. I approached the big dahara with caution, talking to it soothingly. It shied away – but not before I was able catch its reins. It made a token snap at me – I have never known even the wildest dahara to attack a man – and then it was under my control.

Now we both had mounts and enough weapons to arm me.

A trifle ghoulishly, we stripped the corpses of everything we needed – but it was a pity that the armour fitted neither of us, Hool Haji being a little too large and I a lot too small, but I was able to make a cross-belt to go over my shoulder and take the heavy weapons. I was also, thankfully, able rid myself of the greater part of my encumbering Earthly clothing. Feeling more like a warrior of Mars with my weapons strapped about me and seated on the broad back of the dahara, I galloped along, keeping pace with Hool Haji as we headed once more into the hills.

Now we were at last in Mendishar. The village – called Asde-Trahi – lay only a few miles away.

We soon reached it. I had expected something more primitive than the bright, mosaic walls of the low, semi-spherical houses – many of the mosaics being arranged as pictures, very beautiful and artistic. The village was surrounded by a wall, though as we rode down the hill towards it we could see the whole of the interior. The wall was also decorated, but in paints of strong, primary colours – orange, blue and yellow – with geometrical designs mainly based on the circle and the rectangle.

As we neared Asde-Trahi, figures began to appear on the walls.

The figures were almost all armed and their weapons were drawn. These were Blue Giants, but their armour, if they wore it at all, was of padded leather similar to that which the Argzoon, my old enemies, wore. Their weapons, too, seemed to be whatever they had been able to lay hands on.

When we were closer, one of the figures gave out a wild yell and began to talk rapidly to his companions.

A great cheer rang out then and the warriors held their swords and axes high, leaping up and down in exultation.

Evidently Hool Haji had been recognised and was welcome.

From a flagmast in the centre of the village one banner was run down and another raised. I gathered they were literally raising the flag of rebellion. The heavy yellow-and-black square banner was apparently the old standard of the deposed Bradhis.

Hool Haji smiled at me as the gates opened in the wall.

'It is a homecoming worth waiting for,' he said.

We rode into the village and men and women and the Mendishar children – some of them were almost my height! – flocked around Hool Haji, their voices babbling their welcome.

One of the women – I suppose she was beautiful by their standards – clung to Hool Haji's arm and looked with large eyes up into his face.

'I have waited so long for you, great Bradhinak,' I heard her say. 'I have dreamed of this day.'

Hool Haji seemed rather embarrassed – as I'd have been – and had some difficulty disengaging his arm from the woman's embrace, but was able to do so when he saw a tall, dignified young warrior come towards him, hands outstretched in welcome.

'Morahi Vaja!' the exile exclaimed in pleasure. 'You see, I kept my promise.'

'And I mine,' smiled the young warrior. 'There is not a village in these hills that does not willingly offer its support to you and our cause.'

The woman was still there, though she no longer embraced Hool Haji.

Morahi Vaja stepped towards her. 'This is my sister, Ora

Lis – she has never met you, but she is already your greatest supporter.' Morahi Vaja smiled. Then he spoke to the girl. 'Ora Lis, will you instruct the servants to prepare Hool Haji's friend a bed and food?' The young warrior seemed not at all surprised by the appearance of a stranger – a stranger of a different race, at that – in his village.

Hool Haji realised it was time to introduce me. 'This is Michael Kane – he is from Negalu,' he said, using the Martian name for the planet Earth.

This time Morahi Vaja did show slight surprise. 'I thought Negalu was inhabited only by giant reptiles and the like,' he said.

Hool Haji laughed. 'He is not only from Negalu – but from the future!'

Morahi Vaja smiled a little. 'Well then, greetings, friend – I hope you bring luck to our enterprise.'

I restrained myself from remarking that I hoped I could since I had brought little to my own!

As we dismounted, Hool Haji said: 'Michael Kane saved my life when we were attacked by Priosa earlier today.'

'You are welcome and honoured,' Morahi Vaja said to me.

'Hool Haji forgets to tell you that he saved mine before I saved his,' I pointed out as Morahi Vaja led us towards a large house decorated in the most splendid mosaics I have ever seen.

'Then it was ordained that he should – for if you had not been saved you could not have saved him.'

I could think of no reply to such logic. We entered the house. It was cool and the rooms were large, light and simply decorated.

Ora Lis was already there. She had eyes only for Hool Haji, who seemed both slightly flattered and embarrassed by her attention.

Morahi Vaja was plainly a person of some consequence in the village – he was, it emerged later, a kind of mayor – and we were given the best of everything. The food and drink were delicious, though some of it was plainly produced only in the North, since it was unfamiliar to me.

We ate and drank our fill and all the while Ora Lis paid Hool

Haji every attention, even begging to be allowed to remain when Morahi Vaja told her we were now to talk strategy and logistics.

The reasons for the planned rebellion were twofold. One, the people were beginning to realise that the Priosa were by no means superior beings – too many daughters and matrons had testified to the fact that the Priosa's appetites were scarcely those of enlightened demigods – and two, the Priosa were becoming more lax, more self-indulgent, less inclined to ride out on their patrols.

It seemed to me that this process was not unfamiliar – it seems to be something of a law of nature that the tyrant falls by his own lack of foresight. It has always been that the wise king, no matter what kind of character he may possess, protects his subjects and thereby protects himself. The larger and more complex the society, the longer the process of disposing of the tyrant. Often, of course, one tyrant is substituted for another and a vicious circle is brought about. In the end, however, this means the destruction of the state – its conquest or decline – and sooner or later the enlightened ruler or government will arise. This may take centuries – or a few weeks – and it is, of course, hard to be philosophical when it is your face that is beneath the iron heel.

We talked into the night and I was sometimes amused to see Hool Haji having to refuse a dish of fruit or the offer of another cushion from the attentive Ora Lis.

Our plan was based on the belief that, once a large force of village-living Mendishar attacked the capital city, the townsfolk would join them.

It seemed logical that this would be so. Everything seemed ripe.

It had not been thus not so long ago, Morahi Vaja informed us. The men of the villages and small towns had been wary of following Morahi Vaja, who was, in their eyes, too young and untried. But when he had been able to contact Hool Haji everything had changed. Now they were enthusiastic.

'You are very valuable, Bradhi,' said Morahi Vaja. 'You must protect yourself until the time for the rising, for if we were to lose you we should lose our whole cause!'

Morahi Vaja's face was very serious. Evidently he meant what he said – and knew that what he said was true!

We were given a room each in Morahi Vaja's house. My bed was the plain, unsprung bed that predominates all over Mars. I was soon asleep.

I had gone to bed in a mixed mood of desolation and anticipation. It was not so easy to forget, even for a moment or two, that I was separated from the woman I loved by barriers impossible to cross. On the other hand, the cause of the tyrannised folk of Mendishar was one close to my heart. We Americans always have sympathy with the oppressed, whoever they may be, so long as they themselves are fighting back. Not a very Christian attitude, perhaps, but one which I share with most of my countrymen and probably with most of humanity.

I awoke in a somewhat more philosophical frame of mind. There was hope – faint hope. You remember that I told you of the wonderful inventions of the mysterious Sheev? Well, that was my hope – that some time I might contact the Sheev and ask them for help in crossing time and space once again – this time not from planet to planet but from one time and place on Mars to another.

I resolved to seek out the Sheev – or a member of the race – as soon as I had seen the revolution of Mendishar successful. I felt involved in it, principally because I regarded Hool Haji as a close friend, and anything he did was of interest to me.

A light tap on my door came soon after I had awakened. Sunlight was streaming through the unglazed window and there was a sweet, fresh smell in the air – the familiar scents of the Martian countryside.

I called for the person outside to enter. It was a female servant – the blue females are only a foot or two shorter than the males – with a tray of hot food. This in itself was a surprise, for the Southern Martian breakfast usually consists of fruit and the like.

While I was finishing the breakfast Hool Haji came in. He was smiling. After greeting me he sat on the bed and burst out laughing.

His laughter was infectious and I found myself smiling in response, though I did not know the cause of his mirth.

'What is it?' I asked.

'That woman,' he said, still grinning. 'Morahi Vaja's sister – what's her name?'

'Ora Lis?'

'That's right. Well, she brought me my breakfast this morning.'

'Is that strange?'

'It is very courteous – though a rare custom amongst our people. It was not so much the action, which I should normally have accepted as a compliment, as what she said.'

'What did she say?' I had a feeling of unease then. As I have mentioned before, I seem to be slightly psychic – or whatever you care to call it. I have some sixth sense which warns me of trouble. Some would call it the logic of the subconscious which accumulates and draws conclusions from data which never reaches the conscious mind.

'In short,' declared my friend, 'she told me that she knew our destinies to be intertwined. I believe she thinks I am going to marry her.'

'An infatuation,' I said, still somewhat perturbed, nonetheless. 'You are the mysterious exile returned to claim a throne, and what could be more romantic than that? What girl would not respond to it? It is not an uncommon feeling, I have heard.'

He nodded, 'Yes, yes. That is why I did not treat the declaration too seriously. I was polite enough to her, never fear.'

I fingered my chin thoughtfully, realising suddenly that I had not shaved for some time – there was a heavy stubble there. I would do something about it soon. 'What did you say?' I asked.

'I told her that the business of the revolt was consuming all my attention, that I had noticed she was beautiful… She is, don't you think?'

I did not answer this. All beauty is comparative, I know, but I could not, frankly, tell a beautiful, eight-foot, Blue Giantess from an ugly one!

'I told her that we should have to wait before we could become better acquainted,' the Mendishar continued, chuckling.

I felt slightly relieved by the knowledge that my friend had behaved so tactfully.

'A wise thing to say,' I nodded. 'When you sit the throne of Mendishar as Bradhi, that will be the time to think of romance – or the avoiding of it.'

'Exactly,' said Hool Haji, bringing his great bulk to a standing position once more. 'I don't quite know if she accepted this. She seemed to take it rather as a declaration of my own passion, which troubled me a little.'

'Do not worry,' I said. 'What are your plans for today?'

'We must work speedily and prepare a message to be sent to all the *cilaks* and *orcilaks* calling them to a full-scale meeting here.' The two Martian words meant, roughly, village-leader and town-leader, the suffix *ak* designating one holding power over his fellows or – strictly speaking, in Martian – one who was charged by his fellows to act in their interests. *Cil* meant a small community, *orcil* meant a larger one.

'This is necessary,' Hool Haji continued, 'in order that they should see for themselves that I am who I am as well, of course, as deciding when and how we shall strike and deploy our warriors.'

'How many warriors do you estimate having at your disposal?' I enquired washing myself with the cold water provided.

'About ten thousand.'

'And how many Priosa will they have to contend with?'

'About five thousand, including the warriors not of the Priosa but expected to support them. The Priosa will, of course, be much better armed and trained. My people have a habit of fighting independently of any command. The Priosa have rid themselves of this lack of discipline, but I am not sure if the same can be said for many of the village-dwelling warriors.'

I understood. This was a trait which the Mendishar shared with their Argzoon cousins. The Argzoon had only been united under that arch-villainess Horguhl – and united largely through fear of a common enemy, the N'aal Beast, and superstition.

'That is another reason why my presence is needed,' said Hool Haji. 'They will, Morahi Vaja feels, fight under an hereditary Bradhi, whereas they would be disinclined to take orders from a mere *cilak*.'

'Then Morahi Vaja was right – you are invaluable to the cause.'

'It seems so. It is a great responsibility.'

'It is responsibility to which you will have to become accustomed,' I told him. 'As Bradhi of Mendishar you will have heavy responsibilities for your people all your life.'

He sighed and gave me a wry smile. 'There are some advantages in being a lone wanderer in the wilderness, are there not?'

'There are. But if you are of royal blood you are not free to choose.'

He sighed again and gripped the hilt of his great sword. 'You are more than an able fighting companion, Michael Kane. You are also a friend of strong character.'

I grasped his arm and looked up into his eyes. 'Those words apply to you, Bradhinak Hool Haji.'

'I hope so,' he said.

Chapter Three
Hool Haji's Duty

A FEW DAYS later we received word that all the various leaders of the towns and villages had been given secret word and a great meeting was planned in three days' time.

During that period of waiting we had spent long hours in planning and fewer hours in relaxation. Hool Haji spent a great deal of the time with Ora Lis. Like any man, he was flattered by her adoration and could not resist basking in it. I felt that no good could come of this, but I could not blame him. In circumstances other than mine I might have done the same myself. In fact, I have done it myself more than once in the past, though not nearly so much was at stake then.

It seemed to me that Ora Lis was given good cause to think that her passion was being reciprocated, but I could find no way of warning my friend.

Once I found myself in the same room with her, alone, and I talked with her for a short time.

In spite of what was, to me, her outlandish size and strange face, she was plainly a simple, ingenuous, romantic girl. I tried to speak of Hool Haji, told her of his many obligations to his people, that it might be years before he could think of himself – and the taking of a wife.

Her response to this was to laugh and shrug her shoulders.

'You are a wise man, Michael Kane – my brother says that your counsel has aided them greatly – but I think you are not so wise in matters of love.'

This struck deeper than it should have done for thoughts of my own love, Shizala, were forever with me. But I persevered.

'Have you not thought that Hool Haji may not feel so strongly about you as you do for him?' I asked gently.

Again the smile and the light laugh. 'We are to be married in two days' time,' she told me.

I gasped. 'Married? Hool Haji has told me nothing of this.'

'Has he not? Well, it is so, nonetheless!'

After that I could make no reply but resolved to seek out Hool Haji at the earliest opportunity.

I found him standing on the north wall of the village, looking out over the lovely, blue-green hills, the cultivated fields that sustained the villagers, and the large, scarlet *rhani* flowers that grew in profusion hereabouts.

'Hool Haji,' I said without preliminary, 'did you know that Ora Lis thinks she is to marry you in two days' time?'

He turned, smiling. 'Is that it? She is living out some fantasy in a world of her own, I fear. She told me mysteriously yesterday that if I met her by a certain tree yonder –' he pointed to the north-east – 'that which we both desired would be brought about. A secret marriage! Even more romantic than I guessed.'

'But do you not realise that she sincerely believes you intend to make the rendezvous?'

He drew a deep breath. 'Yes, I suppose so. I must do something about it, mustn't I?'

'You must – and swiftly. The poor girl!'

'You know, Michael Kane, the duties of the past days have left me in a state almost of euphoria. I have spent time in Ora Lis's company because I found it the most relaxing thing I could do. Yet I have hardly heard anything she has said to me – can remember scarcely a word I have said to her. Plainly, things have gone too far.'

The sun was beginning to set, staining the deep blue sky with veins of red, yellow and purple.

'Will you go to see her now?' I described where she was.

He yawned wearily. 'No – I had best do it when I am more refreshed. In the morning.'

We walked back slowly to the house of our host. We passed Ora Lis on our way. She went swiftly by, pausing only to give Hool Haji a secret smile.

I was horrified. I understood my friend's predicament, how the situation must have arisen, and I could sympathise with him. Now he had to do what every man hates to do – put a girl into the deepest possible misery in the most tactful possible way. Knowing something of these situations, I also knew that, no matter how tactful a man tries to be, something always results so that he is misunderstood and the girl weeps, refusing to be comforted by him. Few women do not respond in this manner – and, frankly, those are the ones I admire – women like my own Shizala, who was as feminine as could be but with a will of iron and a strength of character most men would envy.

Not that I did not sympathise with the poor Ora Lis. I sympathised very much. She was young, innocent – a village-girl with none of the unpretentious sophistication of my Shizala, and none of the rigid training that all members of the Southern Martian royal houses receive.

I sympathised with both. But it was up to Hool Haji to do his unpleasant duty. And I knew that he would.

Again, after I had bathed and shaved with a specially honed knife I had borrowed from Morahi Vaja – the blue Martians have no body hair to speak of – and climbed wearily into bed, I was filled with a sense of deep disquiet that would not leave me even in sleep. I tossed and turned throughout the long Martian night and in the morning felt as unrefreshed as when I had gone to bed.

Having risen and splashed cold water all over my body in an effort to rid myself of my feeling of tiredness, I ate the food the servant had brought me, strapped on my weapons and went out into the courtyard of the house.

It was a beautiful morning but I could not appreciate it greatly.

Just as I was turning back to look for Hool Haji, Ora Lis came flying from the house. Tears ran freely down her face and great groaning sobs came from her.

I realised that Hool Haji must have spoken to her and told her the truth – the unpalatable truth. I tried to speak to her, to say some comforting words to her, but she was past me in a flash and running into the street.

I told myself that it was best that it should have happened this way and that, being young and resilient, the poor girl would soon recover from her misery and find another young warrior upon whom she could lavish the passion that was so plainly part of her character.

But I was wrong. I was to be proved very wrong in the events which followed.

Hool Haji came out of the house next. He walked slowly, with head bowed. When he looked up and saw me, I noticed that his eyes reflected pain and sadness.

'You have done it,' I said.

'Yes.'

'I saw her – she ran past me and would not stop when I called to her. It was the best thing.'

'I suppose so.'

'She will soon find someone else,' I said.

'You know, Michael Kane,' he said with a sigh, 'it cost me more than you realise to do what I did. In other circumstances I might have grown to love Ora Lis.'

'Perhaps you will when this is over.'

'Will it not then be too late?'

I had to be realistic. 'Possibly,' I told him.

He seemed to make an effort to dismiss the thoughts from his mind. 'Come,' he said, 'we must speak with Morahi Vaja. He would learn your views on the deploying of the axemen from Sala-Ras.'

If Hool Haji was in a mood of depression, I was in one of utmost foreboding.

More was going to come out of this episode than either of us could have foreseen.

It was to change the entire course of events and fling me into some strange adventures.

It was to mean death to many.

Chapter Four

Betrayed!

THE DAY OF the great meeting dawned and Ora Lis had not returned. Nor had the search parties that had gone seeking her discovered a trace of her. We all became worried, but priority had to be given to the meeting.

The proud cilaks and orcilaks were arriving. They had travelled secretly and always alone. The Priosa patrols were ever wary for large groups of men who might represent danger.

Farmers, merchants, artisans, dahara trainers, whatever their normal occupations they were all warriors. Even the Priosa tyranny had not been able to forbid the countrymen their right to bear arms. And armed they were – to the teeth.

Guards were stationed in the surrounding hills to keep a lookout for any Priosa patrol, though none was expected on this particular day, which was why the meeting had been called now.

There were more than forty village-leaders and town-leaders there, all of them looking eminently trustworthy and with integrity ingrained in their faces. But there was independence too – the kind of independence that would prefer to fight its own battles and not rely on any group effort. Their habitual looks of suspicion changed somewhat, however, as soon as they entered the big room set aside for the meeting in Morahi Vaja's house. They saw Hool Haji there and they said, 'He is like the old Bradhi alive again!' And that was enough. There was no bowing of the knee or servile salute – they held themselves straight. But there was a new air of determination about them now.

Having ascertained that all were convinced of Hool Haji's identity, Morahi Vaja unrolled a large map of Mendishar and hung it on the wall behind him. He outlined our basic strategy and proposed tactics in certain conditions. The local leaders asked questions – very thoughtful and penetrating ones – and we answered them. Whenever we could not answer at once we discussed it. With men like these, I realised, pitched against the unwary Priosa, it would be no difficult feat to win the capital and wrest Jewar Baru's stolen power away from him.

But still the feeling of disquiet was with me. I could not shift it. I was constantly on my guard, glancing about me warily, my hand on my sword.

A meal was brought into the hall at midday and we ate as we talked, for there was no time to lose.

By early afternoon the initial talking was over and smaller details were being discussed – how best to use certain small groups of men with a special fighting-skill, how to use individuals such as the local champion spearmen, and so on.

By dusk most of us were satisfied that on the day set for the attack – in another three days – we should be ready and we should win!

But we were never to make that attack.

Instead, at sunset, we were attacked!

They came on the village from all sides and we were hopelessly outnumbered and outweaponed.

They came in a charge, mounted on daharas, their armour shining in the dying sunlight, their plumes waving and their lances, shields, swords, maces and axes flashing.

The noise was terrible, for it was the baying blood-lust of men enjoying the prospect of wiping out a village, man, woman and child.

It was the cry of the wolverine debased in a human throat.

It was a cry not only to strike terror into the hearts of the women and children, but into the hearts of grown, brave men. It was a cry that was merciless, malevolent, already triumphant.

It was the cry of the human hunter of the human prey!

We saw them riding through the streets, striking at anything that moved. The cruel glee on their faces was indescribable. I saw a woman die clutching her child. Her head was sliced off and the child impaled on a lance. I saw a man trying to defend himself against the battering weapons of four riders – and go down with a shriek of rage and hatred.

It was a nightmare.

How had this come about? We had been betrayed, that was plain. These were the Priosa, unmistakeably.

We rushed into the streets, standing shoulder to shoulder and taking the savage riders as they came at us.

It was the end of everything. With us dead the people would be leaderless. Even if some escaped, there would not be enough to launch any sizeable revolt.

Who had betrayed us?

I could think of no-one. Certainly not one of these village-leaders, men of pride and integrity, who were even now falling before the weight of the Priosa attack.

Night fell as we fought – but darkness did not, for the scene was illuminated by the houses which the attackers had already set ablaze.

If I had had any doubts that Hool Haji had exaggerated the cruelty of the tyrant and his chosen supporters they were quickly dismissed. I have never seen such sadism exhibited by one part of a race for another.

Memory of it is still burned deep in my mind. I shall never forget that night of terror – I wish that I could.

We fought until our bodies ached. One by one the brave hope of Mendishar fell in their own blood, but not before they had taken many of the better-equipped Priosa with them!

I met steel with steel. My movements became almost mechanical – defence and attack, block a thrust or a blow, deflect it, aim a thrust or a blow of my own. I felt like a machine. The events, the weariness, had momentarily driven all emotion from me.

It was later, when only a few of us remained, that I became aware of a shouted conversation between Hool Haji and Morahi Vaja, who stood to my left.

Morahi Vaja was remonstrating with my friend, telling him to flee. But Hool Haji refused to go.

'You must go – it is your duty!'

'Duty! It is my duty to fight with my people!'

'It is your duty to choose exile again. You are our only hope. If you are killed or captured tonight, then the whole cause is destroyed. Leave, and there will come others to take the place of those who have died tonight.'

I at once saw the logic of what Morahi Vaja said and added my voice to his.

We continued to fight, arguing as we did so. It was a bizarre scene!

Eventually Hool Haji realised that this must be so – that he must leave.

'But you must come with me, Michael Kane. I – I shall need your comfort and your advice.'

Poor devil – he was in a strange mood and might do something rash. I agreed.

Pace by pace we retreated to where two men, grim-faced, held mounts for us.

We were soon riding out of the devastated village, but we knew that Priosa would be encircling the place waiting for such an attempt – it was a standard tactic.

I glanced back and again felt horror!

A small group of defenders stood shoulder to shoulder just outside Morahi Vaja's house. Everywhere else were the dead – dead of both sexes and of all ages. Lurid flames licked from the once beautiful mosaic houses. It was a scene from Bosch or Breughel – a picture of Hell.

Then I was forced to turn my attention to the sound of feet thundering towards us.

I am not a man to hate easily – but those Priosa I hated.

I welcomed the opportunity to kill the three who came at us, grinning.

We used warm, much-blooded steel to wipe those grins from their faces.

Then we rode on, heavy-hearted, away from that place of anger and cruelty.

We rode until it was almost impossible to keep our eyes open and the cold morning came.

It was then that we saw the remains of a camp and the outline of a prone figure stretched on the sward.

As we neared the camp we recognised the figure.

It was Ora Lis.

With a cry of surprise, Hool Haji rode up to the spot and dismounted, kneeling beside the woman. As I joined him I saw that Ora Lis was wounded. She had been stabbed once with a sword.

But why?

Hool Haji looked up at me as I stood on the other side of the prone girl. 'It is too much,' he said in a hollow voice. 'First that – and now this.'

'Is it Priosa work?' I asked quietly.

He nodded, checking her pulse. 'She is dying,' he said. 'It is a wonder she has lived so long with that wound.'

As if in response to his voice, Ora Lis's eyes fluttered open. They were glazed but brightened in recognition when they saw Hool Haji. A choking sob escaped the girl's throat and she spoke with difficulty, almost in a whimper.

'Oh, my Bradhi!'

Hool Haji stroked her arm, trying to frame words which would not come. Plainly he blamed himself for this tragedy.

'My Bradhi – I am sorry.'

'Sorry?' Words came now. 'It is not you, Ora Lis, who should feel sorry – it is I.'

'No!' Her voice gained strength. 'You do not realise what I have done. Is there time?'

'Time? Time for what?' Hool Haji was puzzled, though some sort of realisation was beginning to dawn in my mind.

'Time to stop the Priosa.'

'From what?'

Ora Lis coughed weakly and blood flecked her lips.

'I – I told them where you were...'

She tried to rise then. 'I told them where you were... Do you not understand? I told them of the meeting. I was mad. It – it was my grief. Oh...'

Hool Haji looked at me again, his eyes full of misery. He realised now it had been Ora Lis who had betrayed us – her revenge on Hool Haji for his rejection of her.

Then he looked down at her. What he said to her then told me once and for all that he was a man in every sense – a man of strength and of pity also.

'No,' he said, 'they have done nothing. We will warn the – village – at once.'

She died saying nothing more. There was a smile of relief on her lips.

We buried the ill-starred girl in the loamy soil of the hills. We did not mark her grave. Something in us seemed to tell us not to – that in burying Ora Lis in an unmarked grave it was as if we sought to bury the whole tragic episode.

It was impossible, of course.

Later that day we were joined by several more fleeing Mendishar. We learned that the Priosa were hunting down all survivors, that they were hot on the heels of the warriors who had escaped. We also learned that a few prisoners had been taken, though the survivors could not name them, and that the village had been razed.

One of the town-leaders, a warrior in middle age called Khal Hira, said as we rode, 'I would still like to discover who betrayed us. I have racked my brains and can think of no explanation.'

I glanced at Hool Haji and he looked at me. It was at that moment, perhaps – though it might have been earlier – that we entered into a unspoken agreement to say nothing of Ora Lis. Let it remain a mystery. The only true villains were the Priosa. The rest were victims of Fate.

We did not answer Khal Hira at all. He did not speak thereafter.

None of us was in any mood for conversation.

The hills gave way to plains and the plains to desert country as we fled in defeat from the Priosa pursuers.

They did not catch us – but they drove some of us, indirectly, to our deaths.

Chapter Five
The Tower in the Desert

KHAL HIRA'S LIPS were swollen but firmly clenched as he stared out over the desert.

Desert it was – no longer a bare wasteland of cracked earth and rock, but a place of black sand stirred into constantly shifting life by a perpetual breeze.

We no longer found pools of brackish water, no longer knew, even roughly, where we were, save that we had travelled north-west.

Our tough mounts were almost as weary as we were and beginning to flag. Here the sky was cloudless and the sun a throbbing, burning enemy.

For five days we had ridden the desert, rather aimlessly. Our minds were still stunned by the sudden turn of events at the village. We were still badly demoralised and unless we were able to find water soon we should die. Our bodies were grimed with the thick black desert sand and we were slumped in our saddles with weariness.

There was nothing for it but to keep moving, to continue our hopeless quest for water.

It was on the sixth day that Khal Hira keeled from his saddle. He uttered no sound and when we went to his assistance we discovered he was dead.

Two more died on the following day. Apart from Hool Haji and myself, three others remained alive – if 'alive' is the proper word to use. These were Jil Deera, Vas Oola and Bac Puri. The first was a stocky warrior of even fewer words than his fellows and very short for a Mendishar. The other two were tall young men. Of the pair, Bac Puri was beginning to show visible signs of losing his grip. I could not blame him – very soon the beating sun would drive us all mad, even if it did not kill us first.

Bac Puri was beginning to mutter to himself and his eyes were rolling dreadfully. We pretended not to notice, partly for his sake, partly for our own. His condition seemed prophetic of the state we ourselves would soon be reaching. Then we saw the tower. I had seen nothing like it on Mars. Though partially ruined and seeming incredibly ancient, it bore no trace of erosion. Its partial destruction seemed to be the result of some bombardment, its upper sections having great jagged holes blown through them at some stage in the tower's history.

It offered shelter, if nothing else. But it also told us that once there had been a settlement here – and where there had been a settlement there might have been water.

Reaching the tower and touching it, I was astounded to discover that it was of no natural substance – at least none that I could recognise. It seemed to be made of some immensely durable plastic as strong as steel – stronger, perhaps, since it had withstood any sort of damage from the corrosive sand.

We entered, my companions being forced to duck. Sand had drifted into the tower, but it was cool. We collapsed to the ground and, no-one having spoken, almost immediately fell asleep.

I was the first to awake. This was probably because I had not yet became fully used to the longer Martian night.

It was barely dawn and I still felt weak though refreshed.

Even in the condition I was in I felt curiosity about the tower. There was a ceiling about twelve feet above my head, but no apparent means of reaching the upper floor which must obviously be there.

Leaving my sleeping companions, I began to explore the surrounding desert, looking for some sign that water lay somewhere beneath the sand.

I was sure that it must, but whether I would find it was a entirely different matter.

Then my eyes caught sight of a projection in the sand. It was not a dune. Inspecting it, I found it to be a kind of low wall made of the same material as the tower. However, when I scraped away the sand I saw that the wall enclosed a surface also of the same material. I could not make out the purpose of this construction. It was laid out in a perfect square some thirty feet across. I began to walk towards the opposite wall.

I was not cautious enough – or perhaps I was too weary – for I suddenly put one foot upon yielding sand, tried to recover as I lost my balance, failed and fell downwards through the surface. I landed, winded and bruised, in a chamber half filled with sand. Rolling over and looking up, I saw that there was a jagged hole above me through which daylight filtered. The hole seemed to have been caused by the same thing that had torn the holes in the tower. Some attempt had been made to patch it and it was across the makeshift patch that sand had blown. It was through this that I had fallen.

The patch was flimsy, originally a sheet of light plastic. I looked at a piece that had fallen with me. Again I could not recognise the substance, although not being a chemist I could not say whether the process was familiar on Earth of my own time or not. Like the tower, however, it spoke of an advanced technology not possessed by any of the Martian races with whom I had come in contact.

Suddenly my weariness seemed to fall away from me as a thought struck me. The thought had many implications but I confess I did not think of my companions above but of myself.

Was this a dwelling of the Sheev? If so, there might be a chance of being able to return to that Mars of the age I needed to visit – the age in which my Shizala lived!

I spat the harsh sand from my mouth and stood up. The chamber was almost featureless, though, as my eyes grew accustomed to the gloom, I made out a small panel on the far wall. Inspecting this I saw it consisted of half a dozen small studs. My hand hovered over them. If I pressed one, what would happen? Would anything happen? Maybe it was unlikely – yet the hand which had patched the roof might have kept any machinery alive. Was the place occupied? I was sure that other chambers opened off from this one. It was logical. If there were control studs there was machinery.

I pressed a stud at random. The result was rather anti-climactic, for all that happened was that dim light filled the chamber, issuing from the walls themselves. This light revealed something else – a rectangular hairline close to the panel, speaking of a door. I had been right.

And the power – or some of it, at any rate – was still working.

Before exploring further I cautioned myself and returned to my position immediately below the gap in the roof. I heard faint voices. Evidently my companions had awakened, wondered where I was and had come to find me.

I called upwards.

Soon I saw Hool Haji's face staring down at me in surprise.

'What have you found, Michael Kane?'

'Perhaps our salvation,' I said with a passable imitation of a grin. 'Come down – bring the others – see for yourselves what I've discovered.

Soon Hool Haji dropped down into the chamber, followed by Jil Deera and Vas Oola. Bac Puri was the last to swing downwards, looking intensely suspicious and still half mad.

'Water?' said Bac Puri. 'Have you found water?'

I shook my head. 'No. But perhaps we shall.'

'Perhaps! Perhaps! I am dying!'

Hool Haji put a hand on Bac Puri's shoulder. 'Calm yourself, friend. Have patience.'

Bac Puri's tongue moved slowly across his swollen lips and he sank into a mood of sullen gloom. Only his eyes continued to dart about.

'What are these?' Jil Deera waved his hand towards the studs.

One of them brought this light,' I said. 'I presume that another activates the door – I cannot guess which.'

'And what lies beyond the door? I wonder,' put in Vas Oola.

I shook my head. Then I reached out and pressed another stud. The chamber began to vibrate slightly. Hastily I pressed the stud again and the vibration ceased. Pressing a third stud brought no apparent result.

A fourth produced a shrill, whining sound and a grating noise which, I quickly saw, indicated that the door was opening, sliding into the right-hand wall.

At first, peering into the aperture revealed, we saw nothing but pitch-darkness and felt cold, cold air on our faces.

'Who do you think created this place?' I whispered to Hool Haji. 'The Sheev?'

'It could have been the Sheev, yes.' He did not seem very certain.

I reached my hand inside and felt about for a panel that should, logically, correspond with the one in the chamber in which we stood.

I found it. I pressed the corresponding stud and light filled the other chamber.

There was no sand in this one. It was roughly the same shape as the one we were in but there were large, spherical objects set into the walls on one side. Beneath them were what were plainly controls of some kind.

Seeing the remains of what had evidently been a Blue Giant of the Mendishar, Bac Puri let out a shriek and pointed a shaking finger at the bones.

'An omen! He, too, was curious. He was slain. There is some supernatural agency at work here!'

Affecting insouciance, I stepped into the chamber and bent towards the skeleton.

'Nonsense,' I said, stooping and wrenching a short-shafted spear from the remains. 'He was slain by this – look!' I held up the lance. It was light and strong, made all in one piece, again of advanced materials.

'I have seen nothing like that in my life,' Jil Deera said, joining me and looking curiously at the weapon. 'And see – these symbols engraved on the shaft – they are in no language I recognise.'

I also did not recognise the language as the basic common tongue of Mars. There were still similarities – though much fainter – to ancient Sanskrit, however. The essential form of the script was the same.

'What is it, do you know?' I said, passing the spear to Hool Haji.

He pursed his lips. 'I have seen something like it in my wanderings. It is like that of the Sheev, but not quite.' His hand was not completely steady as be handed the spear back to me.

'Then what is it?' I asked, somewhat impatiently.

'It is –'

Then there came a chilling sound. It was high and preternatural – a kind of whisper which echoed through the chambers. It came from beyond the chamber in which we stood – from deep within the underground complex.

It was one of the vilest sounds I have heard in my life. It seemed to confirm Bac Puri's half-insane speculation of some supernatural residents of the place. Suddenly, from being a refuge, the underground chamber became a place full of fear – and a terror which was hard to control.

My first impulse was to flee – and, indeed, Bac Puri was already inching towards the door through which we'd come. The others were less decisive but evidently they shared my feelings.

I laughed – or attempted to, the result being a kind of mirthless croak – and said: 'Come now – this is an ancient place. The sound could be made by some animal that inhabits the ruins; it could have its cause in machinery, or even the wind passing through the chambers...'

I did not believe a word I said and neither did they.

I changed my approach. 'Well,' I said with a shrug, 'what shall we do? Risk a danger that may be no danger at all, or go to certain death in the desert? It will be a slow death.'

Bac Puri paused. Some remnant of his earlier strength of character must have come to his assistance. He squared his shoulders and rejoined us.

I strode past the skeleton and pressed the stud to open the next door.

The door opened smoothly this time and I quickly found the next stud to illuminate the third chamber. This one was bigger.

In a sense it comforted me, for it was full of machinery. Of course, I did not recognise the function of the machines, but the thought that some high intelligence must have created them was comforting in itself. As a scientist, I could appreciate the workmanship alone. This was the work of ordinary, intelligent men – it had not been created by any supernatural being.

If inhabitants still lived in this honeycomb of chambers then they would be folk to whom logic would appeal. Perhaps they would bear us some animosity, perhaps they would possess superior weapons – but at least they would be a tangible foe.

So I thought.

I should have realised that there was a flaw in the argument which I so rationally gave to myself to quiet my feelings of disturbance.

I should have realised that the sound I had heard was animal in origin and malevolent in content. There had been no spark of true intelligence in it.

We moved on, chamber by chamber, discovering more machines and great lockers of materials; cloth not unlike parachute silk; containers of gas and chemicals; strong reels of cord similar to nylon cord but even stronger; laboratory equipment used in experiments with chemicals, electronics and the like; parts of machines, things that were obviously power units of some kind.

The further into the great complex of chambers we moved, the less ordered were the things we found. They were neatly stacked and positioned in the earlier chambers, but in the later ones containers had been overturned, lockers opened and their contents strewn about. Had the place been visited by looters, represented by the dead man in the second chamber?

I don't know which chamber it was – perhaps the thirtieth – which I opened the usual way. I reached in my hand to press the light stud – and felt something soft and damp touch my skin. It was a horrible touch. With a gasp I withdrew my hand and turned to tell my companions of what had happened.

The first thing I saw was Bac Puri's face, eyes wide and full of terror.

He was pointing into the chamber. A strangled sound escaped his throat. He dropped his hand and fumbled for his sword.

The others' hands also went to their swords.

I turned back – and saw them.

White shapes.

Perhaps they had once been human.

They were human no longer.

With a feeling of mingled horror and desperation, I too drew my sword, feeling that no ordinary weapon could possibly defend me against the apparitions that moved towards us out of the darkness.

Chapter Six

The Once-were-men

Bac Puri did not flee this time.

His face worked in a peculiar contortion. He took half a step backwards and then, before we could stop him, flung himself into the darkened chamber, straight at the corpse-white creatures!

They gibbered and fell back for a moment, a terrible twittering noise, like that of thousands of bats, filling the air and echoing on and on through the complex of chambers.

Bac Puri's sword swung to left and right, up and down, slicing off limbs, stabbing vitals, piercing the unnaturally soft, clammy bodies.

And then he was, as if by magic, a mass of spears. He howled in his pain and madness as javelins like the one we had seen earlier appeared in every part of his body until it was almost impossible to distinguish the man beneath.

He fell with a crash.

Seeing the creatures were at least mortal, I decided we should take advantage of Bac Puri's mad attack and, waving my sword, I leapt through the entrance, shouting:

'Come – they can be slain.'

They could be slain, but they were elusive creatures and sight and feel of them brought physical revulsion. With the others behind me, I carried the attack to them and soon found myself in a tangle of soft, yielding flesh that seemed boneless.

And the faces! They were vile parodies of human faces and again resembled nothing quite so much as the ugly little vampire bat of Earth. Flat faces with huge nostrils let into the head, gashes of mouths full of sharp little fangs, half-blind eyes, dark and wicked – and insensate.

As I fought their claws, their sharp teeth and their spears, they slithered about, gibbering and twittering.

I had been wrong about them. There was not a trace of intelligence in their faces – just a demoniac blood-hunger, a dark malevolence that hated, hated, hated – but never reasoned.

My companions and I stood shoulder to shoulder, back to back, as the things tore at us.

When we saw that our heavy swords could affect them – and had in fact already dispatched dozens of them – our spirits rose.

At length the ghouls turned and fled, leaving only the wounded flopping on the floor. We slew these. There was nothing else we could do.

We attempted to follow them through the far door, but it closed swiftly and, when we opened it, the creatures had passed on through the complex.

The light stud worked and showed us the dead creatures better.

Bac Puri, in his madness, had undoubtedly helped save our lives. In attacking the creatures he had taken most of their javelins into his body.

These inhabitants of the underground complex were slightly smaller than me and seemed, though this was incredible, to possess hardly any skeleton at all. Our weapons had sliced through flesh and muscle, had drawn blood – if the thin yellow stuff that stained our blades could be called blood – but had met no resistance from bone.

Steeling myself to inspect the corpses more closely, I saw that there was a skeleton of sorts but the bones were so thin and brittle that they resembled fine, ivory wires.

What strange, aberrant branch of the evolutionary tree did these creatures spring from?

I turned to Hool Haji.

'What race is this?' I asked. 'I think you had guessed earlier.'

'Not the Sheev,' he said with a faint, ironic grimace. 'Nor the Yaksha, either – and I suspected that it was the Yaksha before I saw them. These pitiful things are no real threat, unless it be to the mind!'

'So you thought they were a race called the Yaksha – why?'

'Because the language on their spears and on their instruments and cabinets is the written language of the Yaksha.'

'Who are the Yaksha? I seem to remember you mentioning them.'

'Are? Perhaps *were* is a better word, for they still exist only in rumour and superstitious speculation. They are cousins of the Sheev. Do you not remember me telling you about them when we first met?'

Now it came back! Of course – the elder race who had seduced the Argzoon away from Mendishar in the first place, during the war the Martians called the Mightiest War.

'I think these must be descendants of the Yaksha, however,' Hool Haji continued, 'for they bear slight similarities to that race, if I was told aright. They have probably existed down here for countless centuries, somehow remembering – in ritual form, doubtless – to keep the machinery running and defend the place against outsiders. Bit by bit they lost all intelligence and – you will notice – seem to prefer darkness to light, although light is available to them. It is a fitting fate for the remnants of an evil race.'

I shuddered. I could sympathise in my own way with the creatures that had once been men.

Then another thought struck me.

'Well,' I said, somewhat more cheerfully, 'whatever they are biologically, they must have need of water. That means that somewhere here we shall soon find what we need.'

Our need seemed to have diminished with the finding of the underground chambers, but the fight had weakened us further and water was our prime necessity.

Warily, but with more confidence that we could meet and defeat any of the white creatures that attacked us, we moved on until we entered a chamber larger than the rest through which a little *natural* light filtered!

Looking up I saw that the light seemed to come through a domed roof, much higher than the roofs of most of the chambers.

Sand had filtered in through some cracks in this roof, but the floor was not deep in the stuff.

And then I heard it!

A tinkling sound, a splashing sound. At first I thought that thirst had driven me mad but then, as my eyes grew better accustomed to the gloom, I saw it – a fountain in the centre of the chamber. A large pool of cool water!

We moved forward and tasted the stuff cautiously before drinking. It was pure and fresh.

We drank sparingly, wetting our bodies all over whilst we took turns to stand guard against any possible attack from the local residents!

Refreshed and in good spirits, we filled our belt canteens. The stopper of mine was stuck, clogged by the dust. I took a little skinning knife from the right-hand side of my harness – a knife which every blue Martian carries. It is half hidden in the decoration of the leather so that, if captured by an enemy, the enemy might overlook the knife and give the captured warrior a chance to escape. I worked the stopper loose, and then returned the knife to its hidden sheath in my harness.

What now?

We had no inclination to explore the remaining chambers. We had seen enough for the moment. We took the precaution, however, of going to the far door through which the white things had doubtless fled, and blocked it as best we could with sand and loose masonry.

I next discovered a ladder consisting of rungs let into the wall and leading up towards the roof where a narrow gallery ran around the chamber, at the point where the dome began. I climbed this ladder and climbed onto the gallery. It was just large enough to take me and had evidently been intended simply for the use of workmen either repairing or decorating the dome.

The dome was not made of the same durable synthetic material as the rest of the place. I put my eye to a crack and looked out over a seemingly endless expanse of black desert, shining now, like crystal, in the sun. The dome seemed half buried and was probably all but invisible from outside.

A piece of material came away in my hand. It was in an advanced stage of corrosion and would soon collapse altogether. It was transparent – evidently designed to admit light into the chamber of the fountain. Probably the place had been the central hall for relaxing when the Yaksha had been sane and human. The dome had not been planned for any purely functional purpose so much as for decoration. This must be why it would soon collapse. When it did the sand would come in, the fountain would be blocked, and I did not think the inhabitants of the underground city would have the intelligence to clear the sand away – or, for that matter, repair the dome.

Repairs had been made earlier in the roof, but I guessed by more intelligent ancestors of the present dwellers.

I returned to the ground, an idea slowly taking shape in my mind.

At its base the dome was some thirty feet across – ample space for a large object to pass through.

'Why are you looking so thoughtful, my friend?' asked Hool Haji.

'I think I know a way of escape,' I said.

'From this place? We need only retrace our steps.'

'Or break through the roof, for that matter,' I said, pointing upwards. 'It is very flimsy – eroded from the outside by the sand. But I meant escape from our main predicament – escape from the desert.'

'Have you found a map somewhere?'

'No, but I have found many other things. All the artefacts of a great scientific culture – strong, airtight fabric, cord – gas containers. I hope they still contain gas and that it is the kind I need.'

Hool Haji was completely mystified.

I smiled. The others were now looking at me as if I had followed Bac Puri's example and was losing control of my mind.

'It was the dome gave me the idea, for some reason,' I said. 'It struck me that if we had a – a flying ship we could cross the desert in no time.'

'A flying ship! I have heard of such things – some Southern races still possess a few, I believe.' It was Jil Deera who spoke now. 'Have you found one?'

'No.' I shook my head, still thinking deeply.

'Then why speak of such a thing?' Vas Oola spoke somewhat sharply.

'Because I think we could *make* one,' I said.

'Make one?' Hool Haji smiled. 'We have not the knowledge of the old races. It would be impossible.'

'I have some little technical knowledge,' I said, 'though not as much as was once possessed, evidently, by this vanished race. I had not thought of building an aircraft of so advanced a kind as theirs.'

'Then what?'

'A primitive aircraft could be built, I think.'

The three blue men regarded me in silence – still a trifle suspicious.

There was no word for the kind of aircraft I had in mind – no Martian word. I used the English derivation from the French.

'It would be called a *balloon*,' I said.

I began to sketch in the sand, explaining the principle of the balloon.

'We should have to make a gasbag from the material we found back there,' I said. 'There will be difficulties, of course – the bag must be airtight for a start. From it we suspend ropes attached to a cabin – that will be the thing in which we ride...'

By the time I had finished talking and sketching, the intelligent men of Mendishar believed me and largely understood me – which was remarkable considering they came from a society which was mainly non-technical. Once again I had experienced the robust open-mindedness of the Martian who, on the whole, can be taught any concept in a very short time if it is explained to him in sufficiently logical terms. They were an old race, of course, and had the example of the earlier, highly civilised races – the

Sheev and the Yaksha – to show them that what often seemed impossible need not necessarily be.

Enthusiastically, we returned through the underground chambers selecting the things we needed.

I was not at all sure that the *right* gas would be found in the banks of containers that occupied several of the rooms. I took my life in my hands and began to sniff a little of each gas. The containers had valves which still worked perfectly.

Some of the gases were unfamiliar, but none seemed particularly poisonous, though one or two made me a trifle dizzy for a short time.

At last I found the set of containers I needed. They contained a gas with the atomic number 2, the symbol *He*, atomic weight 4.0023, a gas which took its name from the Greek word for the sun – Helium. Non-inflammable and very light, it was what I had been seeking – the perfect gas for filling my balloon!

The search became intensive after I had ascertained that the basic things we needed were there – the light fabric, the gas, the ropes. Next I began to inspect the motors we had found. I did not take them to pieces since I guessed they had some kind of nuclear base – that the power came from a tiny atomic engine. But I did find out how they operated and saw that they would be very simple to harness to propellers.

There were no propellers, however – nothing that would serve as propellers. These would have to be made, somehow.

Our next great discovery was of a machine that could be keyed to run out sections of the tough, light synthetic material of which so much of the place was built.

The machine was large and evidently connected to some unseen reservoir.

It was a boon to us. On a panel in front one made a careful drawing of the part wanted. This had to be done like a plan – side-view, top-view and front-view. The size of the required piece was selected, buttons were pressed and, within minutes, the part came out into a pan lying beneath the main machine.

We could have as many propellers as we needed – indeed, we

could have our cabin custom-built, too. I wished then that I might have more time to saunter around this fantastic underground city and discover just what powered it, what synthesis of elements produced the super-strong plastic, how the machine worked... I resolved to return as soon as I could, bring with me men who could be trained to work with me on a project that would have as its ultimate end the wresting of all the city's secrets from it, the correlation of information, the analysis of machines and materials.

When that came about, a new age would dawn on Mars! Meanwhile we worked hard, transporting all the things we needed into the domed hall where, apart from anything else, we were close to the water supply.

We also found dehydrated food in airtight containers. This food was tasteless but nourishing.

As the balloon began to take shape our spirits rose higher and higher.

During this time we did not forget to look after our personal appearance. I made a point of shaving regularly – although the only mirror I could find was a great reflector as big as me which I somehow dragged into the domed chamber simply to use as a shaving mirror!

While Jil Deera and Vas Oola worked on the balloon – we had found that the pressure of a warm human hand on the fabric served to weld it together, facilitating the making of the gasbag – Hool Haji and I climbed the wall and began to finish nature's work of breaking open the dome.

In order that the inhabitants of the place might continue to live – if life it was – we had constructed a kind of hatch cover which could be fitted in place of the dome to stop sand drifting down and clogging the fountain.

Soon the helium tanks were fitted to the valve of the gasbag and the four of us watched the great mound of fabric slowly fill out.

We had not yet fitted the driving bands to engine and propeller shaft, but apart from that the balloon was ready. It was in all essential respects a powered airship and, though slower and more vulnerable than the Martian aircraft that I had encountered, would do its job well, I thought.

Soon the gasbag was taut. The balloon began to strain at its mooring ropes and looked as if it could lift a hundred such as us. We began to laugh and slap one another on the back – though it was a bit of a stretch for me to slap Hool Haji's back! We had done it!

The cabin was enclosed, suspended from the strong ropes that covered the outside of the gasbag. It was made of sections of synthetic material and had open portholes. Unfortunately we had found no means of providing transparent panes, so we had to construct shutters instead. Inside it was provisioned with water, spare gas tanks and dehydrated food.

We were very proud of the ship. Crude it may have been, but it was soundly constructed and soon, when we had let her up through the roof a bit and fitted the driving bands to the engine, we should be ready to go wherever we chose. Probably back to Mendishar where, as Hool Haji pointed out, the arrival of their leader, thought dead or chased away from the country, in a flying ship would probably hearten the populace to such an extent that much that had been lost in the attack on the village might be regained by this spectacular return!

Hool Haji and the other two Blue Giants were talking earnestly about this possibility when the opposite door – the one we had blocked against any attempt of the white ghouls to enter – began to melt.

The material which I had regarded as indestructible was bubbling and running like cheap plastic in a fire. A terrible smell – acrid and sweet at the same time – began to come from the door.

I did not know what was happening but I acted nonetheless.

'Quick,' I yelled. 'Into the balloon!'

I pushed at my companions, helping them clamber into the cabin.

Then I turned as the door collapsed completely – and there were several of the white inhabitants of the place.

In their hands was a machine.

Plainly they did not know what it was. All they knew was enough to hold it and point it.

It was an odd paradox – a machine so advanced as that in the hands of those imbeciles.

It was emitting a ray – a ray which struck the opposite wall now, narrowly missing the balloon and me. A heat ray, doubtless. A laser ray!

It was then that I realised no-one had cut the mooring lines.

I sprang towards them, drawing my sword.

I knew, in fact, that the knowledge of portable lasers had belonged to the older race. I should have been prepared for something like this.

In their insensate rage these descendants of the Yaksha had perhaps dredged up some race memory, found the projector and brought it back to deal out death to the interlopers.

Whatever the cause, we should all be dead soon unless I was swift. I sliced the mooring ropes.

Hool Haji yelled at me from the cabin as he saw what I was doing.

The balloon began to rise, gently bumping the roof. Shortly the gas would take them to safety as it sought the air beyond the roof. The aperture created by breaking the dome was just wide enough to take it.

Now the ghouls levelled the laser at me again. I was bound to be killed by it. The ray was sweeping the room, melting or slicing apart everything it touched.

And then the idea came!

Chapter Seven
City of the Spider

AS THE BEAM came closer and closer, weaving somewhat at random in the hand of the moronic ghouls, I suddenly saw the great reflector which I had been using a shaving mirror.

It was a powerful reflector. It might work.

Quickly I rushed towards it and got behind it.

The laser beam sliced away part of the fountain which fell with a splash into the water. The fountain spurted sporadically now.

The beam came closer and melted a whole section of the wall, revealing the next chamber beyond. The white things shuffled closer, their soft, near-boneless arms cradling the powerful projector.

Then the beam struck the reflector.

Laser rays are concentrated light. A mirror reflects light.

This one did.

The mirror bent the ray and spread it for a few moments. Then for a few seconds it turned the whole ray back on those who were directing it.

Most of the white ghouls were shrivelled in a second. The rest yelled in terror, retreated a short way and then came at me yelling!

I dashed for one of the dangling mooring lines just as the balloon began to ascend through the aperture.

I grabbed the last few feet of the line.

As claws scraped at me I began to haul myself up towards the cabin.

Then the balloon was shooting into the air and, in that moment of escaping the danger of the white creatures and finding myself in a new danger, I realised that we had forgotten one vital thing in our haste to escape.

We had forgotten to load our ballast – the balloon was rising too rapidly!

Twice I was nearly shaken from my handhold. I clung desperately to the rope, trying to pull myself towards the cabin.

Then I saw Hool Haji open the hatch of the cabin and, balancing with only a toehold on the outside of the cabin, he stretched out and grabbed the rope from which I was suspended.

The ground was far below, the black, shining desert spinning beneath me.

Hool Haji managed to drag himself back into the cabin, still clutching the rope. Then he and the other two began to haul me in.

My hands were aching and torn by the friction. I was almost ready to let go.

Just as I felt I could hang on no longer I felt their great hands seize me and drag me into the cabin. They closed the hatch.

Panting with exhaustion and relief, I lay on the floor of the cabin until I had recovered my breath. We were still rising far too rapidly and would soon escape the slightly thinner Martian atmosphere – it must be remembered that the atmosphere of that age was much thicker than it is now.

I rose shakily and went to the controls. They were simple, makeshift controls and would have been tested before we took the air if we had had the chance. Now we would have to see if they worked. If they did not, we were done for.

I pulled a lever which controlled the valve of the gasbag. I had to let gas out and hope that it would be just enough and not so much that would send us plummeting earthwards!

Slowly our altitude levelled out and I knew the control was working.

But we were still drifting at random on the air currents. We would have to land and fix the driving bands to the engine. Under power we should be able to return to Mendishar in less than a day.

I was rather annoyed at this waste of our valuable helium, but there was nothing else for it. Very slowly, I began to take the ship down.

We were still some two thousand feet up when it seemed the balloon was suddenly kicked by an enormous foot and buffeted about, sending us all flying. I could not keep my footing and was hurled away from the control panel.

I believe I lost consciousness for some time.

When I came to my senses it was almost dark. There was now no longer the sensation of being the ball in some game played by giants far more huge than my blue companions, but a sense, instead, of speeding along at tremendous velocity.

I rose unsteadily and went to a porthole, sliding back a shutter.

I looked down and at first could not believe what I saw.

We were heading over the sea – a rough, storm-tossed sea. We were travelling at a good hundred miles an hour – probably more.

But what was propelling us?

It was a natural force of some kind. It seemed to be a wind by the moaning and howling sound that reached my ears.

But what kind of wind could have struck so rapidly without warning?

I turned back to find Hool Haji was beginning to stir. He, too, had been knocked out.

I helped him up and together we revived our companions.

'What is it, Hool Haji? Do you know?' I asked.

He rubbed his face with his big hand. 'I should have watched the calendar more carefully,' he said.

'Why?'

'I did not mention this because I felt that we should either be out of the desert or dead – that was before we found the tower and the underground city. I did not mention it while we were underground because I knew we should be safe, there being no sign of damage to the city.'

'What didn't you mention? What?'

'I am sorry – it is my fault. Probably the reason why the city of the Yaksha has not been reported is because of the Roaring Death.'

'What is the Roaring Death?'

'A great wind that periodically crosses the desert. Some think that it was originally the *cause* of the desert, that before the Roaring Death came the desert existed as a fertile place. Perhaps the city of the Yaksha was built before the coming of the Roaring Death. I do not know – but the Roaring Death has crossed the desert for centuries, producing many sandstorms, levelling everything.'

'And where does the wind go?' I asked. 'For we might as well know since we're being borne along by it.'

'Westwards,' said Hool Haji.

'Over the sea?'

'Just so.'

'And where then?'

'I do not know.'

I went to the porthole again and looked down.

The troubled sea, cold and dark, still lay below us, but through the gloom I thought I could make out, very faintly, some sort of land mass.

'What lies beyond the Western sea?' I asked Hool Haji.

'I do not know – a land unexplored, save along its coasts. An evil land by all accounts.'

The land was almost below us now.

'Evil? What makes you say that?' I asked my friend.

'Legends – travellers' tales – exploration parties that never return. The Western continent is a place of jungles and strange beasts. It was the continent worst struck by the struggles of the Mightiest War. When the war was over, so they say, strange changes took place in nature – men, animals, plants were all – altered – by something that was left behind after the Mightiest War. Some say this was a spirit, some say a kind of gas, others a machine. But, whatever the reason, the continent in the West has always been avoided by sane men.'

'All that seems to indicate is an atomic war, radiation and mutation.' I mused. 'And in the thousands of years since the war took place it is unlikely that there is any dangerous radiation. We need not fear from that.'

Some of the words I used were in English since, though there probably were words to describe the things of which I spoke, they were not in the current Martian vocabulary.

The 'Roaring Death' was beginning to abate, it seemed, for our movement became slower.

I felt that our fate was out of my hands as we sped deeper inland.

The two moons of Mars dashed through the sky above us, illuminating the sight of strange, waving jungles of peculiar colourings.

I must admit that the peculiar vegetation did disturb me somewhat, but I told myself that we could come to no harm while we rode the wind at this altitude.

When the wind no longer bore us along we could land at leisure, fix the engines and, under power, go where we wished.

The opportunity did not come for some hours. Where the wind came from and where it finally died I could not tell – unless it circled the globe permanently, gathering force as it travelled. I was no meteorologist.

At last we were able to escape the air-stream and drift towards the huge trees whose dense foliage seemed to form a solid mass below us.

Great, shiny leaves waved on sinuous boughs and the colours were shades of black, brown, dark green and mottled red.

A sense of evil hung heavily on this jungle and we did not like the prospect of having to land in it. But at length, by morning, we found a clearing large enough to take the balloon and we began to descend.

We landed quite neatly for such unskilled aeronauts. We moored the ship and inspected it for damage. The Yaksha building materials had stood up to a wind that would have shaken almost anything else to pieces. There was comparatively little damage, considering the buffeting we had taken.

All we had to do now was spend an hour or so fixing the driving bands and finding something that would serve as ballast. Then we'd top up the helium – and be heading for Mendishar in no time.

We soon had the engines working well and the propellers spinning.

While we worked, however, we began to get a definite sense of being watched. We saw nothing save the dark jungle, its trees rising several hundred feet into the air and all tangled together to form a lattice of twisting boles going up and up on all sides, covered in a tangle of other vegetation – warm and damp-smelling.

How the glade could ever have been formed I do not know. It was a freak of nature. Its floor consisted of nothing but smooth, hard mud almost the consistency of rock. At its edge grew the dark, shiny leaves of the lower shrubs, a tangle of vines that, from the corner of one's eye, tended to look like fat snakes, unhealthy-looking bushes and creepers gathered around the spreading roots of the trees.

I had never seen anything so big in a forest. There seemed to be a variety of levels stretching up and up so that from the outside the forest looked like a gigantic cliff in which were dark openings of caves.

It was easy for one to imagine being watched. I suspected that it was only my imagination at work, for the surroundings were such that they set the subconscious going nineteen to the dozen!

Now all we had to do was find ballast. Jil Deera suggested that logs cut from the branches of trees might do as well as anything. It would be a crude ballast but would probably serve us adequately.

While Jil Deera and Vas Oola aided me in putting the finishing touches to the motor, Hool Haji said he would go and get some logs.

Off he went. We finished our work and waited for him to return. We were impatient to get out of this mysterious jungle and return to Mendishar as soon as possible.

By late afternoon we had shouted ourselves hoarse but Hool Haji had not replied to us.

There was nothing for it but to enter the forest and see if he was hurt – possibly knocked unconscious in some minor accident.

Vas Oola and Jil Deera said they would search with me, but I told them our balloon was all-important – they must stay with it and guard it. I managed to convince them of this.

I found the spot where Hool Haji had entered the forest and began to follow his trail.

It was not difficult. Being a large man, he had left many signs of his passing. In some places he had hacked away some of the undergrowth.

The forest was dark and dank. My feet trod on yielding, rotting plants and sometimes sank to the mire beneath. I continued calling my friend's name, but he still did not reply.

And then I came upon traces of a fight and knew that I had not imagined we were being watched after all!

Here I found Hool Haji's sword. He would never have discarded that unless captured – or killed!

I scouted around for signs of captors but could find none!

This was very perplexing, for I rather prided myself on my tracking ability. All I could notice were signs of some sticky substance, like strands of fine silk, adhering to the surrounding foliage.

Later on I discovered some more of this stuff and decided that, since it was my only clue, I would look for more in the hope that Hool Haji's captors – or murderers – had left it behind them, though why they should and what it was I had no idea.

I hardly realised, as night was falling, that I had come to a city.

The city seemed to be one large building sprawling through the jungle. It appeared to grow out of the jungle, merge with it, be part of it. It was of dark, ancient obsidian and, in crevices, earth and seeds had fallen so that small trees and shrubs grew out of the city. There were ziggurats and domes all appearing to flow together in the half-light. It was easy to believe that this was some strange freak of nature, that rock had simply flowed and solidified into the *appearance* of a city!

Yet here and there were windows, entrances, all obscured by plants.

As night fell the city glowed very, very dimly, catching the few faint moonbeams that were able to penetrate the forest roof so far above.

This must be where my friend's enemies had brought him. It was a daunting place.

Wearily I entered the city, climbing over the heaped, glassy rock, searching for some sign of the inhabitants, some indication as to where my friend was hidden.

I clambered up the sloping sides of buildings, over roofs, down hills, searching, searching. Everywhere were deep shadows and the feel of smooth, lumpy rock beneath my hands and feet.

There were no streets in this city, simply depressions in the roof which covered it. I entered one of these gullies – a deep one – and began to inch along it, feeling desperate.

Something scuttled up the wall to my left and I felt sick as I saw what it was – the largest spider I had ever seen in my life.

Now I saw others. I took a firm grip on Hool Haji's sword and prepared to draw my own as well. The spiders were as big as footballs!

I was just preparing to leave the gully and ascend another sloping wall of green rock when suddenly I felt something drop over my head and shoulders. I tried to strike it away with the sword but it clung to me. The more I moved the more entangled I became. Now I understood why there had been no corpses at the scene of Hool Haji's capture!

The thing that had fallen on me was a net of the same fine, sticky silk I had seen in the forest. It was strong and clung to everything it touched.

Now I had fallen face downwards and was still trying to disentangle myself.

I felt bony hands pick me up.

I looked at those who had trapped me. I could not believe my eyes. To the waist they were men, though considerably shorter than me, with wiry bodies bulging with lumpy muscles. They had large eyes and slit mouths, but were still recognisable as human beings – until you looked beyond their waists and at the eight furry legs that radiated from them. The bodies of men and the legs of spiders!

I now made jabbing movements at the leader – my arms were so restricted it was all I could manage.

The leader was expressionless as he pointed a long pole at me. The end of this pole seemed to be fitted with a needlelike tip some six inches long. He stuck this into me – but only a short way. I tried to fight back and then, almost at once, felt my whole body go rigid.

I could not move a muscle. I could not even blink. I had been injected with a poison, that was plain – a poison that could paralyse completely!

Chapter Eight

The Great Mishassa

LIFTED ON THE backs of the strange, repellent spider-men, I was borne deep into the interior of the weird city.

Lighted by faintly luminous rocks, it was a labyrinth that seemed to have no plan or purpose to it.

We passed through corridors and chambers that sometimes seemed little more than conduits and on other occasions opened out into great, balconied halls.

I became convinced that this was not the work of the spider-men – not the work of men at all, but of some alien intelligence created, perhaps, by the effect of atomic radiation. That intelligence – half mad ever to have conceived this city – had probably perished long since, unless these spider-men were their servants.

Somehow I thought not, because the corridors and halls were full of dirt, cobwebs and the decay of centuries. I paused to wonder just how these spider-men had come into being – whether they were cousins of the huge spiders I had seen outside. If they were related, what unholy union in the distant past had produced such fruit as these?

They scuttled along, bearing me in their strong arms. I did not dare speculate what Fate had in store for me. I was convinced they intended to torture me, perhaps eat me in some ghastly rite – that I was, in fact, to be the fly in their parlour!

My guess was closer than I at first realised.

At length we entered an enormous hall, far bigger than anything else. It was all dark and illuminated only by the dim radiance of the rock itself.

But now I could feel the drug beginning to wear off and I flexed my muscles experimentally – as much as was possible since the sticky web – drawn, I now guessed, from the actual bodies of the spider-men – still restricted my movement.

And then I saw it!

It was a vast web stretching across the hall. It shimmered in the faint light and I could just make out a figure spreadeagled in it. I was certain then that it was Hool Haji.

The spider-men themselves were evidently unaffected by their own sticky webs, for several of them began to haul me up strands of this web towards the other victim who was, I saw, indeed Hool Haji.

And there, hanging in space, they left us, scuttling away into the gloom on their furry legs. They had made not a sound since I had first encountered them.

My mouth was still stiff from the drug but I managed to say a few words. I had been placed below and to one side of Hool Haji and so could see little of him save his left foot and part of his calf.

'Hool Haji – can you speak?'

'Yes. Have you any indication what they intend to do with us, my friend?'

'No.'

'I am sorry I led you into this, Michael Kane.'

'It was not your fault.'

'I should have been more cautious. If I had been we should all have been away by now. Is the aircraft safe?'

'As far as I know.

I began to test the web. The actual net in which I had been caught was becoming brittle and broken until I was at last able to fling out my hand. But my hand was immediately trapped immovably on the main web.

'I tried the same thing,' Hool Haji said from above. 'I can think of no possible means of escape.'

I had to admit he was probably right, but I racked my brains nonetheless. I had begun to get a feeling that something horrible was in store for us unless I could devise a means of escape.

I began to try to work my other arm loose.

Then we heard the noise – a loud, scraping noise like the sound of the spider-men moving, but magnified greatly.

Looking down, we suddenly saw two huge eyes, at least four feet in diameter, looking blinkingly up at us.

They were the eyes of a spider. My heart lurched.

Then a voice sounded – a soft, rustling, ironic voice which could only have issued from the owner of the eyes.

'Sso, an appetissing morssel for today'ss feasst…'

I was even more stunned to hear a voice coming from the creature.

'Who are you?' I demanded in a none too firm voice.

'I am Mishassa – the Great Mishassa, lasst of the folk of Shaassazheen.'

'And those creatures – your minions?'

There came a sound that might have been an unhuman chuckle.

'My sspawn. Produced by experimentss in the laboratoriess of Shaassazheen – the culmination of… But you would know your fate, would you not?'

I shuddered. I fancied that I guessed it already. I did not reply.

'Quake, little one, for you are to be my ssupper ssoon…'

Now I could see the creature more clearly. It was a giant spider – plainly one of many produced by the atomic radiation that had affected this part of the country all those thousands of years before.

Mishassa was slowly beginning to climb the web. I felt the thing sag as his weight went onto it.

I continued my effort to release my other arm and at last managed to free it of the net without trapping it on the web. I remembered the little skinning knife in my harness and decided I must try to reach that if I could.

Inch by inch I moved my hand towards the knife… Inch by inch…

At last my fingers gripped the haft and I eased the knife from its sheath.

The spider-beast was coming closer. I began to hack first at that part of the web holding my other arm.

I worked desperately but the web was tough. Then at last it parted and I was able, moving cautiously, to reach my sword.

I stretched my arm upwards and sliced away as much of the web around Hool Haji as I could reach, then turned again to face the giant spider.

Its voice whispered at me:

'You cannot esscape. Even if you were abssolutely free you would not esscape me – I am sstronger than you, sswifter than you...'

What he said was true – but it did not stop me trying! Soon its horrible legs were only a few inches from me and I prepared to defend myself against it as best I could. Then I heard a yell from Hool Haji and saw his body fly past me and land squarely on the back of the spider-beast. He clung to its hair shouting for me to try to do the same. I was only dimly aware of what he intended to do, but I leapt, too, breaking free of the last of the strands and dropping towards the spider-beast's back to land there and hang tightly with one hand to the weird fur. In my other hand I held my sword.

Hool Haji said, 'Give me your sword – I am stronger than you.'

I passed it to him and drew my knife.

The beast yelled in fury and shouted incomprehensible words at us as we began to hack at its back with our weapons.

It had probably been used to more passive offerings in the shape of its own minions – but we were two fighting men of Vashu and were prepared to sell our lives dearly before allowing ourselves to become a banquet for a big, talkative spider!

It hissed and cursed. It darted about in fury, dropping from web to ground. But still we clung on, still driving our weapons into it, seeking a vital spot.

It reared up and nearly toppled over so that we should have been crushed beneath its great bulk. But perhaps it had the instincts of the originals of the species – many of which, once on their backs, cannot get to their feet again. It recovered its balance just in time and began to scuttle backwards and forwards at random.

Sticky, black blood was spurting from a dozen wounds but none had, it appeared, been effective in slowing it down. Suddenly it began to run in a straight line, a thin, high wailing sound coming from it.

We lay flat as its speed increased, looking our puzzlement at one another.

It must have been moving at a good sixty miles an hour – probably more – as it darted along the tunnels, carrying us deeper and deeper into the city.

Now the wailing increased in volume. The spider creature had gone berserk. Whether it was exhibiting a madness, a heritage of its mad ancestors that it had only now failed to control, or whether our wounds were driving it berserk with pain we were never to know.

Suddenly I saw movement ahead.

It was a pack of the spider-men – whether they were the same who had taken us to the hall of the web I could not guess – looking plainly panic-stricken as we rushed at them.

Then the huge, intelligent spider paused in its mad rush and began to fall on them, biting them to death, taking a head in its jaws and snapping it off at the neck, or biting a torso in two. It was a grisly sight.

We continued to cling as best we could to the furry back of the incensed beast. Occasionally it would shout a recognisable word or phrase but they made no sense to us.

Soon every single spider-man had been destroyed and nothing was left but a heap of dismembered corpses.

My arm was aching and I felt I could not hang on to the fur much longer. Any moment I was going to drop and become prey to the spider-beast. From Hool Haji's grim expression I could see that he, too, was feeling the strain and could not bear it much longer.

And then, quite suddenly, the spider-beast began to sag at the leg joints. The legs were slowly drawn up under its body and it sank down amongst the broken bodies of its servitors.

It had destroyed them, it seemed, in its death throes, for it cried one word: 'Gone!' – and died.

We made sure that the heart had ceased to beat and then virtually fell from the beast's back and stood looking up at it.

'I am glad it died and not us,' I said, 'but it must have realised it was the last survivor of its aberrant species. What actually went on in that crazed, alien brain, I wonder? I feel sorry for it in a way. Its death was somehow noble.'

'You saw more than I did,' Hool Haji broke in. 'All I saw was an enemy that nearly destroyed us. But we have destroyed it – that is good.'

This pragmatic statement from my friend shook me from my somewhat speculative frame of mind – possibly out of place in the circumstances – and made me begin to wonder how we were to find our way out of this maze of a city.

I wondered, also, if all the spider-men had been killed in the death throes of the beast.

We picked our way through the ruin of corpses and followed the tunnel until it turned into a large hall.

We discovered a further tunnel leading off the hall and plodded on, simply hoping that we should eventually find a room with a window or exit – for there had been some visible from the outside.

The tunnels were difficult for Hool Haji to negotiate most of the time – only a few of them were large enough to take the spider-beast, for instance. This led me to conclude that the creature we had destroyed had been, even amongst his own kind, a 'sport'.

Once again something in me awakened sympathy for the misshapen creature that had been so ill-fitted for the world and yet plainly possessed an excellent intelligence. In spite of its having threatened my life, I could not hate it in any way.

It was while I was still in this philosophical mood that we stumbled upon the vats.

The first indication of their existence that we received was the smell. Breathing in the vapour, we felt a slight stiffness in our muscles. Then we entered a hall over which crude gangplanks had been placed, for the floor, which was sunken, was full of a noisome, bubbling fluid.

We paused beside the gangplank, looking down.

'I think I know what this is,' I said to Hool Haji.

'The poison?'

'Exactly – the stuff which they coated on those needle-poles to paralyse us.'

I frowned. 'This could come in useful,' I said.

'In what way?' my friend asked.

'I'm not sure – I have a feeling that it might. It will do no harm to take samples.' I pointed to the far wall.

On a shelf stood several pottery flasks and a heap of poles with six-inch needles at their tips.

Carefully we crossed the vat by means of the gangplank, heading towards the shelf. We breathed in as little as possible for fear that our muscles would become paralysed altogether, causing us to plunge into the vat, and we should either drown or die from an overdose of the stuff.

At last we reached the shelf, feeling stiffer with every moment that passed. I took down two flasks of good, if weird, workmanship, and handed them to Hool Haji, who stooped and filled them. We rammed stoppers into the flasks and attached them to our belts, then we took a number of poles and left the hall of the vat by the nearest exit.

Now the floor of the tunnel rose and this gave us some hope.

I could see light glimmering from somewhere, though I could not see its direct source.

Just as we turned into a small passage and saw daylight coming through an irregular opening to one side of the passage, the light was momentarily blocked out by the sudden eruption into the place of a number of the large spiders I had seen earlier.

I drew my sword, which my blue friend had returned to me, and he used one of the poles to flail about him at the disgusting creatures. They paused only for a short time to attack us and then scuttled past, disappearing into the depths of the city.

What I had at first thought to be a direct attack was, in fact, nothing more than the nocturnal creatures returning to the darkness of the city.

We clambered out of the window and stood once again on what I can only call the 'surface' or roof of the city – a place of unnatural cliffs and canyons all of the same darkly shining, obsidian stuff. It still looked as if it had been moulded whilst malleable rather than constructed in any fashion men would employ to build a city.

Our feet slipping on the smooth surfaces, we stumbled along, now realising we had no real idea where our ship was in relation to us!

I imagine we would have wandered like this for many more hours – perhaps days – if we had not suddenly caught sight of Jil Deera's stocky figure framed against the jungle beyond. We yelled to him and waved.

He turned, his hand on his sword hilt, his stance wary. Then he grinned as he recognised us.

'Where is Vas Oola?' I asked as we walked towards each other.

'He is still with the aircraft, guarding it,' the warrior replied. 'At least –' he looked distastefully around – 'I hope he is.'

'Why are you here?' asked Hool Haji.

'When you both did not return at nightfall I became worried. I thought you had been captured since I heard no sounds such as a wild beast might make, and as soon as it was dawn I set out on your trail – and found this place. Have you seen the creatures that inhabit it? Huge spiders!'

'You will find the remains of even stranger denizens below the surface somewhere,' Hool Haji said laconically.

'I hope you left yourself markers for your way back,' I said to Jil Deera, thinking myself a fool for not having done just that myself.

'I have.' Jil Deera pointed into the jungle. 'It is this way, come.'

Since ill luck had, for the most part, dogged us since we had left the haunt of the Yaksha, we were in some fear for the safety of our craft. We should have been in a far worse predicament, stranded on a land we had absolutely no knowledge of at all, if the balloon had been attacked and wrecked.

But it was quite safe and so was Vas Oola, who seemed very relieved to see us.

We had paused to cut small logs for use as ballast, and these were soon aboard.

Then, once aboard, we released the mooring lines and began to rise gently skywards.

As soon as we were high enough above the great jungle, which seemed to stretch away to every horizon, I started the engine, set our course and soon we were – or we hoped devoutly we were – on our way to Mendishar to see if something could be saved from the wreckage of the ill-fated revolution.

Chapter Nine

Sentenced to Die!

THANKFULLY WE CROSSED the ocean without mishap and arrived, at length, at the borders of Mendishar.

We landed in the hills and hid our craft.

Twice, as we scoured the hills in the hope of discovering some information, we came upon totally destroyed villages.

Once we were lucky. We met an old crone who had, by luck, escaped the destruction. She told us that whole families of hill-people had been arrested; many, many villages razed and hundreds, possibly thousands, slain.

She told us that the leaders of the revolution who had been captured were due to die in a great ritual personally inaugurated by the upstart Bradhi Jewar Baru. She did not know when, only that it had not yet taken place.

We decided we would have to visit the capital – Mendisharling – ourselves in order to see just what the true situation was, judge the mood of the populace and, if possible, rescue those under sentence of death.

With robes salvaged from one of the ruined villages, Hool Haji disguised himself as an itinerant trader and myself as – a bundle!

I, of course, would draw too much attention in whatever disguise I attempted, so I had to become the 'trader's' goods!

It was in this manner, slung over Hool Haji's shoulder, that I entered, for the first time, the capital city of Mendishar. It was a place of little spirit. Peeping through a small rent in the cloth in which I was swathed I could see that, apart from the swaggering, boorish Priosa, there was not a back that was not bent, not a face that was not lined with misery, not a child that was not emaciated.

We passed through the market and there was little of anything nourishing on sale.

The whole city had an air of desolation about it which contrasted sharply with the bright uniforms of the 'chosen' Priosa.

It was a scene familiar to me from my reading, but I had never seen anything like it in real life. It was a place ruled by a tyrant who so feared for his own security that he did not dare relax his iron rule for a single moment.

Whatever happened now, I reflected as I was humped along by my friend – who was not, I felt, going out of his way to make my ride comfortable – the tyrant must fall eventually, for people can be ground down only for so long. At some time the tyrant – or his descendant – relaxes, and it is at that moment his subjects choose to act.

Hool Haji took a room at a tavern near the square and went to it at once. Then he placed me on the hard bed and sat down mopping his brow as I disentangled myself from the cloth.

I grimaced as I sat up.

'I feel as if every bone in my body is dislocated,' I said.

'I apologise.' Hool Haji smiled. 'But it would look suspicious if an impoverished trader like myself should treat his goods as if they were precious things instead of the few skins and rolls of fabric he told the gate guards he had.'

'I suppose you're right,' I agreed, trying to wriggle the circulation back into my legs and arms. 'What now?'

'You wait here while I go about the city and see what information I can glean – and test the temper of the people. If they are ready to rise up against Jewar Baru – as I suspect they might be, given the right push – then perhaps we can decide a means of destroying Jewar Baru's rule.'

He set off almost at once, leaving me to do little more than fiddle with my fingers. The reason I had come with him – apart from the obvious one of being his friend and ally – was that if he was captured I might have a chance of taking the news back to our friends and because, if we needed the airship, I would be able to operate it in the event of this happening.

I waited and waited until, in the late afternoon, I heard a disturbance in the street below.

Cautiously I went to the window and peeped out.

Hool Haji was down there talking heatedly to a couple of insolent-looking Priosa guards.

'I am simply a poor trader,' he was saying. 'Nothing more or less, gentlemen.'

'You answer closely the description we have of the Pretender Hool Haji. He fled, coward that he was, from a village we investigated some weeks ago, leaving his followers to fight for him. We are seeking this weakling since he has managed to convince a few misguided people that his rule will be better for Mendishar than that of the noble Bradhi Jewar Baru.'

'He sounds a wretch,' Hool Haji said dutifully. 'A positive scoundrel. I hope you catch him, noble sirs. Now I must return...'

'We believe that you are this *hwok'kak* Hool Haji,' one guard said, blocking Hool Haji's path and using one of the most insulting terms in the Martian vocabulary. Literally, a hwok'kak is a reptile of particularly filthy habits, but the implications of this are far wider and impossible to describe here.

Hool Haji controlled himself visibly on hearing this, but probably gave himself away – not that there seemed any chance of the guards letting him come back to the tavern.

'You will come with us for questioning,' said the second guard. 'And if you are not Hool Haji you will probably be released – though the Bradhi has no love for rabble such as wandering traders.'

There was nothing for it, I decided, but to act. There was a spare sword in the roll of cloth – it had been trying to stab me all the way through the city. I went to the bed and tugged the sword free, then returned to my position at the window.

Now was the time to try to help my friend, for once the whole city was alerted to stop Hool Haji escaping there would be little chance of us leaving Mendisharling alive.

I balanced myself momentarily on the window sill and then launched myself with a yell at the nearest guard.

The great warrior was astonished to see what was, to him, a tiny man leaping at him with a naked sword.

I landed only a short distance from him and immediately engaged him.

Realising that my decision had been the only sensible one and that secrecy was no longer possible, Hool Haji attacked the second guard.

Soon the street had cleared as if by magic and only the two Priosa and ourselves were left, battling to the death.

I hoped that the downtrodden populace did not have spies among them who would go and bring other Priosa. If we could finish these, we might just make it from the city.

My opponent was still baffled. He never really recovered his wits. Within a few minutes I had stabbed him through the side of his armour and he lay dead on the cobbles of the street.

Hool Haji also finished his opponent quickly. We turned at the sound of running feet and saw a whole detachment of Priosa coming towards us. Mounted on a great grey dahara was a tall, heavily built Mendishar in golden armour.

'*Jewar Baru!*' The name was an oath on Hool Haji's lips.

Plainly these warriors had not been summoned but had heard the sound of our fight from close by.

Hool Haji prepared to stand his ground, but I tugged at his arm.

'Don't be a fool, friend. You will be overwhelmed in an instant! Leave now and we will return soon to deal out justice to the tyrant.'

Reluctantly, Hool Haji followed me as I ducked back into the tavern and barred the door.

Almost at once the guards were battering at the door and we ran upstairs to the third and top storey of the building, and from there through a hatchway onto the roof.

The houses in this quarter of the city were huddled close together and there was no difficulty in leaping from one flat roof to another.

Behind us the guards – but not Jewar Baru, who had doubtless remained in the safety of the street – had reached the roof and were following us, shouting at us to stop.

I do not think they recognised Hool Haji at that stage – although it was well known by then that he had a man like myself as a constant fighting companion – and would probably have exerted themselves even more if they had realised just who my friend was.

The roofs became lower now and at last we were running across the tops of single-storey buildings.

Near the city wall we dropped back into the street. People were startled at our appearance and we were in time to see a couple of half-drunk Priosa come out of a wineshop and stagger towards their daharas.

We were there first, mounting the beasts, as it were, under their noses, wheeled them about and were off, heading for the gate, leaving the shouting guards still confused.

Near the gates we met four Priosa who possessed faster reactions than their friends. Seeing us on what were evidently stolen mounts they tried to block our path.

Our swords swung swiftly and we left two dead behind us and the two others wounded as we rode hell for leather through the gates and down the long road that led away from Mendisharling.

Already riders were pursuing us as we galloped along the trail and then turned sharply towards the hills on our left.

Into the hills we rode, our enemies close behind us, our beasts beginning to flag.

If night had not fallen soon I think we should have had to turn and fight a force that was far too large to give us any hope. But night did fall and we were able to elude our pursuers before the rising of the moons.

In the comparative safety of a cave we had discovered, Hool Haji told me all he had learned in the city.

The people were beginning to murmur almost openly against the tyrant, but were too frightened to do anything about it – and too disorganised for it to be effective if they did.

He thought that the news of the wanton razing of villages and killing of the innocent had filtered through to the city, though the Priosa were making every attempt to discount the rumours.

Nearly two hundred prisoners of all ages and sexes were even now languishing in Jewar Baru's jails – ready for the great 'sacrifice' to be held in the city square.

All of these had received the death sentence for their supposed aiding of Hool Haji and his supporters. Some of them had known nothing of it – and the children, of course, had no part at all. This was Jewar Baru's example. It would be a bloody example. It might enable him to continue to hold the people down for another two or three years at most – but surely no longer.

'But that is not the point,' I said to Hool Haji. 'These people must somehow be saved – *now.*'

'Of course,' he agreed. 'And do you know the name of one of those in Jewar Baru's jail – the man of whom they intend to make a particular example?'

'Who?'

'Morahi Vaja. He was captured in the fighting. There were special orders to take him alive!'

'When is this "sacrifice" to take place?' I asked.

Hool Haji put his head in his hands.

'Tomorrow at midday,' he groaned. 'Oh, Michael Kane, what can we do? How can we stop this happening?'

'There is only one thing we can do,' I said grimly. 'We must make use of the resources we have. The four of us – you, myself, Jil Deera and Vas Oola – must attack Mendisharling!'

'How can four men attack a great city?' he asked incredulously.

'I will tell you how the attack can be made,' I told him, 'but there is only a small chance of it succeeding.'

'Tell me your plan,' he said.

Chapter Ten
A Desperate Scheme

I STOOD AT the controls of the airship and stared through a porthole at the countryside ahead.

The three Blue Giants behind me said nothing. There was nothing to say. Our plan, a simple one, had already been fully discussed.

It was close on midday and we were making rapidly for Mendisharling. The plan depended primarily on the timing. If we failed, then at least our failure would be spectacular and might at least point the way for future revolutionaries.

The towers of the capital were now in sight. The city was decorated as if for a festival. Banners flew from every tower and mast – a gay occasion, a stranger would have thought. We knew better...

In the city square stood two hundred stakes. Tied to the stakes were two hundred prisoners – men, women and children. Standing by them, with sacrificial knives ready in their hands, were two hundred splendidly dressed Priosa.

In the centre of these circles of stakes, on a platform, stood Jewar Baru himself, clad in his golden armour and carrying a golden knife in his hand. Also on the dais was a stake. Tied to it was Morahi Vaja, his face set, his eyes staring out at nothing but his own terrible fate.

Surrounding the square, ordered there by decree of the upstart Bradhi, was the entire populace of Mendisharling, many rows deep.

Jewar Baru stood with arms raised sunwards, a cruel, nervous smile twitching his thin lips. He was waiting in ghoulish anticipation for the sun to reach its zenith.

There was silence in the square save for the puzzled murmurings of the young children, both in the crowd and at the stake, who did not know what was about to happen. Their parents hushed them but did not explain. How could they explain?

Jewar Baru's eyes were still fixed on the sun as he began to speak.

'Oh, Mendishar, there are those among you who followed the Great Dark One and chose to go against the decrees of the Great Light One whose material manifestation is the Life Giver, the sun. Moved by wretched motives of self-importance and evil, they sent for the murderer and coward Hool Haji to lead them in revolution against your chosen Bradhi. Out of the depths of the dark wastelands came the interloper, out of the night, to fight against the Priosa, the Children of the Sky, the Sons of the Great Light One. But the Great Light One sent a sign to Jewar Baru and told him what was intended, and Jewar Baru went to fight against Hool Haji, who fled and will never be seen again in the daytime, for he is a skulker in the night. Thus the coward fled and the Great Light triumphed. His followers are here today. They will be sacrificed to the Great Light not in a spirit of vengeance, but as a gift to He Who Watches – the Great Light – so that Mendishar may be purified and the death of these will wash away *our* guilt.'

The response to this superstitious hypocrisy was not enthusiastic.

Jewar Baru turned towards Morahi Vaja, his golden knife raised over the warrior's heart, ready to cut it from him in the blood ritual.

The atmosphere was tense. Jewar Baru's sacrifice of Morahi Vaja would be the signal for two hundred knives to rip out two hundred innocent hearts!

The sun was only a few moments from its zenith as Jewar Baru began his incantation.

He was halfway through it and in a state of near-trance when the airship arrived, unnoticed until now, over the city. All eyes were on Jewar Baru, or else were covered – though he had decreed that all must see.

This is what we had counted on – why we had timed the arrival so carefully even though it would give us only a few seconds in which to try and save the victims in the square.

We had cut the engines and were drifting over the square, falling lower and lower.

Then our shadow crossed Jewar Baru's dais just as he was about to plunge the knife into Morahi Vaja's body.

He wheeled and looked up. All other eyes followed his gaze.

Jewar Baru's eyes widened in astonishment.

It was then, from within the cabin, that I raised my arm and flung what I was holding at the upstart Bradhi.

As I had planned, the point of the javelin grazed his throat – but it was sufficient.

Jewar Baru, as if struck rigid by the power of some godlike being, became paralysed in the position he had been when looking up at us.

For the moment we were fighting superstition with superstition so that the appearance of our ship over the square would look like the visitation of some angry god.

Early that morning I had manufactured a crude megaphone and I now bellowed through this, my voice distorted and magnified more by the echoes from the surrounding buildings.

'People of Mendishar, your tyrant is struck down – strike down his minions!'

The populace began to murmur and their mood was plainly angry as well as puzzled – though the anger was not directed at us. It had been a move depending on psychology. We guessed that the paralysis of Jewar Baru would make his followers lose heart and give heart to the ordinary people.

Slowly the crowd began to move inward towards the centre of the square while the Priosa, who began to look round in a panicky way, were drawing their swords.

I brought the airship closer to the dais, giving Hool Haji a chance to leap from ship to platform and stand beside his frozen enemy.

'*Hool Haji!*' gasped Morahi Vaja from where he was tied to the stake.

'Hool Haji!' This came from several Priosa who had recognised the exiled prince.

'Hool Haji!' This from those folk of Mendisharling who had heard the name spoken by the Priosa.

'Yes – Hool Haji!' cried my friend, raising his sword high. 'Jewar Baru would have it that I am a coward who deserts his people. But see – I enter his city all but single-handed to save my friends and tell you to depose him now! Strike down the Priosa who have persecuted you for so long. Now is your chance to avenge yourselves!'

For a moment there was virtual silence. Then began a murmur which grew gradually louder and louder until it became a roar.

Then the entire populace of Mendisharling were moving in on the terrified Priosa.

Many folk died beneath the swinging swords of the soldiers before the Priosa finally went down beneath the sheer weight of numbers. But fewer – far fewer – died than would have died in the sacrifice, or later in Jewar Baru's jails.

We watched as the tide of humanity engulfed the Priosa in what appeared to be a single fluid action. When it was over – in the short space of a few minutes – not one Priosa who had been prepared to sacrifice a victim that day was left alive. Indeed, few of the corpses were whole. They had literally been torn to pieces. A fitting, if bloody, end.

I had missed joining in the action, but our plan had been based entirely on judging the mood of the people, the psychological effect our appearance would have, and the result of my poison-tipped spear – smeared with the paralysing stuff we had found in the vats of the City of the Spider – on Jewar Baru. If our plan had failed we should have been destroyed in as short a time as were our enemies.

I was trembling both with reaction and relief as I swung down a rope ladder to stand beside my friends on the dais. We cut Morahi Vaja free. Down in the square, all around us, the other reprieved victims were being released.

A great cheer now rose up for Hool Haji.

It lasted for many, many minutes. Meanwhile Jil Deera and Vas Oola swung from the ship and moored her to the stake.

I stepped forward and cried to the people of Mendishar: 'Salute your Bradhi – Hool Haji! Do you accept him?'

'*We do!*' came back the voice of the crowd.

Hool Haji raised his hand, moved by this response.

'Thank you. I have saved you from the rule of the tyrant and helped you overcome him and his followers – though the true saviour is Michael Kane. But now you must seek out the rest of the Priosa and capture them, for they must all pay the penalty for their deeds over the past years. Go now – arm yourselves with the weapons of your persecutors and scour the streets for those who still live!'

The men began to stoop and pick up the swords of the fallen Priosa. Then they were rushing through the streets and soon the sounds of conflict echoed again in Mendisharling. As the effect of the poison was beginning to wear off, we bound Jewar Baru securely.

He was mumbling now and foam flicked his lips. He was plainly quite mad – had been mad for some time, but this sudden defeat had tipped the balance completely.

'What do you intend to do with him?' I asked Hool Haji.

'Try and kill him,' said my friend simply.

Now I had a feeling of anticlimax. It was over – our object had been achieved rapidly. Again a sense of aimlessness overcame me.

We established ourselves in Jewar Baru's palace – the building which had housed generations of Hool Haji's ancestors before the populace had misguidedly followed the upstart to their own downfall.

Morahi Vaja took charge of the parties seeking out the Priosa who had escaped the initial coup. He left, but returned shortly to tell us that a great many of the Priosa were still out on patrol or else had fled the city. It would take time to locate them all – and many might well escape.

This gave me an idea. Although doubtless the Priosa who

remained uncaught offered no real threat to Hool Haji, they should not be allowed to go unpunished. Their crimes were manifold – the sadistic killing of the innocent looming large among them.

This would be something in which I could help, I decided.

'I will be your scout,' I said. 'If I take the airship I will be able to travel much faster than the Priosa and work out their exact positions, and so on. Then I can return and tell you roughly where to find those who have escaped.'

'A good plan,' Hool Haji nodded. 'I would come with you, but there are too many things still to be done here. Start in the morning – you need a little rest.'

I saw the sense of this. A bedroom was placed at my disposal and I was soon asleep.

Next morning I climbed into my ship, waved to Hool Haji and told him that I would probably be away a few days. The great body of the Priosa, I was told, had fled south, so that would be the best direction in which to go.

The near-silent engine began to pulse, the propellers began to turn, and soon I had left Mendisharling and Hool Haji behind.

I did not realise then what Fate – which has, I feel, taken an inordinate interest in my affairs – had in store for me.

Chapter Eleven
The Flying Monster

TWO DAYS LATER I was very far south indeed. I had seen several small bands of Priosa and noted their positions and the general direction which they were heading.

I had gone past the borders of Mendishar and saw in the distance a range of tall, black mountain peaks that seemed familiar.

Having, I felt, located all the Priosa I was likely to find, I decided to investigate the mountains and see if these were indeed what I suspected.

The mountains were what I had thought. The Mountains of Argzoon where earlier – or was it yet to happen? – I had fought against the minions of that wicked renegade Horguhl, and the beast which she had somehow hypnotically controlled.

I felt emotion stir in me – a sense almost of nostalgia – as I flew over those bleak mountains. I felt no love for the mountains themselves, of course, but they reminded me of my earlier adventures on Vashu and, more particularly, of the short period of happiness I had enjoyed with that beautiful girl Shizala. It was difficult to convince myself that she was as yet unborn.

I wondered if it would be worth flying down, but reasoned that the Argzoon had not yet been defeated and were likely to make short work of me. Then I would die for nothing.

I was just turning the ship when I saw the thing suddenly appear from a dark gorge and come flapping up towards me.

It was a monster of such astounding proportions that at first I believed it must be some weird kind of flying machine. Nothing could lift that bulk off the ground, let alone fly so swiftly, but a man-made device, I thought.

But it was not man-made.

It had the appearance of a two-headed heela – the small, savage beast that inhabited the forest further south – with great fangs and blazing eyes. From its shoulders sprouted vast, leathery wings. It was evidently a cousin of the heela in appearance and temperament. The heela was dangerous enough, but this creature was many times its size. It was flying towards me, great taloned paws outstretched as if to seize me, both mouths of both heads gaping wide.

I rammed over the speed lever to 'full' and pulled another lever to let the ballast out of its cradles slung beneath the main cabin.

Climbing rapidly, I managed to put some extra distance between the beast and myself. But now the creature was gaining height and speed also.

I had not had time to turn the ship and was still heading almost due South. I wished for some weapon other than the poison-tipped lances still in the cabin and my sword. A machine gun loaded with dum-dum bullets might have had some slight effect on the beast. Better still, a large, rapid-fire artillery piece or a bazooka, or a flame-thrower, or one of those laser-projectors...

I had nothing of the sort. I was beginning to feel that I did not even have speed on my side as the monster clung to its trail and began slowly to shorten the distance between us.

The airship was not the most manoeuvrable of craft, but the aerobatics I managed to perform would have astounded anyone who knew anything about the possibilities of manipulating a balloon-type vessel!

Below me – far, far below – I saw the heela forest that I had ventured through once with Darnad, Shizala's brother.

Then I was past that and still travelling due South.

I strained every ounce of energy from the motor so that I feared the propellers must shake themselves loose sooner or later.

Nearer and nearer flapped the monster. It was larger – including its vast wings – than my ship and I knew that a couple of rips from its claws alone could destroy the gasbag and send me dropping like a stone to the ground far below.

It refused to give up. Surely, I thought, any ordinary animal would have tired by now. But no. Doggedly it pursued me, sensing perhaps that victory and a meal were in sight – though I could only feel he would be disappointed in the meal.

I circled higher. Soon, unless I was careful, I would be in an atmosphere too thin to breathe. Then I would no longer need to worry about the flying heela – or indeed about anything. I would be dead.

I wondered if, for all its ferocity, this creature were as cowardly as its smaller, land-bound cousins of the forests. If it were, there might be a way to scare it.

I racked my brains but could think of nothing. What *did* scare a two-headed flying mammal of several tons in sheer weight? The humorous answer presented itself – *another*, larger, two headed flying mammal! I had no such ally, however.

Now the heela – or whatever it was called – was much closer so that I could make out its features clearly.

By reflex more than by anything else, I reached for one of the poison-tipped lances and flung it through the porthole at the thing.

I think it must have entered one of its throats, for the mouth closed, chewed – and there was no longer a spear. Now it was almost upon me and I decided that I might as well die fighting, however futilely.

I flung another spear, this time missing altogether. What happened next was astonishing. The beast reached out and snapped the falling spear in its mouth. Again it chewed, again it swallowed.

I felt chagrin then. It was not only unaffected by my puny weapons – it was enjoying them as a meal!

The spears served to slow it a little, at any rate, as it paused to snap them up! I flung the rest, trying for one of its eyes, but failed miserably.

The last thing I remembered was the beast finally catching up with the ship! A huge black shadow seemed to engulf me. I remember a ripping noise and realising that I was doomed along with my ship – either to being eaten, gasbag, cabin and all, in mid-air by a predator that seemed literally omnivorous, or to fall thousands of feet and be smashed to small fragments on the ground.

The cabin swung crazily and I fell back, hit my head on the side of the control panel and, as dizziness overcame me, I remember thinking that at least I would not be aware of my own dying.

Chapter Twelve
New Friends

I FELT THAT every bone in my body was broken. As it happened – though every bone should have been – not one was! I was badly bruised and cut – that was all.

But where was I?

Alive? Just about. How? I could not guess.

I began to disentangle myself from the contents of the cabin. As far as I could tell it was not badly damaged – that building material of the Yaksha must be incredible stuff.

I got the hatch – which was above me now – open and crawled out into the comparative darkness of the Martian night, lit as it was by the twin moons.

The gasbag bobbed on the ground, half empty. Had I dropped so rapidly that, once having released much of the contents of the gasbag, the heela had been unable to follow me?

I did not know, but my tentative answer as to how I was saved was not very convincing.

I went back into the cabin, repressing a groan of pain from my bruising, and got a patch and a tin of the sticky substance we had found in the Yaksha city. Helium was still escaping from the bag but only slowly, since it had folded in on itself, forming a kind of pocket from which the gas was seeping less quickly than it would normally have done.

Hastily I patched the balloon and reflected thankfully that there were still enough spare tanks of helium to fill it.

Just as I was finishing my work I saw something to my right. It was a large object.

I approached it cautiously – and discovered the monster! How had it died? I stepped forward to see if I could tell and then realised that it was still breathing!

Breathing with difficulty, to be sure, but breathing nonetheless!

I guessed that it had swallowed too much of the paralysing poison even for its incredible digestive system to absorb. In the act of attacking me it had been seized by paralysis and had veered away, flopping earthwards to land here. My damaged balloon must have followed it down and landed near it shortly afterwards.

I thanked providence for giving the heela its weird appetite. Then I ran back to the ship for my sword, which must have fallen from my belt as I hurtled downwards.

While the beast slept – and feeling something of a coward, though the creature needed to be slain lest it attack any other traveller – I pierced its faceted eyes, hoping that I had reached the brain. It threshed about, flinging me off twice, but I persevered until finally it was dead.

Then I returned to the airship and attached containers of helium to the valve of the bag.

I soon felt little worse, except for my bruises.

I decided to sleep in the cabin, having moored the ship to the ground, and try to get my bearings in the morning.

Still rather dazed and wearied from the previous day's experience, I took the air next morning without quite knowing what I planned.

Below me now I saw a broad river winding. I did not recognise the countryside at all, but decided to follow the river in the hope that I would spy some settlement on it where I could ask just where I was.

I followed this river, as it happened, for four days without sighting a single settlement.

When I eventually did see something it was not a settlement – but a fleet!

There were some dozen or so finely made sailing galleys of graceful beauty beating up the river. Flying lower, I saw that the ships were crewed by men like myself, only darker skinned.

I began to drop down towards the leading galley which, judging by the size and decoration of its single, lateen-rigged sail, was the flagship.

I caused some consternation before I found my megaphone and shouted down:

'I mean you no harm. Who are you?'

In the common language of Mars, though in an accent that was only barely familiar, one of the men shouted up:

'We are men of Mishim Tep bound for the Jewelled City! Who are you?'

Mishim Tep! That was Karnala's oldest ally – and Karnala was the land from which my Shizala came. I felt I was among friends!

I replied that I was a traveller from the North – a tribeless man who would welcome company if I were allowed to board the ship.

Their curiosity now seemed to be aroused and they also believed me when I said I offered no danger. So they allowed me to tether the balloon to their mast and descend my rope ladder to the deck – a difficult operation which, I pride myself, I accomplished with some dexterity.

The young captain, a pleasant warrior called Vorum Saz Hazhi, told me that he had been away for many months on an expedition to the coast, where a small ally of Mishim Tep's had been plagued by raiders. They had destroyed the raiders and were now on their way home to Mih-Sa-Voh, the Jewelled City, capital of Mishim Tep.

Rather than complicate matters, there and then I told him that I was a scientist, inventor of the airship we now had in tow, looking for commissions in the South. I said that I had journeyed from the Western continent – which was, strictly speaking, true.

'If you could invent *that*,' Vorum Saz Hazhi said enthusiastically, 'then you will be more than welcome at the Court of our Bradhi and you need not fear going hungry. He will give you all the commissions you need.'

I was pleased to hear that and made up my mind on the spot to set myself up as what I had said I was – a freelance scientist!

I was not too worried about the Priosa I had failed to report. The mission had only been to occupy my time really, and the Priosa would probably be tracked down soon enough. I would, of course, return to Mendishar soon to ensure Hool Haji that I was safe. But, in the meanwhile, I could not resist the prospect of dwelling for a short while with people of my own size and general appearance – people, moreover, who had strong affinities of custom and tradition with my adopted nation, the Karnala.

Some days later the towers of the Jewelled City came in sight.

It was the most magnificent place I have seen in my life. Every tower and roof was decorated with precious or semi-precious gems so that from a distance the city looked like one vast blaze of scintillating colour.

Its harbour was made of white marble in which crystals sparkled, reflected in the dancing water of the river. A bright sun shone from a clear blue sky, the scents of shrubs and herbs were sweet, the sight and sound of happy, intelligent and well-cared-for people was a joy to my senses.

Many folk had come to welcome the arrival of the ships after their long expedition. The people were dressed in bright cloaks which matched the brave display of banners from our masts. Many gasped to see the airship in tow.

The delicate music of the Southern Martians began to sound in the air, welcoming the return of the fleet. The sun was warm, the scene peaceful. It was the first time since I had arrived on Mars again that I had felt close to happiness.

Although Hool Haji and the Mendishar had been cultured and noble people, their civilisation had had a touch of savagery about it, a faint echo of their links with their cousins the Argzoon, which the societies of the South did not possess. More than this, the Mendishar, like the Argzoon, were physically so strange to me that the feeling of being among men of my own breed again was good.

We set foot on the quay and Vorum Saz Hazhi's relatives came forward to greet him. He introduced me and they said I was welcome to be their guest until I could find a place of my own.

Vorum Saz Hazhi said that on the morrow he would seek an audience with the Bradhi.

Looking around the dock I saw that there were many warriors – more than I had noticed at first. Also there seemed to be hasty preparations in progress. Vorum Saz Hazhi noticed this too and was as puzzled as I was. He asked his parents about it.

They frowned and said first we must return home, then they would tell him the bad news.

It was not until evening, when we sat at table, that Vorum Saz Hazhi's parents began to tell him that Mishim Tep was preparing for war.

'It is a black day and I cannot understand how it should have happened,' my new friend's father said. 'But…'

Just then a man and a woman entered. They were about the same age as Vorum Saz Hazhi's parents. They wanted to learn all about the balloon, hear about my adventures and so on.

Thus the talk went away from politics as I politely told of my experiences in the North and on the Western continent. By the time the guests had left I was very much ready for bed and wasted no time using the room which the young warrior's parents had prepared for me.

In the morning Vorum Saz Hazhi went to the palace, where he was to be congratulated by the Bradhi for his victories, and I went to the harbour. We had arranged that he should speak to the Bradhi on my behalf while I was getting the balloon. Already the news would have reached the Bradhi, of course, but he would plainly want to see my ship for himself. I was to steer it to the palace and moor it there.

While making my way slowly to the harbour, dawdling a little – for I had plenty of time to spare – to look in shops and chat with those citizens of Mih-Sa-Voh who recognised me as the pilot of what was, to them, a marvellous flying machine, I saw a small procession pass me.

It consisted of tired-looking warriors mounted on dahara. They had evidently just come back, also, from an expedition, for they were dusty and bore minor wounds.

They had a prisoner – a wild-looking man with a long, thick beard and very blond, long matted hair. He, too, bore many recent scars and had his hands tied behind him as he sat his dahara.

In spite of his savage appearance, he bore himself well.

Although I dismissed the idea as a trick of the mind, I was sure there was something about him very familiar to me. Since that seemed impossible, I refused to waste my energy trying to puzzle out why I should feel this, but I asked a passer-by if he knew who the prisoner was.

The man shook his head. 'Doubtless one of our enemies – though that is not their normal appearance.'

I continued on to the harbour and found my balloon still waiting for me, now moored to one of several iron rings in the quayside.

I climbed into the cabin and started the engine – that marvellous little unit which seemed to require no fuel.

Then I steered just above the rooftops of the sparkling City of Jewels towards the palace, a large building that was more magnificent than any of the rest. It seemed literally built of precious gems!

I had learned that many kinds of jewels were mined in Mishim Tep and, though they were useful trading commodities, no special value was placed on them by the populace.

I reached the palace steps and dropped down a little to where guards ran forward at my shouted instructions to take my mooring lines, and make them fast.

Vorum Saz Hazhi now appeared at the top of the steps and greeted me as I mounted the steps.

'I have told the Bradhi of your offer,' he said, 'and he would interview you now. He thinks that you have come at an opportune moment – ships like this could be useful in fighting our enemies.'

As I joined him I noticed that he looked worried.

'What troubles you?' I asked.

He took my arm as he led me into the palace. 'I do not know,' he said. 'Perhaps it is the cares of this terrible war we are about to mount, but the Bradhi does not seem himself. There is something strange going on and I cannot think what it can be.'

That was all he had a chance to say for then the huge jewelled doors of the throne room were opened and I saw a vast hall, lined with great, colourful banners and with tiers of galleries stretching up to the roof, high above, and the walls flanked with nobles, men and women, all looking towards me in polite curiosity.

On the throne dais at the far end were three figures. The Bradhi was in the middle, a careworn man with grey-streaked hair and a massive, impressive head that seemed carved from rock.

On his left, his hands still bound, stood the wild man I had seen earlier.

But it was the person who sat on a stool beside the Bradhi whom I recognised – and recognised with loathing. Yet, at the same time, that person's presence aroused in me a feeling of jubilation.

It was Horguhl, that evil woman who had, both directly and indirectly, been the cause of most of my troubles on my first trip to Mars.

Horguhl!

This could only mean that my calculations about time had been right, even if I had slipped up slightly on those about space.

If Horguhl was here then, somewhere, so was Shizala!

Both Horguhl and the wild man turned to look at me. And they both spoke at once, saying the same two words:

'Michael Kane!'

Why had they both recognised me?

Chapter Thirteen
Horguhl's Treachery

I ADVANCED NO further, aware that I was in danger.

And then, suddenly, I recognised the wild man's voice and knew why he had seemed so familiar to me. It was Darnad – Shizala's brother with whom I had parted what seemed years before in the Caverns of Argzoon.

If he was a prisoner then it was my duty to free him, for he was a close friend.

I drew my sword and instead of turning and running from the hall ran towards Darnad before the astonished courtiers could act.

Horguhl was screaming and pointing to me. 'That is the one – that is he! He is the sole cause of this war!'

How I, in my absence in another time and space, could have caused a war, I did not pause to work out. I cut Darnad's bonds and then wheeled as a courtier came at me with his sword.

Using a trick taught me as a boy by my old fencing master, Monsieur Clarchet, I hooked the tip of my sword in the basket hilt of his, flipped the weapon out of his hand and sent it spinning towards me. Then I flung it to Darnad – and we were both armed. The trick would not have worked on anyone but a man taken off his guard – but it had worked and that was the important thing.

The whole throne room was in confusion. I was sure that there was some awful mistake and that Horguhl was responsible for it, and I did not want to kill any of the folk who had treated me so hospitably.

Darnad and I fought a defensive action from our corner of the throne dais and the courtiers were cautious about attacking us too hard in case their Bradhi should be wounded.

This gave me an idea for a bluff which would prevent any blood being spilt – including ours.

I leapt behind the Bradhi and seized the man by his harness. Then I raised my sword above his head.

'Harm us – and you slay your Bradhi,' I said in a loud, clear voice.

They paused and lowered their weapons.

'Do not listen to him,' Horguhl screamed at them. 'He lies, he will not kill your Bradhi!'

I spoke as sternly as I could – though Horguhl, knowing me better than they did, was perfectly right in what she had said – and addressed the courtiers.

'I am a desperate man,' I said. 'I do not know why you should hold the son of the ruler of your oldest ally a prisoner or why you should allow this evil woman to occupy the throne dais of your Bradhi. But, since you do, I must protect myself and my friend. Do you not recognise him as Darnad of the Karnala, Bradhinak and Pukan-Nara?'

'We do!' one courtier shouted. 'And that is why we hold him! We are at war with the Karnala!'

'At war?' I could hardly believe my ears. 'At war with your friends since the ancient days? Why?'

'I will tell you why,' screamed Horguhl. 'And you should know, since you were partly the cause of all this. Your wanton Bradhinaka Shizala had the Bradhi's son, Telem Fas Ogdai, damned and murdered so that she might marry – *you*!'

I was astounded at the enormity of the lie. It was Horguhl who had been responsible for Telem Fas Ogdai turning traitor and eventually being killed in fair fight.

'Surely it is common knowledge that Telem Fas Ogdai betrayed the Karnala?' I said, turning to the courtiers. But they groaned and muttered, unconvinced by what I had said.

Their spokesman said: 'She has told us the whole despicable plot that you and Shizala of the Karnala devised between you. The honour of Mishim Tep has been affronted, her favourite son destroyed, the Bradhi attacked and humiliated – these are things only blood can wipe out!'

'You speak nonsense!' I said. 'I know the truth – Horguhl has hypnotised you as she has hypnotised so many before. You believe a story that would not stand up to analysis for a moment if your minds had not been dulled by her power.'

The Bradhi struggled in my grasp. 'If it had not been for her we should never have known the truth,' he said. He spoke mechanically and I was sure that he was totally in Horguhl's power.

'Your Bradhi has been mesmerised by her!' I said desperately.

'You lie!' Horguhl screamed. 'I am only a simple woman who was deceived by Michael Kane just as he tries to deceive you. Kill him! Kill him!'

'How can one woman have convinced a whole nation of an enormous lie?' I shouted, turning to her. 'What have you done, you evil creature? You have set two great nations at each other's throats. Have *you* no sense of shame for what you do?'

Although she continued to act her part, I saw a glimmer of irony in her eyes as she replied. 'Have you no sense of shame? You interloper who trampled on all the great customs and traditions of the Southern nations in order to have the woman you loved.'

I could see that convincing them was impossible.

'Very well,' I said. 'If I am the villain you say I am, then you know that I will carry out my threat and slay the Bradhi if you try to attack me.' I began to move forward and she stepped reluctantly backward to let me pass.

Darnad covered my back as we went through the hall towards the doors and thence through the entrance chamber to the palace steps and my airship.

I forced the Bradhi to climb the ladder and Darnad followed me. Once inside the cabin I turned to the old man.

'You must believe us when we deny what Horguhl has said,' I told him urgently.

'Horguhl always speaks the truth,' he said in a flat voice, his eyes glassy.

'Do you not realise that she has hypnotised you?' I asked him. 'The Karnala and the men of Mishim Tep have been friends for so long that a war between them could destroy everything that Southern culture stands for!'

'She would not lie.'

'But she *does* lie!' Darnad spoke now for the first time. 'I do not understand everything of which you speak, but I do understand that neither my sister nor Michael Kane would ever do the things of which you accuse them.'

'Horguhl is good. She tells the truth.'

I shook my head sadly. Then I led him towards the hatch and showed him the ladder.

'You may go, you poor deluded thing,' I said. 'Is this that I see – the shadow of a once-great Bradhi?'

Something seemed to spark in his eyes for a moment and I could see the kind of man he really was when not in Horguhl's hypnotic power. Grief for his son's treachery and death must have sapped his powers for a time – and in that time Horguhl had managed to reach him and work on his mind until his will was submerged.

I had underestimated her. I had thought her defeated in the Caverns of Argzoon but instead she had immediately hit upon a scheme to gain her ends and revenge herself on all her enemies – and one of those enemies, though they did not realise it, was Mishim Tep!

We waited until the Bradhi had reached the ground and then, as the courtiers and guards surged forward, drew in our ladder, sliced our mooring lines and rose into the sky above the Jewelled City.

Now that I knew the truth – that I was really in the same time-period that I had been drawn away from earlier – I was determined to return to Varnal, City of the Green Mists, and see my Shizala. Also we had to discover what the Bradhi Carnak – Shizala's and Darnad's father – knew of this business and what he was preparing to do.

The great battle which had taken place at Varnal between the Karnala and the Argzoon had badly depleted the Karnala force and wearied them. I did not think they could stand a chance of winning a war with the stronger Mishim Tep.

Neither, I thought, would their hearts be in it, for while those of Mishim Tep were convinced that Horguhl spoke truth, the Karnala knew otherwise and must feel more than sympathy for the delusions of their friends.

It would take us some time, even at full speed, to reach Varnal, but at least Darnad would be able to guide me.

As we sped towards the City of the Green Mists, Darnad told me what had befallen him since we had parted at the Caverns of Argzoon.

You will remember that Darnad and I had decided that one of us should return to the South to get help to rescue Shizala, who was Horguhl's prisoner in the Caves of Argzoon, if I was unsuccessful in my attempt.

He had left, riding as swiftly as he could over the hundreds of miles we had crossed. But his mount had gone lame shortly afterwards and he had found himself without a dahara in the heela-infested forests.

Somehow he had fought off those heela which had attacked him – though his beast had not been so lucky – but had lost his bearings a little and had stumbled on to a village of primitives who had captured him with the intention of eating him.

He managed to escape by burrowing out of the hut in which he was imprisoned but, weaponless and half starved, he had wandered for some time before meeting up with a band of nomadic herdsmen who had helped him.

Many more adventures followed and at length he was enslaved by brigands, who sold him to the representative of a Bradhi of a small nation that had somehow managed to survive in the South, though it was far behind most of the Southern nations in terms of civilisation.

He had seized his first opportunity to escape from the working party and had headed for Mishim Tep, it being the nearest friendly nation – or so he thought.

Reaching Mishim Tep and telling the villagers of a small settlement near the border who he was, he was driven off as an enemy! He could not believe what had happened and had decided that a mistake had been perpetrated.

He had found himself hunted by those he regarded as his nation's greatest allies. For weeks he had eluded the guards who sought him, but had eventually been cornered. He had fought well but had finally been captured.

The guards had taken him to Mih-Sa-Voh, where I had first seen him.

It was a story to match my own – which I told him at his request.

Soon we were flying over the vast plain which I recognised at once, from the weird, crimson ferns which covered it, undulating slowly in the breeze like an endless ocean – the Crimson Plain.

I welcomed the sight for it meant we were fairly close to the Calling Hills in which lay Varnal, City of the Green Mist, home of the Bradhis of Karnala – and Shizala, my betrothed.

The Calling Hills were reached next morning and it was no time before we had reached the valley where lay Varnal.

My heart leapt in joy as I saw again the tall white buildings of Varnal. Here and there some of the buildings were of the strange blue marble which is mined in the hills. Traceries of gold veined the marble, causing the buildings to glitter in the sun. Pennants flew from the towers. It was a simpler city than Mih-Sa-Voh, the Jewelled City, and not so large, yet to me it was infinitely more beautiful – and an infinitely more welcome sight!

We dropped down into the city square and guards came forward at once, very alert, preparing to treat us as enemies.

The Bradhi Carnak hurried down the steps of his palace, Shizala following him.

Shizala!

She looked up and saw me. Our eyes met and locked. We stood there with tears of joy coming to our eyes, then I was leaping from the cabin and hurrying forward to take her in my arms.

'What happened?' she asked. 'Oh, Michael Kane, what happened? I did not know what to think when you disappeared the night before the betrothal ceremony. I knew you would not leave me of your own volition. What happened?'

'I will tell you soon,' I promised. 'But first there are other things to discuss.' I turned to the Bradhi. 'Did you know that Mishim Tep plans to march against Varnal?'

He nodded grimly, sorrowfully. 'The declaration arrived by herald yesterday,' he said. 'I cannot understand how Bolig Fas Ogdai came to believe these perversions of the truth. He accuses me and mine – and you, Michael Kane – of the most heinous deeds known to our society. We were friends for many years, our fathers and forefathers were friends. How could this be?'

'I will explain that, too,' I said. 'And now, let us try to forget these problems – we are united once more.'

'Yes,' he agreed, trying to smile, 'this *is* a day of joy – to see you both return together is more than I dared hope for. Come, come – we shall have a meal and will talk and learn everything.'

Hand in hand, Shizala and I followed her father and brother into the palace.

Soon the meal was prepared and I began to talk, telling them of my return to Earth, my journey back to Mars and my adventures in the North. Darnad then told of his adventures and we discussed what had been happening in Varnal since we had left.

In spite of the black cloud of imminent war that was forever present, we could not disguise our joy at being reunited and the talk went on long into the night. The next day would bring two things – the ceremony of betrothal between Shizala and myself, necessary before a marriage could take place, and plans of war…

Chapter Fourteen
An Unwelcome Decision

'SO HORGUHL HAS deceived Bolig Fas Ogdai as she deceived his son,' said Carnak next morning.

'She has him totally in her power,' Darnad said.

We were eating breakfast together – a rare custom on Mars, but there was little time to waste.

'There must be some way of convincing the Bradhi that she is lying,' Shizala said.

'You have not seen him,' I told her. 'We tried to convince him, but he was hardly aware of what we said – he was like a man in a dream. This war is her doing – not Bolig Fas Ogdai's.'

'The question remains,' said Darnad, 'how can we avert this war? I have no wish to shed the blood of my friends and no wish to see Varnal destroyed, for they would undoubtedly win.'

'There is only one way I can think of.' I spoke softly. 'It is an unwelcome solution – but there seems nothing else for it. If all else fails, someone must kill her. With the death of Horguhl will come the death of her power over the Bradhi and his subjects.'

'Kill a woman!' Darnad was shocked.

'I like the thought no more than do you,' I said.

'You are right, Michael Kane.' Carnak nodded. 'It must be our only chance. But who would take on such a repugnant task?'

'Since I reached the decision, then the onus must be on me,' I murmured.

'Let us discuss this later,' said Bradhi Carnak hastily. 'Now it is almost time for the betrothal ceremony in the throne room. You and Shizala must prepare yourselves.'

I returned to my chamber and Shizala to hers. There I found arranged a variety of accoutrements and clothing. In a short while Darnad arrived to show me how I must wear all this.

There was a harness made of finely beaten links of gold and silver, studded with gems, and a sword that also shone with jewels, with a matching dagger.

There was a thick cloak of dark blue lined with rich scarlet. The cloak was decorated with delicate embroidery in yellow and green thread depicting, symbolically, scenes from the history of the Karnala.

There was also a pair of sandals of soft, shiny black leather that laced up to just below the knee.

Soon I was dressed in all this and Darnad stepped back admiring me.

'You make a fine sight,' he said. 'I am proud to have you as a brother.'

There was no such term as 'brother-in-law' in the Martian vocabulary. When one married into a family one automatically became of the same status as a blood relative. I would become Carnak's son and Darnad's brother – their brothers and cousins would become mine. It seemed strange that, by this logic, Shizala would not only become my wife but also my sister and my niece! But that was the custom of Mars and I would accept it.

Darnad led me to the throne room where a few chosen courtiers awaited us. The throne room was not unlike that at the Jewelled City, though simpler and less pretentious. On the dais stood the Bradhi Carnak in splendid robes of black fur, a circlet on his head.

Like most of the important customs of Southern Mars, the ceremony was short and yet impressive.

Carnak announced that we were to be married and we affirmed that it was our wish and the wish of no-one else that this should be. He then asked if there was any objection to this marriage. There was none.

Carnak concluded: 'Then let it be that my daughter Shizala, the Bradhinaka, and my son, Michael Kane of Negalu, be wed when it should please them after the period of ten days from this.'

And so I became engaged to that wonderful girl.

*

There was nothing for it but to prepare for the worst. On a balcony in a tower of the palace we looked down at the square beneath as our pitifully depleted army began to assemble.

I had divested myself of the ceremonial robes and was now clad in a simple warrior's harness, with a workmanlike sword and one of the somewhat inaccurate, air-powered pistols of the Karnala. Over my shoulders was draped a cloak of dark green cloth. I might remark, too, that I was beginning to let my hair grow longer, in the fashion of the Southern Martians. Though this custom is frowned on in our society to some extent, short hair on Mars is conspicuous and one is inclined to be questioned about it. Thus, to conduct myself as much as possible like my hosts – whom no-one could call unmanly! – I was allowing my hair to flow! It was kept from my eyes, also in the Southern Martian manner, by means of a simple metal circlet. Mine was of gold and had been a betrothal gift from Shizala. I stood now with my arm around her as we looked into the square.

As chief Pukan-Nara of Karnala's warriors, Darnad was in the square, but Carnak was with us on the balcony.

'Have you been able to judge the strength of Mishim Tep?' Carnak asked me.

'I have,' I replied. 'To some extent, at least. They must outnumber you five or six to one!'

'Our strongest ally turned against us! This will mean the destruction of the South as we know it,' Shizala said wearily. 'For centuries the balance of power has been held by what we choose to call the "benevolent nations", Mishim Tep and Karnala chief among them. This war will weaken us to such an extent that the South will become prey to all kinds of enemies.'

'Doubtless that is exactly what Horguhl is hoping,' I pointed out. 'In the anarchy that must follow this war – and it cannot matter to her who wins it – she will gain the power she lusts for. She failed in her attempt to smash us by use of the Argzoon – now she tries this. She does not give up easily.'

'She is a strange woman,' Shizala said. 'I spent much time in her company – forcibly, of course, since I was her prisoner.

Sometimes she appears so innocent and bewildered, at other times she is a monster! And that weird power of hers – that ability to make others do what she chooses – it is inhuman.'

'It is not inhuman,' I said, 'since many must have a similar power, though not so well developed. It is the use to which she puts it that is perverted!'

'She seems to blame all Southern nations for some crime committed against her,' Shizala said. 'Why is that?'

'Who can explain the motives of a sick mind?' I said. 'She is insane – and if insanity were easily explained by logic, then perhaps there would be no insanity!'

'This plan of yours,' said Shizala with a slight shudder. 'The one to kill her. How do you plan to make the attempt?'

'It is so distasteful to me,' I said, 'that I have not thought much about it. First we must wait until the main army of Mishim Tep is on the march. I do not think that Horguhl will risk her own life by riding with the army. She will remain behind. I would only – only kill her, of course, in the last resort – that is, if I could find no other way of convincing the Bradhi that she lies. Or, better still, forcing her to admit that she has not told the truth!'

'And when the army is on the march – what then?'

'I will enter Mishim Tep in secret.'

'How?'

'I will travel most of the distance by airship, then stain my skin roughly the same colour as the men of Mishim Tep, entering the city as a mercenary. I believe there are bands of mercenaries who seek employment in Mishim Tep.'

'They are the Jelusa – cousins to the men of Mishim Tep.'

'Then I shall become a Jelusa.'

'And what then?'

'Ask to speak with Horguhl alone, telling her I have secrets...'

'She will recognise you!'

'Is it not a custom amongst the Jelusa mercenaries to mask themselves so that none shall know who has been hired?'

'It is.'

'Then I shall be masked.'

'And when – if your attempt succeeds – you are alone with her?

'I will try to kidnap her and get her to write out the truth. Then I will imprison her and take the statement to the Bradhi of Mishim Tep. If he still refuses to accept the truth I will show it to his nobles. I am sure they will see it, not being directly under her spell...' My voice tailed off as I saw Shizala's expression.

'It is a daring plan,' she said – 'but it is almost bound to fail, my love.'

'It is the only plan I have,' I said, 'the only one with the slimmest hope of succeeding.'

She frowned. 'I remember Telem Fas Ogdai once telling me of an almost forgotten object which they have at Mih-Sa-Voh, in their treasure house. It is a shield with a polished surface that transfixes anyone who gazes into it.'

I was interested in the tale, since it seemed to have affinities with our own tale of Perseus and the Gorgon – and, perhaps, since our race is descended from that of Mars, that was the origin of our legend. 'Go on,' I told my betrothed.

'Well, this shield has another property. Anyone who looks into it is forced to speak the truth. It is something to do with the mesmeric effect of the surface. I do not know the scientific explanation, but it was probably designed by the Sheev or the Yaksha, and their science was far ahead of my knowledge.'

'And mine, too,' I said.

'I think it is only a legend – an amusing story Telem Fas Ogdai told to while away an hour.'

'It sounds unlikely,' I agreed – then dismissed the thought from my mind. I could not afford to waste time on speculation.

Shizala sighed.

'Are we never to know peace, Michael Kane?' she said. 'Has some other power decided that a love so rich as ours may not be enjoyed in tranquillity? Why must we continually be parted?'

'If I am successful, perhaps we shall have a chance to spend long years together in peace,' I said comfortingly.

Again she sighed and looked into my eyes. 'Do you think that is likely?'

'It is worth striving for,' I said simply.

The next day we stood again on the balcony!

'The army of Mishim Tep must be on the move by now,' she said, 'and marching towards Karnala. It will take many days before they reach us.'

'That gives me so much longer to do what I must,' I said. I knew she was hinting that we could spend a few more days together, but I could not afford to risk anything going wrong – must give myself as much margin of time as possible.

'I suppose so,' she said.

I kissed her then, holding her close.

Later, looking down again into the square, I watched the tiny force that only recently had to fight off a far larger force of Argzoon Blue Giants, making their preparations.

It had been decided to meet the army of Mishim Tep on a battlefield rather than wait for it to lay siege to the city. If possible the city, and its women and children, would be preserved. The army of Mishim Tep were not barbarians and once they defeated the army of the Karnala they would not make any further reprisals for any supposed insults and treachery we of Varnal had subjected them to.

Seeing the army making ready, I decided to waste no more time and to leave that very night for the Jewelled City.

I bade farewell to Carnak and Darnad. I said goodbye to Shizala.

I also said a silent goodbye to that lovely city as the waning sun stained its marble red as blood.

And then, the brief period of peace over, I was heading back towards Mih-Sa-Voh.

Chapter Fifteen

Assassin's Mask

I STOOD AT the gates of the Jewelled City and answered the challenge of the guard.

'What do you want within? Know you not that Mishim Tep is in a state of war?'

'That is why I come, my friend. Can't you see that I am of the Jelusa?'

In my mask of thin, filigree silver covering my whole face, my blood-red cloak and my sword carried in a sheath – a strange custom on Mars – I looked a perfect mercenary of the Jelusa. Or so I thought. Now that the guard gave me a careful appraisal I was not so sure.

Then he seemed satisfied.

'You may enter,' he said. After a moment's delay the gates swung back and I strode through jauntily, a pack slung over my back.

The guard came down from the wall and confronted me.

'You have no dahara.' he said. 'Why is that?'

'It went lame on the journey here.'

He accepted this and pointed up the street through the evening gloom.

'You will find the rest in the House of the Blue Dagger,' he said.

'The rest? The rest of whom?'

'Why, the rest of your companions, of course. Were you not with the party?'

I did not dare risk denying this, so I went in some trepidation up to the House of the Blue Dagger – a lodging house and tavern – and entered. Seated inside were several Jelusa mercenaries in masks of bronze, silver and gold, some of them modelled in the shapes of alien faces, some studded with tiny jewels.

Since they did not acknowledge me, I did not acknowledge them.

I asked the tavern keeper if there was a room available but he shrugged. 'Your fellows have them all. Would you share a room with one?'

I shook my head. 'No matter. I'll find another tavern. Can you recommend one?'

'You could try the House of the Hanging Argzoon in the next street.'

I thanked him and left. It was very dark now and I had difficulty finding my way through the streets. Street lighting seemed non-existent, even in the most civilised Martian cities.

I lost my way and never did find the tavern with the somewhat bloodthirsty name. As I quested around for another tavern I began to sense that I was being followed.

I half turned my head, trying to see out of the corner of my eye if there was anyone behind me, but the mask obscured my view – and I did not want to risk removing it.

I continued to walk on and then took a narrow side street, little more than an alley, and flattened myself in a doorway.

Sure enough, a figure passed me somewhat hurriedly. I stepped from my hiding place, drawing my sword.

'Is it polite, friend,' I said, 'to follow a man about in this way?'

He turned with a gasp, his own hand reaching for his shield.

Moonlight flashed on something and I realised he was wearing a Jelusa mask.

'What's this?' I said, speaking as jauntily as possible. 'Do you seek to rob a comrade?'

The voice that issued from the mask was cool now. The man did not bother to draw his sword.

'It is against the code of the Jelusa to do any such thing,' he said.

'Then what do you want of me?'

'A peep behind the mask, *friend*.'

'That, too, is against our code,' I pointed out.

'I do not know what your code is, *friend*, but I know the code of the Jelusa well enough. Do you?'

Evidently I had made some mistake and this man had noticed it. Perhaps there was some secret sign that Jelusa exchanged without apparently seeming to acknowledge one another.

It appeared that I would have to kill this man if he threatened to reveal my secret. Too much was at stake to risk his giving me away and thus ruining my whole plan.

'Draw your sword,' I told him grimly.

He laughed.

'Draw!'

'So I was right,' he said. 'You are masquerading as a Jelusa.'

'Just so. Now draw your sword!'

'Why?'

'Because,' I said, 'I cannot let you betray my secret – I must try to silence you.'

'Did I say I was going to tell anyone what I know?'

'You are a Jelusa. You know that I am not, that I only pretend to be.'

Again he laughed. 'But the Jelusa might be flattered that you should wish to be one of them. There is nothing in our code that says we must betray a man or kill him simply because he pretends to be one of us.'

'Then why were you following me?'

'Curiosity. I thought you were a thief. Are you?'

'No.'

'A pity. You see – as you might know – the Jelusa Guild of the Masked is not only a guild of mercenaries and assassins, but of thieves also. It had struck me, my friend, that you might be here on the same errand as myself.'

'What is that?'

'To rob the treasure vaults of the palace. After all, there are so few guards that it is an ideal opportunity. They are supposed to be impossible to rob, you know.'

'I am no thief.'

'Then why do you lurk behind a Jelusa mask?'

'My own business.'

'You are a spy for the Karnala.'

Since I was not a spy, I shook my head.

'This is very mysterious,' said the Jelusa in his mocking voice.

Something occurred to me then. 'How do you plan to enter the palace?' I asked him.

'Ah, so you have the same object as me, after all!'

'I told you, I am no thief – but I would enter the palace without the necessity of approaching the guards.'

'What is it then? Assassination?'

I shuddered. There was no point in lying – as a very last possibility, I was prepared to kill Horguhl if it would stop the two great nations from destroying one another.

'So that is it,' the Jelusa murmured.

'It is not what you think. I am not a paid killer.'

'An idealist! By the moons, I beg your pardon – I must be on my way. An idealist!' The Jelusa gave a mocking bow and pretended to try to hurry past me.

'A realist,' I said. 'I am here to try to stop the war which is imminent.'

'An idealist. Wars come and go – why try to stop them?'

'That is scarcely an objective judgement coming from one who makes his living from war,' I said. 'But I'm tired of this. Will you swear silence about me, or will you draw your sword?'

'In the circumstances, I will keep silent,' said the masked man, his golden, jewelled mask suddenly flashing as a ray of moonlight caught it. 'Though I have a suggestion. I promise I will pry no more into your object for entering the palace – and I think my proposal will be to our mutual advantage.'

'What is it?'

'That we help each other to gain entrance to the palace, then we go our different ways – you to the – er – victim, me to the treasure house.'

It was true that I could do with an ally, though whether this cynical thief was exactly the ally I would have chosen I did not know.

I thought over his suggestion.

Then I nodded.

'Very well,' I said. 'Since you are probably more experienced in these matters than I, I will do as you say. What is your plan?'

'Back to the House of the Blue Dagger,' he said, 'and the privacy of my room. Some wine, some rest – and some talk.'

Somewhat reluctantly, I followed him back through the maze of streets, marvelling at his sense of direction. Perhaps this thief would be more than useful, after all.

The thief did not remove his mask when we reached his room, though I removed mine. He cocked his head on one side. His mask was moulded to resemble a strange bird and gave him a grotesquely comical appearance.

'My Guild-name is Toxo,' he said.

'My name –' I hesitated. 'My name is Michael Kane.'

'A very strange name. Yes, I have heard it, as you suspected.'

'What do you think of the name?'

'I think it very strange, as I said. If you mean what have I heard and what do I think of that – well, what is the truth? I tell you, my friend, I believe nothing and everything. I am not a good Guild-member – others who had given you the sign and received no recognition would have been angrier than I.'

'What is the sign?'

Casually, with his right thumb, he traced a small cross on his mask.

'I did not notice,' I admitted.

'That sign is necessary when all wear masks,' he said. 'I should not have told you that, either. Many have tried to pose as Jelusa. It is the best disguise there is.'

'Did anyone else notice?' I asked.

'I told them you had given me the sign but that you might need help finding a tavern. That was my excuse for following you.'

'You are something of a renegade,' I said.

'Nonsense – I simply live how I can. I do not believe in these stuffy guilds and the like.'

'Then why don't you leave it?'

'The mask, my friend – the protection. I survive.'

'Are there no penalties for speaking openly of the Guild's secrets?'

'We are more lax than we used to be, all of us – just a few fanatics keep up the old traditions. Besides, I cannot stop talking. I must talk all the time – so some of my talk must give away secrets. Still, what is a secret? What is the truth?'

This last seemed something of a rhetorical question so I did not bother to answer it.

'Now,' said Toxo. 'What about the palace?'

'I have only been in the main hall,' I said. 'I know little of its geography.'

Toxo reached under the bed covering and produced a large roll of stiff paper. He smoothed it straight and showed it to me. It was a detailed plan of the palace, showing all windows and entrances, all floors and everything on them. It was an excellent map.

'This cost me my ceremonial mask,' said Toxo. 'Still, I never used it – and I can have another made when I am rich.'

I was not sure of the morality of helping a thief rob a royal treasure house, but I thought the whole of Mishim Tep's jewels would be a small price to pay to avert the bloodshed that was about to happen.

'Why is there a guarded treasure house?' I asked. 'Why, when jewels can be prised from the walls of the city and the inhabitants treat them like ordinary stones?'

'It is not so much the jewels themselves, which would fetch an excellent price some thousands of miles north or east of here, but the workmanship of the objects stored in the treasure house,' said Toxo.

He bent forward, his eyes gleaming at me from behind his ornate mask.

'Here is the best way into the palace,' he said. 'I rejected this means when I thought I was on my own.'

'Would none of the other Jelusa help you?'

'Only one – and I know him of old for a bungling oaf. No, I am the only thief here at present – apart from the man I have mentioned. All the rest are simple fighting men. You should be able to tell by the mask.'

'I did not know there were differences in the masks.'

'Of course!'

'Then what is mine?'

'The mask – as it happens – of an assassin,' Toxo told me brightly.

I felt a shudder run through me. I begged providence that I would not be forced to kill a woman, no matter how evil she was.

Chapter Sixteen
Woman of Evil

IT WAS VERY still in the streets of the Jewelled City and Toxo and I, both masked, hugged the shadows near the palace.

There was a distinct disadvantage to the masks in that they both caught far too much of the little light there was.

Toxo had unwound a loop of rope from his waist. It was thin rope but very strong, he assured me. He pointed silently up at the roof where a flagpole stood close to the edge. The reason two men were needed was because the rope had to be looped around the pole so that both ends dangled in the street.

One man had to hold the rope while the other climbed and secured it, allowing the second man to climb up.

The guard on the roof passed. There was only one doing a circuit, taking twenty minutes. In normal times there would be three guards.

Toxo flung the rope expertly upwards. It went snaking away to encircle the pole and one end flopped down on the other side, dangling over the edge of the roof. Now Toxo began to make little jerking movements on the rope and the short end, which had been weighted, began to slide down the wall.

Soon both ends were of equal length. I tied one round my waist and took the weight as Toxo began to climb. There were still more than ten minutes left before the guard was due to return – but it was slow climbing.

At last, after what seemed an age, Toxo reached the roof and tied the rope round the flagpole. I began to climb. I felt as if my arms were dropping off by the time I had reached the top.

Quickly we untied the rope and, ducking, ran towards the shadow of a small dome on the roof.

The guard came past. He had noticed nothing.

The roof, though flat, seemed rough and slippery. Reaching down to touch it, I realised that it was encrusted with polished gems!

Toxo was pointing mutely at the dome. This, too, entered into our plan. It was of glass – coloured glass on a soft metal frame. Noiselessly, we had to remove enough of the glass to let ourselves in.

We began carefully to prise the frame open and bend it back after first removing the glass.

Twice the guard passed. Twice he did not see us – his attention was on the street!

Finally, we had made a hole large enough for us to pass through. Toxo went first, dangled by his hands for a moment and then dropped downwards. I heard a soft sound as he landed. Then I squeezed through the hole, dangled and let myself fall.

We were on a catwalk high above a darkened room – perhaps a banqueting hall, for it was not the throne room where I had first confronted Horguhl.

Toxo began to run along the swaying catwalk and it was only then that I realised if I had missed the catwalk I would have fallen to my death!

Now we reached a door, bolted on our side. We slid back the bolts and went through the door into a small chamber off which led stone stairs.

Down the stairs we darted but then slowed our pace when we saw light filtering upwards. The dim, blue radiance of the Sheev near-everlasting light-globes. Almost all the Southern Martians had these.

We peered downward into a larger room – a servant's simply furnished room by the look of it. On a bed a fat man lay, sprawled in sleep. Beyond him was the door.

Our hearts were in our mouths as we crept past the sleeping servant and gradually eased the door open. We managed to do it without waking him.

Now we came, further down, to a larger room. This was better furnished and seemed to be the living room of a larger apartment – perhaps a noble retainer who lived in the palace. The man we had passed was probably his servant.

Just as we set foot on the floor of this room the door opened – and I saw the noble who had encountered me earlier in the throne room!

With an oath, he turned – probably to summon help – but I was across the room in an instant, my sword out, slamming the door and cutting off his exit!

'Who are you? Jelusa, eh? What are you doing here?'

He seemed a little shaken but not frightened – very few of the Southern Martians are cowards. He made to draw his sword but I placed my hand on his and nodded to Toxo.

While the noble was still puzzling out what was happening – he may have been brave, but he was far from clever – Toxo unhooked his scabbarded sword from his belt and raised it by the scabbard, striking the noble on the head with the hilt.

He dropped without a murmur, and we tied and gagged him.

To Toxo's surprise, I had insisted that there must be no bloodshed. The folk of Mishim Tep were misguided and had been influenced by an evil, clever woman, but they did not deserve to die for believing her lies.

Opening the noble's door we found ourselves on a landing. Several other doors led off it.

This was where Toxo and I had decided to part. Judging by his map – which he had bought from a dishonest servant of the palace – Horguhl's apartments were on this floor.

Toxo had no interest in Horguhl but every interest in the treasure vaults below.

Silently we parted, Toxo taking the stairs that led down from the landing, and I creeping further along the landing to the door I sought.

Cautiously, I turned the handle and the door did not resist. The room was in darkness.

Had I made a mistake?

I can usually sense if a room is occupied, even though I cannot see.

This room was not occupied. I crept to the door leading off the room and found that the adjoining room was empty also – as were all the rest in the apartment.

I decided to risk switching on the light.

Surely I had not been wrong? Looking about me, I was sure that this was Horguhl's apartment – and yet she was not in it though it was late at night.

Had she ridden with the army after all?

I was sure she would not have done. She was brave enough, I will credit her, but it did not seem to fit into what I guessed of her scheme. She would prefer to sit back and watch the two old friends fight one another to the death.

Then where was she? In the palace, I was sure. Now I would be forced to seek her out.

I left the apartments and went out onto the landing. Evidently the palace was for the most part deserted. All the usual occupants had left with the army and only a few guards and servants remained – with the noble we had encountered probably left to supervise them.

I decided to risk a visit to the throne room, since instinct told me it was a likely place for Horguhl to be.

With a wary step I made my way down the stairs for several flights, until I reached the ground floor, coming to the entrance hall I recognised.

I ducked hastily back into the shadows as I saw that a guard was on duty by the doors of the throne room. Only one dim, blue bulb burned above his head. He seemed half asleep.

Somehow I had to distract his attention so that I could enter the throne room.

In my belt was a small knife I had used to prise away the soft metal of the dome on the roof. I took this out and threw it from me. It landed near the opposite staircase on the other side of the hall. The guard jerked himself into full wakefulness at the sound and peered towards the other staircase. Slowly he began to walk towards it.

This was my chance. Swiftly, I ran across to the doors of the throne room, my feet almost silent on the smooth floor. I inched open the doors, which I had noted earlier opened inward, and closed them softy behind me once I was through.

I had done it.

And there – on the throne of Mishim Tep – sat the woman of evil, that wild, dark-haired girl who was so beautiful and yet so peculiarly twisted in her mind. As Shizala had said, partially an innocent, partially a woman of preternatural wisdom.

She hardly saw me. She was sprawled in the throne looking upwards and murmuring something to herself.

I had a little time to act before she called the guard. If she called, more than one were sure to come. I sprinted up the hall towards the throne.

Then her eyes dropped and she saw me. She could not have recognised me, for I still wore the silver mask. But, of course, she was startled. Yet her curiosity – a strong trait in her – stopped her from immediately calling for help.

'Who are you?' she said. 'You in the strange mask.'

I did not reply but began to walk towards her with a measured pace.

Her large, wise-innocent eyes widened.

'What do you hide behind the mask?' she said. 'Are you so ugly?'

I continued to advance until I had reached the foot of the dais.

'Take off your mask or I will summon the guards, and they will remove it for you. How did you get in here?'

Slowly I raised my hand to my mask.

'Do you really wish me to remove it?' I said.

'Yes. Who are you?'

I snatched off the mask. She gasped. Several emotions flashed across her face and, strangely, not one of them was the hatred she had exhibited earlier.

'Your Nemesis, perhaps,' I said.

'Michael Kane! Are you here alone?'

'More or less,' I said. 'I have come to kidnap you!'

'Why?'

'Why do you think?'

She literally did not seem to know. She put her head to one side and looked into my face, searching for some sign – I knew not what.

Regarding her, I found myself unable to believe that this girl-like person sitting on the throne could be capable of such hatred that it could bring down whole nations. Already she had been responsible for using the Argzoon to weaken the power of half a dozen Southern nations – and destroyed the Argzoon nation in the process. Now Karnala and Mishim Tep faced one another in warfare and she sat with innocent eyes quizzically staring into my face.

'Kidnap me...!' She seemed to find the idea almost attractive. 'Interesting...'

'Come,' I said brusquely.

Her eyes widened and I averted my own from looking at them directly. I knew her powers of hypnotism already.

'I would still know why, Michael Kane.'

I hardly knew what to say. I had expected many things from her but not this near-passive mood. 'To have you testify that you lied to the Bradhi about his son, about Shizala, about me – and so stop the war before it is too late.'

'And what will you do for me if I do this for you?' She was almost purring now and her eyes had become hooded.

'What do you mean? Do you want to make some kind of bargain?'

'Perhaps.'

'What bargain?'

'You should know, Michael Kane. You might almost say that it was because of you and for you that I created this situation.'

I still did not understand.

'What do you propose?' I asked. It would be a relief if this was all she wanted.

'If I tell the Bradhi I lied, I want – you,' she said, flinging her arms towards me.

I was shocked. I could not answer.

'I am leaving here soon,' she said. 'I need do no more than what I have done. You could come with me – there would be nothing you would want for if you did.'

Playing for time, I said: 'Where would we go?'

'To the West – there are lands in the West which are warm and dark and mysterious. Lands where strange secrets may be found – secrets that will bring us great power, you and I. We could rule the world!'

'Your ambition exceeds mine, I am afraid,' I said. 'Besides, I have had some experience of the Western continent and would not return there again willingly.'

'You have *been* there!' Her eyes lighted and she stood up, stepping off the dais to stand close to me and look up into my face.

I was still at a loss for something to do or say. I had expected a screaming mass of hatred – but found her in this weird mood. She was too subtle, perhaps, for me.

'You have been in the West,' she went on. 'What did you see?'

'Things I would not wish to see again.' I said. Now I was involuntarily looking into her eyes. They drew all my attention. I felt my heart beating strongly and she pressed her body against mine. I could not move. A voluptuous smile played about her lips and she began to stroke my arm. I felt dizzy, unreal, and I heard her voice coming to me as if from a distance.

'I swear,' she was saying, 'that I will adhere to my side of the bargain if you will adhere to yours. Be mine, Michael Kane. Your origins are as mysterious as the origins of the gods. Perhaps you are a god – a young god. Perhaps you can give *me* power, not I you.'

I was sinking deeper and deeper into those eyes. There was nothing else. My flesh felt like water. I could hardly stand. She reached up and began to run her fingers through my hair.

I swayed and stumbled backwards and the movement helped me break her spell. With an oath, I pushed her away, shouting:

'No!'

Her face changed then, contorted with hatred.

'Very well – let it stand,' she said. 'I will enjoy putting you to death myself before I leave. Guards!'

A single guard entered.

I drew my sword, cursing myself for a fool. I had let Horguhl beguile me as she had beguiled the Bradhi! Her powers had even increased since the last time I had encountered her. If they increased any more, heaven only knew what would happen. She had to be stopped by some means – any means!

The guard swung his sword at me and I parried it easily. I do not boast when I say I am a master swordsman and easily the match for an ordinary palace guard. I could have finished him speedily but I was still wishing not to have to kill. I tried the trick of flicking his sword from his hand, but he held on to his blade too tightly.

While I was wasting time trying to disarm him several more guards rushed in.

Horguhl was at my back as I defended myself now against six swords – and I still fought an entirely defensive action since I was anxious not to kill.

It was my undoing, for while I engaged the guards Horguhl had come up behind me with some heavy object – I never knew what it was – and struck me a glancing blow on the head.

I fell backwards. My last memory was of cursing myself roundly again for the fool I was.

Now everything seemed lost!

Chapter Seventeen
The Mirror

I AWOKE IN a dank cell that was plainly somewhere under ground. It was not primarily a prison cell – the Bradhis of the South are not like the old medieval robber barons of Earth – but had probably been used for storage purposes. The door was strong, however, and no matter how I tried to shift it I could not. It was barred on the outside.

My weapons had been taken away from me. I wondered what fate Horguhl planned for me. In refusing her proposals of love I had redoubled her hatred for me. I shuddered. Knowing what sort of thoughts her mind could turn to, I did not enjoy thinking of the prospect of torture at her hands.

There was a small chink in the door through which I could see the bar. If I had had a knife I could have lifted the bar, I was sure – but I had no knife.

I began to feel my way around the cell. There were bits of refuse here and there – crates of vegetables seemed to have been stored in the cell.

My hand touched a wooden slat and then passed on – until I realised what the slat might promise. I picked it up and took it back to the door, but it was too thick to pass through the chink.

The wood was not hardwood but quite soft. This gave me an idea. Carefully, with my thumbnail I began to try to split it sideways.

Little by little I worked at the slat until I succeeded. Then I returned to the door and the tantalising chink and – my piece of wood went through.

Thanking my stars that the cell had not been designed with the idea of imprisoning anything more than a few crates of vegetables, I began to inch the bar upwards, praying the thin slat would not break.

After some time of this I finally managed to lift the bar.

It fell with a thud to the floor outside and I pushed the door open.

The corridor was in darkness. There was another door at the end of it. I walked up to this door, not expecting danger, and found myself confronted by a guard who was only just awakening from a doze. Evidently he had been disturbed by the noise of the bar falling.

He leapt up, but I flung myself at him. We began to wrestle across the littered floor, but then I got an armlock round his throat and squeezed the air from him until he passed out. Then I rose, took his sword and dagger, and continued on my way.

The corridors beyond the first one were a maze, but at length one widened out into a rather impressive corridor, high and roomy, leading towards a pair of heavy doors which seemed to be of solid bronze or some similar metal.

Perhaps these led to the stairs up to the main palace, I thought hopefully.

I opened the doors – and was confronted by one of the strangest sights of my life.

It was the treasure house of Mishim Tep, a huge vault with a low roof. In it were stacked works of the finest craftsmanship – indeed, artistry would be a better word. There were jewelled swords and chalices, chairs and great tables, pictures made of precious stones that seemed to give out their own light. All were dusty and piled at random. Careless of their treasures, the Bradhis of Mishim Tep had stored them in darkness and all but forgotten about them!

I gasped at the wonder of it and could only stand there staring.

Then I saw Horguhl. She was absorbed with something, her back towards me. Even as I walked through the heaps of art treasures she did not seem to notice me. I took my dagger out and reversed it planning to knock her on the head.

Then my foot slipped on a jewelled mosaic and I stumbled against one of the piles with a crash. It fell – and I fell with it.

From the corner of my eye I saw Horguhl turn and snatch up one of the swords.

I tried to rise, but my feet slipped again. She raised the sword and was about to bring it down into my heart when she suddenly stood transfixed.

Her mouth gaped open. She was not paralysed – not in the way I had been when injected with the poison of the spider-men – but her muscles became slack and the sword dropped from her nerveless fingers. I turned my head, wondering what she had seen, but a shout sounded suddenly:

'Do not move!'

I recognised the voice. It was Toxo's. I obeyed his urgent order.

A little later the voice came again. 'Stand up, Michael Kane, but do not look back.'

I did as he said.

Horguhl still stood transfixed.

'Move to one side.'

I did so.

A little later I saw the bird-mask and the bright little eyes gleaming behind it.

'I found the treasure vaults.' Toxo patted a large sack he carried over his shoulder. 'But this young woman disturbed me. Evidently she was engaged in a similar project.'

'So this is what she planned,' I said. 'She told me that if I went with her we should want for nothing. She was not only scheming to bring catastrophe to Mishim Tep and Karnala, but to escape with the treasures as well. But what did you do to her?'

'I? Nothing. I was trying to come to your aid when I, too, slipped and grabbed at the nearest support. I seized some fabric – it must have been very old – and it ripped in my hand. I exposed some kind of mirror. I was just going to look and see what I had done when I noted the effect that mirror had on the young woman, so I thought it wise not to look after all. Then I shouted a warning to you.'

'The mirror!' I gasped. 'I have heard about it – an invention of the Sheev. Somehow it manipulates light so that whoever looks into it is mesmerised. More than that, it will destroy their will so that any question asked of them will bring forth the truth.'

This gave Toxo the opportunity to repeat his favourite rhetorical question: 'Ah, but what is truth? Do you think the mirror can really do all that?'

'Let us try,' I said. 'Horguhl – did you lie to the Bradhi of Mishim Tep about Michael Kane, Shizala and the rest?'

The voice that answered was weak but the word was clear enough.

'Yes.'

I was jubilant. A scheme was forming in my mind. Keeping our backs to the mirror and our faces towards Horguhl, Toxo and I bound the girl, gagged her and – a precaution against her own hypnotic powers – blindfolded her. The moment her eyes were covered she began to struggle – but she was far too securely bound for her struggling to get her free!

For good measure I wrapped her in my cloak.

'We shall need your cloak too, Toxo,' I said. We made a wide detour through the heaped gems until we were behind the mirror. Like all the treasures of Mishim Tep this, too, had been forgotten. How many centuries had this subtle invention lain gathering dust? Many, by the feel of the rotten fabric.

We draped Toxo's cloak over the mirror and wrapped it up. It was about a foot in diameter and was set with only a few gems. It was circular in shape and very heavy, with a handle like that of a shield. Perhaps it had been used as a weapon by the Sheev, but I thought not. Probably, if it had been used in war at all, it had been designed as a method for getting information from prisoners.

Somehow we managed to get both girl and mirror – and also Toxo's loot – out of the chamber and make our way to the roof without being seen.

The guard was still patrolling – or if it was not the same guard it was one very like him. We tapped him on the head – we had no time for caution – and left him dreaming on the roof as we used the rope to lower our bundles to the street.

Once in the street we sneaked along, pausing every so often to rest.

I was praying that having so far succeeded, we should not now be caught. Everything depended on me reaching the airship. I told Toxo of this and he was interested.

'We shall need mounts to reach it,' he said as we came to the House of the Blue Dagger – which was at sleep, thankfully. We took our prizes to our room and Toxo left. He was away for half an hour and when he returned his eyes were gleaming with pleasure.

From somewhere he had stolen a carriage – a fast one, by the look of it – to which was harnessed a team of six daharas.

Toxo bundled Horguhl and me, together with his loot, into the back, covered us with a blanket, drew a hood over his face and whipped up the daharas.

I remember only being jolted along at an almost incredible speed. I remember an angry shout – from the guard at the gate, Toxo told me later – and then we were bumping over open countryside.

It was morning when I poked my head out from under the blanket. Somehow, in spite of the jolting. I had fallen asleep. Toxo was nudging me.

'You must guide me now,' he said.

I guided him willingly to where I had hidden the airship. We drew aside the brush and there she was, unharmed. We began to load everything into the cabin, Toxo telling me that he would like to be dropped on the borders of the Crimson Plain near the robber city of Narlet – a city I knew well, a place of thieves and brigands where Toxo doubtless felt at home.

I agreed, since this was on my way. I was hoping to reach the two armies before they became engaged in conflict.

We were soon in the air and I stopped only once to allow Toxo to disembark with his sack of treasure, waved my thanks to the masked thief and then was rising again.

A few groans from Horguhl did nothing but assure me that she still lived – which was all I wanted to know at that stage.

Would I be in time?

Chapter Eighteen

The Truth at Last!

THERE THEY WERE! I could not have left it any later!

The two armies – the large one of Mishim Tep and the smaller one of Karnala – were camped opposite one another on the Crimson Plain. It was a strange place to fight a battle, but doubtless the army of Mishim Tep had not expected to meet the Karnala at all – and the Karnala had simply marched until they encountered the Mishim Tep.

I could see their battle lines drawn up ready for the charge.

I could even see Carnak seated on his great dahara, with Darnad beside him, at the head of his men.

And there was the Bradhi of Mishim Tep, stern-faced, less glassy-eyed from what I could see – evidently Horguhl's hypnotising powers did not last indefinitely – at the head of his large army.

As my airship began to descend they all looked up – recognising it at once. A few spears were flung at it from the ranks of Mishim Tep, but the Bradhi raised his hand to stop his men. He seemed curious.

I took my makeshift megaphone from its locker and shouted down to the Bradhi.

'Bradhi, I bring you proof that Horguhl lied – that you are about to engage in a senseless war entirely because of the lies of one evil woman!'

He passed a hand across his face. Then he frowned and shook his head as if to clear it.

'Will you allow me to descend and prove this to you?' I asked.

After a pause, he nodded wordlessly.

I lowered the ship until the cabin was bumping the tops of the crimson ferns. Then, unceremoniously, I threw out the bundle that was Horguhl and, clutching the covered mirror in my hands, leapt after her. Swiftly I moored the ship and then dragged both the bound, gagged and blindfolded girl and my mirror over until I was standing in front of the ranks of Mishim Tep. First I uncovered Horguhl and was rewarded by a gasp and a murmur. The Bradhi cleared his throat as if to speak but then changed his mind. Grim-lipped, he nodded at me again.

I took off the girl's gag, forcing her to stand upright.

'Will you believe the truth from Horguhl's own lips, Bradhi?' I asked.

Again he cleared his throat.

'Y-yes,' he said. Already his eyes were brightening visibly.

I pointed at the wrapped mirror. 'I have here the legendary Mirror of Truth which the Sheev invented millennia ago. You have all heard of its magical properties. I shall demonstrate one of them now!'

With my back towards the men of Mishim Tep, I lifted the mirror-shield by its handle and pulled away the covering. Then I reached out and removed Horguhl's blindfold.

At once the mirror drew her eyes and she stood again slack-mouthed.

'You see?' I said. 'It works.'

They began to crowd closer to see that I spoke the truth. 'Do not look directly into the mirror,' I warned them, 'or you will suffer the same effects. Are you ready to see if Horguhl told truth or lies to the Bradhi and seduced you all into launching this needless war against your age-old allies?'

'We are,' said the Bradhi's voice from behind me, surprisingly deep and firm now.

'Horguhl,' I said slowly and clearly, 'did you lie to the Bradhi?'

The low, now spiritless, mindless voice said: 'I did.'

'How did you convince him?'

'By my powers – the powers in my eyes and my head.'

A gasp and a murmur at this. Again I heard the Bradhi clear his throat.

'And what lies did you tell him?'

'That Michael Kane and Shizala planned to kill and disgrace his son.'

'And who was really responsible for this?'

'I was!'

A roar went up then and the men began to move forward. I was sure many of them – none had really wished to fight this battle against their ancient allies – were ready to tear her to pieces. But the Bradhi stayed them.

Then the old man spoke. 'It has been proved to me that I was prey to this woman's evil powers. At first I believed that my son was a traitor – but then, when she came to me with another story, I would rather believe that one. It was a lie. I believed her first lie. I believed all her other lies. Michael Kane was right – she is evil – she almost brought utter ruin to the South.'

Then Carnak and Darnad cantered forward and Carnak and Bolig Fas Ogdai laid hands on each other's shoulders and spoke quietly to one another in terms of friendship. There were tears in the eyes of both men.

Horguhl was tied, gagged and bound again and placed in a supply wagon in which she would eventually be taken back to the Jewelled City, to be tried there for her crimes.

Then Bolig Fas Ogdai and a few of his nobles returned with us in our airship to Varnal – and Shizala.

There is little more to tell you save that the Bradhi of Mishim Tep was an honoured guest at the wedding of Shizala and myself. We spent a blissful honeymoon as guests of the Bradhi and later returned to Varnal, where I began supervising the building of more airships.

In order to get supplies of helium gas we organised an expedition to Mendishar and the desert beyond. In Mendishar a rule of great happiness had begun, with Hool Haji on the throne.

What a welcome I received from him! He had become convinced I was dead.

When we arrived at the Yaksha city we found the fountain blocked and the last of the ghouls lying dead near it. They had not had the sense to clear it!

It was on our third expedition to Mendishar's desert – this time with a full fleet of airships! – that I decided to try a more complicated experiment, using the machines I had found in the forgotten city of the Yaksha.

You will remember that the work on my matter transmitter was connected with earlier work on laser rays. By investigating the construction of the Yaksha laser I was able to devise a method of building a matter transmitter that would send me back to Earth at almost the same instant I left.

That is how I am able to tell you my story.

Epilogue

'So THAT IS the explanation!' I gasped, looking at Michael Kane. 'You can travel at will now between Earth of our age and the Mars of yours!'

'Yes,' he replied with a smile. 'And, moreover, I have sophisticated the whole technique. There is no need to shift the transmitter around – it can be kept in your wine cellar!'

'In that case, I shall have to find a new place to keep the wine,' I said. 'And what do you intend to do on Mars now?'

'Well, I am a Bradhinak now, you know.' He half smiled. 'I am a Prince of the Karnala – a Prince of Mars. I have responsibilities. Karnala is still weak. Since it will take time to build up her man-power, I am concentrating on building up her new *air*-power!'

'And is the excitement all over – will there be no more adventures?'

Kane's lips quirked. 'Oh, I am not so sure. I think there will be many more adventures – and I promise that if I survive them I will pay you more visits and tell you of them.'

'And I will publish them,' I said. 'People will regard them as fantasies – but let them. You and I know the truth.'

'Perhaps the others, too, will realise it some day,' he said.

Very soon after that he left, but I could not forget almost his last words to me.

'*There will be many more adventures!*' he had said.

I looked forward to hearing them.

Barbarians of Mars

For Mr Chip Delany of San Francisco and Sister Mary Eugene of Bon Secours Convent, Derby, Pennsylvania

... The sickness is Fear and the remedy is Faith...

Prologue

SITTING IN MY study one autumn night, a small fire burning in the grate taking the chill off a room filled with the scents of oncoming winter, I heard a footfall in the hall below.

I am not a nervous man, but I can be an imaginative one, and I had thoughts of both ghosts and burglars as I left the leather armchair and opened the door. The hall was quiet and the lights were out, but I saw a shadowy figure coming up the stairs towards me.

There was something about the size of the man, something about the jingle he made as he walked, that I recognised instantly. A grin began to spread across my face as he approached, and I held out my hand to him.

'Michael Kane?' It was hardly a question.

'It is,' replied the deep, vibrant voice of my visitor. He came to the top of the stairs and I felt my hand enclosed in a firm, manly grip. I saw the giant smile in return.

'How is Mars?' I asked, as I led him into the study.

'A little changed from when we last spoke,' he said.

'You must tell me,' I said eagerly. 'What will you have to drink?'

'No liquor, thanks. I'm not used to it any longer. How about some coffee? That's the one thing I miss on Mars.'

'Wait here,' I told him. 'I'm all alone in the house today. I'll go and make some.'

I left him slumped in a chair beside the fire, his magnificent, bronzed body completely relaxed. He looked strangely incongruous in his Martian war-harness, studded as it was with unfamiliar gems, his huge longsword with its ornate basket hilt resting with its tip on the floor.

His diamond-blue eyes seemed much more humorous and even less full of tension than when I had last seen him. His manner had relaxed me, too, even in my excitement at seeing my friend again.

In the kitchen I prepared the coffee, remembering all that he had told me of his past adventures – of Shizala, Princess of the Karnala and of Hool Haji, now ruler of Mendishar, his wife and his closest friend respectively. I remembered how his first trip to Mars – an ancient Mars, far in our own past – had been made accidentally because of a malfunctioning matter transmitter, a development of laser research he had been pursuing in Chicago; how he had met and fought for Shizala against the fearsome Blue Giants and their leader Horguhl, a woman of her own race who had a secret power over people, across the lush landscapes of a strange planet. I remembered how he had sought my help and I had given it – building a matter transmitter in my own basement. He had returned to Mars and had faced many dangers, discovering the lost underground city of the Yaksha, helping to win a revolution and fighting strange, spider creatures before finally finding Shizala again and marrying her. Using the forgotten scientific devices of the Yaksha – a race now supposed to be extinct – he had built a machine capable of flinging him across time and space again to a transceiver in my basement.

Evidently he had, as he had promised before he left the last time, returned to tell me of his latest adventures.

I went back with the coffee and set it in front of him.

He poured himself a cup, tasting it a little suspiciously at first, then added milk and sugar. He took his first swallow and grinned.

'One thing I haven't lost my taste for,' he said.

'And one thing I haven't lost *my* taste for,' I replied eagerly. 'I want to hear your latest story from beginning to end.'

'Have you published the first two adventures yet?' he asked.

At that time I had not, so I shook my head. 'Someone will believe me sufficiently to publish them,' I told him. 'People believe I wrote them cynically for one reason or another – but we know that I did not, that you are real, that your exploits actually happened. One day they will realise this, when governments are prepared to release the information that confirms what you have told me. They will realise that you are no liar and that I am no crackpot – or worse, a commercial writer trying to write a science fiction novel.'

'I hope so,' he said seriously, 'because it would be a shame for people not to be able to read the story of my experiences on Mars.'

As he finished his first cup of coffee and reached forward to help himself to another, I fixed the tape recorder so that it would take down every word he said. Then I settled back in my chair.

'Is your marvellous memory working at full capacity as usual?' I asked.

He smiled. 'I think so.'

'And you're going to tell me of your recent adventures on Mars?'

'If you wish to hear them.'

'I do. How is Shizala, your wife? How is Hool Haji, your friend the Blue Giant? And Horguhl – any news of her?'

'None of Horguhl,' he said. 'And Fate be thanked for that!'

'Then what? Surely things can't have been so uneventful on Mars!'

'They certainly were not. I am only just recovering from everything that happened. Telling you about it all will help me, as usual, to bring it into perspective. Where shall I begin?'

'The last I heard from you was that you and Shizala were living happily in Varnal, that you had designed airships to supplement the Varnalian air force, and that you had made several expeditions to the Yaksha underground city to study their machines.'

'That's right.' He nodded thoughtfully. 'Well, I can begin with our sixth expedition to the Yaksha city. That was when things really started to happen. Are you ready?'

'I am ready,' I replied.

Kane began his story.

E.P.B.,
Chester Square,
London, S.W.1.
August 1969

Chapter One

The Aerial Expedition

I KISSED SHIZALA farewell, little realising that I would not see her again for many Martian months, and clasped the ladder leading into the cabin of my airship – a vessel designed to my own specifications.

Shizala looked lovelier than ever, a womanly woman who was, without doubt, the most beautiful human being on the whole planet of Mars.

The slender towers of Varnal, the city of which I was now a Bradhinak, or prince, rose around us in the light of the early-morning sun. There was a smell of scented mist – the green mist which came from the lake in the centre of Varnal, sending delicate green traceries through the air to mingle with the pennants of lovely colours floating at masts rising from the towers. Most of the buildings are tall and white, though a number are of fine blue marble, while others have veins of gold running through them. It is a delicate, beautiful city – perhaps the finest on Mars.

This was where we had lived since our marriage and we had been exquisitely happy there. But I am a restless soul and my mind was eager for new information about the forgotten machines of Mars in the vaults of the Yaksha, which still needed investigation.

Thus, when Hool Haji had flown from Mendishar, far in the North, to visit me, it had not been long before I had suggested an expedition to the Yaksha vaults, partially for the sake of old times.

He had agreed eagerly, and so it had been decided. We should only be away for the equivalent of an Earthly week, and Shizala, loving me with a deep and abiding love which I fully reciprocated, did not object to this venture.

Now Hool Haji, the Blue Giant who had become my firmest

friend on Mars, waited above in the cabin of the airship as it swayed gently in the breeze.

Once more I kissed Shizala without speaking. There was no need for speech – we communicated with our eyes, and that was sufficient.

I began to climb the ladder into the ship.

The interior was comfortably furnished with couches of a stuff rather like red plush, and the metalwork was similar to brass and polished in the same way. There was something vaguely nostalgic and Victorian about the design and I had encouraged the motif throughout the ship. The ropes criss-crossing the gasbag, for instance, were of thick, red cord and the metal cabin had been painted in bright greens and reds, with scrollwork picked out in gold. The controls of the ship were at the front, and once again these were of the brasslike metal, enamelled in black.

I started the engine as I climbed into the seat next to Hool Haji, whose massive, blue-skinned bulk dwarfed me.

My friend watched with interest as I pulled a lever, releasing the cords which held the ship near the ground, and I began to steer her away from Varnal – not without a pang, for I knew that I should miss both Shizala and the City of Green Mists.

I did not know then that I was to be separated from them for a very long time, that circumstances were so to arrange themselves that I would face death, endure enormous discomforts and experience hideous dangers before I should see them again.

It was, however, in this slightly melancholy mood, yet with mounting excitement at the prospect of studying the Yaksha machines again, that I set course northwards. It was going to be a long journey, even in my comparatively speedy airship.

The journey to the Yaksha city in the desert was not to be without interruption, however, for on the second day of our trip the engines began to falter. I was surprised, for I trusted my engineers.

I turned to Hool Haji. My friend was looking down at the country far below. It was a predominantly yellow landscape, of great flowers similar to gigantic irises, swaying below us as if in a graceful, though monotonous, dance. Every so often the sea of yellow flowers was broken by effusions of blue or green, each splash of colour a bloom like a marigold in general appearance. Even at this distance above them, they sent up languorous scents that delighted my nostrils. Hool Haji seemed entranced by this beauty and had not even noticed the change of note in the engine.

'It looks as if we might have to land,' I informed him.

He glanced up at me. 'Why, Michael Kane? Would it not be unwise?'

'What do you mean, unwise?' I asked.

He pointed downwards.

'The flowers.'

'We could find a clearing.'

'That is not what I am trying to say. Have you not heard of the Flowers of Modnaf? They are attractive at a distance but highly dangerous when you come close to them. Their scent from here is pleasant, but when approached more closely it induces first a lethargy, then a creeping madness. Many have been trapped by these flowers and their vitality sapped, leaving them dry of everything human, to become mindless creatures wandering eventually to the Quicksands of Golana, where they are sucked down slowly and never heard of again.'

I shuddered. 'No human being should suffer such a fate!'

'But many have! And those who have survived have become little more than walking dead men.'

'Then let us steer a course away from both Modnaf and Golana and hope that our motor does not give up until they are far behind us,' I said, making up my mind to avoid the dangers below us at all costs, even if it necessitated drifting in the wind until we had passed them by.

As I nursed the engine along, Hool Haji told me the story of an old, desperate man who had once dreamed of power, one Blemplac the Mad, who was still supposed to wander below. He had imbibed so much of the scents that they no longer affected him as they did others and he had managed to survive the quicksands – because he had been their original creator. Apparently he had once been a benevolent and beneficent man who had acquired a little scientific knowledge from somewhere and had dreamed of greatness. Knowing little of what he handled, he had tried to use his knowledge to build a vast, gleaming tower that would inspire men with its beauty and grandeur. The foundations had been laid and it had seemed for a long time that he would succeed. Sadly, something had gone wrong and his mind had become affected. His experiment had gone out of control and the result was the quicksands, which had peculiar and unnatural properties found nowhere else. At length, and with a feeling of tremendous relief, we passed over the flowers and the quicksands. I had only observed the quicksands at night, by the light of the moons that hurtled above, but the glimpse was enough to tell me that Hool Haji had not exaggerated. Strange cries had risen from the slowly shifting muck below, insane ravings that sometimes seemed to be words, but I could make no sense out of them, nor did I try very hard.

By morning we were crossing a series of deep, gleaming lakes dotted with green islands and the occasional boat scudding across the vast expanse of water.

I remarked on the welcome contrast to Hool Haji and he agreed. While we had crossed the previous territory he had been more disturbed than he had admitted. I asked if it was sensible to try to land, since the engine was now working in fits and starts and was soon bound to give up altogether. He said it would be safe, for these were the islands of enlightened and intelligent folk who had the ability to entertain and delight any visitor to the lakes. He pointed out names as we passed over them. There was one lush island, set somewhat apart from the rest.

'That is an island called Drallab,' Hool Haji explained. 'Its folk have only rare contact with their neighbours, but though they appear to play little part in the activities of the other islands they exert a great artistic influence on them and are really extremely benevolent. They entertained me once, when I travelled the islands, and I enjoyed every moment of my stay.'

Another island appeared. This was a strange-looking place of peculiar contrasts for so small an island. I could make out a small forest, a mountain, a barren area and other features. This was

K'cocroom, Hool Haji informed me, an island that had only in the last few years emerged from the lake and was still largely unpopulated, though the few people who lived there seemed a folk of strange contrasts, sometimes friendly to strangers, sometimes not. We decided not to land there and passed over several other islands, with Hool Haji naming them all with great affection. There was S'Sidla, a gentle landscape of strong, straight trees and rich, dark glades, and Nosirrah, a rugged, healthy-looking place with, Hool Haji informed me, great treasures yet unmined.

I was eager to hear all this, even though part of my attention was on the engine, for everything I heard told me more about a world I had still only partially explored, and the more I knew the better I would be equipped to survive in it.

At length we had managed to nurse the airship over all the islands and saw ahead of us on the mainland – which we decided was a better place to land in case the engine proved unrepairable – a city which was called, Hool Haji told me, Cend-Amrid. The people, he said, were well known for their craftsmanship and skill with the few technical devices in circulation on Mars. They would help us more than the islanders, though the islanders were possibly more friendly.

I manipulated my controls and we began to drop down towards Cend-Amrid.

Later I was to regret not landing on one of the islands, for Hool Haji was to find Cend-Amrid changed from the place he had known when, as a wandering outcast, he had spent some time in the city.

But it was with relief in our hearts that we drifted over the city as evening came, bathing its dark towers in deep shadow.

It was a silent place and few lights burned, but I put this down to the fact that its inhabitants were a hard-working folk, according to Hool Haji, whose pleasures were simple and did not extend to any kind of night-time festivities.

We descended on the outskirts of the city and I released the grappling anchor which imbedded its sharp prongs into the earth and enabled me to climb down the ladder and secure the ropes to a couple of stunted trees that grew nearby.

Chapter Two
City of the Curse

As we walked towards Cend-Amrid, Hool Haji's hand went instinctively to his sword hilt. Knowing him so well, I recognised the gesture and found it puzzling.

'Something wrong?' I asked.

'I am not sure, my friend,' he said quietly.

'I thought you said Cend-Amrid would be a safe place for us.'

'So I thought. But I am uneasy. I cannot explain it.'

His mood conveyed itself to me and a trace of darkness clouded my brain.

Hool Haji shrugged. 'I am tired. I expect that is all it is.'

I accepted the explanation and we walked towards the gate of the city, feeling a little less perturbed.

The gate was open and no guards protected it. If the people were so generous-spirited to allow this, then this would mean we should have little difficulty in finding help.

Hool Haji, however, muttered something about this being unusual. 'They are not a gregarious folk,' he said.

Into the silent streets we walked. The tall, dark buildings seeming without a trace of life, like stage sets built for some extravagant production – and the stage seemed empty now.

Our feet echoed as we stepped along, Hool Haji leading the way towards the centre of the city.

A little later I heard something else and stopped, putting my hand on Hool Haji's arm.

We listened.

There it was – a soft footfall such as would be made by a man walking in cloth slippers or boots of very fine leather.

The sounds came towards us. Again Hool Haji's hand went instinctively to his sword hilt.

Round the corner came a figure swathed in a black cloak, folded over his head to form a rudimentary hood. He held a bunch of flowers in one hand and a large flat case in the other. 'Greetings,' I said formally, in the Martian manner. 'We are visitors to your city and seek help.'

'What help can Cend-Amrid give to any human soul?' the swathed man muttered bleakly, and there was no note of interrogation in his voice.

'We know your folk to be practical and useful when dealing with machines. We thought...' Hool Haji's statement was cut off when the man voiced a strange laugh.

'Machines! Speak not to me of machines!'

'Why so?'

'Do not stay to find out, strangers. Leave Cend-Amrid while you may!'

'Why should we not speak of machines? Has some taboo been imposed? Do the people hate machines now?' I knew that in some Earthly societies machines were feared and that popular thought rejected them since people feared their lack of humanity, that too much emphasis on automation and the like made some philosophers uneasy that human beings might become too artificial in their outlook, and that as a scientist on Earth I had sometimes encountered this attitude at parties where I had been accused of all sorts of wickedness because of my work concerning nuclear physics. I wondered if the folk of Cend-Amrid had taken this reaction to its ultimate conclusion and banned the machines some feared, and this was why I felt encouraged to ask the question.

But again the man laughed.

'No,' he said. 'People do not hate machines – unless they hate one another.'

'Your remarks are obscure,' I said impatiently. 'What is wrong?' I was beginning to think that the first man we had met in Cend-Amrid was a madman.

'I have told you,' he said – and his head turned and he glanced around him, as if he was nervous. 'Do not stay to discover what is wrong. Leave Cend-Amrid at once. Do not remain a second longer. This is the city of the curse!'

Perhaps we should have taken his advice, but we did not. We stayed to argue, and that was to be, in the short term, a mistake which we were to regret.

'Who are you?' I asked. 'Why are you the only man abroad in Cend-Amrid?'

'I am a physician,' be said. 'Or *was*!'

'You mean you have been expelled from your physician's guild?' I suggested. 'You are not allowed to practise?'

Again the laugh, infinitely bitter – a laugh that hovered on the brink of insanity.

'I have not been expelled from my guild. I am simply no longer a physician. I am known in these days as a Servicer of Grade 3 Types.'

'What are these "types" that you service? Are you a mechanic now, or what?'

'I am told to be a mechanic. I service human beings. These are the Grade 3 Types – human beings!' The words came out as a cry of misery. 'I used to be a doctor – my whole training was to give me sympathy for my patients. And now I am –' he sobbed – 'a mechanic. My job is to look at the human machine and decide if it can be made to function with minimum attention. If I decide that it cannot be made to function in this way, I must mark it down for scrapping and its parts go to a bank for use by the healthy machines.'

'But this is monstrous!'

'It *is* monstrous,' he said softly. 'And now you must leave this cursed city immediately. I have said too much.'

'But how did this situation arise?' Hool Haji asked insistently. 'When I was last in Cend-Amrid the people seemed an ordinary, practical folk – dull, perhaps, but that is all.'

'There is practicality,' replied the physician, 'and there is the human factor, the emotional factor in Man. Together they mean Man. But let one factor be encouraged and the other actively discouraged, and you have one of two ultimates – in so far as humanity is concerned.'

'What are they?' I asked, interested in this argument in spite of myself.

'You have either the Beast or the Machine,' he said simply.

'That seems an oversimplification,' I said.

'So it is. But we are dealing with a society that has become oversimplified,' he said, warming a little to his subject in spite of his nervous glances up and down the street. 'Here the Machine in Man has been encouraged and, if you like, it is the stupidity of the Beast which has encouraged it – for the Beast cannot predict and Man can. The Beast in Man leads him to create Machines for his well-being, and the Machine adds first to his comfort and then to his knowledge. In a healthy land this would all work together in the long run. But Cend-Amrid's folk cut themselves off from too much. Now Cend-Amrid is not a healthy place in any way whatsoever.'

'But something must have caused all this. Some dictator must have brought this madness to Cend-Amrid,' I said.

'The Eleven rule in Cend-Amrid – no one man dominates. But the dictator who holds sway over the city is the dictator who has always ruled mankind through the ages – unless the stories of the immortal Sheev are true.'

'You speak of Death,' I said.

'I do. And the form Death takes in Cend-Amrid is one of the most awesome.'

'What is that?'

'Disease – a plague. The dictator Death brought fear – and fear led the Eleven to their doctrine.'

'But what exactly *is* their doctrine?' Hool Haji asked.

The physician was about to reply when he suddenly drew in his breath with a hiss and began to scuttle back the way be had come.

'Go!' he whispered urgently as he fled. 'Go now!'

His fear had so affected us that we were almost ready to obey his imperative when down the long, dark street towards us came an incredible sight.

It was like a giant sedan chair, a huge box with handles on all four lower sides, borne on the shoulders of some hundred men who moved as one. I had seen armies on the move, but even the most regimented detachment of soldiers had never moved with the fantastic precision of these men carrying the great box on their shoulders.

Seated in the box and visible through the unglazed windows on the two sides that were most clearly visible to me were two men. Their faces were immobile and their bodies stiff and straight. They did not look in any way alive – just as the men who bore this strange carriage did not look alive. This was not a sight I had ever expected to see on Mars, where the human individual, no matter what battles and tensions arose in ordinary life, was respected and regimentation of the sort I now observed had hitherto seemed totally alien. Every instinct in me was outraged by the sight and tears of anger came into my eyes. Perhaps this was all instinctive then; perhaps I have rationalised my feelings since. But no matter. I was offended by the sight – deeply, emotionally and psychologically – and my reason was offended, too. What I saw was an example of the insanity the almost insane physician had spoken of. I could feel that Hool Haji, too, was offended in the same way, reacting against the sight.

Happily we are men of sense and controlled our instincts for the moment. It is a good thing to do this but a bad thing to use this control – which, as rational human beings, we have – to convince ourselves that action is never needed. We simply bided our time and I decided to learn more of this dreadful place before I began to work against it.

For work against it I was going to. That I decided, there and then. If the cost was my life and all I held dear, I swore an oath to myself that I would eradicate the corruption that had come to Cend-Amrid, not only for my own sake but for the sake of all Mars.

I did not then, as the carriage approached us, understand to what ends I would be driven in order to carry out my personal vow. I did not realise the implications of my oath.

Even if I had it would not have diverted me from my path. The decision made, the vow sworn – and I sensed Hool Haji's own personal vow sworn, because he was my friend and because I knew just how much we had in common – I stood my ground and waited for the carriage to reach us.

Reach us it did, then it stopped.

One of the men leaned forward and in a cold voice, devoid of emotion, said:

'Why you come Cend-Amrid?'

I was momentarily taken aback by the form of the question. It went so well with the dead face.

Something in me made me reply in a more flowery manner than the one which I normally employ.

'We come with open hearts to ask a favour of the folk of Cend-Amrid. We come with nothing to offer but our gratitude, to ask you for help.'

'What help?'

'We have a motor that is malfunctioning. A flying ship of my own construction with a motor of a kind unlikely to be found on Vashu.'

'What kind motor?'

'The principle is simple. I call it an internal-combustion engine – but that will mean little to you.'

'Does it work?'

'It is not working at present, and that is why we are here,' I explained, quelling my impatience. The malfunctioning engine was decreasing in importance after what I had observed in the place that the physician had so aptly termed the City of the Curse.

'Do principles work well?' asked the dead-faced man.

'Normally,' I replied.

'If it works it good, if not work then bad,' came the emotionless voice.

'Can you work?' I said angrily, hating the implications of the questions.

'Cend-Amrid work.'

'I mean – can you repair my motor?'

'Cend-Amrid do anything.'

'Will you repair my motor?'

'Cend-Amrid think will repair of motor be good for Cend-Amrid?'

'It will be good for us – and therefore ultimately good for Cend-Amrid.'

'Cend-Amrid must debate. You come.'

'I think we'd prefer to stay outside, spend the night in our ship and learn your decision in the morning.'

'No. Not good. You not known.'

I was struck by the incredibly primitive reasoning of the man who spoke and saw at once to what the physician had been referring when he mentioned the Beast creating the Machine and leaving Man out of it altogether. Perhaps, looking back, this was good for me, for I realise now exactly what my Mars means to me in logical terms. Make no mistake, the curse which had come to Cend-Amrid was even more alien to the Mars I love than it would be to Earth. And, perhaps because Mars was not prepared against the dangers inherent in Cend-Amrid, I felt that it was my duty to eradicate the disease as soon as possible.

'I think it would be best, however, if we left Cend-Amrid and waited outside,' I said. It was my intention, of course, to try to repair the motor and get back to Varnal as soon as possible, there to get help. One part of me was aware that just as I resented an intrusion on my own personal liberty, the rulers of Cend-Amrid would resent an intrusion of mine, but the decision had been taken and in my heart I knew I was right, though I decided there and then that if violence could be avoided then it would be avoided, for I am fully aware that violence produces nothing, in the end, but further violence, and to react in terms of violence is only to create more violence in the future.

The dead-faced man's reply was, in fact, an illustration of this when he said:

'No. Best for Cend-Amrid you stay. If not stay then Cend-Amrid make stay.'

'You will use force to make us stay?'

'Use many men make two men stay.'

'That sounds like force to me, my friend,' said Hool Haji with a grim smile, and his hand went to his sword. Again I stayed his arm.

'No, my friend – later, perhaps, but let us first see what we can of this place. With luck they will see no reason in not helping us. For the moment let us curb our emotions and go along with them.' I muttered this rapidly and the dead-faced man, whose partner beside him had not moved or spoken at any time, did not appear to hear.

'For the moment,' he growled.

'Only for the moment,' I assured him.

The dead-faced man said: 'Do you come?'

'We'll come,' I said.

'Follow,' he ordered, and then to the carriage-bearers, who had remained as expressionless and immobile as he and his friend, he said: 'Bearers go back to Central Place.'

Then came another horrifying and unexpected event.

Instead of turning round, the carriage-bearers began to run backwards.

Was this efficiency, even in the limited terms of the rulers of Cend-Amrid?

It was not. It was madness, pure and simple. Sight of this madness almost made me lose the control I had been fighting to maintain, but noticing Hool Haji's stance and knowing that he, too, was about to break, made me restrain him again and thus restrain myself.

In a mood of outraged horror that made me understand just why the physician had seemed insane we followed the carriage.

Chapter Three
The Eleven

THE CENTRAL PLACE had obviously been created by careful calculation of the exact centre of Cend-Amrid, then knocking down existing buildings and putting up a structure that was square and squat, contrasting unnaturally with the other buildings. The Central Place also showed signs of having been erected only recently, and I marvelled at how speedily it must have been built and at what cost – since it must have been created primarily by human labour!

The Central Place had been built by the blood of men – men subjected to a tyranny far harder to understand than that created by some power-mad dictator!

The carriage stopped and was lowered to the ground outside the main entrance – a perfect square let into the side – and from it, walking like robots, the two men descended, leading the way into the building.

Inside it was dim, poorly illuminated by simple lamps that seemed roughly the same as our oil lamps. This surprised me since most Martian peoples still use the almost everlasting artificial lighting that was one of the benefits left behind by the Sheev – the super-scientific race that had, according to legend and the little history that remained, destroyed themselves in a monstrous war many centuries earlier, leaving just a few immortals who had learned the error of their ways and rarely became involved in the affairs of men, fearing perhaps that they might repeat their errors.

I remarked on this to Hool Haji and he said that they had once had these lights, but in attempting to make more like them had taken them all to pieces and hadn't been able to put them together again.

This information added to my impression of the people of Cend-Amrid and helped me to understand why they had become what they were. In sympathising with the causes of their insanity, it did not alter one whit my intention to attempt, in the best way I could, to eradicate this insanity.

We walked behind the two into a chamber where we found nine more men, all having the same unnaturally erect bearing and immobile expression as the first two. They differed, of course, in physical appearance.

The first two took their places at a circular table where the other nine already sat. In the centre of the table, which had been hollowed out, was a grisly sight. In this place it seemed strange that it should be there – until I realised the exact significance of it.

It was a human skeleton.

A *memento mori*, in fact.

Originally – and perhaps even the Eleven had now lost sight of their original motive – it had been placed there to remind them of death. If the physician had been right, it was fear of the plague which had caused them to create this unnatural system of government.

The next thing I noticed was that there was one place short at the table. Yet if there were twelve seats around the skeleton, then where was the twelfth? For the rulers of Cend-Amrid called themselves the Eleven.

I hoped that I might find an answer to this later on.

In the same flat voice, the man I had originally spoken with told the other ten exactly what had passed between us. He made no personal comment on this and did not seem to be trying to convey anything but the precise information.

When he had finished, the others turned to regard us.

'We talk,' said the first man after a moment.

'Shall we go, so that you can decide?' I asked.

'No need. We consider factors. You here not matter.'

And then began an incredible conversation between the eleven men. Not once did anyone state an opinion depending on his own personality. To some this might sound attractive – reason ruling emotions – but to experience it was horrifying, for I suddenly realised that a man's personal point of view is necessary if any realistic conclusion is to be reached, no matter how imperfect it might seem.

To repeat the whole conversation would bore you but, in essence, they debated whether by being of use to us they could get something good for Cend-Amrid.

Finally they came to a conclusion – a conclusion which I couldn't help feeling a more balanced human being would have come to in a matter of moments. Briefly, it was this: If I would explain how an internal-combustion engine was constructed and explain, in general, how it worked, they would help me repair mine.

I knew how dangerous it could be if I started this unhealthy society on the road to real technical advancement, but I pretended to agree, knowing also that they did not have the tools necessary to build many internal-combustion engines before I could be back with help and attempt to cure the sickness that had come to Cend-Amrid.

'You show?' queried one of the eleven.

'I show,' I agreed.

'When?'

'In the morning.'

'Morning. Yes.'

'Can we now return to our airship?'

'No.'

'Why not?'

'You stay, you not stay. We not know. So you stay here.'

I shrugged. 'Very well. Then perhaps we can sleep somewhere until the morning.' At least, I thought, we could conserve our energy until we had decided how to act.

'Yes.'

'Is there an inn we could stay at?'

'Yes, but you not stay there.'

'Why not? You could guard it if you didn't trust us.'

'Yes, but you die, not die. We not know. So you stay here.'

'Why might we die?'

'Plague make die.'

I understood. They did not want us to become infected with the plague, which still held sway, we gathered, in the city. This place was better protected, perhaps, than the rest of the city.

We agreed to stay.

The first man then led us out of the chamber and down a short passageway, at the end of which a flight of steps ran downwards into the cellars of the Central Place.

We descended the steps and came to another passage with many doors on both sides. They looked suspiciously like a row of cells in a prison.

I asked the man what they were.

'Malfunctioning heads kept here,' he told me.

I knew then that this was probably where the people who were still useful to Cend-Amrid, in the city's terms, but who had been judged insane, again in the city's terms, were imprisoned.

Presumably we were thought to be in this class. So long as they did not remove our weapons I was willing to let them lock us up for the night if, by allowing this, we could eventually get our motor repaired and make the journey back to Varnal, there to decide how best we could overcome the double curse lying on Cend-Amrid – the curse of physical and mental disease. A combination, I could not help thinking, that was rare on Mars – where disease is rare – but far less so on Earth. Another thing I could not help considering was whether, if there had been more disease on Mars, the people would be the same. I concluded that they would not have been. I think I am right.

I am a scientist, I know, but I am not a philosophical man – I prefer action to thought. But the example of Cend-Amrid affected me deeply and I feel I must take pains to explain just why I prefer the society of Mars to the society of Earth. Mars, of course, is not perfect – and perhaps it is partially why I have found my true home on Mars. For there the people have learned the lesson of trying too hard for perfection. There, on the whole, they have learned the great lesson – to respect the human individual above all things. Not merely to respect the strong but to respect the weak as well, for the strengths and the weaknesses are, to a great extent, in us all. It is circumstance more than anything else which creates the one we would term weak or the one we would term strong.

This was another part of the reason why I so hated what the men of Cend-Amrid had become.

In the end, perhaps, it was to resolve itself into a matter of wits and swordplay. But you must know that my mind was at work before my sword-arm.

And if Mars is a preferable place to Earth you must understand why. The reason is this: Circumstances are kinder to Mars than Earth. There is little disease on the planet and the population is small enough to allow every man the chance of becoming himself.

The dead-faced man now opened a door and stood back to allow us to enter.

I was surprised to see another inhabitant of the small cell, which was fitted with four bunks. He was unlike the Eleven, but there was something about his haunted eyes that made me think of the physician we had first met.

'He not good for others here,' said the dead-faced man, 'but this only place for you. Not talk to him.'

We said nothing as we entered the cell and watched the door close on us. We heard a bar drop and knew we were imprisoned. Only the fact that we still had our weapons comforted us.

'Who are you?' asked our cell-mate when the footfalls of the other man had died. 'Why has Six imprisoned you and let you keep your swords?'

'He was Six, was he?' I smiled. 'We were never introduced.'

The man got up and came towards me angrily. 'You laugh – at *that*?' He pointed towards the door. 'Have you no understanding of what you are laughing at?'

I became serious. 'Of course,' I said, 'but it seems to me that if action is to be taken against *that* –' I nodded in the direction he had pointed – 'we must keep our heads and not become as mad, in our own way, as those we intend to fight.'

He looked searchingly into my face and then cast his glance to the floor, nodding to himself.

'Perhaps you are right,' he said. 'Perhaps that is where I went wrong in the end.'

I introduced my friend and myself. 'This is Hool Haji, King of the Mendishar in the far North; and I am Michael Kane, Prince of Varnal, which lies to the South.'

'Strange friends,' he said, looking up. 'I thought the folk of the South and the Blue Giants were hereditary enemies.'

'Things aren't quite so bad now,' I said. 'But who are you and why are you here?'

'I am One,' he said, 'and I am here because of that, if you like.'

'You mean you are the missing member of the council which rules Cend-Amrid?'

'Just so. More – I formed the council. Have you seen where they sit?'

'A bizarre place – yes.'

'I put the skeleton in the centre of the table. It was meant to be a constant reminder of what we fought against – this horrible plague which still ravages the city.'

'But what caused the plague? I have heard of no deadly disease on Vashu.'

'We caused it – indirectly. We found an ancient canister not far from the outskirts of the city. It was so old that it was obviously a creation of the Sheev or the Yaksha. It took us many months before we got it open.'

'What was inside?' Hool Haji asked curiously.

'Nothing – we thought.'

'Just air?' Hool Haji said, unbelievingly.

'Not just air – the plague. It had been there all the time. In our foolishness we released it.'

Hool Haji nodded now. 'Yes, I remember half a story,' he said. 'Something about how, in their war of self-destruction, the Sheev and the Yaksha used diseases which they somehow managed to trap and release on their enemies. That must be what you found.'

'So we discovered – and at what cost!' The man who had called himself One went and sat down on his bunk, his head in his hands.

'But what happened then?'

'I was a member of the council governing Cend-Amrid. I decided that in order to control the plague we must have a logical system. I decided – and, believe me, it was not a decision that I enjoyed reaching – that until the plague was wiped out we must regard every human being simply as a machine, otherwise the plague would spread everywhere. If the plague did not affect the person very badly – and its effects vary, you know – then he could be considered a potentially functioning mechanism. If the plague affected him badly, then he was to be regarded as a useless mechanism, and thus to be destroyed, his useful parts to be stored in case they could contribute to a functioning, or potentially functioning, mechanism.'

'But such a concept suggests that you have a much more sophisticated form of surgery than your society indicates,' I said.

'We have the Sheev device. An arm, a hand, a vital organ may be inserted or attached where it should be in the human body, and then the Sheev machine is switched on. Some kind of force flows out of the machine – and knits the parts together.' The man spoke wonderingly, as if I should have known this.

Hool Haji broke in. 'I have heard of such a machine,' he said, 'but I had no idea that one existed in Cend-Amrid.'

'We kept it a secret from other folk,' said the man. 'We are inclined to be a secretive people, as you might know.'

'I knew that,' Hool Haji agreed. 'But I did not realise to what extent you guarded your secrets.'

'Perhaps if we had not been so secretive,' said One, 'we should not be in this position today.'

'It is hard to say,' I told him. 'But why are you now in prison?'

'Because I saw that my reasoning had produced something as dangerous as the plague,' he replied. 'I tried to reverse the course on which I had embarked, tried to steer us all back to sanity. It was too late.'

I sympathised with him. 'But they did not kill you. Why?'

'Because, I suppose, of my mind. In their own strange way they still respect intelligence – or, at least, intelligence of a certain kind. I don't think that will last.'

Neither did I. I was moved to loathe and at the same time sympathise with the tragic man who sat on the bunk before me. But sympathy got the upper hand, though I privately cursed him for a fool. Like others before him, on Earth and on Mars, he had become victim of the monster he had created. 'Did it not occur to you,' I said, 'that if the ancient people – the Sheev or the Yaksha – could devise this plague-canister, they might also have had another device that could cure the plague?'

'Naturally, it occurred to me,' said One, looking up, offended. 'But does it still exist? If so, where is it? How do you contact the Sheev?'

'No-one knows,' Hool Haji said. 'They come and they go.'

'Surely it must be possible,' I said, looking at Hool Haji quickly, wondering if the same thought had struck him, 'to discover this device – if it still exists.'

Hool Haji looked up, his eyes lighting. 'You are thinking of the place we were originally destined for, are you not?'

'I am,' I said.

'Of course. Cure the plague – then cure the madness!'

'Exactly.'

One was looking at us wonderingly, obviously utterly unaware of what we were talking about. I thought it expedient at this stage not to tell him of the treasure house of machines that lay hidden in the vaults of the Yaksha. Indeed, by mutual consent earlier, Hool Haji and I had agreed that the place should be secret and that only the minimum of trusted people should be told where it was. In this, we shared the apparent anxiety of the Sheev, feeling that there was a danger inherent in releasing such knowledge all at once. If the Sheev took the benevolent interest in humanity that I believed they did, then they were obviously waiting for the society on Mars to mature thoroughly before allowing them the benefits of the previous society which had destroyed itself.

One asked: 'What are you saying? That there is a chance of finding a cure for the plague?'

'Just so.'

'Where? And how?'

'We cannot say,' I told him. 'But if we manage to get away from Cend-Amrid, and if we do find such a machine, I assure you we shall be back.'

'Very well,' he said. 'I accept this. You offer hope, at least, when I had thought all hope had gone.'

'Tell us your real name,' I said. 'And restore a little hope in yourself.'

'Barane Dasa,' he said, rising again and speaking a little more levelly. 'Barane Dasa, Master Smith of Cend-Amrid.'

'Then wish us well and wish us luck, Barane Dasa,' I said, 'and hope that the Eleven will be able to help us repair our engine.'

'We understand machines in Cend-Amrid,' he said with something like a former pride coming into his eyes. 'It will be repaired.'

'Perhaps you did not understand them quite enough,' I reminded him.

He pursed his lips. 'Perhaps we did not make enough distinction between the machines we loved and the people we also loved,' he said.

'It is a distinction we should always make,' I told him. 'But it does not mean we should reject the machines altogether. Distinctions are useful, rejections are not so useful, for the distinction comes from a love of knowledge while rejection of something comes from a fear of it, when all's said and done.'

'I will think about that,' he said, a faint smile touching his lips, 'but I will think for some time before I decide whether or not to agree with you.'

'It is all we should ask,' I replied, returning his smile.

Then we went to sleep, Hool Haji stretching himself out on the floor of the cell, since the bunks were not designed for ten-foot-high Blue Giants!

Chapter Four
Flight from Cend-Amrid

In the morning, soon after the sun had risen, we all went out to look at the engine – Hool Haji, myself, and the Eleven. I had learned from Barane Dasa that every member of the council had been at the top of his particular trade before the coming of the plague and understood that these were the best people to put the engine right if anyone could.

I brought the airship right down to the ground and stripped off the plates covering the engine housing. I could see almost immediately that the trouble was simple and swore at myself for a fool. The fuel pipe was in several sections and one of these had come loose. Somehow a piece of rag – perhaps overlooked by a mechanic – had worked its way into the pipe and was clogging it.

It is invariably the simple explanation that one ignores. I had assumed – quite fairly, since the mechanics I had trained in Varnal were normally very trustworthy and conscientious – that something was intrinsically wrong with the engine.

Still, I had found Cend-Amrid because of this mistake, and it was probably just as well, since I now had the chance to do something about it. It was not only the good of Cend-Amrid that I had at heart, but the good of the whole of Mars. I knew that both disease and creed could spread, in much the same way that the Black Death and Black Magic had been linked in the Middle Ages, and I wished to counter this at any cost.

I thought it expedient, however, to pretend that there was still something wrong with the engine and allowed the Eleven to inspect it, their faces as blank as ever, while I drew up the plans I had promised them. I was fairly certain that whatever fuel source they used, it would not be sufficiently sophisticated to allow them to get very far before I returned, since even steam-power was only understood by them in elementary terms. This, of course, made them very different from the rest of the folk of Mars, who had never bothered themselves with physics, save the theoretical kind, since the Sheev machines were highly sophisticated and, to them, beyond understanding. Once again I could sympathise with the folk of Cend-Amrid, but still felt that the situation existing throughout the rest of Mars to my knowledge was, in the end, for the best.

In short, curiosity only sometimes kills the cat, and then it usually happens because the cat hasn't found its feet properly.

I felt better for the knowledge that I could now leave Cend-Amrid without too much difficulty and watched for some sign of puzzlement on the faces of the Eleven as they studied my drawings.

There was none. The only impression I received from them was an impression of their confidence in themselves.

Inevitably, they came to ask me about the fuel and I showed them some of the gasolene which I had had refined in Varnal. I would point out that the Varnalians themselves did not really understand anything of the principles behind the engines I used for the airships, just as they did not understand the much more complicated principles behind the original Sheev engine I had used to power my first airship. This again, I felt, was at the moment for the best.

One of the Eleven – he called himself Nine – asked me about gasolene and where it could be found.

'It is not like this in its natural state,' I told him.

'What is it like in natural state?' came the emotionless question.

'That is difficult to say.'

'You come back Cend-Amrid and show. We have many liquids we keep from old discoveries.'

Doubtless he meant that they had found other things left behind by the Sheev and preserved them in one way or another.

Now my curiosity got the better of me and I did not wish to miss the chance of seeing these 'liquids' that Nine mentioned. I agreed to go back.

Leaving Hool Haji in the ship, I returned with the entire Eleven to their laboratory building which lay just behind the Central Place. By daylight it was possible to see evidence of the plague everywhere. Carts creaked through the streets, loaded with corpses. But whereas one would have expected to see signs of grief on the faces of those who lived, there were few. The Eleven's tyranny did not allow such – to them – inefficient emotions as grief or joy. I gathered that signs of emotion were regarded either as indications of 'insanity' or that the plague had infected another victim. I shuddered more at this than I would have done had anyone shown a sign of grief.

The Eleven showed me all the chemicals they had discovered amongst the ruins of Sheev cities, but I told them that none was anything like gasolene – although I lied.

They asked me to leave a little gasolene with them, and I agreed. I intended to make sure, however, that it would not work when they tried it.

I had refused to be borne in one of their dreadful carriages, and so we walked back the way we had come.

This, although they did not show it, seemed distasteful to the Eleven and I realised exactly why when one of them paused. At the end of the street we were walking down I saw a man stagger from a house and come stumbling towards us.

There was bloody foam on his lips and his face had a greenish patch coming up from his neck to his nose. One arm seemed paralysed and useless, the other waved about as if he was trying to keep his balance. He saw us and an inarticulate cry came from his lips. His eyes were fever-bright and hatred shone from them.

As he drew close to the Eleven he shouted: 'What have you done? What have you done?'

The Eleven turned as one man, leaving only myself to face the plague-stricken wretch.

But he ignored me and ran towards them.

'*What have you done!*' he screeched again.

'Words mean nothing. Cannot answer,' Nine replied.

'You are guilty! You released the plague. You imposed this wicked government upon us! Why will so few realise this?'

'Inefficient,' came the cold, dead voice of Six.

Then, from the same doorway, a girl came running. She was pretty, about eighteen, and dressed in the normal Martian harness. Her brown hair was in disarray and her face was streaked with tears.

'Father!' she shouted, running towards the wretch.

'Go away, Ala Mara,' he cried. 'Go away – I am going to die. Let me use the little life left in me to protest to these tyrants. Let me try to make them feel something human – even if it's only hatred!'

'No, Father!' The girl began to pull at his arm.

I spoke to her. 'I sympathise with you both,' I said. 'But wait a little longer. I might be able to help.'

One of the Eleven – I believe he called himself Three – turned. There was a dart gun in his hand. Without even blinking, he pulled the trigger. The things only worked at short range – and this was almost point-blank. The man fell with a groan.

The girl gave a great shriek and began to hammer at Three's chest with her fists.

'You've killed him. You might at least have left him the little life he had!' she sobbed in rage.

'Inefficient,' said Three. 'You inefficient, too.' He raised the gun.

I could stand no more.

With a wordless cry I leapt at him, knocking the gun from his hand and putting my arm around the girl.

I said nothing.

He said nothing.

We simply stood there regarding each other silently as the other ten members of the council turned.

With my free hand I drew my sword.

'A dead man is the most inefficient of all,' I said. 'And I can make several of you that if you move a step.'

The girl was now weeping with reaction and my heart went out to her now even more than it had done before.

'Do not worry, Ala Mara,' I said, remembering the name her dead father had used. 'They will not harm you.'

Now the furthest away from me put a whistle to his lips, ignoring my threat. Its note pierced the air and I knew that the whistle was intended to summon guards.

Heaving the girl onto my shoulder, I began to dash down the street. I knew that the gate was around the next bend and that if I could put enough distance between myself and the Eleven fast enough their dart guns could not harm me.

I ran panting around the corner and rushed towards the open gate.

Guards were coming at me as I went through the gate and I prayed that I could reach the waiting airship before all was lost.

Hool Haji must have seen me being chased by the guards because he suddenly appeared at the entrance to the airship's cabin. I half flung the girl at him and turned just in time to engage the first couple of swordsmen.

They were inexpert with their weapons and I easily defended myself at first. But soon others joined the fight and I would have been hard-pressed had not Hool Haji's massive bulk dropped down beside me.

Together we held them off until several lay dead or wounded on the ground.

Hool Haji muttered to me: 'Get aboard. I'll join you at once.'

Still fighting, I managed to clamber into the cabin.

Hool Haji made one last thrust, killing a guard and, in that split-second lull in the fighting, jumped into the cabin.

I was ready with the door and slammed it shut. Leaving Hool Haji to bolt it, I went past the still-frightened girl and seated myself at my airship's controls.

It was only a matter of moments before the engine roared into powerful life. I released the anchor ropes and we were soon rising into the air.

'What now?' Hool Haji asked, glancing at the girl as he seated himself in his specially large chair.

'I am tempted to return at once to Varnal,' I said, 'and get the taste of that place out of my mouth before doing anything more. But it would probably be best to go at once to the vaults of the Yaksha and see if we can find a machine to cure the plague. Better yet – if we could contact the Sheev, they might help.'

'The Sheev involve themselves rarely in our affairs,' Hool Haji reminded me.

'But if they *knew*!'

'Perhaps they do.'

'Very well,' I said. 'We go to Yaksha. Perhaps there we will also find a means of contacting the Sheev.'

'What about the girl?' Hool Haji asked.

'There is nothing for it but to take her with us,' I said, 'after all, in helping her in the first place I have made her my responsibility.'

'And mine, my friend.' Hool Haji smiled, gripping my shoulder.

From behind us, Ala Mara said weakly: 'I thank you, strangers. But if I am to be any trouble to you, put me down where you will. You have done enough.'

'Nonsense,' I said, setting course for the North and Yaksha. 'I want to be able eventually to return you to Cend-Amrid – and when we do return it will be with some effective means of destroying both the tyrannies that dwell there.'

Perhaps moved by this, and obviously remembering the death of her father, the girl began to sob again. I, too, found it hard to remain completely unaffected by her emotion and it was a long time before I could begin to work out what method I was going to use to find the machine that could cure the plague – assuming that it existed in Yaksha at all!

It would be several days yet before our destination would be reached. And in that time I would have to train myself to think very coolly indeed.

I did not know then, of course, just what was in store for me. If I had, I might have returned to Varnal.

As it was, things were to complicate themselves even more and I was going to find myself in desperate straits soon enough – as were we all!

Chapter Five
The Barbarians

AT LAST WE were crossing the desert, having decided not to visit Mendishar, Hool Haji's homeland, on our way back. This was partly my friend's decision, since he explained he had only recently left there and was sure that there was little to concern him at present.

We dropped down just outside the entrance we had cleared earlier. We secured the airship, leaving Ala Mara in charge of it.

At the entrance, which had been covered with a great sheet of non-corrosive metal alloy which we had found earlier, we saw signs that it had been disturbed.

Hool Haji pointed at the ground.

'Men have been here since we last left,' he said. 'Here are footmarks – and there signs that heavy objects have been dragged over the ground. What do you make of it, Michael Kane?'

I frowned. 'No more than you at this stage. We had best enter carefully. Perhaps inside we shall discover signs of the identity of the strangers. Who would have been likely to come here?'

Hool Haji shook his head. 'The footprints show that they were not folk of my race but of yours – and yet no small ones dwell in these parts. They must have come from afar.'

We lifted the covering and passed into the cool interior. It was illuminated by the seemingly everlasting lights of the ancient race.

We had made wooden steps on our last visit, and these were now chipped and battered, again indicating that heavy objects had been dragged up them.

As we progressed further into the vaults of the Yaksha, we gasped in anger at the destruction we saw. Machines had been overturned and smashed, jars of chemicals had been spilt and broken, artefacts of all kinds had been partially destroyed.

On we went, through the many chambers of the underground city, finding further evidence of insensate vandalism, until we stepped into a particularly large chamber and found it almost empty. I remembered that the place had contained many of the most interesting machines of the Yaksha, machines which would have produced much interesting knowledge when I got round to investigating them. But they were gone!

Where were they?

I could not guess.

Just then my ears caught the sound of movement ahead of us and I drew my sword, Hool Haji following suit.

We had just done this when, from the opposite entrance to the one we had entered, a number of men came running, brandishing swords in their hands, round shields of crudely beaten metal on their arms.

The thing that struck me most about them, however, was the fact that they were all bearded. Almost everyone I had seen on Mars was clean-shaven.

These men were squat, muscular, with heavy leather harness completely unadorned. Their only decorations were necklaces and bangles of hammered metal, something like iron, though a few wore what appeared in that light to be gold or brass.

They came to a ragged halt as we prepared to meet them, our swords at the ready.

One of them, a squint-eyed individual even hairier than most of the others, cocked his head to one side and said in a harsh, insolent voice:

'Who are you? What are you doing here? These are our looting grounds. We found 'em first.'

'Did you, indeed?' I replied.

'Yes, we did. You're a funny pair to be here together. I thought you Blue Giants were always fighting people like us.'

'People like you need to be fought, judging by what you have done to this place,' Hool Haji said in a tone of distaste.

'I mean people like *him*, too,' said the bearded one, waving his sword in my direction.

'That is beside the point,' I said impatiently. 'What is more to the point is – who are *you*?'

'None of your business!'

'We can make it our business!' Hool Haji growled.

The bearded man laughed harshly and arrogantly. 'Oh, can you? Well, you can try if you like. We're the Bagarad, and Rokin the Gold's our leader. We're the fiercest fighters on both sides of the Western sea.'

'So you come from over the Western sea,' I said.

'You've heard of us?'

I shook my head but Hool Haji said: 'The Bagarad – I've heard a little of you from my father. Barbarians – looters – raiders from the land beyond the Western sea.'

I had only visited the Western continent once, and then by accident, when I had encountered the strange City of the Spider and Hool Haji and I had barely escaped with our lives. So these, too, were from that mysterious continent, unexplored by most civilised Martian nations.

'Barbarians!' Again the man voiced his guttural laugh. 'Maybe – but we'll soon be conquerors of the world!'

'How so?' I asked, a suspicion dawning.

'Because we have weapons – weapons undreamed of by human beings. The weapons of the gods who once dwelled here!'

'They were no gods,' I said. 'Pitiful demons, perhaps.'

The man frowned. 'What do you know of the gods?'

'I told you – those who built this city-vault were not gods, they were simply men.'

'You talk heresy, smoothskin,' the barbarian growled. 'Watch your step. Who are you, anyway?'

'I am Michael Kane, Bradhinak of Varnal.'

'A Bradhinak, eh? Hmmm – could get good ransom for you, eh?'

'Doubtless,' I said coldly. 'But it would be ransom for a corpse, for I'd die fighting rather than have hands such as yours laid on me.'

The barbarian grinned, enjoying the insult for its own sake. 'And who's the other?'

'I am Bradhi Hool Haji of Mendishar, and I need not repeat my friend's words, since they are the same as mine would be.' Hool Haji shifted his stance slightly.

The barbarian lowered his squinting gaze thoughtfully.

'Well, well. Two good prizes if we can get you alive, aren't you? I'm Zonorn the Render – my name well-earned. I've torn men limb from limb in my time.'

'A useful accomplishment,' I said mockingly.

His face became serious. 'Aye, it is – where the Bagarad rule. Nobody dare spit in Zonorn's eye – save the only man stronger than me.'

'The way you speak, there isn't one,' I said.

'I'm talking about our own Bradhi – Rokin the Gold. You can insult me and I'll judge the insult on its merits. Only if it's a weak one I'll complain. But say a word against Rokin – a true War Bradhi – and I'll tear you apart. I need no sword or shield when I deal with a man.'

'So you, under Rokin's orders, have stolen the machines. Is that it?'

'That's it, roughly.'

'Where are the machines now? Still on this side of the Western ocean?'

'Some are, some aren't.'

'You are fools to tamper with them, you know. They could destroy you as easily as they could those you plan to use them against.'

'Don't try to worry me with talk like that,' Zonorn rasped. 'We know what we're doing. Never call a man of the Bagarad a fool until you look for your beard.' He burst into laughter, obviously enjoying what was a common jest amongst his people.

'I have no beard,' I reminded him. 'And you would be wise if you returned what you have stolen. You cannot understand the implications of what you have done, nor would you understand them if I explained them to you.'

'We're not afraid of you,' he muttered. 'And we're not afraid of your big friend. There are a lot of us – and we're the best fighters any side of the ocean.'

'Then we'll bargain,' I said.

'What's the bargain?'

'If we beat you in fair fight, you bring back the weapons.' I thought this would probably appeal to his simple, barbaric instincts.

'Can't do that,' he said, shaking his head as if disappointed. 'Rokin would have to decide anything of that sort.'

'Then what do we do?'

'I'm a fair man,' Zonorn said thoughtfully. 'And we're under-strength at present. I'll let you go. How's that?'

'You're afraid to fight us, is that it?' Hool Haji laughed, hefting his sword.

It was the wrong thing to have said.

If Zonorn had let us go we could have returned with a force of Mendishar to stop them before they embarked in their ships for the Western continent.

But Hool Haji had attacked Zonorn's barbarian pride.

It could only be settled in blood now.

With a roar of anger, Zonorn was already rushing at Hool Haji.

His men came at us, too.

Soon the pair of us were fighting several whirling blades apiece. The barbarians were hardy, powerful fighters, but lacked finesse in their swordplay.

It was fairly easy to defend ourselves, even against so many, but we both knew we should be killed very soon unless we were remarkably lucky.

Our backs were against the wall as we fought, and our blades were soon stained from tip to hilt with the blood of our attackers.

I dodged a clumsy thrust and stabbed over a shield rim, taking my assailant in the throat. It was only when I had killed him and was already engaged with another opponent, that I realised I had killed Zonorn himself.

Alter a time my sword-arm began to ache, but I fought on desperately, knowing that there was much more at stake in this fight than our own lives.

The fate of Cend-Amrid was in the balance. Perhaps even the fate of the whole of Mars.

We had to find the right machine, either in the vaults or in the possession of the untutored barbarian who called himself Rokin the Gold.

I blocked a blow from above and was half winded when my attacker shoved at my chest with his shield.

I slid my sword down to his hilt, suddenly disengaged and then thrust forward again, contriving to take him in the heart.

Yet it seemed that as fast as we killed them there were others to take their places and, as usual, I soon lost all thought of anything but the fight. I became, for all that I loathed it, a fighting machine myself, my whole attention focused on preserving my life, even though it meant taking so many other lives in the process.

For all my fine ideas, when it came down to it I was as much a killer as others I despised for that reason.

I say this only to show that I do not enjoy killing and avoid it where I can, even on Mars – that warlike world.

On and on we fought, until all sense of time was lost and it seemed, over and over again, that we escaped death by a hair's breadth.

But it seemed at last that our assailants were tiring, too. I saw a break and decided that, in this case, we would serve our purpose best if we tried to escape.

With a roar to Hool Haji, I dived through the gap, seeing from the corner of my eye that he was following me.

Then, from somewhere in the shadows, I saw another man dart at Hool Haji's side. I knew instinctively that Hool Haji would not see him in time.

With a yell of warning I turned to save him. I turned too sharply and lost my footing in slippery blood.

I remember a grinning, bearded face and a shield smashing forward into my own.

I tried to keep a grip on my senses, struggled to rise. I saw Hool Haji clutch at his side, grimacing with pain. Then my vision clouded.

I fell forward, certain that I would never wake again.

Chapter Six
Rokin the Gold

I DID WAKE again, but it was not a comfortable awakening. I was being jolted along on the back of an animal.

Opening my eyes, blinking in the glare of harsh sunlight, I saw that I was tied hand and foot, strapped over the back of a large *dahara*, the universal riding animal and pack beast of all the Martians I had ever encountered.

The sun was shining directly in my eyes, I had a headache and every muscle in my body ached. But I seemed generally in one piece.

I wondered what had become of Hool Haji.

And then I wondered what had happened to Ala Mara, whom we had left in charge of the airship.

I prayed that the coarse barbarians had not discovered her.

I closed my eyes against the sunlight, beginning to think of ways of escaping from my captors, ways of finding the machine – if it existed – for curing the plague in Cend-Amrid. I was so tired that it was difficult to think logically.

The next time I opened my eyes I was staring into the leering face of a barbarian.

'So you live.' He grinned. 'I thought you Southern folk weak – but we learned otherwise back there.'

'Give me a sword and untie my hands and you'll learn that lesson personally,' I said thickly.

He shook his head wonderingly. 'Give you a beard and you could be a Bagarad. I think Rokin the Gold will like you.'

'Where are we going?'

'To see Rokin.'

'What happened to my friend?' I deliberately did not mention the girl.

'He lives, too – though he got a slight flesh wound.' We were still moving as he spoke – he was riding a dahara. I was filled with relief that Hool Haji had survived.

'We could not find your daharas,' said the barbarian. 'How did you get here?' I was further relieved on hearing this question, because it meant they had not discovered Ala Mara. But where was she? Why had they not noticed the airship? I tried to reply in a way that would answer these questions for me, at least partially.

'We had an air vessel,' I said. 'We flew here.'

The barbarian guffawed.

'You've got guts,' he said. 'You can lie like a Bagarad as well as fight like one.'

'You saw no airship?'

He grinned. 'We saw no airship. You call us barbarians, my friend, but even we know enough not to believe in children's stories. Everyone knows that men aren't meant to fly – and can't, therefore.'

I smiled weakly back. He did not know that I smiled at his naïveté and because this certainly meant they had not seen either my airship or Ala Mara. But I still wondered what had happened to the girl.

Perhaps the airship had somehow drifted away. I could not guess. I could only hope that both were safe.

After a while my exhaustion caused me to fall asleep in spite of the rough ride I was having.

When next I awoke it was dark and the dahara was moving at a slower pace.

Above the murmur of the barbarians' conversation I heard another murmur – the murmur of the sea.

With a sinking heart I realised that we had come to the barbarians' base and I was soon to face their much admired leader, Rokin the Gold.

The dahara stopped after a while and heavy hands hauled the straps away from my body and dumped me on the ground. One of the barbarians, perhaps the one I had spoken to earlier, put a skin of tepid water to my lips and I drank thirstily.

'Food soon,' he promised. 'After you've been looked over by Rokin.'

He went away and I lay on hard shingle, listening to the nearby sounds of the sea. I was still half in a daze.

Later I heard voices and there was a thump. I turned my head and saw the great bulk of Hool Haji lying beside me. I noticed his wound and saw that at least the barbarians had had the grace to dress it, though crudely.

He turned his head and smiled at me grimly.

'At least we live,' he said.

'But for how long?' I said. 'And will it be worth it? We must escape as soon as possible, Hool Haji. You know why!'

'I know,' he said evenly. 'Thoughts of escape are well in my mind. But at present we can only bide our time. What of the girl you rescued from Cend-Amrid – where is she?'

'Safe, as far as I know,' I told him. 'Or, at least, she was not captured by the barbarians.'

'Good. How did you discover this?'

I told him the little I had learned.

'Perhaps she saw something of what happened and went for help,' he said, though clearly not convinced.

'She could not operate the controls unless she had watched me very carefully indeed. I can think of no explanation. I just hope that she will be all right.'

'Have you noticed one thing?' Hool Haji asked then. 'The one real chance we have?'

'What's that?'

'The secret skinning knife is still in my harness.'

That was something! All blue Martians carry small knives hidden in their ornate war-harness. To someone not used to looking for such things, it seemed part of the general decoration of the harness, but I had had cause to thank those secret knives once before. Unfortunately, I now wore a Southern-style harness that did not contain a knife. Still, one was better than none. If I could reach it with my teeth, I might be able to cut Hool Haji's bonds.

I was rolling towards him with this intention when suddenly there came a sound from above. I rolled back and looked up.

Framed against the sky, which was lit only by Phobos, I saw a gigantic figure, clad all in bright metal. The metal was gold, crudely fashioned into armour, with great, bent rivets plainly visible, holding it all together. It was a splendid picture of barbarian grandiose ostentation, and the man wore it well enough. He had a finely combed yellow beard and hair to match, long and flowing and plainly cleaner than that of his fellows. At his hip he wore a huge broadsword, the hilt of which he gripped as he looked down at me, a vast grin spreading across his face.

'Which are *you*,' he said in a deep, humorous voice, 'the Bradhi or the Bradhinak?'

'Which are you?' I said, though I guessed the obvious.

'Bradhi, my friend, as you well know if you've talked as much to my men as they say. Bradhi Rokin the Gold, leader of these hounds, the Bagarad. Now – be civil and answer me.'

'I am the Bradhinak Michael Kane of Varnal, City of the Green Mists, most beautiful in the whole of Vashu.' I spoke as grandiosely, using the Martian word for their planet.

He grinned again. 'And you – the other one. You must be the Bradhi, then, eh?'

'Bradhi of a long line,' Hool Haji said proudly. 'Bradhi of the Mendishar – there is no greater boast.'

'You think not, eh?'

Hool Haji did not reply. He looked at Rokin with an unblinking stare.

Rokin did not seem to mind.

'You killed a lot of my men, I'm told, including my finest lieutenant, Zonorn the Render. I thought him unkillable.'

'It was easy,' I said. 'It was incidental. I did not realise he was one of those I killed until after I had done it.'

Rokin roared with laughter. 'What a boaster! Better than a Bagarad!'

'Some, I've been told,' I said. 'It is not difficult to believe if they are all like Zonorn.'

He frowned a little, though he still grinned, pointing at me, his golden armour creaking at the joints. 'You think so? You'll find there are few to beat the Bagarad.'

'Few what?'

'Eh? What d'you mean?'

'Few what? Children?'

'No! Men, my friend!' His face cleared. Like many primitive people he seemed to appreciate an insult for its own sake, whether levelled at him or not. I knew, however, that there was a point that could be overstepped and it was not always easy to see it. I did not bother to worry about it.

'What are you going to do with us now?' I asked him.

'I'm not sure. They say you seemed concerned about the weapons I've removed from that place we found. What do you know about them?'

'Nothing,' I said.

'They say you seemed to know a great deal about them.'

'Then they were wrong.'

'Tell him to give them back,' growled Hool Haji. 'Tell him what we told his friend – they're fools to meddle with such power!'

'So you do know something.' Rokin mused. 'How much?'

'We only know that to tamper with them will mean death for you all, at the very least. It could mean the destruction of half of Vashu!'

'Do not try to frighten me with such threats,' Rokin smiled. 'I am no little boy to be told what is bad for me and what is good.'

'In this case,' I said urgently, 'you are as the smallest child. And these are no toys you are playing with!'

'I know that, my friend. They are weapons. Weapons that will win me half Vashu if I use them well.'

'Forget about them!' I said.

'Nonsense. Why should I?'

'For one thing,' I told him, 'there is a plague in a city some distance from here. One of the machines you have might be capable of checking it. If it is not checked it must soon escape the confines of the city and begin to spread. Do you know what a plague is? A disease?'

'Well, I've had one or two complaints myself – so have others I know. I was coughing for a couple of days when I lost myself swimming in the ocean when I was a lad. Is that what you mean?'

'No.' I described the symptoms of the green plague that was destroying the folk of Cend-Amrid.

He looked rather green himself when I had finished. 'Are you sure it's that bad?' he said.

'It is,' I said. 'What would you think if something like that swept throughout this continent, eventually spreading to your own?'

'How can it "spread"?' he said unbelievingly.

I tried to explain about germs and microbes, but it meant nothing to him. All I succeeded in doing was weakening my case and leaving him shaking his head.

'What a liar! What a liar!' he repeated. 'Little creatures in our blood! Ho! Ho! Ho! You must be a Bagarad. You must have been stolen from us as a baby!'

'Believe what I tell you about the plague or not,' I said desperately. 'But believe its effects, at least – even Rokin the Gold is not safe from it.'

He tapped his armour. 'This is gold – it protects me from anything – man or magic!'

'You seem to respect us,' I said. 'Then will you release us?'

He shook his head. 'No.' He grinned. 'I think we'll find you useful – if only for ransom.'

It was impossible, plainly, to reach the barbarian by appealing to his reason. There was nothing for it but to hope we could make an early escape, after seeing just what machines he had stolen and, if possible, making sure he could never use them. This gave rise to another thought.

'What if I can help with the machines?' I said. 'Would you release us then?'

'Perhaps,' he said, nodding thoughtfully. 'If I decided to trust you.'

'I am a scientist,' I informed him. 'I might throw in my lot with you if you made it worth my while.'

This line of attack seemed to be getting better results, for he rubbed his jaw and nodded again.

'I'll think about all this,' he said, 'and talk to you again in the morning.' He turned and began to stride down the beach. 'I'll have some food sent to you,' he called, as an afterthought.

The food was brought and it was not bad – honest, plain meat, herbs and vegetables. It was fed to us by two grinning barbarians whose weak jokes we were forced to put up with as we ate.

When they had gone and the barbarian camp seemed still, I again began to roll towards Hool Haji, intent on getting at the knife in his harness.

Being tied so firmly, it was hard to tell if anyone could see us or not. I decided to take the chance.

Inch by inch I got closer to my friend, and at last my teeth were in the pommel of the secret knife.

Slowly I worked it out of its hiding place until it was firmly clamped in my teeth.

Hool Haji's hands were tied behind his back, so that now he had to roll over while I tried to saw at his bonds.

After what seemed an age the first strand parted, then the second. Very soon his hands would be free!

I was just starting on the last piece of rope securing Hool Haji's hands when there came a gruff laugh from above and I glimpsed gold as the knife was snatched from my teeth.

'You're game, the pair of you,' came Rokin's voice, full of rough laughter. 'But you're too valuable to let go. We'd better send you to sleep again.'

Hool Haji and I made a desperate attempt to get to our feet and attack him, but our bonds had checked our circulation.

A sword pommel was raised.

It descended.

I blacked out.

Chapter Seven

Voyage to Bagarad

We were at sea when I awoke in the musty-smelling hold of a ship whose sides did not seem to be of wood, as I had expected.

My bonds had been cut, and apart from slight cramp in my muscles I was feeling much better physically. I was also thinking with greater clarity. The recent experiences with the barbarians seemed to have drained me of much of my original emotion and, while I knew it would return in time, I felt detached and, in some ways, in a healthier state of mind. Perhaps it was the ship. The space is confined, the possibilities limited, and thus one feels more in control of one's environment, particularly in contrast to the seemingly limitless horizons existing on Mars of the age I know.

Whatever the reasons – and they were probably an amalgam of all those I have suggested and more – I could work out better what I must do. The first objective must be to inspect all the machines Rokin had looted and check if one of them had properties capable of acting against the plague. If one could prove to have this property then I should have to think of ways of getting it away from Rokin and – the thought appalled me but it was going to be necessary – destroy the rest. If none of the machines could provide me with what I wanted, then I could destroy them all. The latter would be the easier task, of course.

The ship was rolling and I was forced to brace myself against the sides of the hold. The hull seemed made in one piece, of a kind of durable plastic that I had discovered earlier in the Yaksha stronghold. It was dark, but as my eyes became accustomed to it, I could make out objects that might once have been engine mountings. But there were no engines now. Here again was an artefact left over from what the Martians call the Mightiest

War – the war that almost totally eliminated both the Yaksha and the Sheev and virtually destroyed the planet itself.

I heard a stifled groan from the opposite corner. I thought I recognised the voice.

'Hool Haji?' I said. 'Is it you?'

'It is I, my friend – or what is left of me. One moment while I make sure I am all in one piece. Where are we?'

Through the dimness I saw my comrade's huge shape rise from where he had been lying, saw him stagger and fall against a bulwark.

As best I could, I made my way towards him as the ship pitched about dreadfully. Though little sound permeated the hold, I had the impression that we were in the middle of a particularly unpleasant storm. I had heard that the Western ocean was not thought a healthy place for seafarers, which was probably why it was so infrequently crossed.

Hool Haji groaned. 'Oh, the Mendishar were never meant to travel on the sea, Michael Kane.'

He shifted his position as the ship was struck by another great wave.

Suddenly light streamed into the hold and sea water rushed in with it, soaking us at once. Framed in the opening above was a bearded barbarian.

'On deck!' he ordered curtly, his voice just heard above the howl of the storm.

'In this!' I said. 'We're not seamen!'

'Then this is the time to become seamen, my friend. Rokin wants to see you.'

I shrugged and made my way to the ladder now revealed in the light of the open hatch.

Hool Haji followed me.

Together we climbed out onto the slippery deck, clinging to the rope that ran along the centre of the deck, looped between the two large masts, their sails now reefed.

Spray swirled in the air, water slapped the deck, the ship was tumbled about by the great grey mass of heaving water. Sky and sea were grey and indistinguishable – everything seemed to be moving below us and about us. I had never experienced such a dreadful storm.

If a Blue Giant can turn green, then Hool Haji's face was green, his eyes showing a kind of agony that seemed to come as much from a deep-rooted disturbance in his soul as from the physical discomfort.

We edged our way towards the bridge of the ship, where Rokin, still in his golden armour, clung to the rail, looking about him as if in wonderment.

Somehow we managed to join him on the bridge.

He turned to us, saying something I could not catch in a tone that matched the wonderment in his gaze. I indicated that I had not heard him.

'Never seen one like this!' he shouted. 'We'll be lucky if we stay up.'

'What did you want to see us for?' I asked.

'Help!' he shouted.

'What can we do? We know nothing of ships or seafaring.'

'There are machines in the hold, forward. They're powerful. Couldn't they calm the storm?'

'I doubt it,' I yelled back.

He nodded to himself, then looked into my face. He appeared to accept the truth of what I said.

'What are our chances?' I asked.

'Poor!'

He still seemed to show little fear. He was, perhaps, more incredulous at the intensity of the storm.

Just then another great wave struck the ship and water came crashing down upon me. Then I felt Rokin's weighted bulk fall on me.

I heard a cry.

Then I knew that I had been hurled off the ship and was totally at the mercy of the raging ocean.

I struggled desperately to stay afloat, keeping mouth and nostrils as closed as possible.

I was hurtled crazily upon the crests of waves, crashing into valleys with walls of water, until I saw a trailing rope. I did not know if it was attached to anything or not – but I grabbed and caught it. I clung to the rope and felt the comfort of resistance at the other end.

I do not know for how long I clung to the rope, but whatever it was attached to the other end kept me afloat until the storm slowly abated.

I opened salt-encrusted eyes in the watery light of an early sunrise.

I saw a mast floating in the water ahead of me. My rope was fastened to it.

I hauled myself towards the broken mast, dragging myself wearily through the water. Then, as I neared it, I could see that several others were clinging to the mast.

When at length I grasped the mast, with a feeling of relief out of all proportion to the safety the mast offered, I saw that one of those who clung there, barely conscious, was Hool Haji, his great head lolling with exhaustion.

I reached out to touch him, to give him comfort and to let him know I still lived.

At that moment I heard a distant cry to my left and, looking in that direction, saw that the hull of the ship was miraculously still afloat.

Sunlight flashed on gold and I knew that Rokin had also survived. Clamping the rope between my teeth, I struck out towards the ship. At length the rope ran out before I had reached the ship but, luckily, it was drifting in my direction.

Soon I was being dragged on board and some of the barbarians were hauling in the rope and the mast.

It was not long before Hool Haji was also being helped aboard and we lay together, utterly weary, on the deck. Rokin, seemingly just as weary, was leaning on a broken rail and looking down on us.

From somewhere a hot drink was brought to us and we felt recovered enough to sit up and view the ship.

Virtually everything had been stripped from the deck by the fury of the storm. Only the miraculous hull had survived, relatively undamaged. Both masts had been ripped away, and most of the rails and all the deck furniture, including one of the hatch covers, had been swept overboard.

Rokin walked towards us.

'You were lucky,' he said.

'And you,' I replied. 'Where are we?'

'Somewhere on the Western sea. Perhaps, judging by the direction of the storm, closer to our own land than yours. We can only hope that the currents are in our favour and that we shall soon reach land. Most of our provisions were ruined when yonder hold filled.' He pointed to the hold that had had its cover ripped off. 'The machines are down there, too – also half immersed – but safe enough, I'd guess.'

'They will never be safe – to you,' I warned him.

He grinned. 'Nothing can harm Rokin – not even that storm.'

'If I am right about the power of those machines,' I told him, 'they threaten far more danger than the storm.'

'To Rokin's enemies, perhaps,' retaliated the barbarian.

'To Rokin, too.'

'What harm can they do to me? I have them.'

'I have warned you,' I said, shaking my head.

'What do you warn me about?'

'Your own ignorance!' I said.

He shrugged. 'One does not have to be so full of knowledge to use such machines.'

'Certainly,' I agreed. 'But one needs knowledge to understand them. If you do not understand them, then you will fear them soon enough.'

'I do not follow your reasoning, Bradhinak. You are boring me.'

Once again I gave up trying to argue with the barbarian, though I knew that in this case, as in all things, it is not enough to know that something works. One must also understand how it works before it can be used to advantage, and used without personal danger.

Chapter Eight
The Crystal Pit

THE SHIP REACHED land the next day – whether the mainland of the Western continent or an island I did not then know.

We leapt from the ship into the shallows, plunging thankfully up to the firm shore, while Rokin directed his men to beach the hull.

When this was done and we sat in the shadow of the hull, recovering from what we had endured in the past two days, Rokin turned to me with a faint trace of his old grin.

'So now we are all far from home – and far from our glory,' he said.

'Thanks to you,' said Hool Haji, echoing my own sentiments.

'Well,' said Rokin, fingering his golden beard, now clogged with salt, 'I suppose it is.'

'Have you no idea where we are?' I asked him.

'None.'

'Then we had best strike off along the coast in the hope of finding a friendly settlement,' I suggested.

'I suppose so.' He nodded. 'But someone must stay to guard the treasures still in the ship.'

'You mean the machines?' Hool Haji said.

'The machines,' Rokin agreed.

'We could guard them,' I said, 'with the aid of some of your men.'

Rokin laughed aloud. 'Barbarian I may be, my friend, but fool I am not. No, you come with us. I'll leave some of my men to guard the ship.'

And so we set off along the shore. It was a wide, smooth beach, with an occasional rock standing out from the sand and, far away, its foliage waving gently in the mild, warm breeze, was semi-tropical forest.

It seemed a peaceful enough place.

But I was wrong.

By mid-afternoon the shore had narrowed and we were walking much closer to the forest than before. The sky was overcast and the air had become colder. Hool Haji and myself had no cloaks and we shivered slightly in the still, chill air.

When they came, they came suddenly.

They came in a howling pack, bursting from the trees and running down the beach towards us. Grotesque parodies of human beings, waving clubs and crudely hammered swords, covered in hair and completely naked.

I could not at first believe my eyes as I drew my own sword without thinking and prepared to face them.

Though they walked upright, they had the half-human faces of dogs – bloodhounds were the nearest species I could think of.

What was more, the noises they made were indistinguishable from the baying of hounds.

So bizarre was their appearance, so sudden their assault, that I was almost off my guard when the first club-brandishing dog-man came in to the attack.

I blocked the blow with my blade and sheered off the creature's fingers, finishing him cleanly with a thrust at his heart.

Another took his place, and more besides. I saw that we were completely surrounded by the pack. Apart from Hool Haji, Rokin and myself, there were only two other barbarians in our party and there were probably some fifty of the dog-men.

I swung my sword in an arc and it bit deep into the necks of two of the dog-men, causing them to fall.

The hounds' faces were slobbering and the large eyes held a maniacal hatred which I had only previously seen in the eyes of mad dogs. I had the impression that if they bit me I would be infected with rabies.

Three more fell before my blade as all the old teaching of

Monsieur Clarchet, my French fencing master since childhood, came back to me.

Once again I became cool.

Once again I became nothing more than a fighting machine, concentrating entirely on defending myself against that mad attack.

We held them off far longer than I had expected we could until the press became so intense I could no longer move my sword.

The fighting then became a thing of fists and feet, and I went down with at least a dozen of the dog-men on top of me.

I felt my arms grasped, and still I tried to fight them off but at length they had bound me.

Once again I had become a prisoner.

Would I survive to save Cend-Amrid?

I had now begun to doubt it. Ill luck was riding me, I was sure, and I felt that I would meet my death on that mysterious Western continent.

The dog-men carried us into the forest, conversing in a sharp, barking form of the common Martian tongue. I found it hard to understand them.

Once I glimpsed Hool Haji being carried along by several of the dog-men, and I also saw a flash of Rokin's golden armour, so I assumed he lived, too. But I never saw the remaining barbarians again, so I concluded they had been slain.

Eventually the forest opened out onto a clearing and there was a village. The houses were only roughly made shelters, but they had been built on, or among, the shells of far older stone buildings that did not seem to have any association with either the Sheev or the Yaksha. The buildings must once have been massive and durable, but they had been erected by a more primitive race than the ancient race which had destroyed itself in the Mightiest War.

As we were carted into one of the shelters and dumped on the evil-smelling floor – half of stone, half of hardened mud – I wondered about the race that had abandoned the settlement before the dog-people had discovered it.

Before I could say anything to Hool Haji or Rokin about this, a dog-man, larger than the rest, entered the shelter and looked down at us out of his large, canine eyes.

'Who are you?' he said in his strange accent.

'Travellers,' I replied. 'We offer you no harm. Why did you attack us?'

'For the First Masters,' he replied.

'Who are the First Masters?' asked Hool Haji from where he lay beside me.

'The First Masters are they who feed from the Crystal Pit.'

'We do not know them,' I said. 'Why did they tell you to attack us?'

'They did not tell us.'

'Do they give you your orders?' Rokin said. 'If so, tell them they have made a prisoner of Rokin the Gold and his men will punish them if Rokin dies.'

Something like a smile touched the heavy mouth of the dog-man.

'The First Masters punish – *they* are not punished.'

'Can we speak to them?' I asked.

'They do not speak.'

'Can we see them?' Hool Haji asked.

'You will see them – and they will see you.'

'Well, at least we might be able to reason with these First Masters,' I said to Hool Haji. I returned my attention to the dog-man who seemed to be the leader of the pack.

'Are these First Masters like you?' I asked. 'Or are they like us?'

The pack-leader shrugged. 'Like neither,' he said. 'Like that one more.' And he pointed to Hool Haji.

'They are folk of my race?' Hool Haji said, brightening a little. 'Then surely they can see that we wish them no harm.'

'Only like you,' said the dog-man. 'Not the same as you. You will see them in the Crystal Pit.'

'What is this Crystal Pit?' Rokin growled. 'Why can't we see them now?'

Again the dog-man seemed to smile. 'They do not come yet,' he replied.

'When will they come?'

'Tomorrow – when the sun is highest.'

With that the dog-man left the shelter.

Somehow we managed to get some sleep, hoping that the mysterious First Masters would be more forthcoming and more open to reason than the dog-men, who were apparently their servants in some capacity we could not understand.

Just before noon on the next day several dog-men entered the shelter and picked us up, hauling us from the place and out into the daylight.

The pack-leader was waiting, standing on a piece of fallen masonry, a sword in one hand and a stick in the other. At the tip of the stick gleamed a rubylike gem of incredible size. I did not understand its significance, save that perhaps it was some sign of the dog-man's leadership over the rest.

We were borne out of the clearing and into the forest again, but it was not long before the forest gave way to another and much larger clearing, with the farther trees a great distance away. Here lush grass waved, rising waist-high and brushing my face as they carried me.

The grass soon became sparser, revealing an area of hardened mud in the centre of which was a great expanse of some gleaming substance which made my eyes ache.

It scintillated, flashing in the sun like a vast diamond.

It was only as we came closer that I realised that this must be the Crystal Pit.

It was a pit. Its sides were formed of pure, faceted crystal that caught the light from so many angles that it was almost impossible to guess what it was at first.

But where were these First Masters who looked like Hool Haji? I saw no-one but my companions and the dog-men who had brought us here.

We were carried to the edge of the blinding pit and our bonds were cut. We looked about wondering what was to happen and none of us was prepared for the sudden shoves we received. Luckily the pit's sides were not particularly steep. We slid down to the bottom, barely able to check our descent, and landed in a heap at the bottom of the Crystal Pit.

As we picked ourselves up we saw the dog-men retreating from the edge of the pit.

We were unable to guess why we were there, but we were all of us uneasy, suspecting that we were not merely to be imprisoned in the Crystal Pit indefinitely.

After about an hour, during which we were forced to keep our eyes closed most of the time, we gave up trying to scramble up the sides of the pit and began to try to work out some other means of escaping.

There seemed none.

Then we heard a sound from above and saw a face peering down at us.

At first we thought this must be one of the First Masters, but the face did not fit their description.

Then we saw that it was the face of a girl.

But perhaps girl is the wrong word, for the face, though intelligent and pleasant to look at, was the mutated face of a cat. Only the eyes and the pointed ears were evidence of the girl's non-simian ancestry, but it was as much a surprise to see this cat-girl as it had been to see the dog-men earlier.

'Are you enemies of the Hounds of Hahg?' came the whispered enquiry from the cat-girl.

'It seems that they think of us as such,' I replied. 'Are you, too, their enemy?'

'All my people – and they are few these days – hate the dog-folk of Hahg,' she replied vehemently. 'Many have been brought here to meet the First Masters.'

'Are they your masters, too?' Hool Haji asked.

'They were – but we rejected them.'

'Have you come to save us, girl?' came Rokin's voice, practical and impatient.

'I have come to try, but there is little time. Here.' She reached over the edge of the pit and slid some objects down the sides. I saw at once that they were three swords, unlike those we had seen used by the dog-folk, but still strange. They were shorter than the swords I was used to, but of excellent workmanship. Picking one up and handing the others to my companions, I inspected it.

It was light and beautifully tempered. A little too light for my taste, but far better than nothing. I felt a little better.

I looked up and saw that the cat-girl's face had suddenly become anxious.

'Too late to help you from the pit,' she said. 'The First Masters come. I wish you well.'

And then she was gone.

We waited tensely, swords in hand, wondering from where the First Masters would appear.

Chapter Nine
The First Masters

THEY CAME FROM above, their vast wings flapping noisily in the still air.

They were somewhat smaller than Hool Haji, but very like him in basic appearance, though their skins were of a much paler blue, a strange, unhealthy blue that contrasted oddly with their red, gaping mouths and their long, white tusks. Their wings spread partially from their shoulders, partially from around their hips.

They seemed more like beasts than men.

Perhaps, as the beasts had become men in the shape of the dog-folk and the cat-girl who had given us our swords, these men had become beasts. There was a strange, insensate glow in their eyes that did not seem to reflect the madness of men but the madness of the beast.

They hovered above us, their huge wings beating the air, causing a stiff wind to ruffle our hair.

'The Jihadoo!' Hool Haji gasped unbelievingly.

'Who are they?' I asked, my gaze fixed on the weird creatures above.

'They are legends in Mendishar – an ancient race, similar to my own folk, who were shunned from our lands because of their dark, magical experiments.'

'Magic? I thought no-one in Mendishar believed in such stuff!' I said.

'Of course not. I told you, the Jihadoo were simply a legend. But now I am no longer certain of anything.'

'Whatever you call them, they mean us ill,' Rokin the Gold growled, blinking his eyes against the glare of the Crystal Pit.

One by one the First Masters – or Jihadoo, as Hool Haji called them – began to cluster downwards into the pit.

Horrified, I prepared to defend myself.

The first one came sweeping down uttering a shrill scream, red mouth gaping, fangs bared, claw-fingered hands extended to clutch me.

I slashed at the hand and drew blood. At least the Jihadoo were mortal, I remembered thinking as it swerved in the air and attacked me from another direction. Now others had joined the first and my comrades were as beset as myself.

I stabbed with the slim sword at the face of my first attacker and had the satisfaction of taking him in the eye and killing him.

The First Masters were plainly unprepared for armed resistance and this was why we survived the first encounters with comparative ease.

Another came at me, exposing his chest for a perfect stab.

The fairly narrow base of the pit helped us, since not too many of the Jihadoo could get at us at one time, but now we were forced to clamber onto the corpses of those we had already slain. In some ways this gave us a firmer footing as we fought.

All was a confusion of beating wings and fanged faces, gleaming eyes and clutching claw-hands. I lopped another's head off, recoiling as sticky, evil-smelling blood spurted at my face.

Then, suddenly, as I engaged yet another of the monsters, I felt my shoulders seized in a painful grip.

I tried to turn, to slash at my attacker, but even as I did so I was hauled into the air and lost my balance for a moment.

I was being borne upwards into the air by one of the flying man-beasts.

High above the forest now, I still tried to destroy my captor, even if it meant my own destruction, so abhorrent did it seem to me.

I saw that Hool Haji and Rokin were in a similar plight to my own, but the few First Masters who followed us made me realise with a grim satisfaction just how many of their fellows we had killed.

Twisting in the painful grasp of the claws half-embedded in my shoulders, I tried to stab backwards at the arms or the torso.

To my right I saw Rokin attempt the same thing and, because of his golden armour, manage to twist one shoulder out of the Jihadoo's clutches.

Hanging by the arm which the Jihadoo still clasped, he began to slash at the creature's chest.

The creature did not retaliate, as I had expected. It simply released its grip on Rokin's other arm.

In horror I saw the barbarian yell and began to hurtle towards the rocky ground that had given way to the forest.

I saw his golden armour twisting in the sunlight, falling rapidly earthwards.

Then I saw it strike the ground.

I saw the armour split open on impact and a red corpse roll for a moment before becoming still.

I was sickened by the sight.

I knew that Rokin had been a barbarian and an enemy, but he had been a warm-blooded and, in his own way, generous man – a human being in the full sense.

And, with Rokin gone, we might never discover the rest of the machines he had stolen from the Yaksha – assuming, of course, the unlikely event of our surviving our present predicament.

I swung myself back now, curling my legs around one of the trailing legs of the Jihadoo. He did not seem to have anticipated this. Neither had I. It had been sudden inspiration, and now I at least had some chance of clinging on if he decided to release his grip.

Next, I managed to shift my position so that I was able to stab at his side with my sword. I began jabbing.

The wounds I was able to inflict were not serious, but they were sufficient to set him screaming and hissing.

I felt his grip begin to weaken and readied myself for what must happen next.

I stabbed several more times.

He screamed even more loudly. One claw released my shoulder and I ducked as he began to flail at me with it. I slashed at the clawed hand – and severed it.

This was too much for him. He dropped his remaining grip and I fell forward.

Only my legs, twisted around one of his, prevented me from joining Rokin.

I hurled my body through the air and managed to get another grip on his leg, this time with one of my arms.

He shook the leg, losing his equilibrium in the air and slowly beginning to descend, in spite of himself, as his wings beat to keep him up.

Bit by bit, and to my intense satisfaction, we began to go lower and lower as he struggled now to free himself. But I still clung to him, stabbing with the light sword.

He was bleeding profusely and getting weaker all the time.

Then, suddenly, with one final convulsion, he managed to loosen my grip.

With a feeling that all had been for nothing, I lost my hold and began to fall.

I did not fall for long, luckily, for once again the rocky ground had been replaced by forest and I fell into the branches of a tree. The supple boughs held me like a soft hammock and after a moment I was able to climb out and begin to clamber to the ground.

I was worried about Hool Haji.

How had he fared?

I prayed that he had, like me, been able to save himself from the clutches of his captor.

The forest was quiet for a moment, then I heard a tremendous crash to my right.

I ran in the direction of the sound and discovered the corpse of the Jihadoo which had borne me here. It appeared to have died of its wounds.

I shuddered as I looked at the ghastly half-beast and decided that my best plan was to climb a tree quickly again to see if I could catch sight of Hool Haji.

Up the nearest tree I clambered until I was looking over the tops of the foliage.

I saw a speck in the distance, then another – flying creatures, but so far away that I could not make out whether they were Jihadoo or, indeed, if they carried anyone with them.

With a sinking heart I returned to the ground. Somehow I had to discover the lair of the Jihadoo and set off to rescue my friend, hoping that they would not kill him immediately.

But how?

That was a question my mind refused to answer.

I wondered if the cat-girl who had first helped us would be able to help us again if I managed to contact her. I decided that to seek her out was the best thing I could do, and I set off in the general direction of the Crystal Pit.

Even if I did not find the cat-girl, I might be able to capture a dog-man and get the information I needed from him.

Chapter Ten
The People of Purha

I MUST HAVE walked for many *shatis* – the Martian basic measure of time – crossing the rocky plain where Rokin had crashed to his death, and entering the next stretch of the forest before I heard some sign of life.

It was a crashing noise in the undergrowth.

It was the sound of some large beast moving about.

Deciding to be cautious, I drew my sword and withdrew into the shade of a bole.

Suddenly, from out of the forest, came yet another weird sight – again almost unbelievable, though this time because the creature bore such a peculiar resemblance to an Earthly animal.

The animal that I confronted, and whose gleaming eyes had fixed on me in spite of my attempt at seeking cover, was almost identical to an earth vole.

But this vole was large. It was very large.

It was the size of a half-grown elephant.

And it was hungry – and doubtless omnivorous.

It stood hunched up, regarding me with its nose twitching and its eyes glittering, preparing perhaps for a spring.

I was so weary, what with my experiences since Cend-Amrid and the walking I had done to get this far, that I gave myself only a faint chance of having the strength to defeat the giant vole.

Suddenly, with a peculiar shrill scream, the creature rushed at me. I ducked behind the tree and this seemed to confuse it for a moment.

It plainly was not particularly intelligent, which relieved me a little – though its bulk, I felt, would be more to its advantage in my present state of weariness than my wits would be to me.

For a moment it paused. Then it began to edge round the tree again.

I edged, also, following the trunk of the tree and keeping it between myself and the gigantic creature that was doubtless bent on making a supper from me.

Suddenly it made a movement towards the tree, flinging its huge body at it. The tree groaned and swayed and I was spun backwards, lying helplessly, for a moment, on the ground.

I began to scramble up as the vole came towards me, its relatively small jaws open ready to seize me in a bite that would have severed any part of my body it snapped.

I slashed at the muzzle with my sword, staggering wearily, my vision focusing and unfocusing as I strove to gather what little strength I had left.

The teeth only narrowly missed. I could not run, for the massive creature was faster than I was, and I knew I would not be able to hold it off much longer.

I knew that I was going to die.

Perhaps this knowledge helped me summon my last reserves of strength, and I slashed again at the muzzle, drawing blood. The creature seemed puzzled but it did not retreat, simply holding its ground while it decided how best to attack me.

Again I swayed with utter tiredness, striving with everything I had left to remain on my feet and die fighting.

Then, from above and behind the creature, a rain of slender arrows came pounding into the gigantic vole's body, causing it to scream and convulse in agony. Several arrows whipped into its eyes as it turned towards its new attackers.

I really thought I must be dreaming, that my ill luck could not have changed so rapidly.

The vole screeched and flailed about. I was knocked flat by its lashing tail as it turned about and began its death throes.

I lay on the springy grass, wide-eyed for a moment, thanking providence for my rescue and praying that I was not to fall into the hands of yet another tribe of barbarians.

As if in the distance, I heard soft voices talking, and had the vision of graceful figures leaping around the dying vole. They gave the impression of cats and, before I finally lost grip on consciousness, I remember reflecting on the paradox of a number of cats attacking a huge mouse!

Then welcome darkness came. Perhaps I had passed out, perhaps not – perhaps I merely slept.

I awoke to the touch of a warm, gentle hand on my head and, opening my eyes, I looked up into the face of the cat-girl who had originally been responsible for my salvation.

'What happened?' I asked somewhat thickly.

'We hunted the *rheti* and found our prey,' she replied softly. 'Our prey hunted you – and we were able to slay the *rheti* and save you at the same time. Where are your friends?'

I shook my head. 'One was killed by the First Masters,' I replied. 'The other was borne off by them, I think. I do not know how he fared.'

'You fought the First Masters and lived!' Her eyes shone with admiration – and something else. 'This is a great day. All we had hoped for when I brought you the swords was that you would be able to die fighting. You will be a hero among our folk.'

'I have no wish to be a hero,' I told her. 'Merely a live man – and one who, with luck, still has a chance to find his vanished friend.'

'Which friend was carried off?' she asked.

'The Blue Giant – Hool Haji, my closest friend.'

'There is little hope for him,' she said.

'But is there any?'

'Not now – the First Masters would have feasted last night.'

'Last night!' I sat up. 'How long have I slept?'

'For nearly two days,' she said simply. 'You were very weary when we brought you here.'

'Two days! So long!'

'It is not so long considering what you did.'

'But too long,' I said, 'for I lost my chance to save Hool Haji.'

'You would never have reached the place of the First Masters in time, whatever you did,' she soothed. 'Salute your friend as a valiant hero. Remember how he died and what that means to those who have suffered the tyranny of the First Masters all these centuries.'

'I know that I cannot truthfully blame myself for Hool Haji's death,' I said, controlling the emotion I felt at my great friend's passing, 'but that does not stop me mourning him.'

'Mourn him if you will, but honour him also. He slew many of the First Masters. Never was such a battle fought in the Crystal Pit. Even now the corpses of the First Masters pile its floor. Half of them, at least, lie dead. Tell me of the fight.'

As briefly as I could, I told her what had happened. Her eyes began to shine even more brightly and she clasped her hands together.

'What a great story for our poets!' she gasped. 'Oh, what is your name, hero – and the names of your friends?'

'My friends were called the Bradhi Hool Haji of Mendishar from across the ocean, and –' I paused, for Rokin had been no real friend to me, though a valiant comrade in arms in our fights – 'the Bradhi Rokin the Gold of the Bagarad.'

'Bradhis!' she cried. 'And you? What are you – a Bradhi of Bradhis? You could be no less.'

I smiled at her enthusiasm. 'No,' I said. 'My name is Michael Kane, Bradhinak by marriage to the Royal House of Varnal that lies far to the South, across the sea.'

'From the South – from across the sea. I have heard tales of those mythical lands, the countries of the gods. There are no gods here. They have abandoned us. Are they returning to save us from the First Masters?'

'I am no god,' I told her, 'and we of the South do not believe in gods. We believe in Man.'

'But is not Man a kind of god?' she asked innocently.

I smiled again. 'So he sometimes thinks. But the men of my land are not supernatural creatures. They are like you, of flesh and blood and brain. You are no different, though your ancestry is not the same as ours.'

'That is not what the First Masters told us.'

'The First Masters can speak?' I was astonished. 'I thought them reasonless beasts.'

'They do not speak to us now. But they left their writings and it is these we read and these we used to follow. The folk of Hahg still worship the First Masters, but we do not.'

'Why do they worship the First Masters? I should have thought they would have fought such creatures,' I said.

'The First Masters created us,' she said simply.

'Created you – but how?'

'We know not how – save for a few scraps of stories that speak of the First Masters as once having served even earlier masters, a race of great magicians who have now passed from Vashu.'

I guessed that she spoke of the Sheev or the Yaksha, who had once ruled the whole of Mars – or Vashu, as they called it. Perhaps the winged blue men who had fled from Mendishar in the old days had sought out some remnant of the older race and learned some of their science.

'What do your stories tell you of the First Masters?' I asked.

'They say that the First Masters created our ancestors by putting spells on their brains and shaping their bodies so that they thought and walked like men. For a while our folk – the people of Purha – and the other folk – the people of Hahg – dwelled together in the City of the First Masters, serving them and being sacrificed for their magical purposes.'

This sounded like a particularly horrific form of vivisection to me. I interpreted the cat-girl's story in more scientific terms. The First Masters had learned science from a even older race. They had applied it, perhaps by some form of sophisticated surgery, to creating manlike creatures from cats and dogs. Then they had used their creations both as slaves and subjects for their experiments.

'And what happened then?' I asked. 'How did the three peoples become separated?'

She frowned. 'It is hard to understand,' she said. 'But the minds of the First Masters turned more and more in upon themselves. The magic they had discovered by sacrificing us was applied to their own brains and bodies. They became... like animals. A madness overcame them. They left their city and flew to their caverns in the mountains far from here. But every five hundred shatis they return to the Crystal Pit – a creation either of their own or of the old ones they served – to feed.'

'What is their usual food?' I asked.

'Us,' she said bleakly.

I was disgusted. I could partly understand a psychology that allowed the dog-men of Hahg to sacrifice strangers to their strange masters, but I could only loathe the mentality that let them hurl their cousins, the cat-folk, into the Crystal Pit.

'They eat the people of Purha!' I shuddered.

'Not just the folk of Purha.' She shook her head. 'Only when the men of Hahg capture us. When they have no prisoners they select the weakest among themselves to provide the food of the First Masters.'

'But what inspires them to commit such dreadful crimes!' I gasped.

Again the girl's answer was simple and, it seemed to me, quite profound.

'Fear,' she said.

I nodded, wondering if that deep emotion was not the essential cause of most ills. Were not all political systems, all arts, all human actions channelled towards creating that one valuable sense of security we all, in our own ways, sought – an absence of fear? It was fear that produced madness, fear that produced war. Fear, indeed, that often produced the things we feared most. Was this why the fearless man was lauded – because he did not represent a threat to others? Perhaps, though there were many kinds of fearless people, and a total fearlessness produced a whole man, a man who had no need to display his fearlessness. The true hero, in fact – the often unsung hero.

'But there are more of you in one of your tribes than exist among the First Masters,' I said. 'Why do you not band together to defeat them?'

'The fear the First Masters exert is not on account of their numbers,' she replied. 'Nor on account of their physical strangeness, though that may have something to do with it. The fear goes deeper. I cannot explain it.'

I thought perhaps I knew what she meant. We call it by a simple term on Earth. We call it fear of the unknown. Sometimes it is a man's fear of a woman whom he feels he cannot understand; sometimes it is a man's fear of strangers – of people of a different racial type, or even from a different part of his own land. Sometimes it is fear of the machines that he manipulates. Whether the lack of understanding is on a personal plane or a more general one, it creates suspicion and fear. It was their fear, I thought, not their antecedents that made the dog-men of Hahg something less than human.

I said some of this to the cat-girl and she nodded intelligently. 'I think you are right,' she said. 'Perhaps that is why we survive and grow and the dog-men revert more and more to becoming like their ancestors.'

I was struck by her quick brain. Though I hesitate to make such judgements about animals, it seemed to me that the essential cowardice of the dog and the essential courage of the cat might be reflected in the types which had developed from them. Thus I could not blame the dog-men for their brutality quite so much, though this did not alter my deep loathing for what they had become. For, I thought, just as there could be courageous dogs – on Earth there were many stories about them – so could these people have once *found* courage.

I am an optimist, and it occurred to me that just as I might eventually find a means of curing the plague infecting Cend-Amrid, I might also help the dog-men by destroying the cause of their fear – for there was certainly no hope for the First Masters. They were evil. Evil is only another word for what we fear. Go to your Bible if you wish to see the fear of women that inspired the old prophets to call them evil – and evil creates evil. Destroy the first source and there is hope for the rest.

Again I mentioned some of this to the cat-girl. She frowned and nodded. 'It is hard to sympathise at all with the men of Hahg,' she said. 'For what they have done to us in the past has been terrible. But I will try to understand you, Michael Kane.'

She got up from where she had been sitting cross-legged beside me.

'My name is Fasa,' she said. 'Come, see where we live.'

She led me from the building in which I had been lying in semi-darkness and had been unable to observe clearly, out into a miniature city built among the trees. Not a tree had been cut in the building of the cat-folk's city. It merged with the forest, thus offering a much subtler kind of protection than the more commonplace clearing and fence used by most jungle-dwelling tribes. The dwellings were only of one or two storeys, fashioned from mud, but mud fashioned into beauty. Here were tiny spires and minarets, painted decorations in pale, lovely colours, a blending of pleasing shapes and colours amongst nature's rich creations.

Some of the darkness in my mind was cleared by the vision and Fasa looked up at me, delighted to see how fascinated I was by the beauty of her settlement.

'You like it?'

'I love it,' I said enthusiastically. In its own simple way it reminded me of Varnal of the Green Mists more than anything else I had seen on Mars. It had the same air of tranquillity – a vital tranquillity, if you like – which made me feel so much at home and at ease in Varnal.

'You are an artistic people,' I said, fingering the sword which I still wore. 'I saw that at once when you first brought us these blades.'

'We try,' she said. 'I sometimes think that if the surroundings can be made pleasing they help the soul.'

Again I was struck by the simple profundities – common sense, if you prefer – coming from this beautiful girl. But what is the deepest wisdom but the soundest kind of common sense, *true* common sense? Living in isolated conditions, beset by enemies of two kinds, these cat-people seemed to have something more valuable than most nations, even on Mars and certainly on Earth.

'Come,' she said, taking my arm. 'You must meet my old uncle,

Slurra. He will like you, I think, Michael Kane. He already admires you – but admiration does not always produce liking, wouldn't you say?'

'I agree,' I said feelingly, and let her lead me towards one of the beautiful buildings.

I had to duck my head to enter and there I saw a old cat-man, sitting relaxed and at ease in a delicately carved chair. He did not rise as I entered but his expression and his inclination of the head seemed more to respect me than any empty gesture of politeness I might have received on Earth. 'We were not aware of the benefits we would bring to the people of Purha when we sent Fasa to you with the swords,' he said.

'Benefits?' I enquired.

'Immeasurable ones,' he said, gesturing for me to sit in a chair close to him. 'To see the First Masters defeated – and they *were* defeated in a deeper sense than you may realise – to be shown that they could be killed, was the thing my folk needed most.'

'Perhaps,' I said, nodding agreement to show that I knew what he meant, 'this will help the Hahg, also.'

He debated this for a moment before replying. 'Yes, it might, if they have not gone too far down the road. It will make them sceptical of the First Masters' power, just as we became sceptical long years ago, well before my great-grandfather's time, in the age of Mispash the Founder.'

'A wise man of your folk?' I enquired.

'The founder of our folk,' replied the old cat-man. 'He taught us one great truth – he was the wisest of prophets.'

'What was that?'

'Never to seek prophets,' Slurra smiled. 'One should be enough – and he a wise one.'

I reflected how true this was and how well Slurra's words applied to the situation on Earth where, because prophets had been found, whole nations now sought new prophets rather than study the teachings of the few whose universal message had always been, *know thyself*. Not knowing themselves, perhaps even fearing to, these nations allowed artificial prophets – Adolf Hitler was an example who came to mind at once – to cure their ills. All such prophets did was to plunge those who listened to them into a worse situation than any they had been in before.

I talked at some length with the old cat-man and found the conversation rewarding.

Then he said: 'But all this is fine enough. We must do something to help you.'

'Thank you,' I said.

'What can we do?'

I remembered the machines left behind in the beached ship. That would be my first objective, I decided. If the cat-people could help me it would make things much easier. I told the old cat-man, Slurra, of the reasons for my being here.

He listened gravely and when I had finished he said: 'You have a noble mission, Michael Kane. We should be proud to help you carry it out. As soon as you are ready, there will be a party of my people to come with you to this ship and the machines can be brought back here.'

'Are you sure you want these fated machines among you?' I asked.

'Machines are only dangerous, I believe, in the hands of dangerous men. It is such men we must be wary of, not their tools,' said Slurra. I had already explained the power and implications of the ancient machines.

And so it was agreed. In a short time an expedition, led by me, would set off for the coast.

It was not my intention to engage the cat-folk in battle with the barbarians – or, indeed, to set out to harm the barbarians, who had been led into danger by Rokin. I hoped that a display of strength and some sensible words, coupled with the information that Rokin was now dead, would encourage them to fall in with us.

Things were not to happen quite like that, but I did not realise it at the time.

Chapter Eleven

'The Machines are Gone!'

IT TOOK US some time to reach the coast, and a little longer to retrace my steps to where I had left the ship.

As we neared the ship I noticed that something seemed wrong. No guards moved on the deck, all appeared as still as the grave.

I began to trot faster, the cat-men following me. There were some twenty of them, well armed with bows and swords, and they hardly realised what a tremendous comfort they were to me on this Western continent.

When I reached the ship I saw signs that some kind of fight had taken place.

Two dead barbarians were next revealed, savagely beaten to death.

Zapha, the captain commanding the cat-men, inspected the ground. Then his intelligent cat's face looked up at me thoughtfully.

'More victims for the First Masters, if I'm not mistaken, Michael Kane,' he said. 'The men of Hahg have been here – they have taken prisoners.'

'They must be saved,' I said grimly.

He shook his head. 'The men of Hahg must have wondered where you came from and followed your tracks back. This happened two days ago. The First Masters will not go back to the Crystal Pit yet, but you were only saved from the sport of the men of Hahg because your appearance coincided with the latest visit of the First Masters.'

'What sport is that?'

'A grisly one – torture of a dreadful kind. I do not think you will find your friends alive in the mind now – though they'll live until the next visit of the First Masters.'

I felt horrified and then depressed. 'Still, we shall have to do what we can,' I said firmly.

I clambered up the side of the ship and walked across the sloping deck towards the hold where I knew the machines were stored.

I looked down.

I saw nothing but brackish water.

'*The machines are gone!*' I cried, running back to the broken rail and calling to the cat-men.

'The machines are gone!'

Zapha looked up at me with surprise in his eyes. 'They have taken them? It is not like them to do anything but capture victims for the First Masters.'

'Nonetheless, they are gone,' I said, climbing down the side of the ship.

'Then we must hurry back to the village of the Hahg and see if we can recover them,' Zapha said boldly.

We turned and began to go back the way we had come.

'We must get additional forces before we do that,' I said.

'Perhaps,' said Zapha thoughtfully. 'But this number has been enough in the past.'

'You have attacked the Hahg before?'

'When necessary – to save our own folk usually.'

'I cannot draw you into this fight,' I said.

'Do not worry. This fight is ours and yours – it is linked because the cause is common,' said Zapha firmly.

I respected his words and understood his feelings.

Thus we set off hurriedly for the Hahg encampment.

As we neared the encampment, Zapha and his followers began to show more caution and Zapha signed to me to follow him.

I could not move with the grace of the cat-folk, who now advanced completely silently through the forest, but I did my best.

Soon we lay in the undergrowth, peering at the squalid Hahg village, which, I had learned, was built on the ruins left behind by the First Masters when they had gone to the mountains.

From somewhere we heard mindless cries of agony and I knew what they signified.

This time Zapha stayed my hand as, impulsively, I made to rise.

'Not yet,' he said, only just audibly.

I remembered a similar warning I had given Hool Haji and realised that Zapha was right. Action we would take – but only at the right moment.

Looking about the camp I suddenly saw the machines. They were surrounded by a group of grunting dog-men, who were poking at them in what appeared to be mystification.

What impulse had led them to go to the trouble of hauling the machines here? Some atavistic memory? Some association with the First Masters whom they tried, at such pitiful and inhuman cost, to please?

Perhaps that was half the answer. I did not know.

The fact remained that here they were and we must somehow recapture them. We must also rescue what remained of the tortured barbarians.

Suddenly there came a disturbance in the air above us and I was astonished to see the First Masters descending into the village.

Zapha was as astonished as I was.

'Why are they here?' I whispered. 'Surely they only go to the Crystal Pit to feed every five hundred shatis?'

'I cannot imagine,' Zapha said. 'We are witnessing something important, I think, Michael Kane, though I cannot understand at this point what it signifies!'

With a great noise of feathery, beating wings, the First Masters landed near the machines and the dog-folk withdrew obsequiously.

Again I got the impression of some atavistic impulse working in the First Masters as they strutted, like stupid birds of prey, among the machines.

Suddenly one of them reached out and touched part of a machine that seemed to me merely ornamentation. Immediately a weird humming began to fill the air and the machine that had been activated began to shudder.

The dog-folk cowered back. Then the First Master who had originally touched the activating stud touched it again. The humming ceased.

As if disturbed by this, the First Masters began to take to the air again, disappearing as rapidly and as mysteriously as they had come.

We watched as the dog-people slowly returned to sniff at the machines.

The pack-leader barked out some kind of order. The vines which had been used to haul the machines to the village were picked up and the dog-men began pulling them away in the opposite direction.

'Where are they taking them?' I whispered to Zapha.

'I only heard a little of what the leader said,' replied Zapha. 'I think they are going to the Crystal Pit.'

'They are taking the machines there? I wonder why.'

'It does not matter at this moment, Michael Kane. What does matter is that they are leaving the village almost undefended. This will give us a chance to rescue your friends first.'

I did not quarrel with his description of the barbarians. They had been no real friends to me, but I felt I owed them something as human beings who had shown their prisoners at least some kind of rough respect.

We walked boldly into the village when the dog-men hauling the machines had gone. Those who remained saw that we outnumbered them and allowed their women and children to draw them back into their dark shelters.

Poor creatures! Cowardice had become their way of life.

The cat-folk did not bother them, but went to the shelter from where the moans had come earlier. There was none now and I assumed the barbarians had passed out.

But the two barbarians in the shelter had not passed out.

They had killed themselves.

From the beam of the shelter a rope hung. It had been looped over and a noose formed at either end.

Hanging, with their necks in the nooses, were the two barbarians.

I leapt forward with the idea of cutting them down but Zapha shook his head.

'They are dead,' he said. 'Perhaps it is best.'

'I am tempted to avenge them here and now,' I said harshly, turning towards the entrance.

'It was you who told us of the real cause of all this, Michael Kane,' Zapha reminded me.

I controlled my emotions and left the place of death.

Zapha came out with me.

'Let us follow the Hahg to the Crystal Pit now,' he said. 'We might learn something. Perhaps that is where the First Masters have gone, too.'

I agreed, and we left the village and the stench of fear behind us.

Chapter Twelve
The Dance of the First Masters

THE LONG GRASS hid our approach up to the Crystal Pit and we lay observing the weird sight before us.

The dog-people had by this time almost dragged the machines up to the brink of the scintillating pit.

I watched, uncertain what to do, as they heaved them over the edge. I heard them slide down, some of them seeming to protest with a screaming noise created by the friction as they slid into the pit.

Just a they had done with us, the dog-people began to back away from the edge once the last machine had been deposited. I knew that the Yaksha machines were durable enough not to have been harmed by the way they had been handled.

Then, in the distance, I saw the First Masters come winging to settle into the pit like vultures upon a corpse.

For a moment all of them were obscured from our view by the sides of the pit; then they came flapping up again, in some sort of order, until they had formed a circle, hovering again in the air above the Crystal Pit.

Now they began to perform a weird, aerial dance, following a pattern which I could not at once understand.

The dance went on, becoming more and more frenetic, and yet keeping its order, no matter how fast the First Masters flew.

There was something almost pathetic about this dance and, not for the first time, I could sympathise a little with the long-forgotten impulses which had driven the First Masters to become the mindless things they now were.

On and on went the dance of the First Masters; faster and faster they whirled in the air above the Crystal Pit. Whether it was a ritual of homage to the machines or a dance of hatred I shall never know.

What I do know, however, is that some of their insensate emotion was reflected in me, and I watched in awe as it went on.

Finally one of their number dived swiftly into the pit. A second followed, then another and yet another, until all were once again hidden from our view.

I assumed that they must have activated something in the machines.

Suddenly there came a vast eruption from the Crystal Pit, a pillar of fire that rose hundreds of feet into the air.

The atmosphere was torn by a great, screaming roar. The dog-people had not had time to retreat to a safe distance. Every one of them was consumed in the blast of energy from the pit.

For a few moments the pillar of fire continued to rise higher and higher. Then it subsided.

The air was still.

Nothing moved.

Zapha and the other cat-folk said nothing. We simply exchanged glances that showed our deep bewilderment at what we had just witnessed.

There was no longer any possibility of discovering if one of the machines was the one I needed. I would just have to hope that the one I wanted – if it still existed – survived somewhere else.

The First Masters were dead, taking most of their servants with them.

Back in the cat village, we told the folk of Purha what we had seen.

There was an atmosphere of quiet jubilation about the village then, though the cat-people were contemplative enough to brood on the significance of what we told them – though its true significance was hard to fathom.

Some death-wish had been tapped in the First Masters, some ancient drive which had taken them to the destruction of themselves as human beings – and now as entities.

A cycle seemed to have been completed. It would be best to forget it, I felt.

My next objective must be to find Bagarad.

There the other stolen machines remained – or so I hoped. There I might find what I sought.

I discussed this with the cat-people and they told me that they felt it their duty to go with me to Bagarad. I told them that their company would be welcome, particularly since I still mourned the loss of Hool Haji. But I did not wish to get them involved in any fighting.

'Let *us* decide whether the fighting should involve us or not,' said Zapha with a quiet smile.

Fasa now spoke up. 'I would go with you, Michael Kane, but it is hard for me to leave at the moment. Take this, however, and hope it brings you luck.'

She handed to me a needle-thin dagger which could be fitted behind my harness. In some ways it resembled the hidden skinning knife of the Mendishar and it was intended to be used for the same purpose – if danger threatened.

I accepted it gratefully, commenting on the weapon's precise workmanship.

'A little rest,' I said, 'if I may, and we'll be off to seek Bagarad.'

The wise old cat-man, Slurra, brought out some tablets which he had told me of earlier.

'Here is the only map we have,' he said. 'It is probably inexact, but it will show you the general direction to take in order to reach the country of the barbarians.'

I accepted this also with an expression of thanks. He raised his hand.

'Do not thank us – let us thank you that we can repay all you have done for us, both with your actions and your words,' he said. 'I only hope that you will return to Purha some day, when the world is tranquil.'

'It will be one of the first things I shall do,' I promised, 'if I ever accomplish my mission and remain alive.'

'If it is possible, Michael Kane, you will do it – and live.' He smiled.

*

Next morning, myself, Zapha and a party of cat-men set off for Bagarad which lay to the south of the land of the cat-people.

Our journey was a long one, and involved crossing a mountain range where, to our sorrow, we lost one of our number.

But on the other side of the valley we encountered a land of friendly, farming folk who willingly gave us daharas in exchange for some of the cat-folk's artefacts, which they had brought along for this purpose.

The cat-folk were not used to riding, but their quick intelligence and sense of balance helped, and soon we were all riding along like old cavalrymen!

The going was fairly easy for several days until we came to a land of marshes and lowering skies. Here we had difficulty picking our way along the ribbons of firm ground which criss-crossed the marshes.

It seemed to be drizzling permanently and it was much colder.

I would be glad when we left this area and found a pleasanter land.

We spoke little as we rode, concentrating on guiding our daharas through the marshes.

It was towards evening on the third day of our journey through the marsh when we first discovered we were being watched.

Zapha, with his quick cat's eyes, noticed it first and rode up to warn me.

'I have only seen glimpses of them,' he said, 'but there are a number of men out there in the marsh. We had better be wary of attack.'

Then I began to notice them and began to feel uncomfortable.

It was not until night had fallen that they suddenly rose from all around us and came silently towards us. They were tall men, well-shaped but for their heads, which were smaller than they should have been in proportion to their bodies.

They bore swords – heavy, wide-bladed affairs which they swung at us and which we met with our lighter weapons.

We were able to defend ourselves well enough, but in the

darkness it was confusing, for these people evidently knew the marsh and we did not.

I struck about me, keeping them at a distance, my dahara rearing and snorting and becoming difficult to control. These beasts were harder to control than the variety found on Southern Mars and part of my concentration had to be used to quiet my beast as best I could.

I felt a blade nick my arm, but paid little attention to the wound.

Through the darkness I caught glimpses of my comrades fighting, and every so often one would go down. So I decided that it would be best if we made a dash for it, hoping to keep firm ground under our beasts' feet.

I shouted to Zapha and he yelled back his agreement. We urged our daharas forward and began to gallop recklessly away from the men who had attacked us.

On through the night we rode, praying that the swamp would not take us. The small-headed men behind us appeared to give up the chase quite soon, and at length we were able to slow down. We decided that, since the moons had risen, we should continue rather than make camp and risk a further attack at night.

By morning we were still safe, although once or twice we had narrowly escaped riding into the marsh, and were very tired.

My wound was aching a little, but I soon bound it up and forgot about it. We were now near the edge of the marsh and could see firmer ground ahead of us.

Also we could see the outlines of what appeared to be a series of buildings, but it was hard to decide whether they comprised a city or not.

Zapha suggested that we should approach the place cautiously, but he also thought that it would be a safe place to make camp if it were uninhabited.

As we approached the buildings we noticed that they were, in fact, ruined shells of houses. Weeds grew in the streets. It looked as if, long ago, a fire had destroyed the city.

But when we approached closer we saw a party of mounted men to the west of the city. They were riding full tilt at it with bared weapons – swords and axes mainly. They were yellow-skinned men and were wearing bright cloaks and highly decorated war-harness. The yellow of their skins was not like that of the Oriental, but a deeper, brighter yellow, somewhat like lemon-yellow.

From somewhere within the ruins we heard a yell – the voice of one man – and we gathered that it was he the yellow men were attacking.

We were undecided how to act, not knowing what situation had arisen, but rode in closer to get a better view of what was happening.

Then I saw the man whose voice we had heard – and I could not believe my eyes.

The man whom the yellow warriors attacked with such ferocity was none other than Hool Haji!

The Blue Giant looked weary and travel-stained. He seemed to have a half-healed wound in his shoulder, but he bore a great, wide sword of a kind I had seen in the hands of the yellow-skinned warriors.

As the yellow riders bore down on Hool Haji, I gave a great shout and urged my dahara towards him.

Zapha and his men followed and soon we were face to face with the yellow warriors.

They seemed dismayed by our sudden appearance. They had expected to have to fight only one man and now found nearly twenty riders coming to his rescue.

We had killed and wounded only a few before the rest turned their mounts about and rode away. They mounted a hill and were quickly lost from our view on the other side.

I swung myself off my dahara's broad back and walked towards Hool Haji. He seemed as astonished to see me as I was to see him.

'Hool Haji!' I cried. 'You are alive! How did you get here?'

He laughed. 'You will think me a liar when I tell you – but tell you I must. I had thought you dead, also, Michael Kane. Have you any food? We must feast and celebrate our coming together again!'

We posted guards and the rest of us built a fire and cooked some provisions.

While we ate, Hool Haji told me his story.

He had, as I suspected, been carried to the mountain lair of the First Masters. It was a dark warren of caves in the highest peaks and there they nested like strange birds.

He had not been harmed at first, but had been deposited close to the central nest, where a young creature of the same species rested.

From the way that they protected this youngster, Hool Haji gathered that this was, in fact, the last of their species, since he saw no females while he was there.

He had been left as food for the young one by the First Masters and expected them to kill him but, just as they were coming towards him, something had disturbed them. He didn't know what it was. They had suddenly taken it into their heads to fly off.

Left alone with the young one, who was actually not very much smaller than himself, he had conceived the idea of training it and thus escaping from the eyrie.

Using his sword, which the First Masters had not had sense enough to take from him, he prodded the young creature to the edge of the outer cage. He clambered upon its back and, by many pricks from the sword, had taught it to obey him.

He had meant to return in the direction of the Crystal Pit and see if he could find any trace of me, but the young Jihadoo – as Hool Haji called it – had revealed a mind of its own after its initial bewilderment, and had resisted him.

It had begun to fly very fast until it had become very tired.

Lower and lower it had sunk, by this time just managing to brush over the tops of the trees.

Then some kind of weariness caused it to turn in the air and begin snapping at Hool Haji. A fight developed. Hool Haji was forced to kill the creature to protect himself and they had both fallen to earth, where Hool Haji had escaped with only a few bruises. But the creature was dead.

Hool Haji had landed in the swamp we had just crossed, but had managed to haul himself to firm ground, and began crossing the marsh.

Then the men with small heads had attacked. Hool Haji called them the Perodi.

They had overwhelmed him after a desperate fight and taken him overland to a city which lay many shatis to the west.

Here the men with small heads had sold him as a slave to the yellow-skinned people who lived in the city – the Cinivik, as they called themselves.

Hool Haji had refused to work as a slave for the Cinivik and had at length been chained in one of their prisons, of which, apparently, they had many.

He was displayed, because of his physical peculiarities, as some kind of zoo specimen, but bided his time until he had recovered all his strength.

Then he had managed to wrench his chains out of the wall and throttle his jailer, taking the man's sword and escaping, after a fight or two, from the city.

As luck would have it, his only route of escape was into the marshes. He had had several encounters with the Perodi but had managed to beat them. He had won several swords from them in these fights and had snapped two while getting the chains off his arm.

Apparently a reward had been offered for him and the Perodi had told the Cinivik where he was. He had taken to using the ruins as his main base.

A small party of warriors had been sent out to find him, but he had killed several and beaten the rest off.

He would have been killed or recaptured, he believed, if we had not arrived on the scene just as the second expedition were about to attack him.

'And that, in brief, is the sum total of my adventures until today,' he told me. 'I am sorry if I have bored you.'

'You have not,' I told him. 'And now let me tell you my story. I think you will like it.'

I told Hool Haji everything that had happened since our forced parting and he listened attentively.

After I had finished, he said: 'Of the two of us, the most has happened to you. So you are on the way to Bagarad now, are you? I will be pleased to rejoin you and help as best I can.'

'Discovering you alive is the best thing that has happened yet,' I told him sincerely.

That night I slept well and deeply.

In the morning we rode on for Bagarad, which was still several days' journey away.

The terrain was easier now and made travel lighter. The whole party of us rode along, talking and joking among ourselves, while a great plain stretched away in all directions, giving us a sense of security, since no enemies could approach without warning.

But there were no enemies on the plain, only herds of strange-looking animals which, Zapha informed us, were quite harmless.

Soon the plain gave way to hilly country that was just as pleasant, for the hills were covered in bright, orange grass, with red and yellow flowers growing in profusion.

It was strange how, on Mars, one would discover a landscape quite similar to Earth's and then, suddenly, come upon another that one might never expect to find on any planet.

Soon now, if the map was accurate, we should come to Bagarad and the long-missing machines.

Chapter Thirteen
The Remains

BY THE NEXT afternoon we had left the hills and were crossing a rugged landscape of rock and coarse turf, with twisted trees springing from anywhere that a little earth had deposited itself amongst cracks in the rocks.

This was the land where Bagarad lay.

But before we reached Bagarad we came upon a party of barbarians whom I recognised as being similar to those who had followed Rokin to eventual destruction.

They were gaunt-eyed men, women and children – and they merely waited for us to pass without challenging us in any way.

I stopped my dahara and spoke to one of them.

'Do you know where Bagarad lies from here?' I asked.

The man mumbled something which I did not catch.

'I do not hear you,' I said.

'Do not look for Bagarad,' he said. 'If you would see where Bagarad lies, go that way.' And he pointed.

I was a little perturbed by what he had said, but set my dahara in the direction he had indicated. Hool Haji, Zapha, and the catmen followed.

It was nearly evening by the time we came to Bagarad.

There was very little of it left.

There were only ruins and the ruins were deserted. A pall of dusty smoke hung over them.

I knew instinctively what had happened. We had come too late. The barbarians had tampered with the machines and destroyed themselves.

Those we had seen must have been the remnants who had survived.

I climbed down from my dahara and began to pick my way through the ruins.

Here was a piece of metal, there part of a coil. It was evident that all the Yaksha machines had been destroyed. I noticed a small metal tube and picked it up. It must have been a part from one of the machines. I tucked it into my belt pouch regretfully – it was the only complete part left.

With a sigh I turned to Hool Haji.

'Well, my friend,' I said, 'our quest is over. Somehow we must now return to the Yaksha vaults to see if anything remains.'

Hool Haji clasped my shoulder. 'Do not worry, Michael Kane. Perhaps it was for the best that the machines were destroyed.'

'Unless one of them held the secret that could have cured the plague,' I pointed out. 'Think of the madness and the misery in Cend-Amrid. How are we going to combat that?'

'We must simply put the case to our physicians and hope they can devise a cure.'

But I shook my head. 'Martian physicians are not used to analysing diseases. There is no cure for the Green Death – or will not be for many years.'

'I suppose you are right.' he admitted. 'Then the Yaksha vaults are our only chance.'

'It seems to be so.'

'But how are we to return to our own continent?' was his next question.

'We must find a ship.' I pointed to the east, where the sea could be seen in the distance.

'Finding a ship is not so easy,' Hool Haji said.

'The Bagarad had ships,' I told him. 'They must have a harbour.' I pulled out a map. 'Look. There is a river not far from here. Perhaps they have ships moored there.'

'Let us go there, then,' he said. 'I am aching to set foot in my own land again.'

We rode to the river and, after a while, we discovered a place where several Bagarad ships were moored. They were deserted.

What urge had made the survivors go inland? I wondered.

Why had they not taken a ship? Perhaps they associated ships with the machines that had destroyed their city. I could think of no other explanation.

We decided on a small ship with a single mast that could just about be worked by two men.

Zapha spoke to me after Hool Haji had picked out our boat and we had discussed its merits.

'Michael Kane,' said Zapha, 'we would be honoured if you would take us with you.'

I shook my head. 'You have helped enough, Zapha. You will be needed by your own people, and it is a long journey back. In a way, your journey has been wasted, but I am glad you have lost so few men.'

'That is a relief to me, too,' he said. 'But... but we would follow you, Michael Kane. We still feel our debt to you.'

'Do not thank me,' I told him. 'Thank circumstances. It could have been any other man.'

'I do not think so.'

'Be careful, Zapha,' I said. 'Remember your old prophet. If you admire something in me, look for it in yourself. You will find it there.'

He smiled. 'I see what you mean,' he said. 'Yes, perhaps you are right.'

Soon after that we parted regretfully and I hoped that some day I would be able to return to Purha and meet the cat-people again.

Hool Haji and I checked our boat and discovered that it was well provisioned, as if it had been intended for use just before the explosion.

With some misgivings, Hool Haji allowed me to shove off and soon we were sailing down the river, bound for the open sea.

The sea soon loomed ahead of us and at length we had left land behind.

Luckily, the ocean was not in turmoil. Hool Haji said that he thought this was normally a quiet season on the Western ocean, and I thanked providence for that.

We set a course for a part of the coast nearest to the Yaksha vaults.

Was there still time to save Cend-Amrid?

I did not know.

Some days passed and our voyage had been without mishap. We were just beginning to feel that good luck was now completely on our side when Hool Haji gave a startled cry and pointed ahead of us.

There, heaving itself from the deep ocean, was a monster of staggering proportions.

Water ran from its back and dripped from its great, green head. Streamers of flesh clung to its body, as if it had been lacerated in some mighty underwater fight.

It did not seem to be mammal or fish – a reptile perhaps, though its body was like that of a hippopotamus and its head somewhat resembled that of a duck-billed platypus.

It was not so much its appearance as its size that was so astonishing. It dominated our little boat and could have opened its jaws and swallowed it, had it wished.

Perhaps it did not normally come to the surface but had been driven there by the victor of the fight it must recently have had.

Whatever the reason, we wished that it had not come, for it paddled towards us, seemingly motivated more by curiosity than anything else.

We could do nothing but gape and hope that it would not attack us.

The huge head bent and the great eyes gazed and I had the impression, in spite of my fears, that it was not in any way a savage beast.

Indeed, it seemed more gentle than many much smaller creatures I had encountered on Mars.

Having inspected us, it raised its head again and looked about, as if taking a last look at the surface.

Then it began to dive, leaving behind it a foaming sea, perhaps returning to the fray it had left, perhaps simply disturbed by what it had seen.

Hool Haji and I breathed a sigh of relief.

'What was it?' I asked him. 'Do you know?'

'I have only heard of it. In Mendishar they call it a Sea Mother – because of its gentle nature, perhaps. They have never been known to harm ships. At least, they have never deliberately attacked one, though occasionally they have sunk one by accident.'

'Then I am glad it saw us first.' I smiled.

A little later we saw a shoal of large creatures, much smaller than the Sea Mother, but nonetheless daunting, and Hool Haji spoke warningly.

'I hope they do not come too close,' he said. 'They are by no means as gentle as the Sea Mother.'

I could make out their snakelike bodies and their sharp heads, rather like swordfish.

'What are they?' I said.

'*N'heer*,' he told me. 'They range all the seas in packs, attacking anything they see.' He smiled bleakly. 'Luckily they don't see as much as they might, since they are extremely short-sighted creatures.'

We steered as far away from the *n'heer* as we could get, but it was our bad luck that they should take it into their heads to swim closer and closer to the ship.

Hool Haji drew his sword.

'Be ready,' he said softly. 'I think they will see us in a moment.'

And, sure enough, they did.

They had been moving at a fairly leisurely pace, but now they darted swiftly through the water, their sinuous necks straight out, their pointed heads like so many spears flying at us.

They drove at the ship, but the ancient hull resisted this and for a moment they swam around rapidly in some sort of confusion.

Then they rose further out of the water and began to stab at us.

We slashed at their pointed heads with our swords and they hissed and snapped at us.

Shoulder to shoulder we fought them off as more of them attacked. Our swords pierced their comparatively soft bodies but seemed to have little lasting effect on them.

Some of them had flopped completely out of the water and landed on the deck.

They writhed towards us.

One of them managed to stab me in the leg before I ran my sword into its eye.

Another nearly took my arm off, but I chopped its head open.

Soon the deck was slippery with their blood and I found it difficult to keep my footing.

Just when it seemed that we should soon be food for the *n'heer*, I heard the throb of engines above me.

It was an impossible sound.

I risked a glance upwards.

It was an impossible sight!

There were several airships of my own design. From their cabins floated the colours of Varnal.

What freak of chance had brought them here?

I had not time to think of that then, as we were forced to concentrate on defending ourselves against the *n'heer*.

But help came from the airships. Arrows rained down on the slimy creatures and many died before the rest swam rapidly off.

A rope was lowered from one of the ships. I grabbed it and began to climb.

Soon I was looking into the face of none other than my brother by marriage – Darnad of the Karnala. His youthful face was grinning in delight and relief and he gripped my shoulder warmly.

'Michael Kane, my brother!' he said. 'At last we have found you!'

'What do you mean?' I asked.

'I will tell you later. Let us help Hool Haji aboard first. Luck has been with you.'

As we helped Hool Haji aboard, I was forced to give him an ironic grin. 'Luck has been with me? I did not think so until now.'

Chapter Fourteen
The Green Death

DARNAD SAT AT the controls of the airship I had taught him to navigate and several Varnalian warriors sat around on the couches grinning their joy at seeing us again.

'I would like to know just how you happened to be in this part of the Western ocean at this particular time,' I said. 'The coincidence seems too incredible to be true.'

'It is no coincidence, really,' he said, 'but happy circumstances.'

'Then tell me of them.'

'Do you remember a girl from Cend-Amrid? Ala Mara, her name is.'

'Of course. But how do you know her?'

'Well, you left her in your airship when you went to inspect the vaults of the Yaksha, did you not?'

'We did.'

'Apparently the girl became a little bored and began fiddling with the control panel of the ship. She meant no harm, naturally, but by accident she released the mooring lines of the airship and the craft began to drift in the wind.'

'So that is what happened. Lucky for her that it did, I think.'

'Why so?'

'Because otherwise she would have been found by those who captured us.'

'Who were they?'

'I'll tell you that when I've heard the rest of your story.'

'Very well. The airship drifted on the air currents for many days before it was sighted by one of our patrol craft which had set out with a message for you from Shizala.'

'A message?'

'Yes. I will also tell you of that in a moment.'

'The girl told of the situation in Cend-Amrid and why you had gone to the Yaksha vaults. The ship returned first to Varnal with the girl and its news. Then I headed this expedition to Yaksha to see if we could help since we guessed you would be almost stranded there without any means of transport – though we thought you might make for Mendishar.

'When we arrived at Mendishar they had no news of you, so we went to Yaksha.'

'And found us gone.'

'Exactly.'

'What did you do then?'

'Well, we did discover signs that many of the machines had been removed. Also, we found the corpses of many warriors whom we did not recognise. We gathered that you had been in a fight and had vanquished your enemies. We guessed then that you might have been captured. Travelling overland, we were able to follow a trail through the desert to the coast where we found further signs that a ship had recently left there.'

'What did you do when you discovered that the ship had probably taken us over the sea?'

'There was little we could do, save try to find the ship – and we never did find it. All we could do after that was scour both sea and coast in the hope of finding some clue. We were on our fifth trip back when we sighted your boat and were able to help you.'

'In the nick of time,' I said. 'I'm very grateful, Darnad.'

'Nonsense. But what has happened to you? Did you find a machine that will be able to cure the plague?'

'No, I am sorry to say.'

Then I told Darnad all that had happened to us. He listened avidly.

'I am glad you both survived,' he said. 'And I hope we shall all be able to see the cat-people some day.'

'Now,' I smiled. 'I have been patient enough. What was the message being borne to me from Shizala?'

'A joyful one,' Darnad said. 'You are to become a father!'

That one scrap of news did more for me than anything else. I could hardly contain my enthusiasm, and everyone joined in congratulating me.

It had been worth going through all I had done to hear that Shizala was going to give me a child. I could not wait to get home and see her.

But first there was my duty. I had to visit the Yaksha vaults and seek the device that the Yaksha must have possessed to counter the effects of the Green Death.

Now we were crossing the land and the Yaksha vaults in the desert would soon be reached.

Then we saw them below us and Darnad brought the airship closer to the ground.

The ships were moored and we left a few men on guard while we once again entered the vaults.

This time, with more men, we could make a really thorough search for the device we sought. For all I knew it might be in tablet or even liquid form, but knowing the fantastically sophisticated science of the Yaksha I thought it might be a machine capable of dispensing some kind of ray that would work directly on the disease germs.

We searched for several days. The vaults were vast, and it took time to check everything we found. The barbarians had left a great deal. They had taken, in fact, only those machines that seemed designed for war. Many other types were left, though all the war machines, it seemed, had gone. Now I knew they were destroyed for good, and perhaps it was just as well, though I regretted missing the opportunity of analysing their principles.

But, though we checked everything, we could find nothing that seemed designed to counter the Green Death. At length we were forced to give up and return to the airships.

Now I sat at the controls while Darnad relaxed.

I set a course for Varnal.

'Now what can we do?' Darnad asked gloomily. 'Must we forget Cend-Amrid?'

'If you had seen the horror there,' I told him, 'you would not suggest that. We shall just have to try to find a cure ourselves, though the time that would take must be very long – unless we are very lucky.'

We did not pass over Cend-Amrid on our way back and I was rather relieved, for I did not think I could bear to look on the place, even from such a height.

But it was as we neared the Crimson Plain that lies quite close to Varnal that I noticed a vast procession of people below me.

At first I thought it was an army on the march, but its order was too ragged.

I dropped lower to see it and observed that it was in fact made up of men, women and children of all ages.

I was fascinated by the sight and could not understand why so many people should be on the move.

I guided the airship down lower and then saw in horror what I had half feared since I had left Cend-Amrid.

The Green Death was on them all.

Somehow a traveller must have come and gone from Cend-Amrid and taken the seeds of the plague with him.

Perhaps he had returned to his own city and it had become infected.

But why were they on the move?

I took the megaphone from its place near the control panel and went to the cabin door.

I shouted down at the crowd, who were by this time gaping up.

They were all in rags, with gaunt, haunted faces.

'Who are you?' I bellowed through the megaphone. 'Where are you from?'

One of them shouted back: 'We are the non-functional! We seek refuge.'

'What do you mean, non-functional? Do you come, then, from Cend-Amrid?'

'Some of us do. But many come from Opquel, Fiola and Ishal, too.'

'Who told you you were non-functional?' I shouted. 'The folk of Cend-Amrid?'

'We have a mechanic with us. He, too, is non-functional. He is our head – we are his hands, his motor, his feet.'

I realised then that not only the plague had come from Cend-Amrid – so had part of the dreadful creed that ruled there.

'If he is non-functional, why does he lead you?'

'We are the great non-functional. It is our duty to produce a non-functional world.'

I was experiencing a further perversion of logic whereby someone had convinced those infected by the plague that it was good to have the plague and bad not to have it.

This could mean that the Green Death could spread like wildfire throughout Southern Mars – perhaps across the whole planet – unless it could somehow be checked.

'Where do you go now?' I asked.

'Varnal!' came the reply.

I almost dropped the megaphone in horror.

The Green Death must not reach Varnal.

Now I had something even more intensely personal to fight for. Would I keep my head?

I prayed that I would.

'Do not go to Varnal!' I cried, half pleadingly. 'Stay where you are! We will find a way of curing you. Do not fear!'

'Cure us!' shouted the man. 'Why should you wish to? We are bringing the joys of the Green Death to all men!'

'But the Green Death means horror and agony!' I cried. 'How can you believe that it is good?'

'Because it is Death!' replied the man.

'But surely you cannot seek death. You cannot want to die – it is against all that is human!'

'Death brings the cessation of function,' droned the plague victim. 'Cessation of function is good. The evil man is the functioning man.'

I shut the cabin door against him. I leaned back against the walls of the cabin, sweating.

'They must be stopped!' growled Hool Haji, who had overheard most of the conversation.

'How?' I half moaned.

'If it comes to that, we must destroy them,' he said bleakly.

'No!' I cried.

But I knew I hardly believed what I said. I was becoming a victim of fear.

I must fight that fear, I knew. But what was I to do?

Chapter Fifteen

The Threat to Varnal

WE SPED AS rapidly as we could towards Varnal and at last her slender towers came in sight.

As soon as we had landed I made for the palace and there, waiting on the steps to greet me, was my Shizala, lovely Bradhinaka of the Karnala, loveliest flower of the House of Varnal.

I sprang to embrace her, careless of who saw us.

She returned my embrace and looked into my face with shining eyes.

'Oh, Michael Kane, you are back at last! I had feared you dead, my Bradhinak!'

'I cannot die while you live,' I said. 'That would be foolish of me.'

She smiled at me then.

'Have you heard my news?' she said.

I pretended I had not.

I wished to hear it from her own lips.

'Then come to our apartments,' she told me. 'And I will tell you there.'

In our apartments she told me simply that we were to have a child. It was enough to bring a surge of joy to me just as strong as when I first heard the news, and I lifted her high in my arms with enthusiasm, putting her down again so rapidly when I remembered her condition that she laughed at me.

'We of the Karnala are not delicate.' She smiled. 'My mother was out riding her dahara when I first showed signs of my arrival into the world.'

I grinned back. 'Nonetheless,' I said, 'I will have to make sure you have plenty of protection from now on.'

'Treat me like a baby and I'll be off to marry an Argzoon,' she threatened jokingly.

My elation began to be clouded again as I thought of the carriers of the Green Death moving so steadily towards Varnal.

She seemed to notice that something was wrong and asked me what it was.

I told her, grimly, simply, trying not to dramatise the situation, though heaven knew it was bad enough.

She nodded thoughtfully when I had finished.

'But what can we do about it?' she said. 'We cannot kill them. They are not sane or well – they hardly know they threaten us.'

'That is the trouble,' I said. 'How do we stop them coming to Varnal?'

'There might be one way,' she suggested.

'What is that?'

'We could set the Crimson Plain afire – that would deter them, surely?'

'It would be a crime to destroy the Crimson Plain. And, besides, there are towns and villages on it that would suffer.'

'You are right,' she agreed.

'Moreover,' I said, 'they have probably already reached the Crimson Plain by now. It will not be long before they arrive at their destination.'

'You mean Varnal?'

'Varnal is the city of which they spoke.'

Shizala sighed.

I sat down on a chair and leaned on the table next to it, loosening the war-harness I had worn for so long. Something clattered in my pouch and I drew out what had made the noise.

It was the small tube, the complete part of one of the destroyed machines, I'd guessed, that I had picked up in ruined Bagarad.

I placed it on the table, echoing Shizala's sigh.

'In a few days the Green Death will come to Varnal,' she mused, 'unless something can be done. Something...'

'I have sought a means of countering the effects of the plague,' I said. 'I have sought it for a very long time – across two continents. I do not think it exists.'

'There is still hope,' she said, trying to keep my spirits up.

I rose and hugged her close. 'Thank you,' I said. 'Yes – there is still a little hope.'

The next morning I was in the central hall conferring with my father by marriage, the Bradhi Carnak; his son, Bradhinak Darnad; my wife, the Bradhinaka Shizala; and my friend the Bradhi Hool Haji. I, the Bradhinak Michael Kane, completed this royal gathering.

Our royal minds seemed incapable of constructive thought as we debated the problem of the Green Death.

I clung to my principles, though it was difficult when my wife and unborn child were being threatened.

'We cannot kill them,' I repeated. 'It is not their fault. If we kill them we kill something in ourselves.'

'I understand you, Michael Kane,' said old Carnak, nodding his massive head in agreement. 'But what else can we do if Varnal is to be made safe from the Green Death?'

'I think we shall have to come to the decision in the end, Michael Kane,' said Hool Haji seriously. 'I can see no alternative.'

'There has to be an alternative.'

'There are five minds trying to think of one,' Darnad pointed out. 'Five good minds, too – and not one of them has come up with a constructive idea. We could try capturing them – something like that.'

'But that would mean coming in physical contact with them and risking the plague ourselves,' said Hool Haji. 'Thus we should defeat our object.'

'We could use some kind of big net to trap them,' said Shizala. 'Though I suppose that is an impractical idea.'

'Indeed, it probably is.' I frowned. 'But it *is* an idea, my dear.'

They were all looking at me. I shrugged. 'My mind is as empty as anyone's could be,' I said.

Darnad sighed.

'There is only one thing to do, you know, Michael Kane.'

'What is that? Not to kill them – I must resist that solution.'

'We must go out in our airship and try to persuade them to turn back again,' he said.

I agreed. It was about the only sensible thing we could do now.

So, soon afterwards, we had taken the air again – Hool Haji, Darnad and myself.

It was not long before we had sighted the rabble, pouring raggedly across the Crimson Plain. It seemed, too, that they had taken on some extra numbers, perhaps folk from some of the villages they had passed through.

Green-tainted faces looked up as we began to drop toward them. They stopped moving and waited.

I used the megaphone to address them again.

'People of the Green Death,' I shouted. 'Why do you not stay where you are? Have you thought that you might be wrong?'

'You are the one who spoke to us yesterday,' came a voice. 'You must speak with the mechanic now. It is he who leads us to the ultimate non-functioning!'

The crowd backed away from a man with a green-ravaged face and large, insane eyes. He seemed to resemble in some ways the physician we had originally met in Cend-Amrid.

'Are you the leader?' I asked.

'I am the mind, they are the hands, the motor – all the parts of the moving machine.'

'Why do you lead them?'

'Because it is my place to lead.'

'Then why do you lead them to other settlements, towns and cities when you know that you will spread the plague wherever you go?'

'It is the benefits I bring them – the benefits of death, the release from life, the ultimate non-functioning.'

'Have you no thought for those you infect?'

'We bring them peace,' he replied.

'Please do not go to Varnal,' I urged. 'They do not want your peace – they only want their own.'

'Our peace is the one peace – the ultimate non-functioning.'

It was obviously still impossible to break through the man's insanity. It would take a subtler psychologist than myself even to begin.

'Do you realise that there are those in Varnal who speak of destroying you because of the threat you offer?' I asked him.

'Destroy us and we shall not function. That is good.'

There was no way round it.

The man was totally mad. With heavy hearts we returned to Varnal.

In the City of the Green Mists – soon to be renamed City of the Green Death, I reflected, if the rabble continued its march – we sat beside the green lake and again tried to resolve our problem.

Darnad was frowning as if searching mentally for a forgotten piece of information.

Suddenly he looked up. 'I have heard of one man who might have the skill to devise a cure for the Green Death,' he said. 'Though I believe the man is a legend – he might not even exist.'

'Who is he?' I asked.

'His name is Mas Rava. He was once a physician at the Court of Mishim Tep, but he became afflicted with philosophical notions and went off to the mountains somewhere in the far South. Mas Rava had studied all the old Sheev texts he could find. But something turned him into a contemplative and he was never seen again.'

'When was he supposed to have been at the court of Mishim Tep?' I asked.

'More than a hundred years ago.'

'Then he could be dead.'

'I am not sure. I never listened very carefully to the stories about him in Mishim Tep. But one thing I remember – they say he had given himself immortality.'

'There is a slim chance that he still exists, however,' I said.

'Just a slim one, yes.'

'But the chances of finding him are even slimmer in the time we have at our disposal,' Carnak pointed out.

'We could never find him in time, whatever happened,' Hool Haji said.

Shizala said nothing. She simply bowed her head and looked into the waters of the green lake.

Suddenly there came a cry from behind us and a Pukan-Nara – which was the name used on Vashu for a leader of a detachment of warriors – came rushing towards us.

'What is it?' I asked him.

'One of our scouting airships has returned,' he said.

'Well?' Carnak asked.

'The rabble is moving with unnatural rapidity. They will be at the walls of Varnal within a day.'

Darnad glanced at me. 'So soon?' he said. 'I would never have suspected it. By talking to them we seem to have done ourselves a disservice.'

'They are running,' the Pukan-Nara said. 'From what the scout says, many drop exhausted or dead, but the rest *run*. Something is causing them to rush towards Varnal. We must stop them!'

'We have considered all ways of stopping them,' I told him.

'We must fight them.'

I clung to my rationality. 'We must not,' I said wearily, though I was tempted to agree once again.

'Then what can we do?' the Pukan-Nara asked desperately.

I came to the decision that had always really been there.

'I know what this means to you,' I said. 'It means the same to me – perhaps even more.'

'What are you going to say, Michael Kane?' asked my lovely wife.

'We must evacuate Varnal. We must let the Green Death have her and must flee towards the mountains.'

'Never!' cried Darnad.

But Carnak put a hand on his son's arm.

'Michael Kane has brought us something more valuable than life or even homeland,' he said thoughtfully. 'He has brought us responsibility to ourselves – and thus to all men on Vashu. His logic is inescapable, his reasons clear. We must do as he says.'

'I will not!' Darnad turned to me.

'Michael Kane!' he cried. 'You are my brother – I love you as my brother, as a great fighter, a great friend. You cannot mean what you say. Let Varnal be taken over by that rabble – that diseased people! You must be insane!'

'On the contrary,' I said quietly. 'It is insanity that I fight. I am striving to remain sane. Let your father tell you – he knows what I mean.'

'These are desperate times, Darnad,' Shizala said. 'They are complicated times. Thus it is so much harder to know the right action to take when action is called for. The people of the Green Death, like the people of Cend-Amrid, are insane. To use violence against them would be to encourage a different kind of insanity in ourselves. I think that is what Michael Kane means.'

'It is a great deal of what I mean.' I nodded. 'If we give in to fear now, what will the Karnala become?'

'Fear! But is not flight cowardice?'

'There are varieties of cowardice, my son,' said Carnak, rising. 'I think that flight from Varnal – even though we are strong enough easily to defeat that rabble advancing upon us – is not so great a cowardice. It is a responsibility.'

Darnad shook his head. 'I still do not understand. Surely there is nothing wrong in defending our city against aggression.'

'There are different kinds of aggressors,' I said. 'There were the Blue Giants of the Argzoon who came against Varnal soon after I had arrived on Vashu. These were a folk of comparatively healthy minds. It was a simple thing to fight them off. It was all we could do. But, if violence is used in this case, we lose touch with our whole cause – my whole cause, if you like, though I thought you all shared it. That is to cure the disease at its source; to cure the double disease of body and mind which has infected Cend-Amrid!'

Darnad looked at Hool Haji, who returned his gaze and then looked away. He glanced at his father and his sister. They said nothing.

He looked at me.

'I do not understand you, Michael Kane, but I will try to,' he said at length. 'I trust you. If we must leave Varnal then we must leave her.'

And then Darnad could no longer control the tears that began to course down his face.

Chapter Sixteen
The Exodus

AND THAT IS why I hope you will understand how a great city, healthy and strong, was left bereft of its population.

Warriors, craftsmen, women and children, left Varnal in an orderly procession, bearing their possessions with them, the airships – both of the Sheev pattern and my own design – drifting above them. Some left, like Darnad, weeping, others puzzled, some thoughtful, but all knowing in their hearts that it was right.

They left Varnal for a few diseased and deluded souls to make what they wanted of it, or take what they wanted of it.

It was the only thing to do.

I am not normally a thoughtful man, as I have told you, but I try to cling to certain principles, no matter how desperate the situation or terrible the threat. Not through any dogmatism but, if you like, from a fear of fear – fear of the actions one takes from fear, the thoughts one deludes oneself with from *fear*.

I rode a dahara, side by side with Shizala on my right and Hool Haji on my left. To his left was Carnak, Bradhi of the Karnala; to Shizala's right was Darnad, stern-faced and puzzled of eye.

Behind us rode or walked the proud folk of Varnal, the graceful City of the Green Mists falling further and further behind us.

Ahead were bleak mountains which we would make our home until some hope could be found for those smitten by the Green Death.

It was not merely the physical fate of Mars that was at stake as we made our exodus from the city. It was the moral fate – the psychological fate. We left Varnal so that Mars might still remain the planet I loved and Varnal itself might remain the city where I felt most at home.

We fought against fear and against hysteria and against the dreadful, insane violence that these emotions bring.

We did not leave Varnal to set an example to others. We left in order to set an example to ourselves.

All this may sound grandiose. I only ask that you consider what we did and try to understand its objectives.

Our journey to the mountains was a long one, for our pace was set by our slowest citizen.

At last the cold mountains were reached and we found a valley where we could build crude houses for ourselves, since the sides of the valley were thickly wooded.

This done, we set off in our airships to explore the mountains in the hope that we should find the almost legendary physician who was, perhaps, the only man on Mars who could save our world from the Green Death.

It was not I who eventually found Mas Rava, but he who had first named him – Darnad.

Darnad came back to the camp one night in his airship. He had taken to travelling alone and we sympathised with the necessity he felt for this.

'Michael Kane,' he said, entering the cabin where Shizala and I now lived. 'I have seen Mas Rava.'

'Can he help us?' was my first question.

'I do not know. I did not speak to him, save to ask him his name.'

'That is all he told you?'

'Yes. I asked who he was and he replied, "Mas Rava".'

'Where is he?'

'He is living in a cave many shatis from here. Do you wish me to take you to him?'

'I think so,' I replied. 'Do you think he has become a complete hermit? Will he be affected by our plight?'

'I cannot tell. In the morning I will take you there.'

So, in the morning, we left in Darnad's airship to find Mas Rava. Just as I had earlier sought the machines in the hope that they would save us, now I sought a man. Would the man prove more helpful than the machines? I was not sure. Should I have trusted the machines so much? Should I have trusted another man so much? Again I was not sure.

But I went with Darnad, navigating the ship amongst the crags, until we came to a place where a natural path climbed a mountain to a cave.

I lowered a ladder onto the wide ledge outside the cave and began to climb down until I stood outside the dark entrance.

Then I walked inside.

A man sat there, his back against the cave wall, one leg crooked and the other straight. He regarded me with humorous and quizzical eyes. He was clean-shaven and quite young-looking. The cave was clean and neatly furnished.

He was not my idea of a hermit, nor did his cave resemble a hermit's lair. There was something urbane about the man.

'Mas Rava?' I said.

'The same. Sit down. I had one visitor yesterday, and I was rather rude to him, I'm afraid. He was my first. I am better prepared for my second. What is your name?'

'Michael Kane,' I said. 'It is a long, complicated story, but I come from the planet Negalu,' I told him, using the Martian name for Earth, 'and from a time far in your future.'

'In that case you are an interesting man for my first real visitor,' said Mas Rava.

I sat down beside him.

'Have you come seeking information from me?' was his next question.

'In a way,' I said. 'But first you had better hear the whole story.'

'Make it the whole one,' said Mas Rava. 'I am not an easy man to bore. Proceed.'

I told him everything I have told you, everything I had thought and said, everything that was thought and said to me. It took me several hours, but Mas Rava listened all the time without interrupting.

When I had finished, he nodded.

'You have got yourself and your adopted people into an

interesting predicament,' he said. 'As a physician I am a little rusty, though you were right in one thing. There was a cure for the plague, according to my reading. It was not in the form of a machine – that is where you went wrong – but in the form of a bacteria capable of combating the effects of the Green Death in a mere matter of moments.'

'Do you know of any place where I could find a container of this bacteria?' I asked him.

'There are several repositories on Vashu similar to the Yaksha vaults you discovered. It could be in any one of them – though it is likely that something as relatively unimportant to either the Sheev or the Yaksha might easily have been allowed to corrode away.'

'So you think there is little chance of finding the antidote?' I asked despairingly.

'Yes, I do,' he said. 'But you could try.'

'And what about you – could you prepare an antidote?'

'In time, I might,' he said. 'But I do not think I will.'

'You would not even attempt it?'

'No.'

'Why is that?'

'Because, my friend, I am a convinced fatalist.' He laughed. 'I am sure that the Green Death will pass and that its passage will leave a mark on Vashu. But I think that mark is necessary to society – particularly a society that knows no deep dangers. It will prevent it stagnating.'

'I find your attitude difficult to understand,' I said.

'Let me be honest, then, and put it to you in another way. I am a lazy man – indolent. I like to sit in my cave and think. I think, incidentally, on a very high plane. I am also a man who needs little company. I have my fear, too, if you like – but it is a fear of becoming involved with humanity and thus losing myself. I value my individuality. So I rationalise all this and I become a fatalist. I have no concern with the affairs of the inhabitants of this planet, or any other planet. It is *planets* that interest me – not *a* planet.'

'It would seem to me, Mas Rava,' I said quietly, 'that you, in your own way, have lost your sense of perspective just as much as the rulers of Cend-Amrid.'

He thought over this statement and then looked into my face with a grin.

'You are right,' he said.

'Then you will help us?'

'No, Michael Kane, I will not. You have taught me a lesson and it will be of interest to speculate on what you have said. But I will not help you. You see –' he grinned at me again – 'what I have just realised, without bitterness or despair, is that I am essentially a stupid man. Perhaps the Green Death will come my way, eh?'

'Perhaps,' I said in disappointment. 'I am sorry you will not help us, Mas Rava.'

'I am sorry, too. But think of this, Michael Kane, if the words of a stupid man mean anything to you...'

'What is that?'

'The wish is sometimes enough,' said Mas Rava. 'Keep wishing that you might find the Green Death gone – provided you keep acting as well, even if you do not understand your own actions.'

I left the cave.

Patiently, Darnad was still there, the rope ladder still touching the ledge.

With a feeling of puzzled curiosity rather than disappointment, I climbed back into the cabin.

'Will he help us?' Darnad asked eagerly.

'No,' I told him.

'Why not? He must!'

'He says he will not. All he told me was that a cure for the plague did exist, might possibly exist now – and it is not a machine.'

'Then what is it?'

'A container of bacteria,' I mused. 'Come on, let us return to the camp.'

Next day I had made up my mind to return to Varnal and see what had happened to the city.

I took an airship without saying where I was going.

Varnal looked unchanged – even more beautiful, if anything – and as I landed in the city square there was no smell of death as I had expected, and none of the subtler smell of fear.

I stayed in my cabin, however, for safety's sake, and called out through the empty streets.

In a little while I heard footsteps and a woman with a small child walked round the corner. The woman was an upstanding person and her child looked very healthy.

'Who are you?' I asked in astonishment.

'Who are *you* is more to the point?' she replied boldly. 'What are you doing in Varnal?'

'This is the city where I normally live,' I said.

'And this is the city where I normally live, too,' she said crisply. 'Were you one of those who left?'

'If you mean was I one of the many thousands who left the city when the folk with the Green Death came,' I said, 'the answer is "yes".'

'All that is over now,' she said.

'What is over?'

'The Green Death. I had it for a while, you know.'

'You mean you have been cured? How? Why?'

'I don't know. It was coming to Varnal that did it. Maybe that's why we came here. I can't remember the journey too clearly.'

'You all came to Varnal and it cured you of the plague? What could it be – the water? The air? Something like that? By the Sheev, surely all my questing has not been for nothing. Surely the answer has not lain here all the time!'

'You sound a bit crazy to me,' said the woman. 'I don't know what it is. I only know I'm cured – and so is everybody else. A lot of them have gone back home, but I stayed on.'

'Where do you originally come from?' I asked.

'Cend-Amrid,' she said. 'I miss it, rather.'

I began to laugh uncontrollably.

'Here all the time!' I yelled. 'Here all the time!'

Chapter Seventeen
To Cend-Amrid

BY A STRANGE twist of fortune, it seemed, we were now able to return to Varnal.

It was a joyful occasion and the journey back was swifter even than the journey away from Varnal.

It was not only, of course, because of this that we felt light-hearted. We had discovered a cure for the plague – or, at least, we had discovered that the plague could be cured.

Once we had settled in Varnal, to the surprise of the few people who had made the city their home, we began to inspect the damage. There was nothing serious save that anything vaguely mechanical had been hurled into the green lake.

This must have been part of the mob's insane urge to destroy anything 'functional'.

Now it struck me that something could have been thrown into the lake that had caused the water to turn into an antidote for the plague.

I tried to think what it might be.

But I could not. Only now can I look back and wonder if that small tube I had carried with me from Bagarad, and which I never found again, had contained the antidote.

I shall never know.

The important thing is that the water of the Lake of the Green Mists was now able to combat the plague, and all we needed to do was to get it into containers and carry it to the victims.

This became our most important task.

We designed tanks to hold the green water and devised a means of attaching them to our airships.

Then we set off towards the central source of the plague – the insane city of Cend-Amrid.

With us we took Ala Mara, whom I had seen little of since she had rescued us, but who had begged to return with us.

A fleet of airships – all that we could muster – began the journey and our hopes were high. We flew away from Varnal with its pennants fluttering bravely from her towers again, towards the horror of the plague. In the leading airship were myself, Hool Haji and Ala Mara. In the nearest one to us was Darnad and his men, and behind us came the airships in charge of Varnal's bravest Pukan-Naras.

At several points we discovered towns and villages where the plague raged and were able to dispense the small amount of water needed to cure it.

Finding so many places infected, we concentrated first on helping these, and thus it was some time before we sighted Cend-Amrid ahead of us. It was the source of the plague and now, thanks to the green water, it was the last place where the plague flourished.

We came cautiously to the city and hovered above its houses.

Then we drifted until we were over the Central Place, the squat, ugly building where dwelt the Eleven.

Wooden-stepped and walking more stiffly and slower than when I had last observed and fought his kind, a guard appeared on the roof.

With immobile face he looked up.

'Who you? What want?'

'We bring a cure for the Green Death,' I told him.

'No cure.'

'We have one.'

'No cure.'

'Tell the Eleven that we bring a cure. Tell the Eleven to come to us.'

'I tell.'

The man walked stiffly off. It was hard to believe that a human being still lived under the robotlike exterior, but I was sure one could be found.

Soon the Eleven came onto the roof – though I was astonished to count Twelve of them.

Looking closely at their expressionless faces I could see that one of them was Barane Dasa, the man we had met in prison.

'Barane Dasa!' I cried. 'What are you doing back with these people?' He did not reply.

'You,' I said pointing. 'Barane Dasa! Answer me!'

The blank face remained expressionless.

'I One,' came the cold voice.

'But you – they judged you insane.'

'Mind repaired.'

I shuddered to think what that phrase might imply – even crude brain surgery was suggested by the statement 'mind repaired'.

'What want Cend-Amrid?' said another of the council.

'We bring a cure for the Green Death.'

'No cure.'

'But there is one – we have it – we have proved it.'

'Logic prove no cure.'

'But I can illustrate the fact that we have a cure,' I said desperately.

'No cure.'

I rolled down the ladder. I was going to have to talk to these fear-created creatures face to face, hope that a little humanity could be touched in them.

'Lower the water tank,' I said to Hool Haji. 'Perhaps that will convince them.'

'Be careful, my friend,' he warned.

'I will be,' I said. 'But I do not think they will use physical violence themselves.'

Soon I was standing on the flat roof, addressing the Eleven.

'Why do you call yourselves "Eleven" still?' I asked. 'You are Twelve again.'

'We Eleven,' they said, and I could not shake them. Evidently they had gone even further down the road to unreality than when I had first met them.

I stared into the cold, blank faces, looking for some sign of real life there, but I could find none.

Suddenly one of the Eleven pointed upwards.

'What that?'

'You've seen one before. It's an airship.'

'No.'

'But you saw one when I last came to Cend-Amrid.'

'What that?'

'An airship – they fly through the air. I showed you how the motor worked.'

'No.'

'But I did!' I said, exasperated.

'No. Airship not possible.'

'But of course they are possible. There it is for your own eyes. It exists!'

'Airship not work. Idea of airship non-functional idea.'

'You fools. You can see one working in front of you. What have you done to your own minds!'

One of the Eleven now put a whistle to his lips and blew a shrill note.

Onto the roof the sword-wielding automata who served them came running.

'What is all this about?' I asked. 'You must realise we are here to help you.'

'You make Cend-Amrid Machine non-functional. You destroy principle – you destroy motor – you destroy machine.'

'What principle?'

'The First Idea.'

'The idea that drove you to become what you are? What motor?'

'The Eleven.'

'You are not a motor – you are individual human beings. What machine?'

'Cend-Amrid!'

'Cend-Amrid is not a machine – it is a city created and lived in by people.'

'You make unfactual statement. You be made non-functional.'

Unwillingly, I drew my sword, but it was all I could do.

From above I heard a great yell from Hool Haji followed by a thump as he leapt from the airship and landed beside me.

The Eleven instructed their guards to attack us.

The great press of automata came towards us, raising their swords as one man.

Close to the edge of the roof, it seemed that Hool Haji and I would be toppled over within a few moments by the sheer mass of the guards.

Then, shouting the ancient cries of the Karnala, Darnad and other Varnalian warriors joined me, leaping from their airships until we formed a thin line of fighting men against the horrible, dead things that came towards us, slowly, at exactly the same pace, like a single strange entity.

The fight began.

The bravery of the Karnala is a legendary thing throughout the whole of Southern Mars, but they were never so brave as in this fight, when the thing they fought seemed never to die.

Every guard that went down was replaced by another. Every sword that was knocked from a fist was substituted by another. We had nothing at our backs but thin air, and so we could not retreat.

Somehow, by sheer willpower I think now, we actually began to gain ground from the automata.

We pushed them back, our swords flickering and flashing in the light, our battle-cries rarely off our lips as we shouted to one another to keep our spirits up.

Many of the automata went down.

Not one of our men received more than a minor wound. Somehow we all survived against the might of the men-turned-machines.

But, bit by bit, they surrounded us and crushed us inwards until there was no room to fight.

Then we were captured – not killed, as I had expected – and our swords wrenched from our hands.

What did the Eleven intend to do with us now?

I looked up at our airships. What would they do with those? With the plague-curing water we had brought?

I wondered if there was never to be good health and sanity in Cend-Amrid.

Chapter Eighteen

Hope for the Future

We were imprisoned in the same kind of cell we had found ourselves in before.

There were quite a few of us and it was rather cramped. I could not understand why we had not been killed outright, but I decided to accept this and begin trying to think of a means of escape.

I inspected our cell. It had been well made and designed specifically to imprison men – a rare thing on Mars, where the whole idea is normally abhorrent.

Suddenly I remembered the slim dagger that Fasa the cat-girl had given me earlier.

I removed it from my harness and looked at it, wondering how it might be used to our advantage.

There are only so many ways of escaping from prison – if the prison has been thoughtfully designed in order to afford no entrance but the door. I considered them all, going carefully over the door in particular.

The hinges were its weakest point. I began to work at the wood of the door frame, near the hinges, with the idea of hauling the door inwards.

I must have worked, absorbed in what I was doing, for several shatis.

At length I had succeeded in cutting the wood away from the frame. Then Hool Haji, Darnad and myself hauled at the door. It groaned inwards, the bar on the other side falling down with a clatter.

No-one seemed to have heard us.

Silently, we began to move towards the steps that led up to the first floor of the Central Place.

We had just reached the corridor and were hoping that we

could somehow reach the roof and the airships – if they were still there – when I heard a sound to my left.

I whirled, dagger in hand, crouched and ready for action.

A figure stood there, blank-faced and stiff-bodied. 'One!' I said. 'Barane Dasa!'

'I was coming to cells,' came the cold voice. 'Now it not necessary. You come.'

'Where to?' I asked.

'To main water supply Cend-Amrid,' was the reply. 'Your tanks are there.'

Wonderingly, we followed him, still unsure, still believing this might be some kind of trap.

We followed him through corridors and passages that seemed to lead away from the Central Place, perhaps under ground, until we came to a high-roofed place that was in semi-darkness. Here a great reservoir of water gleamed. On a kind of jetty leading out into the reservoir were the tanks in which we had carried the green water from the Lake of the Green Mists.

Somehow Barane Dasa must have manhandled them here by himself!

'Why do you go against the Eleven?' I asked him, as I checked that the tanks had not been tampered with.

'It is necessary.'

'But when I last saw you, you were a fairly normal human being. What has happened to you?'

For an instant his face relaxed and his eyes had a faint, ironic gleam. 'To help them we must not attack them,' he said. 'I think you taught me that, Michael Kane.'

I was astonished.

This man had pretended to become 'rehabilitated' into the Eleven so that he could try to reverse the effects of the creed he had himself originated. I could only admire him. I thought he might do it – once the plague was cured for good and all.

'But I still cannot quite see why you brought us here,' I said.

'For more than one reason. You saved the life of my niece, Ala Mara, while you were here. That is simple gratitude. But also you showed me how I might best work to correct the crime I began here in Cend-Amrid.'

I reached out and gripped his arm. 'You are a man, Barane Dasa. You *will* do it.'

'I hope so. Now you must all get the antidote into the water supply. All machines need fuel,' he said, 'and the machines of Cend-Amrid must drink.'

His reasoning was sound. We were going to do good, as he hoped to do personally, by stealth.

Soon we had got all the green water into the reservoir and our work was done – or would be done in the course of a day.

Now Barane Dasa said, 'You come,' returning to his original rôle.

We followed him through a series of winding passageways.

Slowly we began to work our way higher and higher until, to my astonishment – for I had completely lost my bearings – we found ourselves on the roof of the Central Place.

And there were our airships.

They were in exactly the place we had left them.

Peering down from the cabin of my own airship was Ala Mara, a smile of relief on her face.

'Uncle!' she whispered excitedly when she saw Barane Dasa. But the man did not look at her, keeping his face rigid and his body straight. He did not even make a gesture to her.

'Uncle –' her voice broke a little – 'don't you recognise me – Ala Mara, your niece?'

Barane Dasa remained silent.

I made a sign for her – a gesture that was meant to comfort her, but I heard her sob as she retreated into the cabin.

'Why did they do nothing to our airships?' I said softly to Barane Dasa.

'Airships not exist,' he said.

'So they cannot see them – or have deluded themselves into thinking that they can't see them.'

'Yes.'

'You have a hard fight on your hands for one man,' I said.

'Plague gone – fight easier,' he said. 'Plague go fast – this take longer.'

'And you will win, if any man can,' I said, voicing the sentiments I had expressed earlier.

I gripped his arm once more and began to climb the ladder up to the cabin. I would need to comfort Ala Mara now, tell her a little at least of what her uncle had been forced to make himself.

Soon we were all swinging up the ladders and entering our cabins.

Our main mission had been a success and some of our earlier exhilaration had returned.

The airships swung in the air, pointing back towards Varnal.

Soon we were speeding rapidly over the lakes, crossing the place of flowers and quicksands.

We were going home. In a sense we were already there, for our hearts were at ease and our minds at rest at long last!

We came back to Varnal on a peaceful morning full of gentle sunlight. The green mists swirled delicately through the city, the marble towers gleamed and glinted, and the whole city scintillated with light like a precious gem.

Far away came a faint sound, as of children singing, and we knew we were hearing the songs of the Calling Hills.

The whole of Mars seemed at peace. We had fought long and hard for that peace, but we were not heroes because of that. All we had done, in a sense, was to make heroes of all those who had fought with us.

It was enough.

Shizala was waiting in the central square near the palace. She was mounted on the broad back of a gentle dahara and she had another beast saddled and ready beside her.

I was not tired and I knew that she would know that.

I was quick to scramble down the ladder and swing from it onto the back of the waiting dahara.

I leaned over and kissed my wife, hugging her close to me.

'Is it over?' she asked.

'Mainly,' I said. 'In time it will be nothing but a memory of sadness and disturbance. It is good that Vashu should have such memories.'

'Yes.' She nodded. 'It is good. Come – let us ride to the Calling Hills as we used to when we first met.'

Together we urged our daharas forward through the quiet morning, riding through the lovely streets and out towards the Calling Hills.

With my beautiful wife riding beside me, and with the exhilaration of the fast ride, I knew that I had won something of immense value – something that I might well have lost if I had not come to Mars as I did.

The cool scents of the Martian autumn in my nostrils, I gave myself up to the joy that comes from true and simple happiness.

Epilogue

I HAD LISTENED with keen interest to Michael Kane's story and it had moved me to a deeper emotion than any I had experienced before.

Now I realised why he seemed so much more relaxed than he had ever been before. He had found something – something rare on Earth.

At that point I was tempted to ask him to let me return to Mars with him, but he smiled.

'Would you really like that?' he asked.

'I – I think so.'

He shook his head.

'Find Mars in yourself,' he said. Then he grinned. 'It is far less strenuous, for one thing.'

I thought this over and then shrugged.

'Perhaps you're right,' I said. 'But at least I'll have the pleasure of committing your story to paper. So others will have the pleasure of sharing a little of what you found on Mars.'

'I hope so,' he said. He paused. 'I suppose you think me rather sentimental.'

'What do you mean?'

'Well, trying to describe all my emotions to you – the bit I told you about our ride to the Calling Hills.'

'There is a great difference between sentimentality and honest sentiment,' I told him. 'The trouble is that people tend to confuse one for the other and so reject both. All we seek is honesty.'

'And an absence of fear.' He smiled.

'That comes with honesty,' I suggested.

'Partly,' he agreed.

'What a mistrusting lot we are on Earth,' I said. 'We are so blind that we even distrust beauty when we see it, feeling that it cannot be what it appears to be.'

'A healthy enough feeling,' Kane pointed out. 'But it can, as you say, go too far. Perhaps the old medieval ideal is not such a bad one – moderation in all things. So often that phrase is taken to apply to just the physical side of mankind, but it is just as important to his spiritual development, I think.'

I nodded.

'Well,' he said. 'For fear of boring you further, I will return to the basement and the matter transmitter. I find that Earth is a better place every time I return – but I find Mars the same, also. I am a lucky man.'

'You are an exceptionally lucky man,' I said. 'When will you come back? There must be more adventures yet to come.'

'Wasn't that one enough?' He grinned.

'For the moment,' I told him. 'But I will soon want to hear more.'

'Remember,' he joked, pretending to wag a warning finger. 'Moderation in all things.'

'It will comfort me as I wait for your next visit,' I said, smiling.

'I will be back,' he assured me.

And then he had left the room – left me sitting beside a dying fire, still full of memories of Mars.

There would be even more memories for me soon. Of that I was sure.

MICHAEL MOORCOCK (1939–) is one of the most important figures in British SF and Fantasy literature. The author of many literary novels and stories in practically every genre, he has won and been shortlisted for numerous awards including the Hugo, Nebula, World Fantasy, Whitbread and Guardian Fiction Prize. He is also a musician who performed in the seventies with his own band, the Deep Fix; and, as a member of the space-rock band, Hawkwind, won a platinum disc. His tenure as editor of NEW WORLDS magazine in the sixties and seventies is seen as the high watermark of SF editorship in the UK, and was crucial in the development of the SF New Wave. Michael Moorcock's literary creations include Hawkmoon, Corum, Von Bek, Jerry Cornelius and, of course, his most famous character, Elric. He has been compared to, among others, Balzac, Dumas, Dickens, James Joyce, Ian Fleming, J.R.R. Tolkien and Robert E. Howard. Although born in London, he now splits his time between homes in Texas and Paris.

For a more detailed biography, please see Michael Moorcock's entry in *The Encyclopedia of Science Fiction* at: http://www.sf-encyclopedia.com/

For further information about Michael Moorcock and his work, please visit www.multiverse.org, or send S.A.E. to The Nomads Of The Time Streams, Mo Dhachaidh, Loch Awe, Dalmally, Argyll, PA33 1AQ, Scotland, or P.O. Box 385716, Waikoloa, HI 96738, USA.